BEYONDERS

SEEDS OF REBELLION

BEYONDERS

SEEDS OF REBELLION

✦ BOOK TWO ✦

BRANDON MULL

Aladdin

NEW YORK LONDON TORONTO SYDNEY NEW DELHI

ALADDIN

An imprint of Simon & Schuster Children's Publishing Division
1230 Avenue of the Americas, New York, NY 10020
First Aladdin hardcover edition March 2012
Copyright © 2012 by Brandon Mull
All rights reserved, including the right of reproduction in whole or in part in any form.
ALADDIN is a trademark of Simon & Schuster, Inc., and related logo is a registered trademark of Simon & Schuster, Inc.
For information about special discounts for bulk purchases, please contact Simon & Schuster Special Sales at 1-866-506-1949 or business@simonandschuster.com.
The Simon & Schuster Speakers Bureau can bring authors to your live event. For more information or to book an event contact the Simon & Schuster Speakers Bureau at 1-866-248-3049 or visit our website at www.simonspeakers.com.
Designed by Lisa Vega
The text of this book was set in Goudy Oldstyle Std.
Manufactured in the United States of America 0212 FFG
2 4 6 8 10 9 7 5 3 1
This book has been cataloged with the Library of Congress.
ISBN 978-1-4424-5969-4 (prop)
ISBN 978-1-4169-9799-3 (eBook)

To Simon Lipskar and Liesa Abrams,
thanks for watching over Lyrian.

LYR

Northern Hinterlands

Seven Vales

Port Hamblin

Elester

Sunken Lands

Felrook

Harthenham

Wodan

Chasset

Trensicourt

Purga River

Lebaria

Unterton

Tamberoon

Kodoba

"As maps of Lyrian can be difficult to procure, not all features are precisely to scale." —Cartographer unknown

WEST LYRIAN

To Island Nation of Meridan

Emery

Ithilum

Outpost Point

Monument Falls

Repository of Learning

Fortaim

Flet

"As maps of lyrian can be difficult to procure, not all features are precisely to scale."—Cartographer unknown

BEYONDERS
SEEDS OF REBELLION

A PROPHECY UTTERED

The prince entered the room. Repulsively sweet fumes pervaded the air. The mellow glow of scattered candles left most of the ancient carvings drenched in shadow. It had cost him much to reach this temple. Friends had perished. His family felt certain that he was neglecting his duties to them and to Trensicourt. But he had to know.

Hooded acolytes hoisted chains to raise the dripping slab from the fragrant pool. Her body encased in clay, only the face of the oracle was visible, the single interruption across the wet, smooth expanse. Her eyes were closed.

The prince waited. The acolytes secured the chains and departed. The room became silent as the slab gradually stopped dripping.

Her eyes opened. A milky film covered them, muting the brown of her irises and lending the whites an iridescent tint.

"Galloran," she said.

"I am listening," he replied, unsure whether he should have spoken, unsure whether she could hear him. Her ears were hidden within the slab.

1

"You are the last hope of Lyrian," she pronounced.

He had suspected this was true. It was why he had come—to hear it spoken definitively. With her utterance, his assumptions hardened into certainty. A crushing weight of duty descended upon him.

"What must I do?" the prince asked.

"Without you, Maldor will triumph. His reign will be terrible. The realm will never recover. You must intervene."

"I alone?"

"Others will rise to lend aid. The way will be arduous. Many shall perish. Success is unlikely. Yet while you remain, hope remains."

"Where do I start? Is the Word the key?"

"The quest for the Word will be a necessary part of your journey. I guard one of the syllables. The road is longer than you can guess."

The prince nodded. "What else can you tell me?"

"Nothing is certain. Many ways lead to destruction. You will be tested beyond your capacity to endure. Should you survive the trials ahead, you will be a husband without a wife, a father without a son, a hero without a quest, and a king without a country. But take heart. Some must lose the way to find it. Some must be empty before they are full, weak before they are strong, and blind before they can see."

⊰⊹⊱ CHAPTER 1 ⊰⊹⊱

THE RETURN

O n a warm August morning, Jason Walker crouched behind a young batter and a little catcher, eyes intent on the invisible rectangle of the strike zone, a mask limiting his view. Some of the umpires in this league braved home plate without the mask, but Jason's parents had insisted he wear one. Based on the symptoms Jason had described back in June, doctors had concluded that a concussion must have initiated the mysterious disappearance that ended when he showed up at a farmhouse in Iowa, claiming he had no recollection of the prior four months.

The small pitcher went into his stretch. He glanced at the runner on third, then at the runner on first. The pitcher was in a tight spot. It was the third round of the summer league playoffs. His team led by one run, this was the final inning, there were two outs, and the count was three balls, two strikes. The pudgy kid at the plate was the second-best hitter on the opposing team.

The runner on first was taking a huge lead. The pitcher stepped off the rubber and winged the ball to the first baseman. The runner dove to make it back to the bag, then asked for time so he could stand.

The pitcher got the ball back. Again the runner on first took a greedy lead. The pitcher threw to first again, but the first baseman dropped the ball. Although the baseball did not roll far, the runner on third dashed for home. The batter backed away.

"Throw home!" the pitcher yelled as the first baseman grabbed the ball.

The ball streaked through the air to the catcher, who had the runner beat. The runner dropped his shoulder, plowing into the catcher as he got tagged before stepping on home plate. The little catcher flopped backward into the dirt, the ball dropping from his mitt.

"You're out," Jason called, pumping his fist.

The players on the field cheered. The coach of the opposing team, a skinny man with a dark suntan and a darker mustache, charged over to Jason. The coach was already hollering before he reached home plate, eyes bulging, spittle flying from his chapped lips. "What's wrong with you, ump? What kind of call was that? This is our season! Are you blind? He dropped the ball!"

Taking off his mask, Jason stared at the outraged coach. Within the past six months, Jason had confronted a giant bloodthirsty crab, outfoxed a brilliant chancellor, dueled a vengeful duke, and defied an evil emperor. He was not intimidated by Coach Leo. The coach kicked dust at him and gestured wildly. Veins stood out in his neck. Apparently he was emulating the tantrum of some major league manager he had seen on television.

Matt, the first base umpire, hurried over. He got between Jason and the furious coach. "Hey, settle down," he insisted.

"It's okay," Jason said, stepping around his friend. "Look, do you want to listen to me or get banned from this league?"

The coach closed his mouth, hands on his hips, eyes smoldering. His expression warned that nothing Jason could say would appease him.

"The rules of this league demand that the runner slide for a close play at home."

"What kind of rule is that?" The coach remained angry, but sounded less certain.

"A rule to prevent nine-year-old catchers from being hospitalized. If your runner had beaten the throw, I'd make an exception, but he was tagged and only made it home because he didn't slide. Next season, learn the rules, then teach them to your players."

"Ump's right, Leo," the scorekeeper drawled from behind the backstop.

The coach sneered but had no reply. He glanced around at the parents staring at him from the aluminum bleachers, then turned to glare at Jason, as if blaming him for the embarrassing display.

Jason raised his eyebrows.

The coach returned to his dugout.

"Good job," Matt said, clapping Jason on the back. "Way to keep cool."

"I have to remind myself these guys are just somebody's dad, desperate to see their kid win. In a way it's nice that they care."

"Sports turn a lot of people into hotheads," Matt said.

Jason took a deep breath, trying to dismiss the incident. "Should we get out of here?"

"Sure." They started walking toward their bikes. The teams huddled up to shout cheers. "Are you coming to Tim's party tonight?"

"The pool party? I don't know. Maybe."

"Come on," Matt urged. "It'll be fun. It won't stay warm forever."

"We'll see."

"Which means no," Matt sighed. "At some point you should consider rejoining the living."

Jason was unsure how to respond. How could he explain what

was really troubling him? His friends assumed that his reclusive behavior was due to his newfound infamy following the four months when he had dropped off the map. His disappearance had made the national news, as had his sudden reappearance after most had assumed he was dead. True, his absence had created some serious hassles. There had been dozens of interview requests. While some reporters were supportive, others had accused him of faking the incident, of deliberately hiding. Plus, the lost time had complicated his schooling. After counseling with his parents and teachers, Jason had spent much of the summer finishing packets of work that would enable him to advance to the next grade in the fall.

His real problem was not being able to tell anyone the truth. He had been to another world. He had made friends there, and enemies. He had risked his life and had accomplished great deeds. And he had returned home against his will, leaving behind tons of unfinished business. He had left a girl from Washington stranded there. And he knew a vital secret that would change how the heroes of that world tried to resist the emperor Maldor.

How could he explain any of this to Matt? To his parents? No matter what evidence he produced or details he supplied, nobody could possibly believe him. These burdens had to remain private. Although his experiences in Lyrian consumed his thoughts, if he tried to share what had really happened, he would wind up in a mental hospital!

Of all his friends, Matt had tried the hardest to be there for him. After returning from Lyrian, Jason had quit playing baseball. His prior goals as a pitcher had seemed insignificant compared to his new concerns. But he still loved the game, so he had volunteered during the summer as an umpire for a couple of the younger leagues. The volunteer gig carried little pressure and required much less time than actually playing and practicing. Matt had volunteered as well, just to hang out with him.

"I'm sorry," Jason said. "I'm no fun anymore. I've warned you, my head is a mess. I wish I could explain."

"Don't worry about it," Matt said, grabbing his bike. "Who wouldn't feel a little different after all you've been though? Nobody minds. Nobody who matters. If you could just relax, you'd see that not so much has changed. Who cares whether you pitch or not? Everyone wants you around again."

"Thanks," Jason said, stuffing his umpire gear into a sports bag. "I'll try to come."

Matt studied him. "We could go together. Want me to swing by?"

"Better not."

Matt nodded knowingly. "How about some lunch? You hungry?"

"I'm good. Maybe I'll see you tonight."

Matt shrugged. "Have it your way. Catch you later."

Matt pedaled away on his bike. Jason climbed onto his own bike and headed home. If he wasn't careful, soon he'd have no friends left. Was he deliberately pushing everyone away? Having unfinished business in Lyrian did not guarantee he would find a way back there. Like it or not, he might need to start living an actual life in this world again. After all, school would resume in less than a month. A regular schedule would make it much tougher to behave like a hermit.

When Jason got home, he left his bike in the garage and looked out back for Shadow, his Labrador. He came up empty. Nobody was home. His parents had grown closer to the dog during Jason's absence and had probably taken him for a walk.

Jason retreated to his room. He had spent a lot of time there lately. He went to his closet and got down a shoe box from the top shelf. From a drawer he collected a spiral notebook and a pen. Removing a pair of rubber bands, he opened the shoe box and took out a human hand. The severed wrist revealed a perfect cross section of bone, muscle, tendon, nerves, and blood vessels.

H-E-L-L-O. Jason traced the letters on the palm. He set the hand down and picked up his pen, ready to transcribe.

Not now, the hand spelled hastily in sign language.

Ferrin must be in some sort of trouble again. Jason had established contact with the displacer not long after returning from Iowa. He had taught Ferrin the sign language alphabet using a book from the public library. The tedious communication was his only link to Lyrian, and Jason had faithfully logged all of their conversations.

Jason felt grateful for the living hand. It represented his only tangible evidence of all that had happened. Without it, he wondered if he would eventually have come to believe his months in a parallel universe had been an elaborate delusion.

Back in June, soon after receiving word from their son, Jason's parents had driven from Colorado to pick him up in Iowa. His father had good insurance, so not long after Jason related his story of a four-month blackout during which he had somehow traveled hundreds of miles to awaken wearing filthy homespun clothes in a cornfield, he was referred to a neurologist. Jason affirmed to the specialist that he recalled nothing after reporting for work the day he was tagged in the head by a baseball, resisting the temptation to fabricate a horrific tale of alien abductors, sterile lights, and invasive probes. When asked how he got to Iowa, Jason had theorized that he might be a narcoleptic sleepwalker.

After an MRI, the neurologist confirmed that if the blow had resulted in a concussion, as she assumed based on the symptoms Jason had described, it had left no lasting visible damage. Jason was diagnosed with some form of anterograde amnesia, which the neurologist explained as an inability to remember events subsequent to brain trauma.

Jason had a hunch that the neurologist didn't wholly believe the story, but she never went so far as to call him a liar. His parents had been perplexed that given all the media attention Jason's disappearance had received, nobody had noticed him wandering the country for months as an amnesiac. They had insisted that Jason see a therapist, who had blatantly tried to investigate whether Jason was telling the truth about his lost months, but all Jason confessed to was a dream involving many of the details from Lyrian. In the end, the scrutiny had finally subsided.

Jason had considered confessing everything to his parents and trying to use the severed hand as evidence. But he had finally decided that although the lively hand was an inexplicable oddity, it was far from concrete proof that he had journeyed to another world. The hand would only raise a more lingering batch of unanswerable questions.

After putting the hand back into the shoe box, Jason went to his computer and turned it on. Besides the hand, he had one other source of evidence that his trip to Lyrian had actually happened. He went into his photos folder, then clicked through a maze of folders within folders until arriving at one marked "Rachel."

Inside that folder, he found images of Rachel Marie Woodruff, a thirteen-year-old girl from Olympia, Washington, who had gone missing in Arches National Park the same day that Jason had vanished. Jason had acquired the images from sites all over the Internet.

Apparently wealth and connections mattered, because Rachel's parents had managed to turn her disappearance into one of the biggest news stories of the year. The case was particularly baffling because the family had been alone with a guide in such remote country. Rachel had vanished quickly and quietly. The huge team of hastily summoned rescuers had found no body and no trace of violence. Her tracks had led to a natural stone arch where all evidence abruptly ceased.

For earning media exposure, it also didn't hurt that Rachel was quite photogenic and her family had dozens of recent pictures to display. Not to mention that her father had offered a no-questions-asked million-dollar reward for information leading to her recovery.

Jason studied a color photo of Rachel looking up from a canvas she was painting. Another showed her beside a skinny blonde, both of them wearing track uniforms. A third was just her head and shoulders, taken in a studio. She looked like the cute girl next door, but with a little extra style, both in her haircut and her fashion.

Jason had considered making an anonymous call to her parents, just to let them know that he had seen her and that she was all right. But such contact posed several problems. First off, Rachel might not be okay anymore. Last Jason had heard, she had been on the run with Tark, pursued by imperial soldiers. Secondly, if her parents somehow traced the call to him, he had no alibi. He had gone missing at the same time, which would make him a very appealing suspect if he was ever connected to the case. And lastly, he had no idea if Rachel would ever make it home, so it might be cruel to give her parents false hope.

Switching off his computer, Jason rose and started pacing. He hated being the only person in the world who knew where Rachel had gone. He hated being the only person in the world who might be able to bring her back. He hated being the only person in the world who knew that the secret word that could supposedly destroy the wizard Maldor was actually an elaborate hoax meant to distract and measure his enemies.

Jason undressed and took a shower. After drying off and dressing, he stood and stared at himself in the mirror. He had not regained much of the weight he had lost in Lyrian. In spite of his absence from baseball, Jason had exercised vigorously ever since returning home. He threw pitches in the backyard. He jogged. He did sit-ups, push-ups, and pull-ups. He bought books on karate and practiced in his room.

"You know where you're going," Jason told his reflection. "You always go there when you're feeling like this. No point in waiting around."

He went and removed the hand from the shoe box and placed it in a plastic grocery sack, which he wadded into a black backpack stocked with provisions. He wore a gray T-shirt and tied a lightweight jacket around his waist. He put on a new pair of sturdy boots, zipped a disposable waterproof camera into a jacket pocket, shrugged into the backpack, and slipped a pocketknife into his jeans pocket, just in case today would be the day.

At the Vista Point Zoo, Jason pulled the season pass from his wallet and flashed it to get inside. Ignoring the crowds, he strode directly to the hippo tank. As he had done on more than twenty occasions since returning to Colorado, Jason took up his regular position leaning against the guardrail.

The first time he had revisited the zoo, Jason had intended to leap into the tank and get swallowed by the hippo again. But as he stood staring at the lethargic beast, doubts had begun to assail him. What if the hippo was no longer a gateway? It could have been a one-time occurrence. What if the hippo refused to swallow him? What if it mauled him after witnesses watched him intentionally enter the tank? He would get locked up.

Jason sighed. Every time he came to the zoo, he wore his boots and brought the hand, the backpack, and the pocketknife. And every time he just stared at the hippo until he eventually went home.

He had considered trying to find the stone archway that had brought Rachel to Lyrian. All he knew for sure was that it was somewhere off in the middle of the Utah badlands. The way Rachel had told the story, it sounded like the gateway was only open for a brief time. He also worried that searching for the arch could end up connecting him to Rachel's disappearance.

One way or another, he had to return to Lyrian. His friends needed the information he knew about Maldor and the fake Key Word. He needed to show Rachel how she could return home. His current life seemed unbearably mundane and insignificant when weighed against the duties awaiting him elsewhere.

Last year, Jason had not understood why Matt's older brother, Michael, had wanted to enlist in the military. Jason and Matt had argued that the decision was impractical and dangerous for a guy with so many other options, but Mike had been determined. He had joined the marines a month after graduation. It had been something Mike had wanted to do, in spite of the potential hazards and inconveniences. Now Jason had discovered something about which he felt much the same way.

Perhaps he could learn to ignore his experiences in Lyrian, to pretend that the information he knew was not crucial to the destinies of countless people, including many he cared about. But Jason had no desire to forget what had happened. He had become involved in a struggle much larger than himself, he had people depending on him, he had found a cause worth fighting for, and just when he had gained information vital to that cause, he had been forced to return home.

The hippo was his best hope for returning. He lay at the bottom of the tank, motionless. Jason sighed. Just because he needed to get back didn't mean the hippo would comply.

A little redheaded kid stood beside Jason on his tiptoes. "Make it come up, Mommy," he complained.

"The hippo's resting," the woman behind him explained. "He can hold his breath for a very long time."

Jason clasped his hands together. Should he go for it, just dive in? Maybe. At least he would wait until he was unobserved. Even though the zoo was fairly crowded today, an opportunity would eventually arise.

Secretly, though he hated to admit it, he knew he would not jump. He had already passed up countless opportunities. It was just too uncertain.

"What's that music, Mom?"

Jason glanced at the kid and then listened.

He heard a distant, basso melody, much like a tuba, but somehow richer. Jason's hands squeezed the railing. How long had it been playing before he had noticed it? The resonant melody was gradually increasing in volume. He looked at the woman beside him.

"You hear that?"

The woman nodded, her brow furrowed. "Is it coming from the tank?"

"I think so." Jason bit his lower lip. He could have elaborated that the music was originating from a separate reality through the hippopotamus.

Jason felt his heart hammering. Here was evidence. The gate was open. If he was ever really going to do this, the time had arrived. He would be foolish to expect a more obvious opportunity. He gripped the railing more tightly.

Did he really want to go? How would his family feel? He wasn't much closer to his parents than he had ever been. They had made a real effort after his return, although the attention had mostly made him feel like a psych patient being handled with kid gloves. He appreciated the intent, and had tried to show it, but he and his parents had never really been on the same wavelength. Once the excitement of his return had faded, the same old patterns of life had resumed. Still, a second disappearance would certainly be hard on them. Poor Matt would be stunned.

This trip to Lyrian didn't have to be permanent, though—he knew a way back. Sure, deadly enemies awaited him. There was a very real chance he would get killed and never make it home. But what he needed to accomplish was worth the risk. He had to let Galloran and Tark and the others know that the Word was a fraud. And he had to rescue Rachel.

Jason glanced back at the Monument to Human Stupidity, a glass case displaying items careless people had tossed into the hippo tank. If the hippo mauled him instead of gulping him into another world, maybe they could hang his corpse in there.

If he succeeded in being swallowed before the eyes of this woman and her son, what would his family and friends think? Surely they'd assume he was dead. They would probably decide he had succumbed to depression and lost his mind. How would people explain the hippo swallowing him whole? Though large, the animal did not look big enough for such a feat.

Then again, as long as he made it back to Lyrian, who cared what others thought? It might be a little harder to explain his reappearance next time, but he could stress about that later.

The volume of the music continued to increase, still just the deep notes of a single instrument. The placid hippo did not stir from the bottom of the tank. Jason rubbed his palms together. He looked over at the woman, who was leaning against the rail, attentive.

She met his gaze and then said, "Isn't that peculiar?"

"Yep. I'm going to investigate." Taking a deep breath, Jason flung himself over the railing and plunged into the water. He stroked down to the hippo, which remained motionless. Hesitantly, he touched him on the snout, receiving no reaction.

Jason surfaced. The woman was screaming and her son was crying. A few people were hustling over, attracted by the commotion. Last time the hippo had swallowed him spontaneously. How could a person coax a hippo into doing something like that?

Jason dove under again. He tried to slap the hippo, but could not get much force behind the underwater blow. He jabbed his fingers deep into the animal's wide nostrils, and prodded at his eyes. The great head suddenly jerked to one side, making Jason flinch involuntarily. The head swung back and forth before becoming still again. Jason gave him a final poke in the nostril, then swam up for air.

Quite a crowd had gathered. The woman continued shrieking. "Get out of there!" a man shouted. "What's the matter with you?"

Treading water and feeling deeply embarrassed, Jason realized how insane all of this must appear to bystanders. He had a feeling there would be more visits to the therapist in his future. The sluggish hippo evidently had no interest in him, and could not be antagonized. But Jason would try one more time.

Something brushed Jason's leg. He glanced down. The hippo was rising rapidly from directly beneath him, jaws agape. As the bloated brown pachyderm broke the surface of the water around him, Jason was already mostly swallowed. Huge jaws clamped shut amid a chorus of horrified screams, abruptly terminating Jason's view of the onlookers.

Sliding feetfirst down a slick, rubbery tunnel, Jason heard the screams recede as the volume of the low-pitched melody increased. All was dark until he came to a jarring halt, his legs protruding from a gap in a dying tree.

He lay inside the hollow trunk, staring up through the top at the stars, his clothes soaked. The deep, resonant melody continued.

Jason scooted out of the gap, his backpack making it awkward, and recognized the scene—the tall trees, the dense shrubs, the wide river. He was back in Lyrian.

He hurried to the riverbank. The night was balmy, so his wet clothes did not really bother him. A gibbous moon hung in the clear sky, illuminating the river. A small craft drifted on the dark water. A single figure stood on the humble raft, wrapped in an enormous horn.

"Tark?" Jason called in disbelief. "Tark!"

The music stopped. "Who's there?" replied a gravelly voice.

"Jason."

The figure on the raft stumbled. "Lord of Caberton?"

"Yes."

"Are you . . . his shade?" The voice sounded awestruck.

"No, it's really me. I'm back." Jason could hardly believe it himself. "Come over here."

The short, robust figure struggled to unburden himself of the cumbersome instrument. Once free of the sousalax, he sculled over to the bank, peering forward suspiciously. The raft bumped against the shore. Tark hesitated. "Come forward so I can see you better."

Jason realized he had been standing in shadow. He stepped sideways into the moonlight.

"How can this be?" Tark gasped. "You were taken by the emperor."

"I escaped to the Beyond. Now I'm back."

Tark sprang from the raft and fell to his knees in the mud before Jason, hands clasped over his broad chest, tear tracks glinting on his cheeks in the moonlight. "My heart is going to rupture with joy," he proclaimed. "How did you escape?"

Mildly stunned at the exuberant reception, it took Jason a moment to answer. "I had help. Where's Rachel?"

"We parted ways," Tark said. "A strategic move, suggested by Drake."

"Drake? Was this before or after he freed me on the road to Felrook?"

"He helped us before and after. Our enemies dispatched a lurker, so the only way to stay ahead of our foes was constant movement."

"A lurker?" Jason exclaimed. "Ferrin told me that lurkers are really bad news."

"The lurker made matters much worse. Eventually we split up to confuse and divide our pursuers. Drake and Rachel took horses one way, I rode off in another direction, leading a second mount, and we set loose a few other horses for good measure."

"What about Jasher?" Jason asked.

"I delivered the amar of the seedman to his people, at one of the gates to the Seven Vales. He should have been planted weeks ago."

Jason stared down at Tark. "Why are you here alone, playing your sousalax?"

Tark looked away. "Not *my* sousalax. Mine is long gone. I got this mediocre substitute from a pawnbroker. You see, once I assured the safety of the seedman, I kept running, and eventually found my way home. I had no idea how to rejoin Drake and Rachel. I could only hope that the lurker had deserted them to follow me."

"They're also called torivors, right? I don't know much about them, except for what Ferrin told me."

Tark shuddered. "The common name is lurker. Since splitting from the others, I've glimpsed a dark presence in the distance from time to time, but never got an honest look."

"So the lurker followed you?" Jason said. "Rachel and Drake may have gotten away?"

"No way to be sure," Tark replied. "Having never met a torivor, I can't be certain what exactly tracked me. I pray that I drew away the worst of Rachel and Drake's pursuers. For the first couple of nights at home, no longer on the move, I expected to be taken. But no enemies ever appeared on my threshold. Instead, I began to stew. My guilt hollowed me out. I would never have left you behind, Lord Jason, had you not entrusted me with the amar. I would have fought to the death at your side."

It took Jason a moment to realize that Tark truly felt bad for leaving him at Harthenham. "You did the right thing, Tark. We had to give Jasher a chance at survival. And you had to help Rachel. You did what I wanted."

Tark's eyes remained downcast. "I couldn't shake the certainty that in abandoning you to be captured, I had performed my culminating act of betrayal. Not only had I let the Giddy Nine sacrifice themselves without me, I had forsaken the person who had revived my dignity and granted me renewed purpose. Part of me wanted to mount a solitary assault on Felrook, but the undertaking felt too hopeless and too grand. So I purchased a secondhand sousalax, built this small raft, and tonight intended to finish what I started months ago with my comrades."

"You were headed for the falls? Tark, you have to overcome—"

Tark raised a hand to interrupt. "Waste no words. Even I can read signs this obvious. You are a specter descended from realms ethereal, and for some unfathomable reason you have condescended time and again to rescue me from self-pity."

"I'm just a regular person."

Tark snorted a laugh. "Whatever you may be, you are no regular person. Do not protest. In gratitude, I formally vow to serve you until my dying breath." He prostrated himself further on the muddy bank, bowing his head low. "I pledge to you my fealty. All I have is yours." The final words were uttered in profound solemnity.

Jason felt touched by the display. He also felt awkward. "Get up, Tark."

Tark arose.

Somewhat troubled, Jason folded his arms across his chest. "Look, there's something I need to tell you."

"What?"

Jason cleared his throat. "It might affect how you feel about me."

"I can't imagine holding you in higher esteem."

"That's not what I'm worried about."

Tark huffed a quick chuckle. "Nothing could make me think less of you."

Jason gave a small shrug. "Remember that night when eight of the Giddy Nine plunged over the waterfall?"

Tark scowled. "How could I forget?"

"Your music summoned me from the Beyond. And once I entered your world, I tried to prevent you from going over the falls!"

Tark sputtered, clutching his head with both hands. "Wait, hold on, you were the accursed interloper who tried to rescue us?"

"I was." Jason knew that Tark blamed the wannabe rescuer for ruining what was supposed to be a majestic sacrifice by the Giddy Nine.

In the moonlight, Tark's rugged countenance slowly became illuminated with comprehension. He spoke like a man beholding a vision. "Then we succeeded." He thrust a finger at Jason. "You were the hero the oracle told Simeon he would summon. And our destruction was not a prerequisite to our success. Quite the contrary . . . you arrived before any of us had perished, and you tried to save us from our folly."

"I'm not sure I'm a hero."

Tark waved the comment away. "This is no occasion for false modesty. I believed that by surviving, I had spoiled the prophecy and hindered the arrival of the hero. But I didn't." He paused. "And they needn't have died." His jaw quivered, and then clenched tight. He swiped his forearm over his eyes.

Jason laid a comforting hand on Tark's sturdy shoulder.

"Wait!" Tark whispered in alarm, slapping himself on the forehead. "I am a buffoon! Quick, onto the raft."

"Why—"

"Hurry, my lord," Tark hissed. "I'll explain on the water."

Jason climbed aboard the small vessel, feeling it rock alarmingly beneath his weight. Tark shoved off, sloshing in the water before vaulting onto the raft, trousers soaked to the thighs.

"What—"

"Stay down," Tark cautioned in a low, urgent tone. Jason crouched beside the sousalax. Tark sculled away from the bank, staring hastily about, narrowed eyes searching the night. "I can't be sure I ever lost the being that has been stalking me."

"The lurker?" Jason whispered, the night seeming suddenly chillier.

Tark glanced at Jason. "We don't want to take any chances. It's a dark, slippery creature. Last time I glimpsed it was yesterday evening. If I were its prey, the villain has had ample opportunities to fall upon me. Perhaps the fiend hoped I would lead it somewhere . . . or to somebody. To you, I suspect, seeing as you've escaped."

"What *do* you know about lurkers?"

Tark shivered. When he continued, his whisper was barely audible. "They're foul personages. Unnatural. Nobody really knows much. Drake advised us not to discuss them."

"If it might be after me, I need to know."

"I'm not sure myself. Folks say that if Death took a physical

20

form, he would be a torivor. Whatever has followed me looks like a living shadow, best I can tell."

Jason furrowed his brow. "What should we do?"

"We must separate. You can't afford a lurker on your tail. They're difficult to shake. Believe me, I've tried. Drake tried too, and that seedman has forgotten more about woodcraft than I'll ever know. If we have any luck, the fiend may not yet realize you accompany me. I hesitate, but I think I'll drop you on the far bank."

"Why do you hesitate?"

Tark frowned. "Nobody goes into the forest north of the river. They say giants dwell there, and that few who enter ever return."

"So why send me that way?"

"It's the last place you would be expected to go. And the last place you would be followed. Aside from the shadowy presence, whatever it is, I have noticed soldiers paying unusual attention to me of late. For all I know, some may be trailing me now. I should have paid closer attention. I wasn't overly concerned. I thought I was going to my death."

They were past the middle of the wide river. Jason studied the approaching bank, lined with trees and ferns and shadows. "What about the giants?"

"I have ventured twice into those woods. Not overly far, mind you, but Simeon, our former leader, was curious. There was a man who relished exploration! Anyhow, we went in on two independent occasions for the better part of a day and saw no giants nor any sign of them. There are stories of the old hamlets near the forest being raided, but once the hamlets were abandoned, the stories ceased. Could be the giants moved on. Could be they never lived there."

They were nearing the far bank. Jason clenched his fists. How was he already in such trouble, not five minutes after returning to Lyrian? Then again, what exactly had he expected? With all of the potential danger, he was lucky to have found a friend so soon, even if they needed to part ways. Jason had an urgent message to share with Galloran, and Tark might be able to help ensure that the message would get delivered.

"If this is our plan," Jason whispered, "I need you to do something for me."

"Name it."

"Do you know where to find the Blind King?"

"Certainly. Fortaim. Same place as ever."

"I've got to tell him something. The secret is so dangerous, I probably shouldn't share it. But it's incredibly important."

"Have no fear. I am your man."

"Only repeat this to the Blind King. Let him decide who else should know. Tell him Lord Jason got the entire Key Word. I used it on Maldor. It's a fake, meant as a diversion. Also tell him I escaped from Felrook."

"You came before Maldor?" His voice was filled with grim wonder. "You used the Word?"

"Yes. It failed. The Word is meant as a distraction. Can you remember the message?"

"Absolutely. We'll have to warn Rachel as well. I shared the syllable you relayed to me. She has the entire Word."

"Exactly. We have to find her. Hopefully, the Blind King can help us."

"If you don't mind my asking, why the Blind King? I mean, he gives good advice, but what do you really expect from him?"

"Maybe he'll tell you. It isn't my place."

Tark tapped the side of his nose. "More to him than greets the eye, I take it. Have no fear, no matter who is hunting me, I'll find a way to deliver your message."

The small craft ran aground. Jason and Tark both hopped out

to crouch in the bushes near the shore. Jason eyed the dreary forest.

"So where do I go?"

Tark rubbed his chin. By the change in his expression, Jason saw an idea strike him. "I'll send you to Aram. Set off to the northeast. Stay on that course until you reach the coast on the northern edge of the peninsula. Do you know the lay of the land north of here?"

"I don't. Except that we're on a peninsula."

"Follow the seashore east toward the mainland until you reach the first big town. That will be Ithilum. Near the southwestern extremity of town, right on the wharf, you'll find the Dockside Inn. Aram works nights there."

"Who's Aram?"

Tark snickered. "A huge fellow, toughest bruiser I've ever met. Used to do a lot of mercenary work. Now he keeps things quiet at the Dockside. Our group performed there regularly. We became good friends. He owes me a couple of favors. Tell him Tark sent you. If anybody can keep you safe, he's the man."

"Okay."

Tark began rummaging through his pockets. He brought out two drawstring bags.

"This has some money," he said, giving one of them a little shake. He then opened the second bag. "And this has some keepsakes from Harthenham."

Jason peered inside. It was full of jewels.

"Despite my recommendation, Aram may resist lending you aid. Though still strong as a bull and no older than I am, he considers himself retired. But every man has a price."

"So I offer him the jewels?"

"Not all of them. A few should be plenty. Keep them hidden. Carrying that much wealth can be fatal, particularly in a town like Ithilum."

"What should I do after hiring Aram?"

Tark scratched his cheek. "Have him escort you to a village called Potsug. It's on the Telkron River, and has a couple of ferries. After I deliver your message, I'll either rejoin you there or send someone to meet you. I'll only stay away if I still have enemies after me. The stableman Gurig is trustworthy. Mention my name to him, then await help in his home."

Jason repeated the names and instructions Tark had related.

"That is right." Tark heaved a sigh. "I'm overjoyed to see you, Lord Jason. Don't dally in the woods. Now I must away. Safe journey."

"Let me shove you off."

Tark climbed in and Jason pushed him away from the shore. Tark remounted the sousalax on his shoulders and began playing while skillfully manipulating the long oar. Jason swept his eyes along the riverbank, looking for living shadows or hidden soldiers. All appeared still. After one last look at Tark, Jason crept away from the river, into the gloom of the trees.

CHAPTER 2

GIANTS

As Jason marched away from the river, the tall leafy trees prevented most of the milky moonlight from reaching the ground. Through the dimness, he pressed between dark bushes with fuzzy foliage, occasionally altering his direction when he encountered thorny brambles and tangled thickets. The farther he waded through the vegetation, the more overgrown the forest floor became. Repeatedly he was corralled by spiny barricades.

He paused several times, crouching beside shrubs or behind trees, listening and watching for enemies. No matter how long he waited, or how intently he strained his senses, he detected no sign of pursuers. Nor did he hear giants stomping around up ahead.

Jason inhaled the scent of little bell-shaped flowers, drooping from a slender stalk. The smell was familiar. He was back in Lyrian, crouched in the darkness, foliage obscuring the moon. Despite the danger, or perhaps in part because of it, his situation felt natural. He could do this. As long as he remembered some of the precautions he had learned from Ferrin and Jasher, alone in the woods he should be very hard to find.

After some time spent gradually climbing away from the river along a clumsily improvised route, Jason blundered onto a narrow footpath. He tried to use the moon to keep his bearings. As his hunger grew, he stopped a few times to get trail mix from his backpack.

Not long after daybreak, with his inner thighs raw from rubbing against wet denim all night, Jason reached a clearing where the footpath vanished into the deep grass of a meadow. Following the perimeter of the meadow, Jason hopped a narrow stream, disturbing a lynx. The sinuous wildcat hissed and bristled, tufted ears quivering, making Jason recoil in surprise. Crouching, he grasped a stone, but the creature sped away, low across the ground, to disappear in the brush.

Not far beyond his encounter with the lynx, Jason found a meager trail running to the northeast. He knelt down behind a thorny bush, just beyond the edge of the meadow, and gazed back across the clearing. After waiting patiently, he saw the lynx slink away into the trees, but otherwise viewed nothing out of the ordinary. Maybe he really had slipped away from the river unnoticed.

Jason pawed through his backpack for a protein bar, which he ate while walking. The sun moved toward its zenith as Jason advanced along the faint trail. Despite his exhaustion, he wanted to keep moving, at least until nightfall. He hoped to leave behind the forest and the threat of giants as soon as possible.

Some time after the sun passed its apex, Jason spotted a bubble-fruit tree not far off the path. Feeling like a veteran adventurer, he climbed the narrow trunk and plucked three pieces of the fruit. Back near the path, he sat with legs folded, enjoying the break and the bitter juiciness of the transparent bulbs. The taste, the surrounding trees, the solitude—it all seemed familiar to Jason and helped him feel firmly back in Lyrian.

While he sat, Jason removed the hand from his backpack, still wrapped in the plastic sack. Ferrin had taught Jason to recognize bubblefruit trees. Might the displacer suspect he had returned to Lyrian? Could he somehow sense his hand more near? Would it be foolish for Jason to contact him? Ferrin had claimed that he was currently on the run from Maldor, which could mean the displacer and Jason were now on the same side.

When Jason had first made contact, after Ferrin speedily mastered the sign language alphabet, the displacer had offered only terse, vague replies. Then one day Ferrin had related that his participation in Jason's escape from Felrook had been discovered, and his messages became more elaborate. Still, because of past deceptions, Jason felt uncertain whether he could believe the information.

Supposedly, after Jason departed from Lyrian, Ferrin had gone undercover to a prison camp to discover how the inmates kept killing guards without leaving a trace of evidence. According to Ferrin, before his work there was complete, a scarlet rider had arrived with a message summoning him back to Felrook.

Ferrin had acted happy to comply, but quietly slipped away in the night, escaping into the western wilderness, eventually making his way to the port city of Weych. He later confirmed that as he had suspected, Maldor had discovered his involvement in Jason's escape. Ferrin had remained in hiding ever since.

Throughout their conversations, Jason never hid his wish to return to Lyrian, and Ferrin had pledged his aid should Jason ever succeed. But Jason had deep misgivings about relying on Ferrin. Everything the displacer had asserted could have been fabricated to gain his trust. For the present, confiding in Ferrin would be irresponsible.

Invigorated by the snack, Jason stuffed the plastic sack with the hand into his backpack and trotted along the trail. He estimated that back home it was the middle of the night. His summer had been lazy so far, with plenty of sleep, so he didn't expect an all-nighter to give him too much trouble. Besides, with the sun up, it felt earlier.

After some time, Jason reduced his pace to a walk. The day was too hot. Despite the humidity, his jeans were almost dry.

The little path he followed bent westward, then southwest. Jason continued, hoping the path would turn back to the north. The vegetation seemed closer and pricklier than ever.

Just when Jason was preparing to double back, the path intersected a larger trail that cut straight to the north. He followed the northward track, surprised at how wide it was for a path out in the wild. He noticed several places where foliage appeared to have been roughly chopped away to keep it from crowding the trail.

At one particularly mangled bush, Jason paused. Who was tending the trail? The maintenance was deliberate and relatively recent. Could it be giants? Or perhaps some industrious hermit?

Jason studied his surroundings. Given the dense undergrowth, if he left the path, his progress would be slowed to a frustrating crawl. Examining the trail, he found no huge footprints, but spotted traces of animal tracks—deer, perhaps. He decided to hurry along the pathway but to remain attentive. If he heard anything suspicious, he could always duck into the undergrowth.

With the heightened caution of a trespasser, Jason proceeded along the trail. The sun descended toward the treetops. Several times he paused at strange noises, and once he dove from the trail to roll under a scratchy shrub.

Every disconcerting sound turned out to be a false alarm, so it came as quite a shock when the trail curved around a tall bush and he found himself confronted by a twelve-foot giant, clutching a spiked club.

The huge man stood on the edge of the path, face twisted into a fierce grimace. Jason froze, deeply startled, then relaxed. The giant was a rough-hewn statue.

As Jason was calming himself, a shrill voice cried, "State your business!"

The order had come from somewhere before him, but Jason could not see the speaker.

"Keep your hands visible. State your business immediately!"

Jason held his empty hands forward. He still could not identify the speaker. The voice seemed to originate from the looming statue. "I'm just passing through these woods on my way up the coast."

"Dispose of your weapons."

"I have no weapons." Jason held out his arms and slowly turned.

A little man emerged from concealment within the bushes between the legs of the giant statue. He had curly auburn hair and was only slightly higher than Jason's waist.

Approaching with a bowlegged waddle, the small man held his hands palms outward. His tone became less demanding. "I am unarmed as well. If you intend to harm me, please end the suspense and do it now."

"I'm not going to do anything to you. All I want are directions, so I can get clear of these woods."

The little man approached cautiously. His simple clothing was a faded green that blended with the forest vegetation. "Pardon my candor, but if you plan to waylay me, I would prefer to have it done with." He turned around. "There. My back is turned and my eyes are closed. I detest anticipation. If you harbor unwholesome intentions, please have the decency to accost me while I am braced for the worst."

"You can open your eyes," Jason assured him. "I'm not here to bother anyone."

The little man cast a sly glance at Jason over his shoulder. "Well, your honor has saved your life."

Three other little people, two men and a woman, emerged from hiding nearby. They were clad similarly to the first little man, but they all carried bows.

"You might be surprised how many strangers fail that test," the little fellow said. "Who are you?"

"I'm Matt Davidson." The lie came smoothly. There was little chance these dwarfs hidden in the woods were in league with Maldor, but since Jason was a wanted fugitive, it did no harm to take precautions.

"Greetings, Matt, son of David," the little man said politely. "I am Peluthe, son of Rogon." He gave a curt bow. "This is my brother, Saul; my wife, Retta; and my cousin, Ulrun." The others nodded in turn. "Where do you hail from?"

"I'm a wanderer, but this region is new to me. I have spent a lot of time near Trensicourt."

"Where are you going?" asked Retta.

"Don't be so inquisitive," chastised Peluthe.

"*You* keep asking questions," she complained.

"That's my duty. I'm in charge."

"Then you can cook your own supper."

"I'm headed for Ithilum," Jason said.

His answer defused the argument. Peluthe returned his attention to Jason. "Have you not heard these woods are infested by giants?"

"Another question," Retta huffed in a low tone.

"In charge," Peluthe growled back.

"I've heard stories," Jason said. "Any truth to them?"

Saul and Ulrun shared a chuckle.

"Come with us," Peluthe said, "and judge for yourself."

The little people led the way along the path, past the tall statue. As they progressed, the trail showed evidence of increasing amounts of grooming. Before long, the foliage along the sides was pruned as neatly as hedgerows. The group passed another large, menacing statue, and then a third.

"Who's the stranger?" came a cry from up in a tree.

"Matt, son of David," Peluthe answered. "We have found him trustworthy."

"Where are you escorting him?" challenged the faceless voice.

"To the village."

"Is that prudent?"

"He is in my care."

"Very well."

A few more paces, and the path emerged into a tremendous clearing occupied by a village. Little people like those who found Jason roamed the streets, but the houses were enormous. The doors rose at least twelve feet high, the windows were huge, and the roofs towered above the ground. The sinking sun cast long shadows.

Jason halted where the forest path became a gravel road. "It looks like giants live here."

Saul and Ulrun laughed.

Peluthe glared at them. "Once they must have. But not now, or else we all would have been spitted and devoured. We are a small race, an experiment by some long-forgotten, misguided wizard. We're ill equipped to defend ourselves against larger folk such as yourself. When we discovered that the forest was abandoned, we inhabited this empty village."

Jason grinned. "And did nothing to discourage the rumors about giants."

Retta winked. "You catch on quick."

"So what now?" Jason wondered.

Peluthe shrugged. "Enjoy our hospitality for the evening, sleep with a roof over your head, and tomorrow we will speed you on your way."

"Thank you."

Jason drew a lot of attention as he strolled into the village. One little woman shrieked. Peluthe and the others repeatedly explained that "Matt" was their guest. They led Jason to a massive two-story house. Three big steps led up to the bulky door. The little people boosted themselves up each stair, and Jason had to take very large steps.

The little folk entered using a small door built into the over-sized one. Jason crouched low to get through. Inside, beneath the lofty ceiling, mingled a bizarre combination of oversized and undersized furnishings. Two little women and one tiny old man appeared busy preparing a meal.

"We have a visitor," Peluthe announced.

"My goodness," exclaimed one of the women. "Is he safe?"

"Quite safe," assured Peluthe. "He is Matt, son of David. This is my sister, Deloa; Saul's wife, Laila; and my codger, Jep."

Those mentioned smiled and nodded in turn.

"Pleased to meet you," Jason said.

Peluthe patted Retta on the shoulder. "If you must make added preparations to accommodate our guest, be quick about it. My stomach is impatient today."

Retta rolled her eyes. "Stop trying to show off in front of our company. I'm either your wife or your slave. You decide."

"I don't want to cause any trouble," Jason said.

"Nonsense," Peluthe said. "Retta is happiest when complaining."

"Must be why I keep you around," she replied.

"He's gargantuan," the old man griped. "He'll eat us all."

"Behave, codger," Peluthe scolded.

The old man toddled toward Jason. "We'll have to butcher a herd of deer just to feed this behemoth." He tapped Jason with a gnarled cane.

"Be kind, Jep," Deloa said, moving between the old man and Jason. She smiled up at Jason with wide eyes.

"Don't you start getting ideas about kissing giants," the old man hollered, using the cane to pat Deloa on the rump. "We don't have a ladder tall enough."

Peluthe, Saul, and Ulrun burst out laughing. Jason covered a smirk. Deloa looked scandalized.

The small front door opened, and two little men entered. "Evening, Peluthe," one of them said, rubbing his palms together.

"Out of here, you two," Peluthe cried, hustling over to the door. "I realize everybody in town wants to dine with our visitor, but we don't have enough as it is. Spread the word."

Dejected, the two men retreated out the door. Peluthe locked it behind them.

Over at the immense fireplace, in front of a huge cauldron, Laila tended a pot on a small bed of coals and ash. "Find a seat," she invited.

The little people gathered around a low table. Moving a chair out of the way, Jason sat on the floor, putting himself at about the proper height.

"Perhaps you would be more comfortable at the big table," Peluthe suggested.

"I'm not that large," Jason said. "Plus, I would miss all the conversation."

Laila carried the pot over, and Deloa walked with her, spooning stew into the wooden bowls on the table. They served Jason first, then worked their way around. Retta collected tough, dark rolls into a pan and offered one to every guest. The little women served themselves last. Once they took a seat, everyone began to eat.

"This is good," Jason said. The thick, meaty broth was loaded with chopped vegetables.

"It better be," the codger griped. "Grew those carrots myself. Best in town. Which gives me an idea." He turned to Peluthe. "What do you say we throw a harness on this great brute and let him plow my field?"

"That is enough, codger," Peluthe admonished, then turned to Jason. "Forgive him."

The codger was shaking silently with laughter.

"No problem," Jason said, after swallowing another mouthful of stew.

Jason remained hungry after finishing his stew, but pretended to be fully satisfied when he complimented the meal.

"Why, thank you," Retta replied. She glanced at Peluthe. "At least some people in the world still have manners."

"Oh, yes, very fine work," Peluthe mumbled.

From the westward windows, golden light streamed in: the final rays of the setting sun. "How far before I reach the northern coast of the peninsula?" Jason asked.

Peluthe squinted. "With those long legs, not more than two days. That about right, codger?"

The old man grunted. "If he fell over, his head would be half-way there."

"Of course, I give you my word to keep your secret," Jason said.

The little people shared sidelong glances.

"Secret?" Peluthe said.

"That the giants have abandoned these woods," Jason clarified.

"Oh, yes, *that* secret." Peluthe glanced up at the windows.

"You know, we have another secret. A bigger one. Retta, close the shutters."

Retta snatched up a pole and moved about the room, using it to secure the shutters. The last ones she closed covered the westward windows. "The sun is almost gone," she said.

"Right," Peluthe agreed. He winked at Jason. "Ready for a shocker?"

Each of the little people rose from his chair and collected a coarse, brown blanket from a folded pile beneath the huge table. Most of their knowing eyes remained on Jason as they began wrapping themselves in the blankets. Jason stood up and backed a few steps away, concerned by the peculiar change in attitude. He did not trust the new atmosphere in the room. Their bearings seemed suddenly menacing. Beneath the large blankets, the little people appeared to be disrobing.

As one, the little people dropped to their knees. They clenched their teeth and tightened their fists. A couple of them groaned.

"Are you all right?" Jason asked, growing distressed.

"Be right with you," Peluthe gasped.

Their small bodies began to swell. As the expansion became more pronounced, they all commenced moaning and crying out. After a slow start, the growth came rapidly. A few staggered to their feet, now the height of regular people. Peluthe and Retta shot up taller than Jason. And the growth continued.

Hoping he was not too late, Jason shrugged on his backpack and dashed for the front door. The little door in the base of the larger one had been locked with a key. He slammed his shoulder against it, but the portal would not give. A large hand caught Jason by the shoulder, hurling him to the floor. Eight feet tall and still growing, Peluthe blocked access to the door. Grimacing and coughing, Peluthe doubled over as his body inflated more.

Panicked, Jason turned in a circle. There were no other doors. The windows were out of reach and shuttered. The stairs to the second floor were now guarded by Deloa and Saul, whose sweaty bodies continued to thicken and grow taller. Jason could now tell that the blankets were actually large tunics.

Jason rushed to the huge fireplace, dodged past the fading coals of the small cooking fire, and raced around the great cauldron. The stones at the rear of the fireplace were rough and fitted imperfectly, offering abundant handholds. A hasty glance over his shoulder revealed the former little people wracked by a final onslaught of painful expansion, completing their transformation into powerful giants. The codger stood up. Jason was no longer much higher than his waist.

With speed born from desperation, Jason scaled the soot-blackened stones, certain that a horrible death awaited if he missed a handhold and fell. After reaching the dark throat of the chimney, Jason climbed higher, unsure how far up the giants could reach.

"He's getting away!" boomed a mighty voice.

"After him, you dunce," called someone else.

The chimney narrowed as he scrambled higher. Jason did not believe the giants could follow him. He heard the cauldron being dragged out of the way.

"Prongs!" spat a voice directly below him. "He climbs like a lizard!"

"Grab him!"

Jason heard hands scuffing against stone not far below his feet.

"I can't reach."

"Well, climb, you oaf!"

"You want to try to squeeze up there?"

Jason reached a narrow ledge where there was a slight elbow in the chimney. He paused, panting, seated as if on a bench.

"Come on down, Matt," suggested the husky voice of a woman—probably Retta—trying to sound sweet. "We mean you no harm."

"You'll have to do better than that," Jason called.

"Blast!" the woman shouted. "Why were you so rough with him?"

"I thought we had the pest cornered."

"Why didn't somebody guard the fireplace?"

"Who knew he'd head up there?"

"He might get away."

"No, he won't."

Jason heard the big front door open and shut. Not long after, he heard the roof creaking. He was trapped.

"Ho, Matt! This is Peluthe. You hear me?" The voice came from above.

"I hear you."

Peluthe spoke calmly. "Why not end this silly game and climb down? You cannot possibly escape. We promise to kill you quickly. No prolonged suffering."

"Think about it," Jason said. "If you were in my position, would you come down?" He shifted on the ledge, legs dangling.

"If I were being reasonable, I just might. Even if you last in there until dawn, there are plenty of us to easily slay you. We have weapons."

"You're only big at night?" Jason verified.

"Now you know our real secret," Peluthe answered. "You can understand why we can't allow you to leave here alive."

"Plus, we haven't had fresh human in ages," the codger called from below, his voice now deeper.

"I promise to keep your secret," Jason tried. "Why not just let me go?"

"Deal," Jep replied. "Come on down."

"No, I mean for real."

"Fresh human is a rare delicacy," Jep explained. "It's nothing personal—you seem like a good enough lad. If you would rather not be eaten, a wise policy is to stay away from these woods, and especially from our village."

Jason stared down the chimney in silence. He really was trapped. His demise was only a matter of time. At least he had sent Tark off with a message for Galloran, so his return to Lyrian wouldn't be a total waste.

"Be reasonable," Peluthe pleaded.

"Sorry for the inconvenience," Jason said, trying to keep the fear out of his voice, "but I'm going to make this as difficult as I can. You should be ashamed for inviting a guest into your home and then trying to eat him."

"Suggestions?" Peluthe asked, no longer addressing Jason.

"Find a pole," someone proposed.

"Smoke him out," growled the codger.

"Saul!" Peluthe called. "Trade places with me. I'm coming down."

A commotion of voices ensued, with some giving directions and others complaining. Jason heard the giants clomping about. A big pair of hands began piling wood into the fireplace.

"Find greenery," Jep instructed. "It makes more smoke."

Jason heard the front door open and close.

He examined the little ledge he was on. If he put his nose against the rear corner of the ledge facing the wall and breathed through his shirt, he might last for some time. But no matter what precautions he took, eventually he would asphyxiate. If they piled the wood high enough and it burned hot enough, he might even cook! Jason had known returning to Lyrian might get him killed, but deep down he had not believed it would happen. At least not so soon!

Down below, green boughs were heaped atop the growing pile of wood.

Jason patted his pockets, considering his options. He had money and jewels from Tark, but the giants would not likely accept a bribe when they could just kill him and rob his corpse. He had Ferrin's hand, but there was no chance the displacer was near enough to offer direct assistance. Were these giants loyal to Maldor? If so, could he pretend to be a displacer by dropping the hand, maybe bluff that he was on an errand from Maldor? He doubted whether the giants would care.

Peluthe called to him again, this time from below. "Are you sure you refuse to come down? This won't be pleasant."

"Not to mention that the smoke will sully your flavor," Jep added.

"We could provide a quick, clean death," Peluthe offered. "Dignified and painless."

Jason wondered if he should keep answering. His responses might only encourage them.

"Don't bother playing possum," Retta said. "We're going to get you down one way or another, even if we have to climb up there in the morning."

"I hope I taste like ashes," Jason snapped.

"He's a rather poor sport about all of this," the codger grumbled.

"I'm going to light it up," Peluthe announced. "I don't mind my humans lightly toasted."

Jason watched Peluthe bend forward over the logs. He was clacking some stones together to make sparks. Whatever Jason was going to try, it had to be quick.

"Use the coals from the other fire," the codger said.

"They were swept aside," Peluthe replied. "They're not hot enough." He kept clacking the stones.

"Let me do it," Retta insisted.

"I have it." Peluthe clacked for a few moments to no avail.

"I do this every day," Retta sighed.

"I have it!" Peluthe snapped.

"I'm a servant of Maldor," Jason called down. "I'm here on official business."

"Little late to claim friendship with Maldor," Peluthe replied disinterestedly. "You didn't have any idea what we were when you met us." He huffed with exasperation. "Fine, Retta, you light it."

Jason decided he should send a final message to Ferrin. He took off his backpack and started rummaging around in it.

"Uh, Peluthe, Saul, we have a visitor," warned a wary female. Perhaps Deloa.

Jason heard multiple gasps.

"Great demons from Beyond!" Peluthe exclaimed, moving away from the fireplace and out of view.

"Get out!" Jep cried urgently. "Don't look at it!"

Jason heard the giants clomp across the floor and out the door. Silence followed. Was it a ruse to fool him into climbing down? A ploy to avoid having him taste too smoky?

"Come down from there, Saul!" Peluthe called from outside.

"Why?" The response came from near the top of the chimney.

"Don't argue. Trust me."

Jason heard the roof creaking, then nothing else. After waiting for a moment, he decided to leave the hand in his backpack, and zipped it back up. The zipper seemed unusually noisy.

If the giants had only pretended to leave, they would pounce on him as soon as he exited the chimney. If they truly had run off, Jason could only conclude that his situation had grown worse. What would frighten away a house full of giants? Deloa had mentioned a visitor. Could it possibly be somebody friendly? A good guy?

Biting his lower lip, Jason peered down the chimney. The fireplace remained vacant. He heard nothing.

"Hello?" Jason called softly. "Anyone there? Anyone who hates giants and likes people?"

The silence continued unbroken.

Time passed. Jason breathed the charred odor of the chimney. He became fidgety. Using his pocketknife, he scratched the sooty stones around him, seeing if he could remove the blackness. He couldn't. Above him, visible through the mouth of the chimney, dusk began to fade into night.

Given the bickering he had heard until they left, Jason did not believe the giants were capable of such patience. Not only was the house silent, the whole village was quiet. Still, he waited. He had no desire to let impatience kill him.

As stars became visible through the mouth of the chimney above him, Jason's little ledge grew very dark. He listened for clues as to what might have frightened the giants, but heard nothing unusual.

Gradually Jason became convinced that the giants were truly gone. He began to worry he might be wasting his only opportunity to escape. Turning around, Jason climbed quietly down the chimney, feeling for little outcrops with his toes, pausing occasionally to listen. There still was no sound.

Toward the bottom, as the chimney began to widen into the fireplace, Jason lost his grip and fell onto the stack of wood. The green branches on top cushioned the fall, although it felt like he'd twisted his ankle.

Rolling off the mound of firewood, Jason sat rubbing his ankle, staring at the dark room. A pallid gleam from the rising moon peeked through the shutters.

Standing in the center of the room was a human shape.

Squinting, Jason studied the stationary form, feeling chills tingle down his back. It was the size of a typical man, but through the gloom, Jason could identify no details. The figure held perfectly still.

His ankle already hurt less, which suggested it was not broken or sprained. Jason arose. The dark figure did not move. All remained quiet.

The personage could not have missed his fall. "Hello?" Jason whispered. The mysterious figure offered no response.

Jason edged along the wall, away from the fireplace. Whoever stood in the center of the room remained unnaturally still—not shifting, not twitching, not moving its head, not even visibly breathing. Reaching the corner of the room, Jason moved along the next wall toward the door.

The big door had been left slightly ajar, and Jason pulled it open and then stepped out into the night. The village was still. No light shone from any windows. The gibbous moon was rising, large and white over the treetops.

Limping slightly, Jason descended the oversized steps to the wide street. In a window across the road, he met the gaze of a large pair of eyes. The eyes ducked out of sight.

Jason turned to look back at the house he had just left, only to see the shadowy figure standing silently outside the door. Gasping, Jason stumbled several steps backward.

Beneath the direct moonlight, Jason could now see that the figure was truly featureless. The being looked like a human shadow made three-dimensional. No moonlight reflected off its matte surface.

Jason stood frozen, staring. Was this what had followed Tark? Was this a torivor? If so, Jason understood why people compared the creatures to the form Death might take. The unnatural presence of the shadowy being filled Jason with dread.

"What do you want?" Jason asked, his voice cracking.

The silent figure remained motionless.

Glancing around, Jason glimpsed another face dropping out of sight behind a window. Whatever this thing was, the giants wanted nothing to do with it.

Jason swallowed dryly.

He started down the street toward the north side of town. Listening intently, he detected no evidence of anything following him, although his own steps crunched noisily against the gravel road. Whirling, Jason beheld the shadow being standing in the road, about ten paces behind. How could it move with such stealth?

Jason turned back around and walked quickly. When he looked back, the creature once again stood less than ten paces behind him. Was this some kind of game? Jason studied the ominous figure. It made no move, threatening or otherwise. Finally, he continued along the road, walking backward, keeping his eyes on the black figure and hoping it might hold still while he watched, since Jason had yet to see it move. The dark form began to walk, advancing with fluid grace. The shadowy entity made no sound.

Facing forward, Jason hurried out of town. The road became a groomed forest path, cutting through the woods to the north.

Repeatedly Jason glanced back, always to find the dark being standing ten paces behind. He remembered that Tark had mentioned lonely nights when the mysterious creature tracking him could have attacked. But Tark had never seen the creature clearly. He had caught only glimpses. This being did not seem interested in hiding.

Pausing, Jason stared at his pursuer. The dark apparition showed no sign of aggression. But given the reaction of the giants, he had to assume it could be plenty dangerous when it wanted.

After a couple of hours, Jason felt his lack of sleep weighing him down. Tonight was less warm than the previous evening, but with dry clothes, he didn't feel too cold. Finding a grassy patch beside the road, Jason stretched out, wadding his jacket under his head. Would the creature kill him in his sleep?

He had a feeling it might be creeping up on him. Sitting up quickly, Jason found the figure still standing roughly ten paces away.

Lying back down, mind racing, he tried to calm his nerves. Either it would kill him, or it wouldn't. Out here alone in the woods, there wasn't much he could do about it either way.

Jason glanced at the creature. It remained the same distance away as before, still as a statue.

"What do you want?" Jason asked.

No answer.

"Are you the thing that followed Tark? You should keep following him. He's the real mastermind. Shoo. Go hide."

No response.

"Okay, how about you stand guard while I sleep. Keep the giants away. Sound good? All in favor, hold perfectly still. Fine, I guess we have a deal."

Jason felt a little silly, like he was conversing with an inanimate object. Bundling his jacket into a makeshift pillow, he closed his eyes and eventually sank into an uncomfortable sleep.

CHAPTER 3

A SHADOWY COMPANION

A cold wind swept across the narrow ridge. On either side of him, a sheer drop fell away into darkness. Unsure of how he had gotten there, Jason sensed that something was deeply wrong. He had to hurry. Crouching low enough to almost touch the rocky ground with his fingertips, he moved forward, choosing his steps with care, trying to remain in the center of the jagged spine, despite the buffeting gusts.

From one side came a monstrous roar, like an approaching landslide. A mighty blast of wind lifted Jason off his feet and hurled him to the edge of the ridge. He landed roughly, with his legs dangling over the void, desperately hugging the rugged ground as a flood of wind rushed over him.

As the gust relented, Jason pulled himself forward, swung his legs up, and got to his feet. His torso and the underside of his arms ached and burned with bruises and scrapes. Returning to the center of the knifelike ridge, he staggered forward, currents of air rising and falling, swirling and whistling.

The fierce wind lashed at him with increasing violence. To keep his balance, he leaned into the gale, which suddenly switched directions, and his own effort helped the new gust shove him toward the dizzying brink. He fell to the unforgiving ground time after time, trying to grip with his entire body to avoid being flung to his doom.

He wanted to lie still and wait until the raging windstorm abated, but he had to press on. What was he doing here again? Was something after him? Was the storm going to worsen? He did not understand the logic of his need, but an innate sense urged him to hurry.

He got to his feet and shuffled onward, unpredictable currents thrusting him in different directions. Ahead, through the dimness, he saw where the ridge ended. At the extremity of the rocky spine awaited a table with one empty chair and an occupied seat.

Shouldering his way against a persistent gust, Jason stumbled to the empty chair and sat down. The other person at the table was Rachel! The wind did not seem to touch her, although it continued to half blind and half deafen Jason.

"Why have you returned?" Rachel asked. He could hear her soft words despite the howling gale. "You should have stayed home. You don't belong here."

"I couldn't just leave you behind!" Jason yelled. "What are you doing here?"

"You should not have come," she whispered, her expression neutral. "You have condemned the both of us."

Jason could hear the sound of the wind rising, louder than ever. He knew it was about to hit them like an avalanche. He stood and shoved the table aside. "We have to go!" He took her hand, shocked by how icy cold her skin felt.

Rachel rose. She stood significantly taller than him. Her hand gripped his firmly, so cold that it burned. Her eyes were black—no whites, no irises. "Stay away from me." She released his hand, and at the same moment, the wind hit, like a tsunami.

Jason tumbled helplessly off the ridge and into the stormy void, arms pinwheeling, legs thrashing. Powerful updrafts slowed his fall, then heaved him sideways and upward. A succession of unpredictable gusts thrust him in various directions, as if he weighed nothing. Had he dropped into a tornado? With wind screaming around him, Jason fell and flew, flipping and twisting, his orientation so disrupted that he lost all instinct for up and down.

Each time he opened his mouth to cry out, wind rushed into his lungs, drowning his protests. Questions surfaced through his panic. How high was the ridge? When would he hit the ground? How hard would he hit it?

The wild fall continued until Jason finally managed a shout. At that instant, his eyelids flew open, and he found himself on his back, beside a path, beneath a sunlit sky. A dark, featureless figure towered over him.

The events of the previous evening returned all at once. Using his heels and elbows, Jason scooted away from the shadowy form without taking his eyes off it. The figure did not move.

After putting a few yards between himself and the dark entity, Jason paused. Fear lingered from the nightmare. His heart raced. Everything had felt much too real. Jason checked his arms, expecting to see scrapes and bruises from the stony ridge. There were none.

He detested that the shadowy figure had been standing over him as he slept. He wondered if the creature had gotten even closer. He wondered if it might have touched him. The thought made him shudder.

The events of the dream left a foul aftertaste. Jason found his hands trembling. There had been other nightmares before the stormy ridge. He could almost remember them. What had they been about? The details dissolved under scrutiny.

Taking a steadying breath, Jason arose. The featureless figure held still, its surface perfect blackness, even under the sunlight, like a void in the shape of a man. Jason had hoped dawn would have driven the apparition away, like a vampire or something. But the inky creature appeared indifferent to the brightness.

Wiping sleep from his eyes, Jason hesitantly approached the creature. "What do you want?"

The tenebrous being offered no indication of understanding.

"Why are you following me?"

Nothing.

"¿Hablas español?"

Nothing.

Jason circled the creature, scrutinizing its smooth shape. They stood about the same height, roughly six feet. The face had no contours to suggest ears or eyes or a mouth. The hands had fingers, but no fingernails or other details. The feet lacked individual toes. The being was like a man reduced to his simplest geometric form.

No matter how Jason positioned himself, the flawless surface of the figure reflected nothing. It was a black that should have been impossible under the light of day. What material could absorb light so completely? Did it have any more substance than a shadow? Maybe that was how it moved so silently.

"I'm not going to harm you," Jason soothed.

He extended a hesitant finger toward the being's shoulder. Would it feel spongy? Hard? Would his finger pass through the surface? The instant before his fingertip would have made contact, the figure moved in a blur, seizing Jason by the wrist and shoulder and flinging him through the air. Jason sailed off the path, turning a three-quarter somersault and landing on a bush.

Stunned, Jason lay quiet for a moment. Would the creature pounce? Follow up the attack? He rolled over, rose to his knees, and saw the figure standing on the road, fifteen yards away, as if nothing had happened. His wrist ached from where it had gripped him. The dark hand had been ice cold.

Jason waded through undergrowth back to the path. "I get it," he said, brushing leaves from his shirt. "Hands off, right? You don't need to tell me twice."

As usual he received no acknowledgment. Jason felt angry. He wanted to strike the calm figure, if for no other reason than to earn a reaction, but he had a suspicion that if he attacked, the shadowy entity would knot him into a pretzel.

"Did you give me those bad dreams?" Jason asked, rubbing his wrist. "Was that you impersonating my friend? You both have really cold hands."

As usual, the being gave no reply.

"Are you a lurker? A torivor? A creepy puppet? Can you speak? Can you understand me?"

No response.

"Nod if you can understand me. You just chucked me into the bushes. You must have a brain. Wiggle a finger if you understand. Tap your foot."

Nothing.

Jason sighed, exasperated. "Well, looks like I can't talk to you and I can't beat you up, and the sun doesn't bother you. I guess you're going to tail me for as long as you want. Don't expect me to smile about it."

Jason took out a protein bar and finished the water in his canteen. He then set off to the north, determined to distance himself from the giants. The dark figure followed less than ten paces behind.

The groomed path dwindled to an indistinct trail, but continued northward. Jason filled his canteen when he crossed a brook, and ate trail mix. He wondered if his parents were freaking out back home. This time witnesses had seen him get swallowed by a hippo. Everyone would think he was dead. He hoped they wouldn't blame the animal.

Where was Rachel right now? Safe? On the run? Captured? He wished he could know that he wasn't too late to help her. What about Tark? If the shadow creature was chasing Jason, hopefully that meant Tark had escaped with his vital message. As he munched on raisins and nuts, Jason wished he had packed a wider variety of food. Maybe next time.

Not long after the path began to run parallel to a little brook, Jason finally spotted a bubblefruit tree. He hungrily devoured some fruit, grateful for something fresh and juicy. Ferrin had once claimed that a watchful wanderer could survive in the wilderness on bubblefruit alone.

Standing near the trunk of the tree, Jason wondered if the shadow creature ever ate. How could it survive otherwise? He watched it. How could something capable of movement remain so perfectly stationary? It didn't seem to breathe. Maybe it absorbed air through its icy skin. Maybe it absorbed food. Maybe it was magical and didn't need air or food. Jason decided to try to get some answers.

Holding up a bubblefruit, he approached the dark figure. "Do you eat? I haven't seen you eat. These are pretty good. Want to try one?"

The figure did not stir.

Jason pantomimed taking a bite of the fruit. "I know I'm supposed to be terrified of you, but I started to wonder whether you might be hungry. Here's some food. I'd hate to have you pass out and then stop following me."

Jason held out the transparent fruit. When the dark being

made no move to accept it, he tossed it underhand. The graceful creature stepped sideways, caught the clear fruit in one hand, and, quick as a blink, flung it back at Jason. There was no time to react. The bubblefruit splatted squarely against Jason's forehead, spraying his face with juice and sending him reeling onto his side. He remained on the ground for a moment, stunned, his head smarting from the impact and his eyes stinging from the juice.

Clenching his fists, Jason calmed himself. If he attempted to retaliate, he knew the creature would dismantle him. In fact, that could be precisely what the creature desired.

"I don't get you," Jason growled, getting up and using his shirt to wipe juice from his face. "If you want to beat the snot out of me, why don't you just do it? I can tell you could."

As expected, the being offered no response.

"Seems like you only react if I invade your space. Don't worry, I won't try to give you anything ever again. I'll leave you alone. I wish you'd return the favor."

The trail flanked the brook for the rest of the day. By the evening the brook joined a larger stream. Near the intersection, Jason found another bubblefruit tree. He offered nothing to his eerie escort.

By sundown, Jason could smell the sea. He felt exhausted after the long day, and curled up near the creek. After getting comfortable, he raised his head to look at the dark figure.

"You keep away from me while I sleep. Don't even think about hijacking my dreams. I'm going to be ready this time, just in case. Fair warning."

Jason rested his head on his jacket and tried to prepare his mind to dream about happy things. He pictured Rachel excited to see him instead of possessed and warning him that he should have stayed away from Lyrian. He told himself that coming here was the right decision, that he would make a difference, that he wouldn't die alone in the woods. And he promised himself that if he had another bad dream, he would recognize it and take over.

Jason stood on Zuma Beach in Southern California. He had been here once before, a few years ago while visiting his brother for a long weekend. But today the beach was deserted, including the light-blue lifeguard stations spaced evenly along the sandy expanse. Low gray clouds muted the sun and made the sea look grayer than he remembered it.

A helicopter came up the coast, flying directly toward him. It hovered loudly above, and a male voice called to him through a loudspeaker. "Sir, you do not belong here. The evacuation has been in force for hours. Your life is in danger."

A rope ladder unfurled from an open door, and the helicopter came closer to the ground. Jason ran forward, the sand hampering his strides. The ladder dangled almost within reach. He squinted as the wind from the rotors blew particles into his eyes. Suddenly the helicopter rose, along with the flimsy ladder. Charging hard, Jason jumped, but barely missed the last rung.

"We're sorry," the voice informed him. "We're too late. We have to climb now or none of us will make it out."

Jason gazed out to sea and saw the horizon curl upward, steadily rising as a mountain of water like he had never imagined approached the shore. Awed by the sight, everything inside of Jason seemed to drop, and despair filled the emptiness.

Turning, Jason recognized that there was no escape. At best he might make it to the parking lot. Looking back at the sea, the leaden water continued to ascend. This wave would break over not just the beach, but the coastal mountains as well. He doubted whether the swiftly rising helicopter could escape it.

Still, he ran away from the oncoming tsunami, panting as he plodded across the sand. Could he possibly ride it out? Hold his breath and hope he might somehow make it to the surface before drowning? No, not through miles of water. This would be like having the whole ocean fall on him.

When Jason reached the parking lot, he turned to look back. The great wave was almost to the shore, curling up so high that the top disappeared into the overcast sky. The water before it had receded dramatically, turning the coastline into a sloping desert of moist sand.

"Not the best way to go," said a gravelly voice at his side.

Glancing over, Jason found Tark beside him, wearing a Hawaiian shirt and sandals. Otherwise he looked exactly as Jason would have expected.

"How'd you get here?" Jason asked, panic giving way to curiosity.

Tark shrugged, staring up at the looming wall of water. "Serves us right, you know. This is what happens when you bite off more than you can chew."

"We can run," Jason said. "We can try."

Tark grasped his arm, his hand so cold, it burned. "Better to accept the inevitable."

Jason tugged and pulled, but couldn't break his grip. For the first time Jason recognized that Tark's eyes were entirely black.

"Wait a minute," Jason said, the realization hitting him hard. "This is a dream. You're not really Tark. I'm not really here."

Tark grinned darkly. "Tell that to the wave."

Looking up, Jason saw the wave curling over him—over the entire coast—the wave to end all waves, falling forward, stretching so far beyond Jason and the little parking lot that he could hardly imagine a place beyond its reach.

The sound was like being at ground zero during an atomic blast, so loud that Jason knew he would never hear again. Then he was tumbling helplessly through turbulent water that surged with unfathomable power. He immediately lost all sense of direction and found it impossible to keep the salt water from painfully invading his nose and mouth.

Jason woke up screaming, eyes squeezed shut, drenched in sweat, his body curled into a defensive ball. He opened his eyes and found himself staring at a faceless black head, inches beyond his nose, and screamed again, recoiling as best he could. The dark figure that had crouched beside him stood upright, took a step back, and held still.

Jason rolled away from it, deeply shaken, grateful that predawn light had begun to illuminate the forest. "I knew it was a dream," he panted, trying to let go of the terror that had owned him. He was on dry ground. He could breathe. "It was horrible and realistic, but I called it. I knew it was you. I couldn't stop it, but I knew what was up."

The shadowy figure remained still. Jason found it infuriating to think that this voiceless, motionless creature was getting inside his head and manipulating his dreams. He despised the thought of it following him sedately all day, only to attack him mentally when he was at his most vulnerable.

Seething, Jason lurched to his feet. The creature did not twitch, but Jason reminded himself how quickly it could move when attacked. If he tried anything physical, he would only get hurt.

Jason stalked over to the figure and stood close, glaring at its blank face. "You're a coward!" he yelled. "Stay out of my dreams! If you're going to kill me, let's get it over with. I'm serious. What's your point? Why are you here? To make nightmares? Or is that just extra credit?"

The figure withstood the tirade without flinching.

"Are you trying to make me doubt my friends? To make me sorry I came back to Lyrian? Are you trying to provoke me into attacking you? Are you a spy? All of the above?"

The figure gave no acknowledgment of Jason's presence.

Disgusted, Jason turned away. Why was he wasting his breath? It was like complaining to a mannequin.

Torn by worry and frustration, Jason kicked a small rock into the bushes. "I'm not sure what you're trying to do," he murmured bitterly, "but I think it's working."

CHAPTER 4

CHARM WOMAN

Rachel sat on a stone, the stub of a candle in one hand. She muttered a quick Edomic phrase. Staring intently at the wick, she willed it to be the focal point referenced in the phrase, and the candle flamed to life.

She blew out the tiny light. A thread of smoke curled upward.

Rachel repeated the phrase, exerted her will, and the little flame flared back into existence. She held her hand above it, feeling the warmth. She had now performed this trick hundreds of times, but she still experienced a fresh thrill each time the candle ignited.

She blew out the flame, then reignited it.

The effort used to tire her. Now it was easier than striking a match.

She blew out the flame.

Brought it back.

Blew it out.

Brought it back.

"You're getting too good at that," a voice said dryly. Startled, Rachel dropped the candle and turned to find Drake standing over her, his dark hair tied back in a ponytail, his flat features impassive.

"You'd better slow down, or soon you'll be instructing me."

The candle had gone out when she dropped it. She picked it up. "You should let me light the next campfire."

"I expect you could by now," Drake agreed. "But we have to keep moving."

"You found more marks?"

"Fresh ones. We've almost caught up to her."

Rachel stashed the candle in her bag. She and Drake had been roaming these hills for more than a week, looking for the charm woman. Drake had insisted she represented their best chance of getting the lurker off their trail.

After splitting with Tark, Drake had led Rachel deep into the wilderness. The seedman had reasoned that since the lurker seemed to be tracking them for their enemies, the farther they got from civilization, the safer they would be. He had further hoped that perhaps the lurker would abandon them to follow Tark or else give up after participating in a fruitless chase with no end in sight.

The strategy had succeeded in avoiding interference from other imperial servants. But even after weeks on the run in the wild, Drake continued to catch glimpses of the torivor tracking them. Rachel had even seen it once—a humanoid silhouette crouched on a high ledge, backlit by the moon.

Drake had been able to provide whatever they needed as they roamed secluded mountain valleys and uninhabited forests—fish, fowl, venison, nuts, berries, mushrooms, and bubblefruit all combined to nourish them. The horses also found plenty of opportunities to graze and drink.

As the days passed, and the lurker neither attacked nor went away, Drake had remembered a woman who had once helped him save a friend from a flesh-eating disease. At the time Drake had asked the charm woman how she managed to use Edomic without drawing the notice of the emperor. She had replied that the emperor was well aware of her, but that she had a way of avoiding even his torivors, which allowed her to practice her craft in peace.

Based on that memory, and the hope that the charm woman still resided in the same vicinity where he had found her years ago, Drake had led Rachel south, into the wooded hills west of a sizable body of water called Jepson Lake. He had explained that the charm woman moved around a lot, but left coded markings to enable those who needed her services to locate her.

After a few futile days of wandering, Drake had recognized her marks on a boulder, and although the trail was cold, over the past several days he had maintained that the marks kept getting fresher. Each collection of marks looked like nonsense to Rachel, but Drake had explained that while most of the marks were meaningless distractions, a few left clear instructions once you knew how to read them. When she asked the secret, he said the charm woman would have to tell her, because he had vowed never to reveal how to decode the marks.

During the past weeks, Rachel had tried her best not to fixate on the negative. She tried not to count how many days it had been since she had slept in a bed. She attempted to downplay how many times she had felt too hot, too cold, too sore, or too dirty. She strove to ignore how regularly she had been forced to ride, run, swim, or climb long after exhaustion would have normally demanded that she rest. She pushed away thoughts of her parents. She endeavored to forget about the endless conveniences of modern America that she had once taken for granted.

And she especially tried to not think about Jason.

Whenever her thoughts turned to him, it was like pressing an infected wound, increasing the pain without any realistic hope of making it better. Yet often she couldn't resist. In moments of fear or discomfort, she wondered how much worse he had it, rotting in some filthy cell in the dungeons of Felrook. She pictured him cold, hungry, alone. She imagined him enduring ruthless torture. And she prayed that he was still alive.

Rachel climbed onto her horse and Drake mounted his. He led the way up a forested hillside and down into the valley beyond. He reined in his stallion near a cluster of boulders. She drew up beside him.

"See the grove on the far side of the valley?" Drake asked.

Rachel nodded. "Are the next markings so close?"

"No. Unless I'm mistaken, we should find our charm woman there."

"Really?"

He flicked the reins, and his horse charged forward. Rachel followed, urging her mare to a gallop. The valley floor blurred by beneath her. She had been a competent horsewoman before coming to Lyrian, but after weeks on the run, most often on horseback, riding had become second nature.

It felt good to let her horse race at top speed, even if she had no hope of keeping up with Drake. He had not brought Mandibar to a full gallop for weeks, and Rachel had almost forgotten how truly fast the stallion could move.

Drake slowed his mount to a walk as he reached the edge of the grove. Rachel slowed as she caught up.

"What was that about?" Rachel asked.

He gave her a crooked smile. "Maybe I wanted to remind you who has the fastest horse."

"Maybe you're just in a good mood."

He shrugged. "There's a first time for everything." He patted the stallion. "He's not even tired. I've never ridden his equal. I may not have particularly liked Kimp, but I owe him for his fine taste in steeds."

"May he rest in pieces," Rachel said solemnly.

Drake chuckled, covering his grin with one hand. "It's bad luck to malign the dead."

She had made the same joke a few times before, and only kept repeating it because it always made Drake smile. "Don't be a sissy. He tried to feed you to his dogs. He had it coming." She had also noticed how it amused him when she talked tough. Deep down, beneath the banter, she remained haunted by the sight of Jasher and Kimp being blown apart when an orantium sphere had accidentally detonated in a grassy field near Harthenham.

Drake dismounted and gathered Mandibar's reins. "Let's lead them well into the trees before tethering them. I don't like how near we're getting to settlements."

Rachel climbed down and led her horse into the grove. "How do we get this charm woman to help us?"

"We ask," Drake replied. "On the only other occasion I've visited her, when she healed my friend Kaleb, she would accept no payment. I take it she'll either aid us or she won't. I expect she will if she can."

They tethered the horses, and Rachel followed Drake deeper into the grove. He kept a hand on his sword. The trees were not very tall, but they had thick trunks with deeply grooved bark. Heavy, twisting limbs tangled overhead. She imagined that after nightfall the place would look haunted.

The undergrowth remained sparse enough to proceed without a trail. At length, Drake waved Rachel to a halt. He pointed up ahead, and she saw a long string of colorful beads looped around the knob of a fat tree. Three feathered hoops hung at the bottom of the strand.

"What is it?" Rachel whispered.

"Charm woman!" Drake called, raising his voice enough to make Rachel flinch. "We have met before! Please console us in our hour of need!"

They waited. Drake held a finger to his lips to discourage Rachel from speaking.

"You may pass" came a reply, well after Rachel had stopped expecting one. The sonorous female voice sounded younger than Rachel had anticipated.

Drake led Rachel past the strand of painted beads. As they advanced, she noticed various trinkets—some fashioned out of metal, some of bone or ivory, others of stone—dangling from other trees and shrubs.

They reached a small clearing. In the center awaited a large tent composed of stitched animal hides in mottled shades of gray and brown. The head of a wolf, still attached to the pelt, lolled over the entrance. Small carvings and graven figures surrounded the tent in a loose circle.

A woman appeared, taller than Rachel, but hunched, with ratty silver hair and a face that looked too young and smooth to match her spotted, wrinkled hands. She wore crude brown garments belted at the waist, and a colorful shawl. In one gnarled hand she held a staff topped by dangling trinkets that clinked when in motion.

"Drake," she greeted, her voice melodious. "I believed we would meet again."

"I would not have bet on it," he answered. "Until recently I expected to rot and die in Harthenham."

"You have brought a visitor," the charm woman said. "What is your name, sweetling?"

"Rachel."

Her attention returned to Drake. "What is your need?"

"We're being chased by a lurker."

The woman squinted. "Yes, I have sensed one nearby. It has been years since Maldor deployed a torivor."

"Can you help us?" Drake asked.

"You have brought a terrible threat my way. But that harm is already done. We shall see if I can help you. Remove your footwear."

Drake took off his supple boots and Rachel squatted to untie hers. The woman slipped strings of dark beads accented with teeth over each of their heads, mumbling quiet phrases.

The charm woman stepped back and invited them into the tent. Barefoot, Rachel ducked through the doorway. Three large bearskins lay on the ground. Elaborate mobiles hung from the ceiling, displaying a variety of gently spinning ornaments and crystals. Simple dolls made of wood and yarn sat opposite the entry in a staggered row. Incense burned inside hollow statues, aromatic smoke filtering through tiny holes, the heady scent mingling with the earthy smells of ashes and old leather.

The charm woman crouched on a low stool and gestured for Drake and Rachel to sit on the bearskins. The thick fur felt soft.

"How long has this torivor been after you?" the woman asked, her eyes on Drake.

"Five weeks," Drake said.

"Has it guided soldiers to you?"

"Yes, until I led Rachel far into the wilderness."

"The torivor has remained with you?"

"I continue to see it. Not clearly or often, but consistently."

The woman rubbed a coin with a hole in the center that hung from a cord around her neck. "When was the last time you saw it?"

"Last night," Drake replied.

"Has it visited your dreams?"

"No."

The charm woman turned to Rachel. "How about your dreams?"

"How would I know?"

"You would know." Her attention shifted back to Drake. "Is it more interested in you or the girl?"

"Almost certainly the girl."

"Why?"

Drake glanced uncomfortably at Rachel. "I'm not sure we should confess why, charm woman. It could place you in greater danger."

The woman laughed, quick and loud. "I could not be in greater danger. The emperor has hunted me for years. You have brought a torivor to my threshold. Speak candidly. The more I know, the better I can help."

"The girl is a Beyonder," Drake said. "She knows all of the syllables of a word that can unmake Maldor."

The woman regarded Rachel with new interest. "I know of this word. You have all of it?"

"Yes," Rachel said. "So did my friend Jason, another Beyonder. He has been captured by Maldor, but it doesn't seem like he's had a chance to use the Word."

"He could be dead," the charm woman said.

Tears clouded Rachel's vision. "He could be."

"Though I expect that he lives," Drake inserted. "He rang the gong and was admitted to Felrook. Maldor has never been quick to dispose of a significant enemy once captured."

"You were close to this other Beyonder?" the charm woman asked Rachel tenderly.

"We became close," she said, trying to bridle her emotions. She had cried enough over Jason. There was no need to make a scene in front of a stranger. "I didn't know him in the Beyond. I met him here."

"By what power did you cross over from the Beyond?" the woman asked. "Most of the ways have long been closed."

Rachel explained how she had followed a butterfly through a natural stone arch and how she had entered Lyrian near the cabin of a spellweaver named Erinda, on the same day the solitary woman had died. Rachel also mentioned how the Blind King suspected that Erinda had summoned her.

"Intriguing," the woman said. "Erinda was a former apprentice of mine. I have long wondered what became of her. She always displayed a profound interest in the Beyond. You have acquired an Edomic key word. Have you any experience speaking Edomic?"

Rachel blinked. "A little."

"The girl can call fire," Drake specified.

"Indeed?" The woman licked her lips, her gaze becoming more intent. "Who taught you this secret?"

Rachel glanced at Drake.

"I did," he said.

"What business does a member of the Amar Kabal have speaking Edomic?" the woman challenged.

"I'm an exile," Drake replied. "I've dabbled in many pursuits uncommon among my people."

"You know the prophecy," the woman pressed. "When the People of the Seed grow familiar with Edomic, their downfall will have commenced."

Drake flashed his crooked grin. "I'm no longer among my people. I prefer to conclude that I don't count. Besides, anyone can see that our downfall has begun. We might as well go down fighting."

"Perhaps," the charm woman mused, stroking her chin, the

liver-spotted hand incongruent against the more youthful skin of her face. "Prophecies aside, the wizardborn normally show little aptitude for Edomic."

"I'm no spellweaver," Drake huffed. "It doesn't come easily. I know a few practical tricks."

"How long did it take her to learn?"

"She saw me call heat to light a campfire one evening. She asked how I did it, and I told her. She lit a candle that same night."

"The same night?" The charm woman gasped. "How long did it take you to light your first candle, Drake?"

"Years of practice. She clearly has an unusual aptitude."

The woman fixed Rachel with a suspicious stare. "Where did you study Edomic before?"

"Nowhere," Rachel replied. "Never. I know the syllables to the word that can kill Maldor. Otherwise, the first Edomic words I heard came from Drake."

"This was how long ago?"

"A couple of weeks."

"You can light a candle whenever you choose?"

"Pretty much."

"Show me." The charm woman arose, collected a long reddish candle, handed it to Rachel, and returned to her stool.

"Now?"

"At your pleasure."

Rachel felt a mild surge of stage fright. She hadn't done this trick under such scrutiny. The woman had made it sound like lighting a candle with Edomic should have been difficult to learn. The skeptical attitude magnified Rachel's nervousness. She took a breath. She had done this hundreds of times. She spoke the words, focused on the wick, and a flame flickered into being.

"Remarkable," the charm woman said. "Blow it out." She

gestured at Drake. "Take the candle to the other side of the room."

Rachel handed him the candle, and he carried it to the opposite side of the tent.

"Light it," the charm woman ordered.

"I've never tried this from so far away," Rachel explained.

"Same idea," the woman said. "Will heat to the wick."

Rachel said the words, concentrating on the wick. She could feel an inexplicable resistance, like the first time she had tried to use Edomic to light a candle. Her attention began to waver, as if some distractive force were willing her eyes away from her target, but she redoubled her effort, pushing mentally, and whispered the words again. Across the room, a new flame was born.

"That was harder," Rachel said, wiping perspiration from her forehead.

The charm woman considered Rachel curiously. "Yet you made it look relatively effortless." The woman looked at Drake. "What are the chances of Rachel remaining with me as an apprentice?"

"You would have to ask her," he replied with a slight frown.

"Well?" the woman asked.

Rachel felt flustered and flattered. Did this mean she showed serious promise with Edomic? It would be amazing to learn more, but the timing seemed off. "I don't think I can. We need to figure out how to rescue Jason, and I need to get in front of Maldor, so I can use the Word. Plus, I need to find a way home."

"I can offer you as safe a sanctuary as you are likely to find in Lyrian," the woman replied. "Study with me for a year, and you will become much more formidable. You learned to call fire with abnormal ease. For most, those words you uttered would convey meaning only. Heat would hear but not respond. If you can continue as you commenced, you could exceed the abilities of any practitioner remaining in Lyrian."

Rachel looked to Drake.

"This is a high compliment," the seedman admitted. "The charm woman would not make this invitation lightly. Nor offer such encouragement."

Rachel pressed her lips together. "Wait a minute. Is this why you really brought me here? To see if she thought I could become a wizard?"

Drake shrugged innocently. "I was interested in her opinion regarding your aptitude. And we needed to lose the lurker. Both needs aligned."

"Only one person in Lyrian could help you become a true wizard," the charm woman said, "but Maldor does not take apprentices. He crushes any who aspire to learn Edomic. Our best lore on the subject has been lost. Only scant fragments of what we once knew are preserved by stragglers like myself. Still, there is much I could teach you."

"What do you think?" Rachel asked Drake.

"You are in a difficult situation," the seedman replied. "Maldor wants to apprehend you more than any rebel in recent memory. The torivor proves that. You hope to return to the Beyond, but we have no idea how. You wish to rescue Jason, but we currently lack any realistic chance of accomplishing that as well. Alternatively, if you could arm yourself with greater power . . . who knows what options the future might hold?"

Rachel bowed her head. To agree to study with the charm woman would mean admitting some uncomfortable things. It meant that Jason would be in Felrook for a long time. It meant that she would remain in Lyrian for a long time. In fact, an apprenticeship like they were discussing might be the first step toward admitting she would remain in Lyrian for the rest of her life.

But wasn't that just accepting the reality of her situation? Jason had been captured. He might be dead. Nobody knew of a way back to the Beyond. The emperor was out of reach. Whether or not Rachel studied Edomic, she was in serious trouble. Her options were limited. If this woman could provide a safe haven while empowering her to have a better chance of surviving on her own, shouldn't she seize the opportunity?

Besides, wasn't she curious to learn what else she might be able to do using Edomic? If lighting a candle brought an exultant thrill, how would it feel when she mastered more ambitious abilities? Didn't she crave the rush that came when a few words supported by her will set the forces of nature in motion?

Rachel wrung her hands. Did she want to study Edomic? Absolutely. Maybe too much. Maybe so much that all the other reasons she had in mind were really just excuses.

"Would you stay with me?" Rachel asked Drake.

"If the charm woman would allow it," he replied.

The woman laughed. "You have changed, Drake. You are completely committed to the welfare of this girl?"

"My seed went bad," he said evenly, rubbing the back of his neck. "This is my final lifetime. I have wasted many. I can think of no finer way to spend it than helping Rachel destroy Maldor. She and the word she possesses represent the best chance we have."

"In that case, I invite you to remain with us throughout her apprenticeship." The charm woman studied Rachel. "There are limits to what I can teach you. Most of my skill is with charms. Such spells require time and patience to weave, along with certain specific Edomic aptitudes that I have not found in another. For all we know, your chief aptitude could involve summoning heat. Only time will tell how far you can take that ability and what else you can learn. But I can certainly teach you some new phrases, help you hone your talents, and advise you about the dangers of Edomic."

"Dangers?"

The woman snorted. "The danger mounts as your ability grows. In short, it is simplest and safest to use Edomic to accomplish tasks you could perform without Edomic. Lighting the candle is a good example. Given the right materials, you could ignite a candle on your own with little difficulty. Edomic is simply more convenient. If you fail to summon a candle flame with Edomic, the modest amount of energy involved tends to dissipate harmlessly.

"However, if you were trying to summon enough fire to consume a haystack all at once, considerably more energy would be in play. If you lost control of that much energy, unintended targets could ignite, including yourself. Also, should an ambitious command go awry, the failed effort could damage your mind, perhaps even permanently crippling your consciousness. There can be numerous unhappy consequences when a significant amount of power is involved."

"Which is why I keep my commands simple," Drake muttered.

"A prudent policy," the woman agreed.

"It was harder to light the candle when it was across the room," Rachel noted. "I had to say the words twice."

"Many factors, including distance, can complicate an Edomic command. Repeating the Edomic words seldom achieves the desired benefit, except perhaps by serving as a crutch to help your mind urge the heat to carry out your command. Once you have spoken, exert your will to demand compliance."

"It's weird to think of arguing with heat," Rachel said.

"Not arguing like you would with Drake," the charm woman clarified. "The heat has no intellect comparable to you or me, but it does comprehend Edomic. Ages ago, this world was created by the great master of this language. Edomic is equally understood by matter, energy, and intelligence. Even so, as you have begun to discover, it is one thing for the heat to comprehend your intent and another for it to obey."

Rachel scrunched her brow. "I sort of have to push with my mind to get the candle to light. It's hard to explain."

"Very hard to explain," the woman echoed. "In the past, scholars have sought to master Edomic as a form of communication. This is what many would call the lower use of Edomic. The higher use of Edomic is to speak with sufficient authority that matter and energy comply. Some, especially the uninformed, call it magic. Call it what you like. While scholars communicated, wizards commanded."

"What's the difference?" Rachel asked. "What made the wizards special?"

The woman shrugged. "None have found a satisfactory answer. Certainly not a teachable one. It has much to do with the will of the speaker. It also has something to do with faith, intelligence, experience, passion, courage, imagination, determination, and many other attributes. Commanding with Edomic also seems to rely on an innate, prerequisite gift that only a few possess. With effort, most could learn to speak at least some Edomic. But no amount of study can elevate a person from speaking to commanding. While training can increase the gift to command with Edomic, apparently nothing can create the raw ability."

"And I have it," Rachel said softly.

"You certainly do," the woman affirmed. "Do you intend to learn more? Will you tarry with me for a season to explore your potential?"

"Yes," Rachel said. "I'll do my best." She glanced at Drake, who gave a nod of approval.

"Very well," the charm woman said, clearly pleased. "Our first order of business must be to divert the torivor. In order for you to remain with me, we will have to part ways."

"What do you mean?"

"The charms that protect me from torivors and other servants of the emperor work mostly on principles of avoidance and misdirection. They won't long protect me or anyone else against intense scrutiny. For all of our sakes, we must mislead the torivor."

"How will that work?" Rachel wondered.

The charm woman winked. "Watch and learn."

CHAPTER 5

LURKER

Jason hiked along a gray beach of smooth, rounded pebbles. The stones magnified the crashing rumble as waves pounded the shore, and shifted underfoot with each step, rattling softly. Ahead, a wide creek crossed his path, emptying into the sea.

When he reached the creek, Jason knelt and filled his canteen, then took a long drink. Breathing deeply of the salt-tinged air, he rubbed his tired eyes. He had reached the beach yesterday morning, but had slept only briefly last night, thanks to the nightmare that had instantly overwhelmed him. He had been riding a roller coaster when a massive tornado touched down at the theme park. Everything had gone horribly wrong and had felt horrifyingly real.

So he had continued east along the northern rim of the peninsula by moonlight, then through sunrise, then under the full light of day. In a few hours, night would fall again. Jason knew he would have to try to sleep, but tired as he felt, he doubted whether he would rest.

He looked back at the featureless creature, standing silently on the stones. Mr. No Comment—the silent invader of his dreams.

Jason had looked back many times while moving along the stony beach. Not a single pebble clicked or clacked as the dark figure trod over them.

Jason removed his boots and socks, rolled up his jeans, and waded across the cold creek. The dark figure did not follow. Jason sat on the far side and let his feet get mostly dry before putting his socks and boots back on.

He marched away, glancing back at the dark figure. Soon the creature was more than a hundred yards behind, and it still did not follow. Was it intimidated by water? They had crossed streams before, but nothing as wide as this creek.

Peering ahead, Jason realized that the seaside stones were getting bigger. Soon the rocky beach would become too treacherous for walking quickly, so he decided to parallel it slightly inland. He glanced back toward the creek, and was startled to find the black figure standing less than ten paces behind.

How long had he looked away? Four or five seconds? Maybe six? This thing was fast. It had traversed the creek and dashed across at least a hundred yards of pebbly beach without a sound. "Are you showing off?" Jason asked.

The expressionless figure supplied no explanation.

After he'd skirted the rocky coastline for an hour or so, the stones dissolved into speckled pink sand, and Jason returned from the scrubby inland undergrowth to the beach. Occasional boulders interrupted the shoreline: tortured shapes pocked with irregular holes. Leafy ropes of translucent seaweed lay strewn across his path in haphazard piles. Spoon-billed shorebirds scuttled in the shallows, taking flight as breakers disturbed their foraging. Colorful fragments of broken shells littered the sand near the water, sometimes crunching under Jason's boots.

Back in America, this sandy stretch would have been a popular vacation spot or else coveted real estate for beach houses. He could visualize little kids piling sand while their older siblings rode boogie boards and their parents sorted snacks under big umbrellas.

Jason continued along the mildly curving beach. Up ahead, a village came into view, situated on a gentle rise not far from the shore. A palisade of upright logs surrounded the settlement, the wood bleached by sun and wind and salt. The village contained perhaps thirty residences, along with a few larger buildings. He felt relieved to see an actual community of people. It made him feel less lost. Too small to be Ithilum, the seaside settlement lacked a real dock, although several small fishing boats huddled in a nearby cove, sheltered by a man-made breakwater.

Leaning against a misshapen boulder, Jason paused to survey the little village. Smoke drifted up from a few chimneys. Somewhere a dog barked.

Jason folded his arms. His eyes itched. He had skipped sleeping his first night in Lyrian and had mostly skipped sleeping last night as well. His food was running out, and he wanted something besides granola. Watching the village, it was hard not to picture beds and warm food.

Towns in Lyrian had routinely brought him bad luck. The people here distrusted strangers, and Jason doubted his wraithlike companion would earn him any extra goodwill. But the village would have resources, and Tark had given him plenty of money.

While weighing whether to visit the village, Jason eyed the boats in the sheltered cove, then glanced at his shadowy escort. The dark figure had hesitated to cross the creek. What if Jason bought passage to Ithilum by boat? Wasn't it possible that traveling over the water could help him ditch the creature? As a bonus, he'd probably reach his destination faster, and he'd get a break from walking. Even if booking such a voyage was irregular, he figured that enough money would inevitably convince some poor fisherman to help him out.

The more he pondered the idea, the better he liked it. If the reaction of the giants had been any indicator, the dark creature following him would probably keep anyone in the village from messing with him. Maybe somebody could confirm whether the entity was a lurker. Or maybe he would get lucky and the creature would simply wait outside the palisade.

Jason started toward the walled settlement. He noticed a few men on the shore near the cove, fussing with large nets. A dirt road meandered from the seaside to a wooden gate in the palisade. Jason approached the entrance, the dark figure less than its typical ten paces behind. A pair of huge white fish jaws gaped at either side of the closed gate, showing jagged triangular teeth. Both sets of jaws appeared large enough to swallow a human whole. Or bite one in half.

Jason neared the gate, which was lower than the rest of the wall. A small wooden guardhouse stood on stilts behind one side of the gate.

"Hello?" Jason inquired.

An older man with bushy sideburns appeared in the guardhouse window. He glanced at Jason, then gaped at the dark figure standing behind him. "What evil walks with you?"

Jason glanced over his shoulder, acting startled. "Yikes! You know, I'm not sure. We're not together."

The man gave Jason a skeptical stare.

Jason peeked over his shoulder again, as if nervous and perplexed. He looked up at the man. "I don't like the look of him. Mind letting me in?"

"Please, pass us by," the man asked, eyes on the shadowy figure. "We're simple folk."

"He isn't with me," Jason insisted. "I assumed he was a local. How about you just open up a little so I can squeeze through?"

"Don't share your doom with our community," the man implored.

"Sorry, I need to come inside. Orders from the underworld."

The man vanished from the window. A bell atop the guardhouse clanged three times, then three times again, then a final three times. Jason heard the man dashing away from the gate, shouting hoarsely. "Run! Hide! Death stands at the gates! Get inside! Bolt your windows! Barricade your doors!"

The gate was only about seven feet high. Jason hesitated. He was clearly unwanted. But the gatekeeper had looked terrified— much too frightened to make trouble. Surely Jason could find some intimidated villager willing to sell provisions. Maybe even somebody to sail him to Ithilum.

Jason climbed the gate without any trouble. He backed away, curious to see how the dark figure would handle the obstacle. It remained outside the gate as Jason walked backward. Jason turned away, then whipped around in time to see the shadowy apparition landing on the ground inside the gate. Jason pointed at the figure. "I saw that. Part of it, anyway. Nice jump."

Turning, Jason directed his attention to the village. The buildings were constructed from weathered wood accented by the same rounded stones prevalent beyond the sandy beach. Most of the dwellings had stone chimneys, and several boasted stone foundations or garden features. Nobody walked the dirt streets.

A few curious villagers poked their heads out of doorways or windows, only to hastily withdraw once they caught sight of Jason and his mysterious escort. Jason heard a panicked woman calling to her children and saw a group of young kids hustle over to a small dwelling on the far side of town.

By the time Jason advanced up the road to the largest building in the village, all was silent except for the swishing of the waves against the shore. He paused to consider the large structure. A splintery, faded sign proclaimed it TAVERN. Jason found the front door locked. He knocked.

Nobody answered.

"Open up!" Jason called, banging harder. "I just want to talk. I'm not here to cause trouble. I need some food, then I'll move along. And if anyone wants to make some money, I'd love a ride to Ithilum."

"Go away," replied a female voice muffled by the intervening door.

"Look, I'm exhausted. I'm just passing through. How about some food? I'll pay double."

"We don't make deals with your kind."

"My kind? I'm not with the creature. It started following me in the woods. I'm hungry. Please help me."

"It's too late for you. Move along. Take a boat if you must, but move along."

"I don't know how to sail," Jason said. "If you send out a sailor who can take me to Ithilum, I'll not only leave, I'll pay him well."

No response.

Jason shoved his hands in his pockets. Maybe he was being too nice. "Hello? I'm still here! Hello? Lady, you better answer me. Not a good idea to make the guy with the shadow demon angry."

He heard a bolt being thrown, and a wide-eyed woman in a beige canvas apron pulled the door ajar, her frizzy brown hair streaked with gray. "What's the matter with you?" she hissed, trying to keep her eyes focused on Jason instead of his dark companion.

"I'm starving."

She said nothing.

Jason tried to make his tone gentle and reasonable. "I need some food. Like I mentioned, I have money. May I please come in?"

Her anxious eyes flicked to the tenebrous figure.

"Don't worry about him. He doesn't eat much."

Tears brimmed in her brown eyes, and she shook her head. "Death has marked you. This burden is yours to bear. Go." She closed the door.

"Now!" bellowed a hearty voice.

The door to a relatively large establishment across the street flew open, and a burly bearded man led out two younger men. Each brandished a weapon.

"Don't!" Jason yelled. He pivoted to face the attackers, raising his palms.

The bearded man threw a hatchet at the back of the dark figure. In a simple, fluid motion, the figure spun, caught the weapon, and hurled it back. The hatchet blurred through the air, striking the bearded man with enough force to bury the entire head into his chest as he flopped to the dirt.

Shocked by the abrupt demise of their comrade, the other men skidded to a stop, looking from their fallen leader to the shadow creature. Jason stared in horror. The black figure did not stir.

One of the remaining men looked jittery—a stout, swarthy guy with youthful features and a stubbly beard. He shuffled sideways and glanced down the road, clearly ready to bolt.

"Stay with me, Vin," the other man encouraged, tall and gangly with hollow cheeks, gripping a pickax. "Take the sword. We'll rush him together."

The bearded man had dropped a short sword when he fell. Vin held a gaff. He set down the iron hook and took up the sword.

"Get out of here, Vin," Jason advised the stocky man. "This thing generally stays tranquil unless people attack it."

"Don't listen to him, Vin."

"Are you blind?" Jason asked the other man, pointing at the corpse. "Did you see what it just did to that poor guy?"

"You mean our uncle?"

Jason frowned. He held up his hands calmingly. "This demon is no friend of mine. It refuses to leave me alone. If you attack it, I promise you'll join your uncle."

The lean man appeared uncertain. "Why lead it into our town? Who would do such a thing?"

"I need help. I don't even know what it is. I didn't imagine anybody would try to fight it."

The tall man glared at Jason. "Our uncle was not about to let his sister become endangered." His eyes shifted to a point beyond Jason's shoulder.

Jason glanced at the tavern door. It had cracked open enough to show half of the face of the woman he had confronted. She held a quivering hand to her lips. Tears streaked her cheeks. Briefly she met Jason's gaze.

"I'm sorry," Jason said around a lump in his throat. "I didn't mean—"

Releasing an inarticulate cry, she raced from the doorway to the fallen man in the street and collapsed atop him, shoulders shaking. Jason stared down at his boots, wishing he could disappear.

"Come on, Gil," the stocky man said, stepping toward the creature, sword raised.

"No!" the woman shrieked, freezing him. "Obey the stranger; leave the demon alone. Help me with your uncle."

"But—"

"No discussion. Gil, Vin, help me with him." The grieving woman turned her head to address Jason without making eye contact. "Help yourself to whatever you can find. Forgive me if I do not cook for you."

The two young men lifted the lifeless bulk of their uncle. The woman gathered the sword and the gaff and the pickax. Jason wanted to express further apologies, but only grossly inadequate words came to mind. They toted the bearded man into the building across the street and then closed the door.

Embarrassed and shaken, Jason entered the tavern. The figure followed him. The common room was empty. Evidently all patrons and workers had vacated the premises.

Jason felt guilty and frustrated. He slumped down at an empty table. He had never thought somebody would attack the creature. Had he suspected something like this might happen, he would have starved to death rather than lead the shadow fiend into this town.

Remaining seated, Jason rounded on the creature. "What's the matter with you? You killed that guy! He was just worried about his sister!"

The figure offered no response.

"How about you hit him in the leg with the hatchet?"

Again, no response.

Jason rubbed his face. Resisting tears, he tried to force from his mind the shocked expression the bearded man had worn as he flopped to the dust. He tried to forget the devastated sorrow of the man's family.

Standing up, Jason glowered at the living silhouette. "If I thought there was the tiniest chance of success, I'd wring your neck. This wasn't my fault. I never asked for some shadow freak to haunt me. You were never welcome. You're the one responsible for anyone you hurt."

The words did nothing to sooth Jason's conscience. It was like scolding a statue.

"I should have stayed away," Jason grumbled miserably. "I should have known better." The damage was done and irreparable. He had come here to eat, and despite the tragedy, his hunger lingered.

One table held a pair of plates with good portions of food remaining, as if the meal had been served shortly before the gatekeeper raised the alarm. One plate contained a cooked fish with a couple bites missing and some vegetables that looked like tiny potatoes. The other plate had several gray, curled shellfish; a pool of beige sauce; and stringy green vegetables.

Jason sat at the table. Despite the hassle of eating around all the spiny little bones, the fish tasted good, the meat flaky and soft. Jason ate carefully. He doubted the dark figure would rush to his aid if a bone lodged in his throat. The gray shellfish were rubbery, but not bad when smeared in the sauce. The miniature potatoes tasted a little like dirt, and the green veggies were too chewy, but Jason ate them for the sake of his nutrition. Anything that terrible had to be healthy.

Although the two meals filled him, Jason wandered back into the kitchen. He found a pot containing pink chowder. Sampling the concoction straight from the ladle, he found it was the tastiest food yet, and slurped some as dessert.

After finishing, Jason leaned against the wall, feeling sluggish. How could he go from feeling so empty to so overfed in such a short time? He studied the shadowy figure. How would he get help in Ithilum with this thing tailing him? Tark had expressed that Aram might be reluctant to aid Jason. With the shadowy apparition at his side, Jason doubted whether the man would even speak to him. The whole town would end up in an uproar, and possibly more people would be killed. But what was the alternative? Give up? Jason needed advice, and in spite of the risks, he could think of only one source.

Jason explored the kitchen. One door opened to a cellar, another to the outside, and a third to a spacious pantry with a small window in the back. Jason shut himself in the pantry and sat on the floor, waiting to see if the creature would follow him. It did not.

Jason fished the severed hand from his backpack. He slapped the palm to get its attention, and then began tracing letters with his finger. CAN YOU TALK?

The hand began signing. Jason preferred to write the letters down as they came, to keep a record of the conversation. Lacking writing utensils, he focused on mentally combining the signed letters into words.

You returned to Lyrian through the hippo.

WHAT MAKES YOU SAY THAT?

You got all wet and have carried my hand in the same backpack for multiple days.

Jason shook his head. So much for secrecy. WHY WAIT SO LONG TO TALK TO ME?

I presumed you were hesitant to trust me, so I waited for you to make the first move.

I AM HESITANT.

You should be. But I have told you the truth. In fact, the last time you tried to contact me, I could not respond because I was on the run. I fled south to a different town.

WHAT TOWN?

A minor village. I will tell you as a token of trust. It no longer has a name. Once it was called Truek. I do not plan to linger here for long.

I AM IN TROUBLE.

Explain.

A DARK CREATURE IS FOLLOWING ME. LOOKS LIKE A LIVING SHADOW.

The hand convulsed. *Is it with you now?*

82

I AM IN A PANTRY. IT IS OUTSIDE THE DOOR. I HAVE KEPT YOUR HAND OUT OF ITS SIGHT.

Good policy with the hand. You are in supreme danger. A lurker has found you.

I THOUGHT IT MIGHT BE A LURKER.

None of Maldor's servants are more powerful. This is calamitous. Do not provoke it. Do not touch it.

I ALREADY LEARNED THAT THE HARD WAY.

Unless a torivor appears bearing swords, it will only attack if provoked. How long has it been with you?

THREE DAYS.

It shows itself openly?

IT JUST FOLLOWS ME AROUND.

Has it visited your dreams?

Jason felt chills. IT KEEPS GIVING ME NIGHTMARES.

It will bring ruin upon you. Lurkers communicate mind to mind with those capable of hearing. Do you hear it while awake? In your thoughts?

NO.

Maldor may already know of your whereabouts. I assume you are in a remote village or farmhouse?

HOW DO YOU KNOW?

You are in a pantry, but the lurker remains near you. You must hasten to a large town. It will not follow you there.

WHY?

They are secretive beings. They have been known to enter remote outposts if on a mission. They almost never venture into a city. Certainly not openly. Do you know where to find a town?

Jason hesitated momentarily. He supposed with a lurker tailing him, his destination would be no mystery to his enemies. I AM GOING TO ITHILUM.

Perfect. How near are you?

I AM MOVING EAST ALONG THE NORTHERN COAST OF THE PENINSULA.

Hurry. You cannot be far off. Contact me again when you arrive. Keep both eyes open. Try to resist the torivor in your dreams. Expect an ambush at any time. Maldor is undoubtedly moving against you.

THANKS.

Jason returned the hand to his backpack. Even without good news, the communication left him in higher spirits. He had underestimated how alone he had been feeling. At least he had confirmed that his mysterious companion was truly a lurker. And it was good to know that it probably wouldn't follow him into Ithilum.

He looked at the small window at the rear of the pantry. Leaving that way might seem predictable, but it was worth a try. He opened it and found the lurker waiting for him. Instead of trying to squirm out, he returned to the kitchen through the pantry door. Again he found the lurker waiting.

"You can really move when you're in the mood," Jason said. "I think we've done enough harm here. How about we get out of town? Any objection?"

Jason scavenged around the kitchen, stuffing bread and cheese into his backpack. He left several drooma on the counter, along with a couple of jewels. He would not be surprised if the suspicious villagers threw the payment into the sea, but he wanted to try to leave some reparation for what had occurred, even though he was painfully aware that no amount of money could replace a lost life.

After exiting through the back door, Jason turned to the dark figure. "Now I know you're a torivor. No need to pretend otherwise. Can you talk to my mind?"

Jason sensed no thoughts besides his own.

"Come on." He saw no one as he returned to the gate and climbed over.

* * *

Jason tramped through moonlit snow up to his knees. The still, frigid air seemed almost brittle. His hooded parka, gloves, and snow pants kept out the worst of the chill. He moved along a slope populated by tall pines shrouded in white, his breath pluming frostily with every exhalation.

A long howl reached his ears from farther down the mountainside, the mournful notes echoing hauntingly. A louder howl answered from higher up the slope, making Jason pause, frozen by primal, instinctive fear.

Where was he going? Somewhere important. How did he get here? It didn't matter. Or did it? If he didn't hurry, he might end up as wolf chow. Or would he?

Jason put his hands on his hips. Why would he come alone into snowy mountains? He wouldn't. Hadn't he been hiking along a beach in Lyrian? This was another dream!

"I'm not playing," Jason announced, sitting down. He stared at the snow in front of him, willing it to melt. Nothing happened. The icy air felt real in his lungs.

From higher up the slope came a distant, thunderous rumbling.

"Avalanche," Jason mumbled. "Didn't see that coming." He remained seated. If he could learn to endure these dreams without panicking, maybe he could finally get some sleep.

"You should not be here," said a male voice behind him.

Jason looked over his shoulder and found Drake standing there, taller than he should have been, hand on the hilt of his sheathed sword, eyes black. Resisting his fear, Jason stood and faced the phantom seedman. "What's with all the snow? Is this the Christmas special? Let's do the roller coaster again."

"You are going to die."

"True, sooner or later. You're the annoying shadow creature

following me. I'm glad we have a place to talk. You shouldn't have killed that guy back at the village. Now I really don't like you."

"You have brought destruction to all you love."

Jason could hear the avalanche building momentum as it drew nearer. The oncoming roar was terrifying, but he tried to think of it as nothing more than impressive special effects. "Another spooky warning. Honestly, after today, this dream feels sort of minor league."

Drake cocked his head, as if perplexed, then pointed up the slope.

Jason could now see the avalanche coming, a massive tide of whiteness devouring everything in its path. It was seconds away. The ground began to tremble.

"I get it," Jason said, deliberately making his expression bland. "I also get that it isn't real. Smell you later."

Drake held up a hand. As the avalanche reached them, it forked, devastating everything to either side, but leaving Drake and Jason untouched. The uproarious sound was unnerving, as was the quaking ground, as were the few stray bits of snow that peppered Jason. Eventually the avalanche passed, leaving a bare field of white to either side, all trees swept away.

"Does this mean we can talk?" Jason asked. "I'd love to know what's really going on. Why are you following me?"

"I obey," the fake Drake said.

"You obey Maldor?"

"You must be taken."

Jason brushed snow off his parka. "Why do you even care?"

"I am indifferent."

Jason stared at the phony Drake. "Are you his slave, Lurky? Do you mind if I call you Lurky?"

"Come. Attack me. You want to hurt me."

Jason almost grinned. "Is that what you're after? No way. I've seen what you do to people who attack you." Jason sat down on the snow.

Drake remained standing. "You should not have returned."

"To Lyrian? You're like a robot. Do you have any of your own thoughts?"

"I am more than you can imagine."

"What I imagine is a shadowy guy who sneaks along behind me on the beach. Then he comes, disguised as my friends, and talks to me while I'm sleeping. At first he's scary, then he just gets annoying."

Drake stared down at him, face impassive. Jason stared back. The flat black eyes betrayed no emotion. Jason winked.

"YOU! WILL! DIE!" Drake shouted, each word exploding with supernatural volume. Jason could hear a second avalanche coming.

Jason narrowed his eyes at Drake. "Not yet. I bet I'll just wake up."

The snow hit Jason like a freight train. Even though he knew it was an illusion, he panicked as his body tumbled amid the crushing force of the freezing onslaught. He tried to cry out, but icy snow filled his nostrils and mouth.

But before too long he awoke.

He was lying on cool sand beneath a gleaming moon. He could hear the waves crashing against the shore. The lurker stood beside him.

Jason felt less rattled than he had after the previous dreams. He stood up and stared at the lurker. Just like in the dream, Jason sensed that disinterest would be his best weapon. "That was actually kind of fun. I've always wondered what an avalanche would feel like. You really shouldn't have hurt that guy. It made all the rest of this less scary. I've got this figured out, Lurky. Seriously, if you take requests, let's do the roller coaster next time."

The lurker showed no evidence of comprehension.

Jason sprawled out on the sand, then went back to sleep.

CHAPTER 6

ARAM

L ate in the afternoon on the following day, while picking his way along some craggy cliffs, Jason viewed a sizable town up ahead. The cliffs descended to a flat plain of solid rock nearly level with the ocean, pitted with tidal pools. Beyond the plain, on higher ground, the city began. Many tall ships were moored to piers projecting into the water, shielded from breakers by a long brown reef. Some of the biggest vessels were painted a menacing black. Out at sea, a ship with three high masts approached the port, a huge whale secured to its side.

The town itself extended away from the waterfront, reaching a good distance inland. The buildings were covered in stucco and roofed with ceramic tile. Dark cobblestones paved the roads. A lofty bell tower stood close to the docks, its yellowed plaster peeling. A thick crenellated wall enclosed every part of the city except the wharf.

Jason descended the diminishing cliffs. Below, on the rocky plain preceding the town, workers gathered shellfish from tidal pools.

Once the cliffs had almost merged with the flatness of the

rocky field, the lurker stopped following. Jason walked on, glancing back every few steps. The shadowy figure stood immobile, flanked by jagged boulders. Between two glances, the lurker vanished.

Jason strode out onto the plain. The entire expanse had the twisted hardness stone acquires after long erosion by the sea. A pair of women, one older than the other, worked in a nearby pool, loading shellfish into sacks, hair bound in rags.

"Hi there," Jason said.

"Good day," the younger one replied, looking up.

"What are you doing?"

She smiled as if the question were silly. "Harvesting abalones." She held up a shell that appeared to be full of living pudding.

"Good luck to you," Jason said before moving along.

Across the wide plain, other workers harvested different sea life. Jason crouched at a shallow pool, marveling at the bizarre creatures inside. He saw a black thorny starfish, conical mollusks topped with bright tufts of grasping tendrils, and fat, chocolate-colored slugs dotted with tiny yellow bumps. Part of him wished he could just sit and study all of the interesting species.

A loud wave drew his attention back to the ocean. The flatness of the plain must allow the water to encroach hundreds of yards during high tide, which explained the abundant tidal pools so distant from where the waves currently expired.

Jason looked back the way he had come. The lurker remained out of sight. He could hardly believe that he had finally ditched the creature, at least temporarily.

"You there! I need to see your permit." Jason turned. A soldier was drawing near, walking briskly. He wore the same armor as the men who had apprehended Jason after he fled from the Eternal Feast at Harthenham.

Resisting the reflex to run, Jason watched the man approach.

"Your permit," the man repeated officiously. He had a crooked nose and stood half a head shorter than Jason.

"I don't have one. I'm not bothering anything."

"Be that as it may," the man replied importantly, "nobody sets foot on the floodplain without the proper documentation. Everyone knows that."

"I didn't."

"Then we have a problem."

"I'm sorry. I've never been here before. I'm just coming up from the south, looking for work. Is this Ithilum?"

"Of course it is." The soldier stroked his chin, sizing up Jason, his stance becoming a bit more casual. "You wear strange apparel."

Jason used a planned response. "My uncle was a tailor. He liked to experiment."

The soldier gave a nod. "Times are hard. Tell you what. Trespassing on the floodplain carries a hefty fine, but if you would rather hire me to escort you across for a fraction of the fee, I might oblige you."

"How much?"

The man regarded him shrewdly. "The fines can reach upward of a hundred drooma."

"How about twenty?"

By the soldier's expression, Jason knew he had offered more than expected. "A man who offers twenty can often afford thirty."

Jason produced one of the small drawstring bags Tark had given him.

"Not here," the soldier muttered under his breath, glancing around.

"Oh." Jason put the bag back in his pocket. "Sorry."

"Act like you're showing me a document."

Jason pantomimed taking a piece of paper from his pocket.

The soldier stepped close to him and pretended to take it. He nodded at the imaginary permit and handed it back.

"Twenty-five?" Jason tried.

"Thirty is much less than a hundred," the soldier pointed out, "and you'll get to avoid prison."

"I need something to live on until I find work." Jason had plenty of money for now, but didn't want to give the impression that paying thirty was no sacrifice.

"Fair enough. Come with me. Pretend we're talking."

"Why don't we just actually talk?"

"Good idea."

There was an awkward pause.

"Tell me about your work," Jason said.

"I'm stationed out here to prevent poaching. This tideland is an important resource. If any vagrant could wander out here and pilfer shellfish, soon none would remain. The harvesting must be controlled."

They were walking past a circular pool. Leaning over it, Jason could not see the bottom.

"That one's deep."

The soldier nodded. "Those are tide wells. Specialists dive deep to retrieve rare delicacies. Dangerous job. Fierce predators prowl the deep ones. In fact, some of them intersect far underground. There's a whole system of tunnels and grottos."

"Really?"

"Sure as I'm standing here. See those two pools?" The soldier indicated the ones he meant, which were separated by maybe fifty yards.

"Yeah."

"They're connected. Some of the divers try to make it from one to the other. I've seen two divers succeed, and one drown in the attempt."

Jason had his hand in his pocket. He managed to open the drawstring bag and work several drooma into his palm. Based on the soldier's previous reaction, he figured it would be better to pay without displaying his bag of money. "What sort of predators are down there?"

The soldier squinted. "I don't know all the names, but I've seen some ugly injuries. One poor woman came up with a big chunk missing from her side. I heard she died. And I saw another fellow who got tangled with some kind of jellyfish. The thing was wrapped around his leg. You should have seen it. His leg was as red as my tongue and had swelled to three times the size of the other one."

"Ouch." Jason slid his hand partway out of his pocket. In his palm were three bronze pellets, two copper, and a silver. He kept the three bronze and fished for different drooma. "Your job sounds exciting."

"On occasion. Most days it gets tiresome, same as any job. Where are you from?"

"A puny no-name village to the south."

"Seeking excitement in Ithilum, are you?"

Jason shrugged. "Not so much excitement as a better life."

They continued in silence for a few minutes.

When they neared a long flight of stone steps that led up to the town from the floodplain, the soldier cleared his throat. "Well, good luck to you. Now that you know about floodplain regulations, have the sense to stay away without a permit."

"Count on it," Jason said. He held out his hand. Five bronze drooma were cupped in his palm.

"How about twenty?" the soldier said, taking four of the pellets. "You seem like a good enough sort."

"Thanks," Jason said with a nod and a smile. He had not experienced much courtesy or kindness from the soldiers in Lyrian.

The small discount left him feeling a surprising amount of gratitude. Pocketing the extra bronze sphere, he mounted the stairs toward a gate in the wall encompassing the town.

The Dockside Inn sprawled along the southern periphery of the wharf, the front door opening onto the worn planks of a long dock. From the window of the upstairs room Jason had rented, he watched the bustling piers grow quieter as the sun descended toward the west.

Jason had inquired about Aram, and the innkeeper had confirmed that he worked exclusively at night. Which had left Jason with little to do for a few hours. In the common room he had ordered some raw puckerlies, a shellfish he had sampled during his previous trip to Lyrian. They had tasted even better than he remembered and had left him feeling very sleepy.

A hammock stretched from one wall to the other. Abandoning the window, Jason reclined in the hanging bed, swaying gently. The prospect of sleeping without having to endure invasive nightmares seemed absolutely delicious. As he drifted toward sleep, Jason tried to program his mind for a short nap.

Had it not been for the music vibrating up through the floor, Jason might have slept the night away. He awoke to a raucous chorus sung by harsh, male voices accompanied by various instruments. His room dark, Jason rolled out of the hammock, shaking his head and slapping his cheeks. Opening the door, he passed down the hall and descended the stairs.

The spacious common room was thronged. All of the tables were full, the bar was crowded, and numerous patrons stood against the walls. There seemed to be at least five men for every woman. Many of the men sang along to the rollicking music provided by three women performing on a small stage in a corner of the room. One of the women strummed a lute; another squeezed squealing notes from a concertina while a third kept time on an oversized tambourine. As the chorus ended, the men fell silent, allowing the women to render the verse in three-part harmony.

> *His ship went down in a violent storm*
> *Amid the booming thunder,*
> *But he held his breath and scoured the sand*
> *In search of hidden plunder!*

> *When he arose from the briny depths,*
> *His pockets full of pearls,*
> *He found the tempest had drowned his wife*
> *So he kissed all the local girls!*

The audience joined in on the chorus.

> *Old Ingrim was a man of the sea,*
> *The sort you'd hope to know.*
> *He'd buy you a drink*
> *If you shot him a wink*
> *Then tell you he had to go!*

The women ceased playing and then curtseyed to rowdy applause. They moved off the stage, and an announcer took their place.

"Give us another one!" a strident voice demanded.

The announcer, a small man with a thin mustache, held up his hands. "They may be back," he hollered over the din. "Our next participant is Wendil the Fantastic, who traveled all the way from Humbid for our competition."

A scrawny man with a round face, holding a wooden lyre,

mounted the stage. He cleared his throat, his demeanor rigid. "This is a song I composed," he explained, casting a bitter glance at the women who had vacated the stage, apparently to remind the crowd that they had not performed original material.

Assuming a sad-eyed expression, the musician began plucking the strings of the lyre and singing in a tremulous vibrato. The pace was much slower than the previous tune, each word drawn out to hang quavering in the otherwise silent room.

> *My love is as the lilies,*
> *Her eyes like sapphires shine.*
> *Harmless as a lamb is she,*
> *Her countenance divine.*

"Is this a punishment?" a harsh voice shouted. Several others chuckled.

The singer paused, glaring.

"Humbid has declared war on Ithilum!" added another heckler. The laughter increased.

"Hold!" the singer cried, raising a hand. "Hold, let me give you the chorus."

"Don't do it," Jason murmured to himself.

The ruckus subsided somewhat. Plucking the lyre, the man went into a high falsetto.

> *But she was taken, taken, taken away*
> *Stolen away, oh so far away . . .*

"I wish someone would take you away!" yelled an onlooker.

The crowd became riotous, hurling objects at the stage and shouting taunts. The singer turned his back to the shower of vegetables and insults. The announcer hurried onto the stage, waving his arms and shouting over the commotion.

"By popular demand, Wendil the Fantastic Waster of Our Time, will be shipped back to Humbid in a barrel of rotten fish."

The crowd hoorayed. Wendil slunk off the little stage.

From his position near the bottom of the stairs, Jason scanned the room, wondering how he would identify one person among the boisterous multitude. Aram was supposed to be big and strong. Jason looked for men who might be bouncers. Sooner than expected, he spotted a likely candidate—a hulking mountain of a man leaning against the bar, primitive features set in a scowl. The only space along the bar not crammed two or three deep with patrons was to either side of him. The man did not look very approachable, but he fit the description Tark had supplied.

While the announcer introduced the next act, Jason descended the remaining stairs and shouldered his way through the crowd. "I present another newcomer to our venue, who also journeyed from afar to be with us, Hollick, son of Mathur."

A skinny man with a long face and big ears mounted the stage, holding a recorder that forked into two tubes. Placing one hand over the finger holes on each tube, he began to play a catchy melody, the instrument harmonizing with itself.

Jason reached the vacant space surrounding the goliath at the bar. He could better appreciate his size up close. The man stood more than seven feet tall. His massive shoulders were bloated with muscle, and a sleeveless tunic revealed thick, bulging arms. He carried no visible weapons, except for a set of iron knuckles on one huge hand. Oily hair pushed back from his brutishly handsome face dangled almost to his shoulders. The man regarded Jason disapprovingly as he drew near.

Even leaning against the bar, the man stood more than a

head taller than Jason. "Are you Aram?" Jason asked.

Aram gave a slight nod, his squinted eyes roving to survey the room.

"I need to hire your sword." Jason thought that sounded like a professional way to approach a mercenary.

Watching the piper, Aram spoke in a deep voice. "You can't afford my sword, let alone me along with it."

"I have a lot of money."

The man continued to watch the performer. "In that case, go wait out back, I'll send some men to rob you."

"I'm not carrying it with me," Jason lied, thinking of all the money and jewels currently in the pockets of his jeans.

"I'm no longer for hire at any price."

"You were recommended to me by Tark the musician."

Aram glanced down, making real eye contact for the first time. "Of the Giddy Nine?"

"The sole survivor."

"They were the most talent this place ever saw. The room would overflow. Is Tark well?"

"Depressed, but holding up."

Aram's scowl deepened. "He knows I no longer accept assignments."

"He said you owe him some favors, and gave me enough money to tempt you."

"Tark supplied the funds to hire me?"

"We're working together. Is there a place we could talk privately?"

Aram snorted. "I'm at work right now. Leaving would draw attention. Meet me out back of the place tomorrow after sunset, and I'll listen to your proposition. I'll turn you down, but I'll listen."

The piper onstage stopped playing, and the onlookers applauded, though not as vigorously as they had for the three women. The man bowed and left the stage.

"My request is urgent," Jason said.

"Look, kid, if you must, wait around, enjoy the entertainment, purchase some food. We might talk later."

The announcer declared an intermission.

"You want anything?" Jason asked.

Aram shrugged his bulky shoulders. "If you're paying. You have enough?"

"Sure."

"Hey, Sandra," Aram called.

"What?" answered a barmaid.

"This character wants to buy me a triple order of sand scuttlers prepared Weych-style."

Several heads swiveled to look at Jason.

"Did he just come into an inheritance?" Sandra laughed.

"Something like that."

"He want anything?"

Aram looked at Jason.

"I'll take an extra order of what he's having," Jason called.

"You got it, Your Majesty." She winked.

At a nearby table, one man roughly overturned the chair of another, depositing him on the floor. The fallen man bounded to his feet and pushed the other guy, growling a threat. Faces near the pair turned toward Aram. The big man coughed loudly into his fist.

The pair of would-be combatants looked up, stricken, all anger vanishing from their expressions. They appeared ready to run.

Aram jerked his head in the direction of the door. The two men nodded politely, then pressed through the crowd, followed by a few of their comrades.

"You want to go watch the fight?" Aram asked. "Should be decent. They look evenly matched."

"I'd rather stay away from trouble."

"What do you know. An ounce of sense. Let's commandeer their table and wait for our meal."

Several people were heading toward the vacated table, and a husky man had already laid hands on a chair, but they all backed away as Aram strode forward. Jason claimed a seat across from the enormous man. There were chairs for four other people, but nobody joined them. The noisy room was not conducive to conversation, so they sat in silence. Aram watched the crowd, paying no attention to Jason.

After a time, the announcer started the show again. A woman imitating bird calls was well received at first, but overstayed her welcome, and was finally booed from the stage. A skilled juggler pretended to be clumsy, stumbling and tripping and flailing his arms, but never dropped a single item. The crowd laughed heartily and gave him warm applause. A man was leading the crowd in a popular sing-along while sawing on his fiddle when Sandra the barmaid served the food.

She set a steaming platter in front of Aram, heaped with fleshy orange strips drenched in a buttery cheese sauce and dusted with seasonings. Jason received a plate holding a lesser portion.

"You emptied the kitchen of scuttlers," she told Jason. "Expensive items are purchased before they're eaten."

"How much?"

"Forty."

That was a lot! Eight times the cost of his room. Aram was grinning. Jason handed the barmaid a silver pellet. She gave him two bronze drooma in return.

Aram took a bite. He closed his eyes in ecstasy. Opening them, he nodded appreciatively at Jason.

Not particularly hungry after the puckerlies he had relished earlier, Jason tried a strip the size of his index finger. The soft flesh melted in his mouth. It tasted incredible. Jason started devouring the food, moderating his pace once he noticed Aram savoring every mouthful.

When the food was gone, Aram rose from the table, returning to his position at the bar. The other patrons parted to give him space. The chairs around Jason quickly filled up. He stayed put through the remainder of the show.

At the conclusion, the announcer summoned four of the most popular acts to the stage and, by audience reaction, determined a winner. When the three women who were singing when Jason came downstairs won, they reprised their song about Old Ingrim.

After the show ended, many of the patrons shuffled out. Some, mostly older men, kept on conversing and eating. A few had fallen asleep.

Moving to a table near a corner, Jason rested his head on folded arms and napped.

A loud noise awoke him.

Blinking blearily, Jason saw a man prostrate on the floor beside him, an overturned chair nearby. Aram had a boot on his back.

"You know better than to try a stunt like that while I'm on the job," Aram growled. "Especially if you intend to insult me with such a clumsy lift."

The man on the ground held up a small drawstring bag.

"And the other one."

The man produced a second bag. It took Jason a moment to comprehend that they were his. Aram crouched, snatching them from the thief.

"Now get out of here," Aram demanded.

The culprit scrambled to his feet and staggered out of the inn.

Aram handed Jason the bags. "Is this the wealth you hid elsewhere?"

"Oh, thanks."

"It's my job."

Jason surveyed the room. It was almost empty. A matronly barmaid was wiping down a table. Two red-eyed men sat huddled in conversation. A fat, drooling man lay slumped in a corner, snoring softly.

"I'm done for tonight," Aram reported. "If you wish to speak briefly, take a walk with me." Aram led Jason out the front door.

A chill breeze blew in from the ocean. Somewhere in the gray morning a gull cried. There was little activity on the docked ships. Jason guessed it was an hour before dawn.

Aram leaned against a wooden railing crusted with guano. "You have my attention," he said.

Jason looked up at the huge man. "I want to pay you a lot to bring me to a village called Potsug. I guess it has some ferries."

Aram folded his muscular arms. "I know the village. It actually straddles the river. It isn't far. Why do you require an escort?"

"For protection. I'm being pursued by Maldor."

Aram waved both arms, shaking his head. "Say no more. This conversation should never have happened. In my most reckless days, I never worked directly for or against the emperor." Aram started walking away.

"Wait, you haven't even heard the offer."

Aram kept walking without a backward glance. "No need. You could offer a golden palace stuffed with riches, and I would turn you down, because what use is treasure to a corpse? Thanks for the food. Seek help elsewhere."

"What's the hurry?" Jason called. "Do you turn into a dwarf at dawn?"

Aram froze, then slowly turned, a strange expression on his face. "What makes you say that?" His voice held a dangerous quality.

"I was only joking," Jason said, surprised by the weighty reaction.

Aram narrowed his eyes. "What spawned the joke?"

"You know, like the giants in the woods that shrink during the day? I guess people don't really know about them. See, you're super big—"

Aram strode near, towering over Jason, his expression grave. "Who sent you?" The quiet way he spoke promised violence.

Jason retreated a step. "Nobody. I mean, besides Tark."

Aram seized Jason's shoulders. "Why are you trying to involve Tark? What have you done to him? Who do you work for?"

"Nothing. Nobody. Settle down. Are you trying to tell me you're a giant?"

The muscles in Aram's wide jaw tightened. His glare threatened murder.

"I've seen them," Jason said, trying to diffuse the situation. "You're big, but they're way bigger."

Aram squinted up at the sky, then grabbed Jason by the front of his shirt, like a bully about to demand lunch money. "Come with me."

"I think I'll just—"

"Now." The way he pronounced the word left no room for argument. The sheer girth of his arm was also pretty convincing.

"But I have stuff in my—"

"Not another word." Aram released his shirt. "You wanted my attention? You have it. Stay beside me. Try anything, and I'll snap your neck."

They started off at a brisk pace.

CHAPTER 7

MOIRA

Aram guided Jason up a series of cobblestone streets away from the sea. They encountered few other people. Jason considered trying to run away, but the large man stayed close.

On a narrow street walled with tall townhomes, Aram thumped on a door.

"Where are we?" Jason asked.

"My place."

"You knock at your own house?"

"My mother keeps it locked."

Jason heard a lock being disengaged. The door opened to reveal a portly female dwarf with curly gray hair and kind, wrinkled features. She reacted to Jason with undisguised surprise.

"Who is your friend, Aram?" she asked sweetly.

"Don't tell me she's a giant," Jason sighed. "Wait, no, the sun isn't up yet."

The little woman scowled at Jason, then threw Aram a questioning glance.

"He approached me tonight," the big man told her. "I'm not sure what he's after."

The short woman stepped aside as Aram shoved Jason through the doorway with casual, implacable strength. By stumbling most of the way across the room, Jason barely managed to avoid falling flat on his face. Aram ushered him into a tidy parlor, motioning for Jason to take a seat on a sofa. Aram and his mother sat in armchairs. The room did not look like the bachelor pad of a hulking bouncer. Everything seemed soft and frilly. Apparently, Mom was in charge of the decor.

"You have a nice home," Jason said, hoping to lighten the mood.

"Thank you," the woman replied. "What's all this nonsense about giants?"

Jason glanced at Aram, who returned the gaze in silence, tacitly seconding the inquiry.

"Well, I made a joke to your son about him shrinking at dawn, and he got really upset. Seemed like a touchy subject."

The little woman considered Jason suspiciously. "Where have you heard about shrinking giants?"

"I was in their village a few days ago."

They both looked at Jason like he was lying.

"I'm telling the truth."

"For your sake, you'd better be," Aram said, leaning forward. "Go on."

"I went there by accident. I thought I had imperials after me. Turned out to be a lurker."

The little woman gasped.

"An actual darkling?" Aram asked.

Jason shrugged. "All black, like a shadow come to life?"

Aram nodded skeptically. "Keep going."

"I got to the giant village not long before sunset. The people were all little, like your mom. The houses were enormous, but they convinced me the giants had left long ago. Seeing all the little people running around, it seemed true. They invited me to dinner, and when the sun went down, they all changed into giants and then wanted to eat me."

"But you battled your way to freedom," Aram said sarcastically.

"No. I climbed up inside the chimney, and they would have gotten me, but the lurker caught up with me and frightened them away."

"How did you escape the lurker?" Aram asked.

"I came here. They hate big towns. It stopped following me on the far side of the floodplain."

"And you claim Tark sent you to me?"

"Yes. To help me rejoin him and Galloran."

Aram chuckled. "Some good liars lean on extravagant details, but you abuse the technique." His expression darkened. "Who are you? You never shared your name. Make no mistake, your life depends on a straight answer."

Jason glanced from Aram to his mother. Neither of them liked that he knew about giants. They were certainly hiding something. If they were somehow affiliated with the giants, it most likely meant that Aram was an enemy. But if he was such a bad guy, why would Tark have recommended him? Could Tark have been totally wrong about him?

"Tark could have sent me anywhere," Jason murmured. "He could have sent me to anyone. Why you? I don't think you're on our side."

Aram frowned, eyes wary. "I'm not on anyone's side. I have a few friends, sure. But I have a hard time believing Tark sent you to ambush me with secrets about my past. You might as well drop the innocent act. We all know where this is heading. Are you after money? Some kind of bribe?"

Jason furrowed his brow. Whatever connection Aram had to the giants was clearly a guilty secret. If Aram thought this was a shakedown, it would explain his paranoid behavior. "You've got this all wrong. I just wanted to hire you based on Tark's recommendation."

"Enough nonsense," Aram's mother interjected. "Who else knows you're here? Who are you, really?"

As Jason looked from mother to son, he realized that they seemed braced for disaster. If he could convince them that he meant no harm, maybe he could still get the help he needed. And avoid Aram pounding him into hamburger meat.

"I'm honestly not here to connect you to the giants," Jason said. "My name is Lord Jason of Caberton. My title was granted by Galloran. I am the former chancellor of Trensicourt. I have been in and out of the dungeons of Felrook, and I come from the Beyond."

Aram smiled and shook his head. "I've never witnessed such shameless bluffing! So you are the mysterious Lord Jason who out-witted Copernum before disappearing into thin air."

"You heard about that?"

"Everyone did, as you well know. You choose a grand alias to accompany a monstrous exaggeration. Except rumor has it Lord Jason accepted an invitation to Harthenham. End of story."

"I broke out of Harthenham, was taken before Maldor, escaped Felrook, and returned to the Beyond. But I'm back. I learned some vital information that needs to be shared, and I left a friend behind in Lyrian."

Aram shook his head, then looked to his mother. "This is absurd. What do we do?"

His mother raised her eyebrows. "Have you any evidence to prove your story?"

"What's your name?" Jason asked.

"Moira."

"Nice to meet you, Moira. I'm still dressed in clothes from the Beyond. See my boots? My pants? Have you ever seen clothes quite like them?"

"No," Moira said. "Go on."

"I can tell you details," Jason said. "I can talk about the gong that grants audience with Maldor, or the inside of the lorevault at Trensicourt, or what a mangler looks like after you blast it with orantium."

"How about the signet ring to Caberton?" Aram asked, holding out a hand.

"I don't have it. I left it with a seedman before I entered Felrook. But the ring has a gem in it that glows when a certain chime is rung."

"You mentioned orantium," Aram pursued. "I don't suppose you have any samples?"

"I used what I had blowing up a mangler." He cupped his hand, fingers curling as if holding an invisible ball. "But the crystal sphere was about this big. The little mineral inside glows intensely for an instant before exploding."

"Have you any physical evidence besides odd clothes?" Moira asked.

"When Tark and I escaped from Harthenham, he snatched some jewels." Jason pulled the drawstring bag from his pocket.

"Tark was in Harthenham?" Aram asked.

"Long story," Jason said. "But that was where we sealed our friendship. He gave me these to help me hire you." Jason dumped the contents of the bag on a nearby end table. Aram and Moira gasped. Even Jason was impressed. He hadn't laid them all out in the open before—diamonds, emeralds, rubies, sapphires, and other precious stones, all cut to glittering perfection.

Aram picked up a red jewel, a green jewel, and a purple one, eyeing them closely. "These are real. This is a fortune." He sounded amazed. "These are meant to hire my services?"

"At least some of them," Jason said. "You seemed to think I was here to blackmail you. It's the opposite. I'm on the run, Aram. I'm in over my head. I've told you enough that I'm at your mercy. I'm trusting you, because Tark told me I should. I only know you have a connection to the giants in the woods because of how you reacted when I teased you."

Aram set down the jewels. "What's to stop me from killing you and then keeping the gemstones?"

"Aram!" his mother exclaimed.

He held out a hand to silence her.

Jason scooted forward in his seat. "Nothing. Except that a lurker followed me here, and people have seen you with me. I know some important secrets, Aram, and Maldor knows I know them."

Aram grunted. "Then you have already brought ruin upon us. What are the secrets?"

"You'll be safer if I keep them to myself," Jason said.

"Mother, step outside the room for a moment?"

"Aram, I deserve to—"

"Mother, just for a moment. If we end up in custody, you may not want these secrets in your mind."

"Neither will—"

Aram held up a hand. "Enough. Please, just for a moment."

She got up and walked out of the room. Aram fixed Jason with a brooding gaze. He spoke softly. "If the emperor traces you here, I'll get treated like you told me whether I know your secrets or not. I want to know how dangerous your knowledge is."

"Fine," Jason said. "Have you ever heard of an Edomic key word that can destroy Maldor?"

"Vague rumors," Aram said. "I never investigated the claim."

"I learned the Word," Jason said. "I had help from Galloran and a few others. The syllables were scattered all over Lyrian. I said the Word to Maldor, and it didn't work. I learned that the Word was actually an elaborate fraud meant to sidetrack his worst enemies. I need to share what I learned with those who helped me, so others don't waste their time."

Aram shifted uncomfortably. "You swear this is true?"

Jason crossed his heart with his finger. "I'm probably the most wanted person in Lyrian."

Aram bowed his head. After a moment he looked up. "You have really met Galloran? The true heir to Trensicourt? You know where to find him?"

"I'm going to Potsug to meet up with him and Tark. And to find my friend, another Beyonder who got left behind when I went home."

"Mother?" Aram called.

A moment later she returned. "You're running out of time," she told him.

"I know. If the secret he shared is authentic, it could not be more deadly. Among other things, our guest may truly have been consorting with Galloran."

"Do you believe him?" she asked.

"I don't know. I'm afraid I might. Could you finish the conversation?"

Moira nodded, taking a seat while Aram arose and then hurried from the room.

"Do you intend us any harm?" Moira asked Jason, her eyes intense.

"No. I mean, harm might follow me here, but I'm not your enemy."

The little woman exhaled and rubbed her thighs. "Harm will inevitably follow," she agreed. "Aram and I have done our best to lay low for many years. Your visit marks the end of life as we've known it."

"I'm sorry."

"There have been rumors for years about Galloran surviving in hiding. He truly lives?"

"Yes."

"You're acquainted with him?"

"Yes."

"He is still striving to overthrow the emperor?"

"He's doing what he can. He has limitations. I've been helping him. So have others."

Moira brushed an errant strand of hair from her eyes with a stubby hand. "It's almost certainly too late." She paused, staring down at her lap, then looked at Jason serenely. "I hope I'm still a good judge of character. You could be the answer to my deepest hopes and wishes."

"What?"

"You see, I am dying. I'm not sure how many days I have left."

"I . . . I'm sorry. That's terrible."

"Sooner or later, it happens to everyone." She rubbed her torso. "Pain has been gnawing inside of me, escalating over time. It began mostly in my joints, and would come and go, but it now fills me, and it is becoming constant. I can no longer keep food down. I seldom sleep. Death would be a relief, except I fear for my son."

"Why?"

"Aram is a special man." Her eyes glazed over with tears. "A unique man. We have secrets too, Jason. We'll keep yours if you keep ours."

"Okay."

"Swear by your life. Swear by all you hold dear."

"I promise."

"You wouldn't be able to spend much time close to him without discovering his secret. You had better hold to your word. Aram will make you pay otherwise. Make no mistake, he is one of the most dangerous individuals in Lyrian. Yet he still has so much untapped potential. I've been waiting for him to wake up and fulfill his destiny. I know Aram could be great. His father was the truest man I've ever known. His father also happened to be a giant."

Jason clasped his hands in his lap and nodded thoughtfully. "So he really does shrink at dawn."

"Not as much as a full-blooded giant, just as he is not so enormous as a true giant at night."

"And he keeps it a secret."

"Only the two of us know," Moira whispered. "And now you. Allow me to share a story. Years ago, in my youth, I lived in a hamlet on the peninsula, not far from the woods where rumors hinted that giants prowled. My father was the leader of the village. My stunted size was an anomaly. My mother, father, and two brothers were all quite tall.

"On occasion, I would venture into the woods. My family was overprotective, so when any chance arose to steal away, I always seized it. When I was a young woman, I met a little man in the forest. He was about my age, and hardly taller than me. His name was Thurwin. I had never seen another human dwarf before. He said he lived in the woods. I asked if he was afraid of the giants, and he laughed, assuring me he had wandered every corner of the forest and had never encountered one.

"We began to meet regularly. Thurwin made his amorous intentions known early on, showering me with compliments and staring at me as if I were a vision of loveliness. I was unaccustomed to that manner of attention, and though I acted coy at first, I had always longed for romance.

"By our tenth meeting we decided to get married. He told me he could never come to the village, nor could I visit where he lived, but instead he built a little cottage where we could rendezvous, and Thurwin devised a simple wedding ceremony consisting of private vows. It was all terribly romantic.

"After our secret nuptials, I still lived at home, but I saw my new husband at least two days out of each week. Months of secret encounters passed. One fine afternoon, in a shaded glen, I told him I was expecting a child. He chuckled, insisting I was mistaken. Perplexed by his confidence, I conceded that I could be wrong.

"Over time, the evidence of my condition grew. A couple of months later, when Thurwin beheld my belly unmistakably swelling with a child, he flew into a jealous tirade. I assured him I had been a faithful wife, and I began to weep. After I convinced him of my fidelity, he became very solemn. He asked me to remain with him until nightfall. We had never been together at night—he had always insisted it was too dangerous for me to roam the forest after dark.

"You can imagine my surprise when the sun went down and Thurwin expanded into a monstrous giant. I was not much higher than his knee. In time, he calmed me, explaining that if I were truly expecting his child, it would mark the first time a giant had successfully mated with a human.

"When I could no longer disguise my condition from my family, I pretended to have briefly eloped with a certain traveling merchant. After my tall tale, my family redoubled their smothering protectiveness. I was unable to visit Thurwin for the remainder of my pregnancy. Eventually, with the aid of a midwife, I became the mother of a healthy infant son.

"Some months after Aram was born, I began stealing away to the woods again, visiting our cottage and other locales I had frequented with Thurwin. It took a few trips before I encountered him. He was overjoyed to see me. I explained why I had been unable to return to the woods for some time, and he was very understanding. It was not long before I brought Aram with me to introduce the infant to his father.

"Then came the night that changed everything. I was nursing Aram, surrounded by my family, when somebody rapped on the door, hard enough to make the walls shudder. My father answered and was struck dumb. I heard a rumbling voice inquire about me. It was Thurwin, bearing a huge club.

"By the time I had rushed to the door, the screaming had begun. Thurwin looked distressed. He told me the giants were raiding our village and that I had to flee. He had tried to divert them elsewhere, but had failed. He had brought a saddled horse and apologized for not being able to warn me earlier.

"Behind him, giants were wreaking havoc. Burning buildings illuminated a variety of murderous atrocities. My father and brothers raced to meet the threat with weapons in hand. My mother dissolved into shrieking hysterics.

"Four giants rushed toward my house, and my father and brothers charged to intercept them. The giants slammed them aside almost effortlessly, hardly slowing to issue the fatal blows.

"Thurwin cried out for the giants to move on, but they came at me without hesitation. Shouting for me to ride away, Thurwin met them with his club. I mounted the horse in a panic, thinking only that I had to save my child. I believe Thurwin slew two of them before he went down. Once he fell, the remaining giants assaulted him mercilessly. I am grateful that I had a limited view.

"I returned the next day, accompanied by men from a

neighboring community, to find my village razed, the populace massacred. Aram and I were the sole survivors. Everything of value that the men salvaged from the rubble was given to me. It amounted to enough for me to move to Ithilum and to begin a new life.

"Aside from having a tiny young mother as his only family, Aram enjoyed a normal childhood. But one night in his eleventh year, he shot up two feet when the sun went down, and I was forced to explain to him about his unusual parentage. From that day forward, he experienced incredible growth at sunset and the opposite at sunrise. We have managed to maintain this secret through all the intervening years, until today."

"I'm sorry if I messed things up," Jason said.

"Don't apologize," Moira insisted. "I have not finished. Aram has used his size to perform mercenary work at night over the years. He built and ran a successful smuggling operation and has seen his share of combat. For a time, he was something of a pirate, hiding in a private cabin during daylight hours, occasionally pretending to be his own assistant. Having retired with plenty of money in reserve, he now uses his bulk to knock heads together at the Dockside Inn.

"I've always known he was special and was meant to do great things." Her voice cracked, and she paused to regain control of her emotions. "He has a hard exterior, a necessary adaptation given the secret he hides. But there is a goodness to him. I always yearned for him to find a way to employ his gifts for something more noble and meaningful than financial profit."

Jason rubbed the arm of the sofa. "You want him to join us in our struggle against Maldor?"

Moira pursed her lips. "If Galloran lives, he must have found a way to strike at Maldor without getting caught. I would rejoice to see my son employing his talents on behalf of a man of such legendary character. Since my death is approaching, I will not dilute my opinion. Maldor is a scourge. Our freedoms are already limited. No individual is safe. Once he conquers all of Lyrian, a day not far off, the vise will tighten until all joy is squeezed from life. Even if Maldor cannot be defeated, the only people who will really live will be those who resist him."

Moira shifted in her chair, looking over her shoulder toward a doorway. "Aram? Son, show yourself."

A small man with a slight build—not quite five feet tall— entered the room. A loose tunic could not conceal the narrowness of his shoulders or the slenderness of his arms. The face was barely recognizable as Aram—the structure of his cheeks, less defined; the brow, less primitive; the jaw, narrower. "I've been listening for some time." His voice had evolved from bass to tenor. "What use is there resisting a foe as invincible as Maldor?"

Moira faced her son. "Because you may discover he is not as invulnerable as you imagine."

Aram huffed. "I imagine nothing. There is a good reason I have never joined either side of that battle. Those who work for Maldor either get drawn into permanent service or end up dead. Those who work against him get caught. The smart ones, the only ones who last, shun tasks directly involving the emperor."

Moira frowned. "I do not have much longer, Aram."

"Don't say such things."

"Whether or not I speak openly about my condition, the reality remains. You know I never approved of your chosen occupation. But neither did I hinder you. When a government becomes unjust, honor is often found among the lawless. Over the years, you have developed many talents that may now prove useful to an honorable cause."

Aram shook his head. "Where's the honor in suicide?"

"More honor than attends a life of indifference, idling away your years quashing brawls in a tavern. Galloran and whatever resistance he creates may represent the final hope, however bleak, of dethroning Maldor. If the emperor succeeds, he will soon bring all of Lyrian into bondage, and with his wars behind him, an age of tyranny beyond our imagination will ensue. Among the first to disappear will be the former pirates, smugglers, and mercenaries—all those with adventuresome and questionable histories. Act now, unite with those who understand how to resist and avoid the emperor, and your abilities could prove useful. Hesitate, and you will be destroyed."

For a moment, Aram seemed taken aback by her intensity. Then he waved a hand toward a shuttered window. "Nobody loves the emperor. We all foresee darker times ahead. But why ensure misery striving for a futile cause? I would rather prepare to weather the storm than throw stones at the clouds."

"You behave as though there is no hope."

Aram turned to Jason. "Do you believe there is hope? Be honest."

Jason shifted in his seat. "Well, yeah. There are still some amazing people who stand up to Maldor. Tark is one of them. I've seen conscriptors and manglers and displacers killed. I've helped the cause, fighting against Maldor, and didn't get caught for a long time. After he nabbed me, I escaped. We've recently unraveled some secrets that were causing a lot of wasted effort. The information could start a revolution."

Aram scowled. "It's too late for resistance."

"You don't know that," Moira said. "You could at least investigate. You know I've been fretting about these concerns for years. Our visitor brings an opportunity to move beyond conversation. A chance that may never come again. I want you to accept the assignment Lord Jason has brought you. If you meet Galloran, my final request is for you to aid his cause, however you can."

Aram looked angry. His diminished size reduced the impact of the emotion to a childish petulance. "If I do anything to defy Maldor, you'll be most at risk. I will not allow you to become endangered."

Moira gave a faint smile. "I won't be alive by the time I could be in any danger. If I was, I'd go into hiding."

"You'll need me with you through your final months."

"Months? I'm probably down to days, Aram. I limit my complaints to downplay my condition, but, Son, agony has become my constant companion. My only hope is for your future. My only relief is in peace of mind. Grant your mother that peace."

Moira stared in silence, tiny hands folded on her lap. Aram bowed his head. "I'll . . . I'll consider it."

CHAPTER 8

EVASION

T he doll did not look much like Rachel. At least she hoped it didn't. Carved from a single block of wood, it was shaped roughly like an owl, all head and body, without arms or legs. Strings of wool served as hair, dull coins doubled as eyes, and a crude dress of plain fabric softened the wooden body. Most of the other features were painted—nose, mouth, ears, eyebrows.

Despite the blatant physical discrepancies, the doll was meant to fool the lurker. Strands of Rachel's actual hair had been woven into the woolen tresses. Small triangles cut from Rachel's clothes had been pinned to the simple dress. The coins were dimes Rachel had carried with her since her arrival to Lyrian. The charm woman had also employed samples of blood, skin, and saliva.

A goat bleated beside Rachel, then bent forward to nibble at the doll, and Rachel pushed its neck. "Shoo! Get out of here."

The goat ambled off, pausing to tear up some weeds. The charm woman owned several goats, a few sheep, some chickens, and a small army of donkeys. All of her possessions—including the tent, its furnishings, and her endless tokens and charms—had already been packed onto the donkeys. None of the animals had been in view before the charm woman had called, but after she beat a drum composed of stretched hides while chanting a few Edomic phrases, most of the livestock had wandered into camp within ten minutes.

Breathing heavily, the charm woman toddled into view, swaying from side to side as she walked, holding a short carved cane in one hand and a tall staff in the other. The skull of a large bird of prey topped the staff, adorned with feathers and teeth.

"I have the last of my talismans," the charm woman announced. "We can proceed once Drake returns."

"He's a big believer in scouting an area before we move," Rachel said. "He sometimes takes a while. But he always comes back."

"May it ever be so," the charm woman muttered, touching beads on her necklace. "Are you ready to grant the doll authority to serve as your substitute?"

"I think so," Rachel said. Learning new Edomic phrases was tricky. The language was quite different from English, with a wider variety of vowel sounds and certain consonants that required a nimble tongue. To further complicate things, speaking Edomic felt almost like singing. The pitch mattered, as did the rhythm. Plus, you spoke the language with your mind as much as with your mouth. To get it right required full concentration, especially as the phrases became more complex. The charm woman had drilled Rachel on this particular phrase since yesterday.

"Just as we practiced," the charm woman encouraged. "Relax and speak true."

Rachel placed two fingers on the doll's forehead. After mustering her willpower, she spoke words that essentially meant "you now have my full permission to represent me." The phrase tasted good leaving her lips. She sensed additional nuances encapsulated in the declaration, including approval of the previous enchantments established by the charm woman, along with a confirmation that the doll was now a symbolic proxy commissioned to exude every characteristic that Rachel embodied.

Rachel had not been studying long with the charm woman, but she already recognized how difficult it was to mentally translate Edomic expressions into English. The English versions always proved less precise, requiring far more words to convey the same meaning as the Edomic, and inevitably falling a little short.

"Well done," the charm woman enthused. "You're a prodigy, Rachel. Some individuals have a natural talent for a particular category of Edomic endeavors, but this undertaking was quite different from calling fire. Making that pronouncement stick was no casual task. The doll should have proven adequate, even without your formal permission, but now I expect the lurker will be thoroughly baffled. With my charms shielding your mind, the lurker ought to follow the decoy with full confidence."

Rachel fingered her braided necklace of bead and bone. The charm woman had custom made one for her and another for Drake. Rachel also wore a bracelet, a ring, and an anklet, all intended to disrupt efforts to perceive her presence.

"What happens if the lurker gets too close to the doll?" Rachel asked.

"The camouflage is strong," the charm woman said. "For a time, the illusion should withstand close scrutiny. Eventually the lurker will recognize the deception. No illusion endures forever. But torivors do not perceive the world the same way we do. Based on my studies, I'm not even sure if they have any faculties comparable to human sight, smell, hearing, or taste. Instead they reach out with their minds. Our decoy is specifically designed to confuse that method of perception. The lurker will sense the doll as a seriously injured or partially shielded version of you. With your actual self heavily cloaked by charms, the lurker should have little reason to doubt the authenticity of the proxy. If fortune favors us, by the time it realizes we pulled a trick, we'll be far away and shielded by charms."

"What exactly are the torivors?" Rachel asked. "Drake wouldn't explain."

"He was trying to keep you safe," the charm woman said. "Ignorance can offer some protection from their psychic abilities. But after the extended exposure you've endured over the past weeks, I expect knowledge will serve you better than ignorance. There has been considerable debate regarding the nature of torivors. The wizard Zokar claimed to have created them, and although most who have investigated the race refute his assertion, none contest that they first showed up as his servants."

"Then where did they come from?"

The charm woman grinned. "I've done my best to understand the torivors. Self-preservation is a potent motivator. I've read extensively about them, shared dreams with them, traded information with others, and spent years practicing how to use Edomic to mislead them. Based on all I've learned, I suspect Zokar summoned them. They don't belong in Lyrian any more than you do."

"You mean they're Beyonders?"

"That's my guess."

"I've never seen anything like them in my world."

"I suspect there is much more to the Beyond than just your world," the charm woman said. "If I'm right, the torivors come from a much more foreign reality than yours."

"Where?"

"I don't know a name for it. But Zokar took great interest in the Beyond. It was a specialty. My best guess is that he somehow lured the torivors to Lyrian from afar and bound them into his service."

"How many torivors are there?"

The woman shrugged. "No less than twenty. Probably no more

than a few hundred. It is difficult to estimate with any certainty. Lurkers are seldom seen abroad anymore, and they tend to show up solo. During the great war between Eldrin and Zokar, torivors occasionally appeared in groups, giving us our only basis for guessing at their numbers."

Oncoming hoofbeats made the charm woman turn.

"A single horse," Rachel recognized. "Should be Drake."

The charm woman nodded. "I still have defenses up that would reveal the approach of an enemy."

Astride Mandibar, Drake burst into view through a pair of tall shrubs and loped over to Rachel, dismounting smoothly. "The lurker has brought soldiers."

"How near are they?" the charm woman asked.

"They're coming from the east and the west, fanned out in wide lines, at least sixty in all; half soldiers, half militia. I watched from the hilltop to the southwest."

The charm woman frowned. "Lurkers are clever. Once this one lost you, it recognized that you had found a way to conceal yourselves. So it has brought others to converge on the area where you disappeared, to flush you out. My charms are meant to divert casual attention, not intense scrutiny."

"We have maybe half an hour before they come within view," Drake said. "If you two go north and I head south, we should avoid discovery."

"We're ready to go," the charm woman said. "This may work to our favor. Just when the lurker is expecting to flush us, you'll run south with the doll."

"If it takes the bait, I'll lead it southwest to the Purga River. After I set the doll adrift, I'll ride hard to the north. We'll meet on the highest ridge above Crescent Valley, to the northeast of Trensicourt."

"That's the plan," the charm woman confirmed. "It's time I uprooted for a change of scenery. I was getting too comfortable here. Don't forget the doll." She gestured toward it while mounting a donkey. Rachel climbed onto her mare.

Drake looked at the doll, and froze. He blinked and squinted, glancing from the doll to Rachel and back. "Uncanny resemblance," he muttered.

"Ha-ha," Rachel said. "Let's just hope it confuses the lurker."

"I'm not jesting," Drake assured her, crouching over the doll. He held out a tentative hand, passing it through the air above the wooden figure.

"It's the power of your permission, coupled with my preparations," the charm woman told Rachel. "The doll is speaking to his mind with more authority than his eyes."

"He sees me?"

Drake fumbled almost blindly for a moment before laying hands on the doll. He patted it, as he might in the dark, to confirm its size and shape. "Masterful work."

"The first layer of enchantment directs attention away from the doll," the charm woman explained. "Under that layer, the decoy registers as Rachel to the mind."

Drake picked up the doll, shaking his head. "Enough to make me hallucinate," he agreed. "And that was with the real girl right in front of me."

"It should suffice," the charm woman said.

With the doll cradled in one arm, Drake swung up onto Mandibar. "Until we meet again," he said. The stallion bounded forward at his command.

"Bye, Drake," Rachel called, sad to see her protector leaving. He had been her sole companion for weeks.

The charm woman shook a rattle and chanted Edomic words.

Rachel had never heard the phrases, but innately sensed the meaning. The words spoke to the animals, releasing them from this area and encouraging them to make their own way to the rendezvous point.

"Can you control animals with Edomic?" Rachel asked as they started northward.

"Not control," the woman replied. "At best, one can influence. You will find that all life generates natural resistance to Edomic tampering. Speaking broadly, the greater the intelligence, or stronger the will, the more potent the resistance. The usual relationships one could form with domestic animals can be hastened and deepened by proper use of Edomic, and communication becomes much clearer. Influencing wild animals can be significantly more challenging, and exercising compulsion is virtually impossible. I build trust with my pets over time, occasionally inviting them to do my will."

Rachel had to hold back her mare to avoid outpacing the charm woman. As they moved north, the other donkeys and animals dispersed. "So they'll just roam and eventually join us at our destination?"

"Essentially," the charm woman said. "They're all protected with various tokens that should guide them back to me while helping them avoid the notice of predators. I've been on the move like this for decades, so I've gained some skill at the relevant enchantments."

"You seem good at what you do."

"Thank you."

"Isn't there an easier way for you to live?"

The charm woman considered the question before answering. "I suppose I could set up an exhaustively protected lair from which I could operate. But I don't think I'm good enough to keep such a stronghold hidden indefinitely. Besides, I enjoy the outdoors. The exercise keeps me young. I suspect I would stagnate if trapped in one place."

"Does it get lonely?"

"My charms are good company. I never tire of creating them. Improving my Edomic is a lifelong challenge. The related efforts keep me stimulated. My only other realistic option would be to take up a false identity and quit using Edomic, which I would never consider."

Rachel nodded. "It's fun to use it. It makes me feel, I don't know, more alive."

The woman gazed up at her from astride the donkey. "Considerable pleasure arises from successfully exerting your will to command natural elements. Something more than the inherent satisfaction of accomplishment. The thrill can become intoxicating. It can lure the unwary into attempting more than they are ready to manage . . . with disastrous results."

"I'll try to be careful," Rachel said, wishing she had kept the thought to herself.

"I'm not advising you to ignore the pleasure of wielding Edomic," the charm woman clarified. "You couldn't if you tried. But keep up your defenses against the tantalizing allure. Chasing the thrill of power is a short path to destruction."

They proceeded in silence for a time, with the donkey in front, Rachel behind on her much larger mount. The donkey showed no interest in hurrying, never advancing at more than a walk.

After some time, the charm woman dismounted and then planted a small stake in the ground, not much bigger than a golf tee. A few copper rings dangled from the top.

"What will that do?" Rachel asked.

The charm woman remounted the donkey. "The purpose is

twofold. The totem will serve as an alarm to let us know if somebody is following our trail. And it should also befuddle and divert any who seek to pursue us."

"You think of everything," Rachel said.

"I try."

"Do you have a name? I feel like I have nothing to call you."

"I have a name. But I don't share it. My most formidable enemies hunt me with their minds. It helps that they don't know where I'm from, or my age, or who my relatives might be. It also helps that they don't have my name. You can assign me a nickname if you like."

"How about Elaine?"

"That will serve. You chose swiftly."

"I've always liked it." Rachel did not add that Elaine had been the name of her favorite stuffed animal, a giraffe with a hat and pearl necklace.

As the day progressed, they rode across low, wild hills and skirted numerous valleys and meadows, never proceeding with any haste. The charm woman planted a couple more stakes. By sundown, they reached a rocky slope above a small lake. Rachel followed the donkey over uneven terrain until they arrived at the wide mouth of a shallow cave.

The charm woman dismounted and removed a few items from the donkey's packs. Rachel tethered her horse and then collected her rolled blankets. Elaine led her into the broad recess. Rachel noticed symbols painted on the walls, and a few crude figurines on the ground. In a rear corner of the shallow cave, the charm woman led Rachel through a narrow cleft into a second chamber.

"I've used this cavity before," Elaine confided. "It offers plenty of shelter to build a fire now that darkness will hide the smoke." She motioned toward a few tidy stacks of wood.

"Are those your dolls out in the first room?" Rachel asked.

"I prefer for my hideouts to remain undisturbed."

"Right."

Elaine piled up some logs in a depression, then added some twigs. "Would you care to do the honors?"

"Sure. I haven't lit a campfire before."

"Concentrate on this stick," Elaine said, indicating a gnarled twig. "See if you can get the entire length to ignite at once."

"Drake used tinder," Rachel hedged.

"Drake didn't have your aptitude. There are words that could direct the heat to gather along the entire stick. But I would rather you used the same verbiage as usual, and simply willed the heat to the entirety of the twig."

Rachel flexed her fingers nervously. "What if I fail?"

"This is not overly ambitious. You'll be fine. Besides, if you fully invest in this task, I don't expect you to fail. Go ahead."

Rachel knelt close beside the modest pile of wood, eyes on the gnarled twig, trying to internalize the texture and shape. She focused her will on it, just as she had on the candle wicks, but instead of narrowing her concentration down to a point, she tried to mentally aim at the entire object.

She spoke the Edomic words and pushed with all of her consciousness, exerting her will much as she had when lighting distant candles. The twig suddenly burst into hot flames, making Rachel lean back. She laughed at the sudden combustion and enjoyed a much more satisfying rush than had ever attended the lighting of a candle.

"Well done, child!" the charm woman exclaimed. "You're really learning to merge the command with your will."

"I gave it everything I had," Rachel said.

The twig continued to burn. The fire she had called had not merely licked across the surface—it seemed to have erupted from within. As the twig burned hotly, flames spread to neighboring wood.

"I couldn't have lit that twig half so impressively," Elaine confessed. "And I have been at this for many years. How did it feel?"

"Good. It actually felt easier than the first time I lit a candle from a distance."

"Come with me."

The charm woman led Rachel out of the cave and over to a little pine. She ran a finger along a slender limb bristling with green needles. "Try to ignite the end of this branch."

"How much of it?" Rachel asked.

She indicated the last couple of inches. "Just this much."

"That's a lot shorter than the twig."

"It'll be harder. But see if you can manage it."

"Okay. It's funny, I feel a little tired after the twig."

Elaine nodded. "You pushed hard to light the twig, probably harder than necessary. Over time, you'll learn how much effort is needed for various tasks, and that will help you conserve your strength. Take a moment to collect yourself."

"I'm all right."

"Don't hold back," Elaine advised. "This will be tough."

"Right," Rachel said softly. She breathed deeply, focusing on the end of the limb, trying to memorize every needle. "Here we go."

Just like in the cave, she spoke the words to summon heat, then pushed with all the will she could muster. She centered her attention on the last two inches of the limb, directing the heat to permeate it. If anything, it felt like she had marshaled more power than ever for this command, but the end of the limb began to feel indefinably slippery. Her concentration wavered. Clenching her fists, she redoubled her effort. The limb quivered, and tendrils of steam trickled up.

After a prolonged, frustrating moment, her focus completely broke. She simply couldn't sustain the internal effort. It felt like she had taken a step off an unseen curb. Damp with perspiration, Rachel fell to her knees. A wave of nausea washed over her, and she found herself short of breath. As she closed her eyes, the ground seemed to twirl and tilt. She bowed forward, putting her palms on the dirt.

She felt steadying hands on her shoulders. "Calm yourself, child. Let the sensation pass."

Rachel felt acutely aware of the smell of the rocks and soil beneath her, the scent of the little pine beside her. She fought down the urge to retch, and the dizziness began to recede. After a moment, she stood.

"That was brutal," she said, feeling too rattled to hide her resentment. "I fell apart. Why'd you ask me to do that?"

"Do you know what made it so hard?"

"The water inside the branch?"

"Think about what I told you before."

The realization hit. "The tree is alive."

"Exactly. All life resists Edomic tampering. The difference between trying to ignite a dead twig and a live limb is extraordinary. I'm not sure if even the greatest wizards could have directly burned a human."

"You knew I would fail," Rachel said.

"I suspected you might fail with the twig. When you succeeded, I gave you a much harder challenge."

"Why would you want me to fail?" Rachel still felt unsteady and short of breath.

"Two reasons. First, I wanted you to feel firsthand the resistance living things have to Edomic. The way life resists tampering is difficult to grasp until you experience it."

"And second?"

"You needed to learn what failure feels like. You needed to experience your concentration unraveling when engaged in a task beyond your capacity. With practice, you will learn to recognize when you have attempted to accomplish too much. Deliberately abandoning a command early can reduce the negative impact of failure."

"So if I hadn't kept fighting to the end, I would have been less jolted?"

"Correct. Anyone who dabbles in Edomic must learn to cope with failed directives. Little by little, you'll be able to handle more ambitious commands. But never forget that the more ambitious the command, the harsher the impact of failure."

"I see how that could be good to know."

"For example," Elaine continued, "had you tried to set the whole evergreen ablaze, and had you pushed with all your might, you would probably be dead."

"I'll be careful," Rachel promised. Her legs still felt a little rubbery.

"Using Edomic can be very rewarding," the charm woman said. "But it is no game. You must learn to stay within your limits. You have great potential, Rachel, but those with impressive native skill often burn out quickly. They attempt too much too soon, and never get to discover what they might have become had they cultivated their talent more patiently."

"I think I've got the idea," Rachel said. "If I'm going to fail, I need to fail doing only a little more than I can handle."

"That is a sane and proven road to progress. If you can hold to that principle, you could go far. If not, you will probably perish."

CHAPTER 9

SMUGGLED

Upstairs, in a spotless guest bedroom, Jason could not sleep. Fingers laced behind his head, he lay atop the covers of a narrow bed, gazing up at the slanted ceiling. Aram was asleep downstairs, and Moira had insisted Jason rest as well, in preparation for a night on horseback.

The night before, Aram had collected Jason's belongings from the Dockside Inn. He had also scouted the town and found triple the usual guardsmen at every gate, complemented by an unusual amount of patrols scouring the city in search of a nameless fugitive who matched Jason's description. Aram had expressed that he couldn't recall comparable interest in a fugitive since Galloran had been abroad.

Jason rolled onto his side, trying to get comfortable. Part of his restlessness stemmed from Ferrin's hand. The dismembered appendage kept fluttering in the backpack. The rustling had persisted off and on for at least an hour. In the past, Ferrin had only drawn such attention when there was something he urgently wanted to share.

Although he felt painfully curious about the message from Ferrin, Jason had been trying to ignore the rustling. After all, the safety of Aram and Moira was in jeopardy, along with his own. There was no guarantee that Ferrin was on his side. The smart course would be to avoid contacting Ferrin until Ithilum was behind him. But as the minutes passed and the fluttering continued, Jason began to question how the displacer could deduce anything useful from letters traced on a palm. If he was careful not to give away information, was there any real harm in exchanging a few words? What if Ferrin had a vital tip?

As the rustling continued doggedly, curiosity finally overcame caution. Jason had to silence the hand, right? With the sun perhaps an hour from setting, Aram might show up before long. The lively hand would be difficult to explain.

Jason rolled out of bed and removed the severed hand from the backpack, slapping it gently to signal he was prepared to receive a message. The hand began signing.

I am in Ithilum. So are you. All routes out of town are under surveillance by agents of Maldor, no doubt summoned by your lurker friend. I will help you escape.

Jason considered the message. With all of these soldiers around, it would be an ideal opportunity for Ferrin to backstab him. Even if the displacer really had burned bridges with Maldor, might he not view this as a chance to repair the damage?

Jason began tracing letters. I FOUND AN ALLY. HE WILL HELP ME GET AWAY.

Who?

BETTER NOT SAY.

I understand your reluctance. Yet I swear I am laboring for your welfare. I have no illusions that nabbing you would offset my crimes. Maldor does not forgive traitors. He would never let me live given what I know. I never had many friends. I want to join you and help you.

WISH I COULD TRUST YOU. I LOOK FORWARD TO THAT DAY. NOW IS NOT THE TIME.

Let me supply some free information to inspire a little faith. The port is under heavy scrutiny, as are the three city gates. You must find a different way out of town. At least one other displacer is in the vicinity, along with many conscriptors and droves of common soldiers.

THANKS. WE WILL BE CAREFUL.

One more thing. The name of your ally is Aram.

Jason stared at the hand in shock. How could he respond without giving away too much?

WHY DO YOU SAY THAT?

I still have my sources. The Dockside Inn has always been a reliable well of information.

ARE YOU THREATENING ME?

This is not a threat. I am trying to create an opportunity for you to trust me. I already have the intelligence I need if I meant to turn you in. I know you are here in Ithilum. I know you have hired Aram to assist you. I know the secrets you carry. And I am across the street.

Could it be true? Jason deliberated how to respond.

Look out a window.

The guest room window commanded a view of the street. Jason sidled over to it and peered outside. Ferrin stood below on the far side of the cobblestone road, arms folded, a patch over one eye, a scruffy beard on his chin. He wore a broad-brimmed hat tilted at a rakish angle. The displacer met his gaze and gave a faint nod.

Jason backed away from the window. WHAT NOW?

Aram has a respectable reputation. But you will need more than a muscle-bound smuggler if you hope to evade a lurker for long. You need my help. This is for your own good. See you in a moment.

A second peek out the window revealed Ferrin crossing the street toward the front door. Flustered, Jason dashed from the room and clomped down the stairs. Moira came out of the kitchen into the entry hall, sleeves rolled back, hands powdered with flour. "What is it?" the little woman asked.

There came a brisk knock at the door.

"An old friend has tracked me down," Jason said.

She blanched. "Is he trustworthy?"

"I hope so. I think so. I didn't invite him. He tracked me on his own. He came here instead of turning us in. At this point, our only choice is to speak with him."

Moira motioned Jason out of sight and cracked the door. "Yes?"

"My close friend is visiting you," Ferrin said politely. "May I intrude?"

Moira glanced at Jason, who nodded. She pulled the door wide, and Ferrin entered.

"We meet again," Ferrin said, grinning. He swept off his hat and tossed it like a Frisbee onto a sofa in the parlor. Striding forward, he embraced Jason, who returned the hug uncertainly. Then the displacer bowed to Moira.

"Are you going to introduce us?" he prompted Jason.

Jason felt off-balance. "Ferrin, this is Moira. Moira, meet Ferrin."

"The pleasure is all mine," Ferrin said. Turning to Jason, he raised an arm that ended at the wrist. "Can you lend me a hand?"

"A displacer?" Moira gasped, raising fingers to her lips.

"Have no fear, I have gone renegade. The emperor is my enemy. I mean you no harm. In fact, I intend to offer vital assistance. Does she know who you are?"

Jason nodded.

"I'm an old comrade of Lord Jason. I rescued him from—"

The door to the cellar burst open, and Aram emerged, hair mussed from sleeping, a long, slightly curved knife in one small hand. His eyes went from Ferrin to Jason and back. "What's going on?"

"Who's that?" Ferrin asked.

"My son, Burt," Moira said.

"Who are you?" Aram challenged.

"Is he in on all of this?" Ferrin mumbled.

Jason nodded.

"As I was explaining to your mother, I'm Ferrin the displacer, a former servant of the emperor who went renegade after I smuggled Lord Jason out of the dungeons of Felrook. I'm here to help him flee Ithilum, no small task considering the host assembling to apprehend him."

Knife pointed at Ferrin, Aram glanced at Jason. "Does he speak the truth?"

"As far as I know," Jason said. "He helped me escape from Felrook, and today he located us on his own. If he wanted to turn us in, he could have already done it."

Aram snorted. "Unless he counts on you leading him to bigger game. No displacer can be trusted."

"There is no larger quarry than Lord Jason in all of Lyrian," Ferrin replied. He turned to Jason. "I understood you were working with Aram."

"What do you know of Aram?" Aram asked.

"Only his reputation."

"What reputation is that?"

Ferrin made a vague gesture. "He was arguably the most reliable mercenary in the business before he retired. He stayed out of imperial matters. He was cautious, smart; a survivor. To be candid, Aram was savvy enough to steer clear of somebody like Jason. I question whether he sincerely means to help. I take it you're a colleague?"

"I'm his brother," Aram said.

Ferrin raised his eyebrows. "Evidently he used up all the size in the family. Where is your brother now? He must realize that he could make more money with less risk by handing Jason over to the authorities."

"My brother values nothing above his reputation. He has never double-crossed a client after accepting a job. He only came out of retirement because he believes in this cause."

Ferrin glanced at Jason. "Money has been exchanged?"

"A lot of money," Jason said.

Ferrin nodded pensively. "I can't fathom how you convinced Aram to commit. But I've learned not to underestimate you. Very well. I repeat the question, Burt. Where exactly is your brother?"

"Out scouting," Aram said, still holding the long knife warily. "He knows about the hunt for Jason, and he is exploring our options."

Ferrin gave a nod. "The three gates out of town are heavily manned. The port is full of eyes. Clever deception will be required to smuggle Jason away."

"We're aware of the complications," Aram said.

Ferrin narrowed his eyes. "I've never heard of a brother. Do you work with Aram often?"

"For years I served as his cabin boy."

"Ah. The infamous cabin boy. It wasn't Burt back then."

"I went by Goya."

Ferrin's lips twitched. "Brothers. I had no idea. Can you speak on his behalf?"

"Aram may have the size, but we're equal partners."

"Fair enough. We should counsel together. I mean to help Jason, so we should factor my services into your plans. As a displacer and a former servant of the emperor, I can do much to help you avoid capture."

Aram shook his head. "I don't work with limb droppers. Help from your kind tends to end badly. Mother?"

Moira had quietly sidled toward the kitchen. Reaching around the corner, she retrieved a heavy crossbow. The weapon almost looked too large for her, but she leveled it coolly at Ferrin.

"I admire your caution," Ferrin said. "Avoiding displacers in these types of arrangements is good for longevity. But every rule has an exception."

Without warning, Ferrin dove and rolled across the floor toward Moira. She fired the crossbow, but the quarrel hissed over his head, and he whipped her legs out from under her with a sweeping kick. Aram charged.

Wrenching the crossbow from Moira's grasp, Ferrin used it to parry Aram's long knife, then sent him to the floor with a sharp kick to the chest. While Aram scrambled to his feet, long knife still in hand, Ferrin drew a dagger and brought it to Moira's throat.

Jason stood paralyzed with shock and uncertainty. Aram glared from Jason to Ferrin.

"You have a reputation for knifework, Goya," Ferrin said. "I have some experience myself."

"This is no way to win friends," Aram spat.

"This is precisely how to court allies under hostile circumstances," Ferrin argued. "I was prepared to be civil. You and your mother pulled weapons on me. If I keep the upper hand, hopefully I can show that I mean you no harm."

"I'll never trust you," Aram growled, knuckles white as he clenched the long knife.

"I just need you to work with me. You and Aram know this city. I am willing to believe you can get Jason out. Unfortunately, a lurker is involved. Even with my assistance, Jason will probably be taken. Without my aid, his downfall is certain."

Aram looked over at Jason. "What do you say?"

"Ferrin has faked friendship in the past. He's a patient liar. On the other hand, he could have shown up here with soldiers and apprehended us. He has lots of talents. If he's really on our side, he would be useful."

"Put the knife down," Aram said. "You have my word that you'll leave here unmolested."

"Finish the conversation first," Ferrin replied. "Forgive me if I'm slow to rely on the word of a smuggler. We must reach an accord. I insist on helping Jason."

"Do you have his hand, Jason?" Moira asked, heedless of the blade at her throat. "When he entered, the limb dropper seemed to suggest you had it."

"I have it," Jason said.

"It may be all he wants," Moira pointed out. "He may only be waiting to turn us in until his hand is returned."

"If all I wanted was the hand, I could have brought guardsmen and taken it," Ferrin said. "I'm not after money, either. My services come free. I've betrayed the emperor for the sake of my friendship with Jason. My only place now is with the resistance."

"Tell you what," Aram said. "I still haven't arranged for horses. Can you meet us at a rendezvous with three fresh mounts?"

"Tonight?"

"Yes."

"Certainly."

"One must be large enough to carry Aram."

"And a fourth for myself."

"I won't be coming," Aram said. "Just Aram and Jason."

"So the third is for me. How thoughtful."

"Aram will inspect the area. He's good. If you're there with the horses, and no enemies lie in ambush, you'll get your hand back."

Ferrin scowled. "I would hate to be left standing alone in the dark all night."

"You have my oath. Some degree of trust is required. This role is vital. It will fill a gaping need. You will find it difficult to obtain the horses without arousing suspicion. Do we have your word?"

"Naturally."

"Say it," Aram pressed.

"You have my word of honor."

The promise made Jason edgy. He knew Ferrin was willing to lie when it suited his purposes.

"There are several groves inland from the cove north of town," Aram described. "One has an old well at the center. It's been in disrepair ever since the water became brackish. Meet us there."

"Done. I apologize, Moira, for holding you at knifepoint."

"I'll forgive you once you prove yourself true," she responded.

"Don't forget, you did pull a crossbow on me." Ferrin stepped away from her, knife ready, eyes on Aram. He retrieved his hat. "Until tonight." He backed to the door and let himself out.

Aram hurried over to Moira. She was standing up. "Are you all right?" he asked.

"I'm fine," she said. "He could have been much more vicious when he took me down. Under the circumstances, he was almost gentle."

"Lucky for his sake." Aram glanced at Jason. "You have charming friends."

"I'm a Beyonder," Jason apologized. "I met Ferrin before I knew what displacers were."

"How did he find us?"

"He's a spy," Jason said. "It's what he does. He said he asked around at the Dockside Inn."

"You have his hand?"

"I stole it when he forced me to return to the Beyond. I used it to keep in touch with him from there."

Aram opened the front door, checked up and down the street, then withdrew. "How much do you trust him?"

"About as much as you do," Jason said. "I expect he'll follow through with the horses. But I'm not sure I want to lead him to Galloran."

"How would you feel about completely avoiding his assistance?"

Jason thought about it. Ferrin might be sincere. But the displacer had suckered him before. No matter how much help Ferrin could provide, there was a real chance it would end with a double-cross. "Might be safer."

"Good. Because we're not exiting town where I described. I'm a man of my word, but I'm willing to make an exception when some limb dropper has a knife to my mother's throat. Besides, no money changed hands."

"He's lied to me before," Jason said. "It was how we ended up traveling together."

"Yet he really freed you from Felrook?" Moira asked.

"He did," Jason confirmed. "He took a huge risk with nothing to gain. It was the sort of thing only a real friend would do. It's possible he really means to help us."

"Any doubt is too much when displacers are involved," Aram said. "We need to leave this house now. There's a secret back exit. I have many hideaways around town."

"I'll gather my things," Moira said.

"How do you plan to sneak us out of town if the gates and port are covered?" Jason asked Aram.

"We'll stage a couple of diversions, then sneak under the wall."

"Under the wall?"

Aram grinned. "How long can you hold your breath?"

* * *

The streets of Ithilum quieted as the shadows of evening deepened. Jason followed several paces behind Aram, who had regained his imposing physique at sunset. Wearing trousers and sturdy sandals that Aram had purchased, along with a hat and a brown cloak, Jason felt much less conspicuous than he had in his jeans. Glancing back down the avenue that sloped up from the sea, Jason saw several people moving about. Out on the point of the reef, a fiery beacon flared. Scattered tendrils of mist shone in the distant firelight.

Earlier in the evening Aram had escorted Jason and Moira to a hidden room less than a block from their townhome. He had reviewed several options with his mother regarding resources she could access, including people who could help her and places she could go. He then requested some additional money and jewels from Jason to pay some bribes.

After Aram became tall and strong again, he set off to perform some final errands. Moments ago, he had returned and exchanged solemn but tearless farewells with his mother, who beamed up at her son after their final embrace.

Jason had almost lost it watching them say good-bye. His throat had constricted, and tears had threatened. It saddened him to think that the half giant would probably never see his mother again. They were obviously close.

The farewell had turned his thoughts to his own parents. Sure, he wasn't especially tight with his mom and dad, but they wanted the best for him and he still loved them. They had worked hard to get him back after he had vanished the first time. They had to be devastated thinking he had been devoured by a hippo. And they might never learn otherwise. At least he knew that his family was home and safe. With a little luck, he might find Rachel and eventually make it back to them.

Up ahead, Aram rounded a corner. When Jason followed him into the alley, Aram stood several paces ahead, gesturing for him to hurry. Jason sprinted to the big man, who boosted him over a wall before following. They crouched together in a courtyard garden. Aram led Jason stealthily to the far side, passing a pond decorated with floating flowers, and hopped up to peer over the wall.

"Some soldiers behind us were showing too much interest," Aram whispered before shoving Jason over the wall. Jason dropped to the far side. The big man landed beside him an instant later. They hurried across a road and down another alleyway. Aram led them at a furious pace around numerous corners, keeping to narrow streets and crooked alleys. Soon they stood panting in a shadowy side street that opened onto a main road running along the western wall of the town. A row of shops lined the far side of the road along the base of the wall.

Leaning forward, Aram scanned up and down the street. He tapped Jason on the shoulder and led him across the road. They strolled casually to the door of one of the shops. The windows were dark. Aram knocked three times, paused, and then rapped twice more.

The door opened immediately, and Aram led Jason inside.

The cluttered shop contained an assortment of curiosities and knickknacks. Jason noticed a large trunk completely encrusted with shells. A huge trophy fish bristling with quills hung on one wall.

A hunched figure wearing a clownish mask silently guided Aram and Jason to a door at the rear of the store. Judging by his hands, he appeared to be an old man. He took a sleek harpoon from a rack on the wall and handed it to Aram. From a pocket in his loose, shabby coat, their guide produced a glowing length of seaweed. Aram took the seaweed, opened the door, and led Jason down a rickety flight of wooden stairs that groaned at their passage.

The masked figure closed the door but did not follow.

The deep cellar was a musty maze of stacked crates and indiscernible objects draped in dusty tarps. With quick strides, Aram wove through the clutter to a pyramid of crates in a corner. Winding the seaweed around his thick forearm, Aram began unstacking the wooden boxes, moving them aside until he uncovered a splintered wooden pallet. Raising the heavy pallet, Aram revealed a circular hole in the stone floor protected by a metal grate. Leaving the pallet upended, Aram knelt, produced a key, unlocked the grate, and pulled it open.

"Down the ladder," Aram instructed.

The gaping hole looked ominous in the turquoise light of the luminescent seaweed. Jason hoped that Aram knew what he was doing. Squatting at the brink, staring down into the darkness, Jason observed iron rungs protruding from the stone. Could this lead to a tunnel under the wall? Turning around, he felt for the first rung with his foot, then began to descend. Aram followed. Jason heard the grate clang softly as it was dragged shut.

The humid odor of seawater permeated the close confines of the shaft. Jason felt like he was climbing down into a well. He counted more than fifty rungs before he could see light from the seaweed reflecting off rippling water below him.

"This passage is one of the best kept secrets in Ithilum," Aram said from above. "The owner charges exorbitant prices, so it is not often used. Fortunately, this escape was well funded. You'll find that the rungs continue underwater, and then along a tunnel. Use them. Periodically we'll encounter barrels chained to the ground. The owner assures me they're filled with fresh air. Even the swiftest diver could not make this swim unaided, but the passage has been prepared to accommodate any man who can hold his breath for roughly a minute at a time. Hesitate at no barrel very long. The air will grow stale. I'll go first, in case any dangerous creatures lurk ahead."

"Creatures?" Jason asked.

"Aquatic predators. Let me worry about them. You just move quickly, and try to look inedible."

Aram pulled a fresh piece of seaweed from his pocket and twisted it, triggering the bioluminescent reaction. The seaweed emitted a sickly green light.

"Fasten this around your wrist," Aram directed.

Jason took the seaweed, then hooked his elbow through an iron rung to maintain his balance while securing it.

"Ready?" Aram asked.

"I guess."

"Wait a moment or two and then follow me."

Harpoon in hand, the huge man released his grip and fell past Jason into the water, illuminating the previously murky liquid. Jason watched Aram find the rungs and use them to hurry downward. As he moved away across the floor of the submerged chamber, the turquoise illumination began to fade.

Clinging to the iron rungs, Jason wondered what was wrong with riding out of town in the secret compartment of a wagon. This seemed almost as dangerous as fighting their way past soldiers. But he supposed there was no turning back now.

Jason blew all the air from his lungs, inhaled deeply, and blew it out again. After another deep indrawn breath, he dropped into the water. He hardly noticed the gentle sting of the cool brine against his eyes as he found the rungs and pulled himself deeper. The bottom of the shaft opened through the roof of an underwater cavern, the regular stonework giving way to natural formations. But the rungs continued.

Within a tunnel branching out from the cavern, Jason saw turquoise light retreating. Using the rungs, Jason worked his way down the wall and across the floor to an overturned barrel chained to the ground. Grasping the chain, Jason surfaced inside the barrel, taking deep breaths. His breathing sounded noisy in the close space. The rich aroma of damp wood filled his nostrils.

Recalling Aram's advice, Jason abandoned the air pocket before too long and continued along the rungs. As he advanced across the cavern floor toward the tunnel, a flurry of motion caused Jason to glance sideways at a flowing tangle of brown tentacles. Although the creature was moving away from Jason, he scrambled even faster from rung to rung.

When Jason entered the narrower tunnel, Aram remained too far ahead to see. Only the faint, bluer radiance of his seaweed hinted at his location. The cave wound left and right, up and down. Jason faithfully followed the rungs.

He came to another barrel, and rose, gasping, into the clammy pocket of air. A few mussels had latched to the insides of this barrel, as had some glossy yellow slime. Jason stayed longer in that barrel than he had in the previous one. He felt like part of a really low-budget deep-sea exploration.

Not far beyond the second barrel, the underwater cave forked. Grateful for the iron rungs showing him the way, Jason veered right. A pipefish longer than a broom hovered across his path. The tubular snout looked too narrow to inflict any damage, and Jason was mostly worried about reaching the next barrel, so he hastened toward the elongated fish. Like a striped pole with eyes, the fish darted at his wrist, stealing the glowing seaweed. Jason reached for it, but the fish arrowed away through the water, speeding off the way Jason had come.

The fish fled rapidly, depriving Jason of the seaweed's greenish radiance. Of course he would have the luck to cross paths with a daring fish that fed on the glowing kelp! Enough light reflected back from Aram to distinguish the rungs, but Jason knew he needed to hurry.

Coming around a curve in the tunnel, he reached the next barrel. Swimming up into it, he rose until he bumped his head against the top. The barrel was full of water! Without the seaweed on his wrist, the inside was quite dark.

Panicked, Jason thrust himself out of the barrel and clambered along the rungs. The tunnel darkened as Aram pulled farther ahead. Jason's aching lungs began to clench for want of air. He focused on progressing from rung to rung at the maximum possible speed.

How far to the next air pocket? He had to stay calm and keep moving. If he proceeded swiftly, he might survive.

The tunnel bent gradually left, then back to the right. He ignored a school of small fish that briefly swarmed around him, glimmering in the dimness. The distant radiance from Aram's turquoise seaweed grew fainter.

The tunnel angled upward, and Jason spied the outline of a barrel ahead. Lungs squeezing, he resisted the urge to inhale and struggled forward.

As his desperate hands grasped the chain below the barrel, a disturbing thought occurred to him. What if this barrel lacked air as well? An image came vividly, his lifeless body drifting through obscure submerged caverns, hungry fish picking at his doughy flesh.

Gasping desperately, Jason entered the air pocket. Eager gulps of air cycled through his lungs. There was no light, but he didn't care. He breathed greedily until he began to wonder if he was hyperventilating. Fighting his instincts, Jason worked to slow his respiration, worried that if he didn't, he might pass out when he held his breath again.

Ducking back into the water, Jason discovered that the cave was no longer much brighter than the barrel. He couldn't make out the rungs, but proceeded by feel without too much difficulty. At least they were regularly spaced.

Jason realized that in the darkness, he might miss the next barrel. The barrels had been chained right next to the rungs, so he spread his legs wide to help ensure one of them would hit the next chain.

He progressed more slowly than before. Just as his breath was beginning to fail, a chain bumped his thigh. Jason followed the metal links into a barrel. The trapped air revived him.

When he left behind the reservoir of air, Jason found that the cave was brighter. As he advanced, the turquoise glow increased until he saw Aram returning for him. Jason waved for him to go back. Aram reversed his direction. Before long the big man swam up into another barrel. Jason entered it after he departed. Aram waited for Jason to come out, then led him to where the tunnel curved upward. Together they rose to emerge from a tidal pool on the floodplain. Cool fog obscured the moonlit night.

"I was worried," Aram panted. "I couldn't see your light. I feared the faulty barrel had overcome you."

A roiling surge of salt water sloshed against them. Jason staggered. The rising tide had already overtaken this pool.

"It was a close call," Jason admitted. "You should ask for a refund."

"I felt a crack. The air must have leaked out. You lost your light?"

"A fish stole it."

Aram blinked. "Hard to plan for everything. You all right?"

Water gushed around them, foaming over the tideland.

"I'm peachy. Let's do it again."

"We should hurry. The floodplain grows treacherous at night."

They jogged diagonally across the tideland, simultaneously heading away from Ithilum and the ocean. The turbulent water occasionally surged as high as Jason's waist and alternated between pushing and pulling. Once, Jason stepped inadvertently into a concealed tide well. Aram immediately hauled him up.

Before long they left the chaotic seawater behind.

"This fog is our best stroke of luck so far," Aram said as they trotted over solid rock, sandals squelching, wet clothes flapping heavily. Already the fog had reduced visibility to less than twenty yards.

Past the outlying tidal pools the ground began to rise. The rocky plain gave way to a brushy hillside. Jason followed Aram up the long slope. Scrub oak became plentiful on the far side of the hill. Aram forced a winding path through the gnarled vegetation.

On occasion Aram paused, eyes closed, listening.

Beyond the hill, Aram rushed along a stream up a narrow ravine. Jason had to run at almost a full sprint to keep up. The exertion helped combat the chill of his wet clothes.

Veering away from the stream, Aram clambered up the wall of the ravine. At the top he lay prostrate for a moment, staring back the way they had come.

"You holding up?"

Panting and shivering, Jason nodded.

"I think we got away clean," Aram whispered. Jason noticed that the big man was not winded. "We're almost to the horses. A fellow called Chancy will be meeting us. He's reliable, but with a lurker in the mix, we should stay ready for anything."

Aram led the way over a rotting fence into an overgrown orchard. The fruit trees remained in orderly lines. Tall weeds and wild shrubs clogged the ground.

At the far side of the orchard, beside a splintery fence, Aram knelt to examine an abandoned farmyard through the mist. Part of the old farmhouse had collapsed. A broken wheelbarrow lay in the middle of the yard, netted with cobwebs. Atop the decrepit barn an owl roosted, head swiveling in the misty moonlight.

"Almost too quiet," Aram murmured. "Wait here."

In a crouch, the big man dashed into the weedy yard. When he was halfway across, a figure bearing a sword emerged from the barn. Aram skidded to a stop. The figure waved for him to proceed. Aram hurried over and ducked into the decaying structure.

A moment later Aram reappeared, signaling for Jason to join him. Jason crossed the foggy yard, stumbling over a discarded plank hidden in the weeds before entering the barn.

Chancy stood off to one side, a nondescript man of medium height and build wearing a woolen hat with earflaps. He had sheathed his sword and now fidgeted with a short length of luminous seaweed. Aram had stripped off his shirt. His Herculean torso bulged gratuitously. Jason saw fresh clothes draped over a moldering stall, and began kicking off his sandals.

"The decoys you hired performed well," Chancy whispered to Aram. "Having that little vessel steal away from the docks was a stroke of genius. It created quite a stir. I could see the commotion from well outside of town."

"How are the roads?" Aram asked.

"Untreadable."

"That bad?"

"I did some investigating. Many eyes watch the ways out of Ithilum. I've been jumping at shadows all evening. How'd you escape?"

Aram pulled on a long shirt scaled with iron rings. "Trade secret."

"Wet as you are, wouldn't be too hard to guess. Not that it's any of my concern." Chancy shifted his attention to Jason. "How are you?"

"Alive." He buttoned his dry trousers. "Thanks for bringing our gear."

Chancy made an indifferent gesture. "When I get paid, I do my part."

Aram hefted an enormous broadsword. From the tip of the blade to the end of the pommel, the weapon was almost as tall as Jason. The wide, double-edged blade looked heavy enough to chop down a tree. In the feeble cyan glow provided by the seaweed, Aram gazed lovingly at the weapon.

"That's quite a sword," Jason said.

Aram smiled in agreement. "I commissioned it from a master blacksmith. The hilt is inlaid with mother-of-pearl and embellished with diamond dust. The pommel is an opal from the isle of Teber. The blade weighs enough to wield it as a mace, but I keep it sharp enough to shave whiskers." Aram swished the blade through the air a few times, swinging the heavy broadsword as though it were a yardstick. He sheathed it and then slung a baldric over one shoulder, so the sword hung across his broad back, then wrapped a hooded leather cloak around himself. The voluminous garment hung to his knees.

Chancy led a pair of horses from shadowed stalls. One was a tremendous brown stallion with a coarse mane and hairy fetlocks. Beside Aram, it seemed not much more than a pony. A smaller chestnut mare stood ready for Jason, his backpack attached to the saddle.

As Jason prepared to mount, Aram placed a hand on his shoulder. "You should also carry a sword."

Jason hesitantly accepted a belt and scabbard. He began looping it over his shoulder as Aram had done.

Chancy smirked. "That one fits better around the waist."

Chagrined, Jason fastened the belt the way Chancy had suggested. "I don't know how to use a sword," he admitted.

Aram folded his arms. "It isn't too complicated. Insert the blade into the body of your enemy."

"Makes sense." Jason drew the sword. It felt good in his hand, heavy enough to inflict damage, but not cumbersome.

"You can hack your way in with the edge or stab with the tip. We can go over some finer points later. Don't go trying to slice up any lurkers yet."

"Okay."

Aram patted Jason on the arm, motioning toward the horse.

Jason sheathed the sword. "Won't the soldiers I face have a lot of training?"

Aram shrugged. "If you have to use that sword tonight, most likely we're both finished. But it beats confronting your opponents unarmed. If it comes to it, I plan to go down fighting."

Jason climbed onto his horse.

"Any parting advice?" Aram asked Chancy.

The man was leading his own piebald mount from a third stall. "Stay off the roads. The countryside looked clear to the southwest."

"Hope so." Aram flicked the reins, and his horse clomped forward over the dusty planks. Jason followed the big man into the gloomy yard, where a breeze stirred the fog.

"Whoa," Aram exhaled, reining his mount to a halt.

Jason stopped alongside the larger man and followed his gaze.

Shrouded in swirling vapor, a dark featureless form stood motionless in the midst of the yard. Gasping, Jason clenched his jaw, squeezing the reins. Was it his imagination, or did his horse stiffen as well?

"Is that the lurker?" Aram whispered. He sounded reverent.

"Yeah." Jason tried to relax.

"Stop fooling around," Chancy chuckled softly, exiting the barn. "I wasn't born yester—"

Jason looked over as Chancy pulled his horse to a stop, eyes widening in alarm.

The lurker raised one hand and extended the other in their direction.

The horse Jason rode stamped and whickered, tossing her head. Aram's big mount reared. Chancy jerked the reins as his horse sidestepped.

"What now?" Aram asked, ignoring his restless steed.

Jason could not respond because his horse began to buck. He wrestled with the reins, gripping hopelessly with his knees as the horse curveted around the yard, rearing and plunging. After surviving a few wild ups and downs, the horse turned and bucked at the same time, catapulting Jason from the saddle. He landed upside down and continued into an awkward roll. Shielding his head, he scrambled away from the hoofs thudding nearby.

When Jason looked up, Aram stood between the stallion and the chestnut mare, holding both horses by the reins. The animals lurched and tugged, as if trying to rear, but Aram would not allow it.

Chancy lay spread-eagle on the far side of the barnyard, his horse no longer in view. The fallen man gaped at Jason in horror. Despite the agitated horses, Aram gazed his way as well.

Turning his head, Jason saw that he was sprawled at the feet of the lurker. The shadowy personage loomed over him. Jason rolled away from it.

"Look at it move," Aram murmured.

Glancing back, Jason glimpsed the lurker streaking away, a dark blur slicing through the mist. He had never seen it run so fast. Thanks to the fog, he didn't get to watch it for long.

"Where's it going?" Chancy asked.

"To report our location," Jason guessed. "Ferrin said the lurker brought reinforcements to Ithilum."

"We must now place speed ahead of stealth," Aram said. "You still in one piece?"

Jason arose, burrs sticking to his cloak. "Let's get out of here."

"What are the odds of me finding my horse?" Chancy mused.

"Not good," Aram replied. "It was spooked and running hard. You'll want to get away from here, Chancy. Find a spot to lay low."

The other man gave a weak smile. "I knew this job paid too well. I swear, never say yes if you get offered more than your contribution merits."

Jason walked over to his horse. "Is it calm enough to ride?"

"She's as calm as we can wait for," Aram replied.

Jason mounted the chestnut mare. She stamped a little. Aram kept a hand on her until she settled down, then remounted his stallion.

Chancy stood up and started dusting himself off. "Give me something to use if I get caught?" he asked miserably. "Some little tidbit? Some secret to trade?"

"Don't get caught," Aram said. "Violent forces are converging."

Chancy sprinted toward the orchard.

Aram gave a soft kick, and his horse cantered away from the dismal farmyard with Jason close behind.

CHAPTER 10

FLIGHT

A persistent breeze shredded the fog into tattered wisps of vapor. Starlight began to penetrate the murky sky as Aram and Jason journeyed south. Their flight took them across desolate terrain, following overgrown trails through woods and improvising paths over fields and low hills.

Aram kept the horses moving at a good pace, but never let them run hard, balancing the desire for haste with the need for endurance. Jason was pleased to find his horsemanship continuing to improve. Riding felt more familiar and enjoyable than ever.

Whenever they came to high ground, Aram would pause to look back. Repeatedly, he detected no evidence of pursuit.

The night wore on uneventfully until they reached a low ridge overlooking their destination. A broad river divided a quiet little town. Similar amounts of buildings huddled near the northern and southern banks.

Peering back the way they had come, Aram moaned. "We won the race to Potsug, but not by much."

Squinting into the night, Jason faintly perceived moonlit

shapes moving along a distant road. "It looks like a lot of them," Jason said.

"Tark wanted you to meet him at the home of a stableman?"

"Gurig."

"I only see one large stable. It's on this side of the river. Come, we must hurry."

Aram led the way down the ridge, after which they loped across a flat expanse to the village. The sleepy town had no surrounding walls or any other apparent defenses.

Even after slowing to a walk, the horses sounded loud as they advanced along a silent dirt road flanked by wooden buildings. They approached a modest residence alongside a large stable. Jason dismounted and knocked on the door.

"Be ready for an ambush," Aram warned, baring the blade of his massive sword.

Jason pounded harder. A moment later a man bearing a candle opened the door. He had a high forehead and a flabby chin. He glanced past Jason at Aram astride his stallion. "Who are you?"

"I'm looking for Tark the musician," Jason replied.

The man blinked in bewilderment. "Tark? I haven't seen Tark in ages."

"You're Gurig?"

"The same."

"Tark hasn't been in touch? Hasn't sent a messenger?"

"Not a word. Are you a friend of his?"

"Yes. If he contacts you, tell him he missed me."

"Who shall I say he missed?"

"It's better if I don't explain. Good night."

"Very well," the man said with another glance at Aram, who did his best to hold his sword out of sight. "Safe travels."

The door closed, and Jason returned to his horse.

"Tark is late," Aram said.

"I hope nothing happened to him."

"We cannot wait. We must cross the river immediately. We'll decide where to proceed from there."

"Lead the way," Jason said.

"I noted two ferries from the ridge, one larger than the other. Both were dark, but enough money should rouse them. We'll try the smaller one first."

Aram kicked his horse to a trot, and Jason followed him to a shanty beside a large, flat raft. The glow of a dying fire seeped through the shuttered window. Aram rapped on the door.

A short, round-faced man with a black eye answered. His cheek was marked by the creases of a pillow. His sour expression faltered as he tipped his head back to gape up at Aram. "What do you want?"

"We need to cross."

"At this hour? Three times the normal fare."

"Four times if you hurry."

"I'll have to fetch the haulers."

"Not necessary."

The ferryman looked Aram up and down. "I suppose not. No discount for hauling it yourself. Payment in advance."

"Fine, but we leave now. What's the standard rate for two men and two horses?"

The ferryman hesitated.

Aram cracked his knuckles menacingly. "If you intend to fib, you need to think faster."

"Ten drooma. A man is one, a horse four."

"Sounds plausible. Do you have two bronze?"

The ferryman nodded. He ducked back inside. When he returned wearing a cap and a long coat, he exchanged two bronze drooma for a silver and then led them to the quay.

Aram and Jason guided their horses onto the flat raft. Jason leaned against a wooden railing. The ferryman reached toward a copper bell.

"Don't sound the bell," Aram said firmly.

"But the regulations—"

"How about you forget this time, and I return those bronze drooma to you."

The ferryman scowled. "I don't care how much you're paying; I could lose—"

"Or I could drown you."

"I'll take the drooma."

The ferryman unmoored the rectangular vessel. A thick rope ran through a device attached to the raft. The ferryman pulled a lever releasing a locking mechanism.

"Ding, ding," the ferryman muttered. "Go ahead and pull."

Standing at the front of the raft, Aram began to hastily haul the guideline hand over hand. The raft lurched forward, progressing rapidly. The moon had just set, and the stars did little to brighten the dark river.

"You aren't looking for employment, by chance?" the ferryman asked.

Silently and tirelessly, Aram kept the ferry advancing swiftly. The shanty and small quay shrunk behind them. As the craft approached the center of the river, Aram showed no sign of flagging.

Near the middle of the wide river, something suddenly splashed aboard the raft. Aram whirled, casting off his cloak and drawing his sword. The ferryman yelped, scampering to the far side of the raft. Jason fumbled for the hilt of his sword.

The sopping figure who had boarded the raft raised a hand and spoke softly. "Pardon the intrusion. I'm a friend."

"Ferrin?" Jason gasped.

"What are you doing here?" Aram rumbled, sword poised to strike.

"No time," Ferrin insisted tiredly, water dripping from his clothes and hair. He clutched a long oar. "Cut the guideline."

"What?"

"An ambush awaits on the far side. Sever the rope."

"Absolutely not," the ferryman asserted, striding forward.

Dropping the oar, Ferrin leaped to his feet and seized the ferryman by the throat. The startled man fumbled for the knife at his belt, but Ferrin released his neck and snatched it first. "You're in no position to issue demands, boatman. Make another squeal at your peril." Ferrin glanced at Aram. "Cut the line or we die."

The broadsword arced through the air, slicing through the thick rope in a single sweep. The raft began to drift with the sluggish current.

"Add what speed you can with the oar," Ferrin whispered, keeping the knife near the ferryman's chin. "Will you keep silent?"

The ferryman nodded, massaging his throat. One hand strayed to a pocket.

"I already have it," Ferrin said, letting a smaller knife fall from the crook of his arm to the deck. "Cover your ears, lie on your stomach, and hum a quiet tune. If you see nothing and hear nothing, you just might live through this."

The ferryman complied.

"That was a quick grab," Aram said, taking up the oar. "Snatching the hidden knife, I mean."

"You should see me with two hands," Ferrin replied.

Aram began using the oar to scull. The ponderous raft sped up and began to rotate. As Aram did his best to compensate for the rotation, the raft fishtailed forward.

"How did you get here so fast?" Jason asked.

"I'm reasonably good at my job," Ferrin said. "I investigated the well Aram described, and the position seemed less than ideal for a rendezvous. After snooping around, I caught wind of a man named Chancy who had bought a pair of horses that matched your needs. He inadvertently led me to the barn where you encountered the torivor. I lingered long enough to confirm your direction, then rode harder than you could have. I led a second mount and alternated between the two steeds. I may have lamed one of them."

"What's the situation on the southern bank?" Aram asked.

"A dozen soldiers lie in wait, half of them conscriptors, led by a displacer. I crossed the river in a stolen canoe to reconnoiter. Once our adversaries ascertained that you were fleeing south, this town became the logical location for an ambush. Helps when you think like the enemy. Helps even more when you trained them."

"How did the news beat us to the ferry?" Jason asked.

"I assume the lurker informed them. Not surprising."

"What now?" Jason asked.

"We let the river carry us some distance before disembarking on the southern bank. How are your horses holding up?"

"Doing well," Aram said. "We haven't overtaxed them." He continued to scull vigorously.

"Good," Ferrin said. "What's our destination? Does it matter?"

Jason thought for a moment. If Tark hadn't made it to Potsug, he may have never delivered the message about the Word to Galloran. "We should head to the castle of the Blind King. Do you know the way?"

"I can get us there," Ferrin said. "So the Blind King is Galloran?"

"I didn't say that," Jason protested.

"You didn't need to. I once suspected as much, but discounted my theory after observing him. He looked too old, sounded too pathetic, acted too eccentric. To think he was actually the famed hero! Felrook took a heavy toll."

"The Blind King really is Galloran?" Aram said, a hint of disillusionment in his tone.

"It appears that way," Ferrin replied.

Jason had not meant to share this information with Ferrin, of all people! But the displacer already seemed certain. Maldor had long known the truth about the Blind King, but the secret had not been widely shared. Jason supposed that if Ferrin joined him and Aram on their way to Felrook, Galloran himself could decide how to deal with the displacer. "I can't confirm your guess."

"No need," Aram muttered.

Ferrin glanced at the ferryman. The prostrated man continued to hum, hands clamped to the sides of his head. Ferrin raised his voice. "I suppose we should kill the boatman. We can't leave witnesses behind."

Jason began to protest, but Ferrin held up his hand and glared. "Let's see, I'll just insert my knife right here and open him up." The man continued to hum without missing a note.

"He had to be certain the ferry operator wasn't eavesdropping," Aram explained, but Jason had already caught on. The raft rotated so much that Aram moved to a different side. "This vessel is unwieldy."

"You're doing a remarkable job," Ferrin said. "Start easing us toward the southern bank. I propose we bind and gag the boatman, then set him adrift."

"Seems like the gentlest option," Aram agreed. "You have rope and a gag?"

Ferrin pulled a length of cord and a wet strip of material from a pocket. "I like to plan ahead. Could I possibly have my hand back? If we get cornered, we all might want me to have it."

"Might as well," Aram said.

Jason dug into his backpack and fished out the hand. He hefted it for a moment, then passed it to Ferrin. The displacer reattached it seamlessly, flexed his fingers, then crouched and bound the ferryman. "It's good to be whole."

"You're still wearing the eye patch," Jason mentioned. "I thought it was part of a disguise."

"Sadly, no," Ferrin said. "I grafted my eye to an alley cat in Weych. The precaution provided an early warning when they came for me, but I couldn't manage to retrieve my eye in time. It's still there."

"Unnatural," Aram muttered in disgust. "Many soldiers are trailing us from the north."

Squatting beside the ferryman, Ferrin secured the gag. "We need only concern ourselves with the forces on the southern bank for now. I sabotaged the other ferry, along with the three largest watercrafts in town."

"Remind me to stay on your good side," Aram said.

"There are still enough enemies on the southern bank to waylay us," Ferrin cautioned. "The cover of darkness will soon be lost. Speed and stealth will be imperative."

The half giant stopped plying the oar long enough to wipe sweat from his brow. The sculling was finally tiring him. "You and Jason should take the horses and flee," Aram said. "I can catch up later."

"Are you serious?" Ferrin asked.

"We only have two mounts, and I'm the heaviest rider."

"I already prepared a fresh horse for myself, along with weapons."

"Impossible."

"I work fast. I beat you here by almost two hours."

From up the river came an angry cry, followed by dismayed shouts.

"Get us to the shore," Ferrin said calmly. "They've finally recognized that we cut the guideline. They can travel much faster by horseback than we can on the water. My new mount is close by."

Aram grunted as the oar sloshed noisily. The commotion upriver continued to escalate.

When the raft reached the bank, Ferrin and Jason led the horses ashore. Keeping the oar, Aram shoved the raft back onto the water. The ferryman continued humming as best he could around the gag.

Ferrin crashed through the riverside vegetation and returned astride a black horse. He had wrapped a long strip of black linen around his head several times to cover his face. Aram studied the horizon, where the oncoming dawn had purpled the starry night.

"Come," Ferrin said. They could hear horses charging along the river in their direction.

Jason and Aram climbed onto their mounts, and the three galloped away from the river into open, brushy country. "Not much cover," Aram called. "How many had horses?"

"I counted eight. They could commandeer others."

"We better find a place to make a stand."

"Three versus eight? Or possibly twelve? Why not run?"

Aram hesitated before answering. "Because they might catch up after sunrise."

"So?"

"I'm no use after dawn."

"What do you mean?"

Aram didn't answer.

"What happens at dawn?" Ferrin pressed.

"This is not something I share lightly," Aram said. "I don't have much choice right now. I'd kill to keep this secret."

"I keep secrets for a living. I won't tell."

"I turn into a weakling during the day," Aram confessed. "I'm half giant."

"There's no such thing."

"You'll feel differently after sunrise. Remember Goya?"

There came a pause in the shouted discussion. Jason felt sorry for Aram. He knew the big man would never have wanted Ferrin to learn his history. But under the circumstances, there was no way to avoid blowing his secret.

"Very well," Ferrin finally said. "Where?"

"How about between those hills?" Aram pointed. "The way narrows right where that boulder offers some cover. Jason can lob stones from a flanking position."

In answer, Ferrin swerved toward the gap between the steep hills.

"What do you mean I'll lob rocks?" Jason called.

"This is no occasion for a first lesson in swordplay," Aram said.

"He's right," Ferrin said. "You'll do much more harm harassing them from the hillside. When we get there, gather a pile of rocks in a sheltered position. We'll place the horses by you. If the giant and I go down, try to ride away."

"Don't call me a giant," Aram growled.

The pair of hills drew closer. Looking back, Jason saw a cluster of riders racing a mile or two behind.

When they reached the gap between the hills, Aram and Ferrin dismounted. "Any objection to fighting dirty?" Ferrin asked.

"Only way to fight when your back is to the wall," Aram replied. "Come on, Jason." Jason dismounted. Looping around somewhat, Aram led two of the horses up the steep side of the hill. Jason led the third, crouching to grab a rock or two. Aram tethered the horses by a thick tree, then walked sideways down the steep slope.

The enemy horsemen cantered nearer. Jason secured his horse and then collected more rocks, trying to pick ones that were small enough to throw hard, but large enough to do damage. A couple hundred yards from the hills, the horsemen reined in to confer with one another.

"I count eleven," Aram said, joining Ferrin in the gap between the hills behind a boulder the size of a minivan.

"So do I."

Aram drew his enormous sword. "Eleven may be too many. How well do you fight?"

"I'm not bad. You?"

"I'm expensive for a reason. Can you commit to taking down two?"

Ferrin was prepping his bow. "Three, maybe four."

"If you're serious, and if they rush into this, we may have a chance."

Nine of the horsemen charged. Several had crossbows. Two horsemen held back, evidently content to watch. The horizon behind them continued to lighten.

Aram fastened his leather cloak shut.

"Thick cloak," Ferrin said.

"Better than some armor." Aram glanced up at the slope and cupped a hand beside his mouth. "Wait until they're close!"

Jason saluted.

"Here they come," Ferrin announced, setting an arrow to his bowstring.

Jason could barely hear the conversation between Ferrin and Aram. He hoped he could surprise them and drop a soldier or two with rocks. He held one in each hand, both stones squarish and a little larger than baseballs. He wished he still had an orantium sphere. This would be the perfect occasion for an explosion!

In the middle of the gap, Aram and Ferrin crouched behind the boulder. There was ample room for the horses to pass between the slope and the boulder at either side. Aram hefted a rough stone bigger than a bowling ball.

Crossbow quarrels zipped past Ferrin as he leaned into view, bow drawn. He ducked back twice, arrows sparking against the boulder, then leaned out farther and released an arrow. It flew true, unhorsing one of the soldiers. Then the thundering horses were upon them.

Jason began throwing stones. The first one missed. The second bounced off a soldier's helm, nearly knocking him from the saddle. Leaning precariously, the soldier clung to the neck of his horse until Aram's huge stone hit him like a cannonball. One rider among the nine slowed to hang back. He wore the armor of a conscriptor. The remaining six swarmed Aram and Ferrin.

Aram hurled another large rock at a charging conscriptor who was bringing his crossbow to bear. The stone struck the horseman in the chest, blasting him from his saddle.

Ferrin had discarded his bow in favor of his sword. Deflecting the blade of a soldier on horseback, Ferrin slashed his thigh. Jason kept flinging stones. He struck the soldier attacking Ferrin in the small of the back. Aram leaped from the cover of the boulder to almost decapitate a charging horse, sending the hapless rider plunging to the hard ground. With a ferocious backhand stroke, Aram cut down another soldier. Losing momentum, the remaining horsemen milled around the boulder ineffectively, and Aram, taking advantage of his great height and long reach, began slaughtering horse and man alike, his weighty sword hacking and bludgeoning without prejudice. Ferrin scrambled up the boulder and sprang from the top to tackle a conscriptor out of his saddle.

Jason doggedly pitched stones into the fray, connecting with several. The conscriptor who had hung back spurred his horse up the hillside toward Jason.

After meeting the gaze of his attacker, Jason desperately hurled rocks at the oncoming threat, missing once and striking the steed in the chest with the other. The horse kept coming. Jason dodged to the far side of the tree, drawing his sword as the conscriptor dismounted.

Jason wore no armor. He had zero experience at swordplay. The tree blocked his view, so Jason backed away as the conscriptor raced around the trunk, brandishing a longsword.

Jason found himself backing down the hillside toward the skirmish. He stopped retreating as the aggressive conscriptor hurtled forward from higher ground, swinging his weapon. Jason swung his sword to block the stroke. The blades connected with a clang that vibrated through Jason's hands to his elbows. With too much momentum behind his lunge, the conscriptor plowed into Jason, and the pair tumbled wildly down the slope, coming to a rest at the fringe of the skirmish. Head swimming, Jason tasted brush and dirt. Blood trickled from his nostrils.

Disoriented from the fall, Jason rose to his knees, eyes darting to locate the sword he had dropped. The conscriptor had also lost his sword, but before he could retrieve it, a blade erupted through his chest, piercing the iron-banded leather of his armor. The sword had been hurled, like a throwing knife, by Aram.

As the conscriptor slumped forward, pawing numbly at the protruding blade, Ferrin sprang atop a horse to pursue the two riders who had held back. All of the other soldiers had fallen. One of the remaining riders retreated at a full gallop. The other cantered forward to engage Ferrin.

The horses converged, and swords clashed harmlessly as they passed. The enemy rider, now headed toward Aram and Jason, veered away, but almost immediately a large stone thrown by Aram thumped against his shoulder, toppling him to the dirt.

The man staggered to his feet, clutching his injured arm.

Ferrin drew up near him, face still obscured behind black linen.

The soldier raised one hand in surrender. The other arm hung useless at his side.

Aram led Jason to retrieve the horses. By the time they rode over to Ferrin, the conscriptor knelt on the ground, his helmet off, unarmed but glaring defiantly.

"The displacer who led them, Rogold, got away," Ferrin explained as Aram and Jason drew near. "This is Corge, a captain among the conscriptors."

"So the rumors are true," the wounded man growled at Ferrin. "You defected."

Ferrin uncovered his face. "The disguise isn't working? I should have kept the hat. You know too much. We'll have to duel."

"Your oaf broke my arm."

"Yes, Corge, he did. You were attacking us. You are now my enemy. Are you going to die fighting or whining?"

"You'd murder an injured prisoner?"

"Whining. Very well. Perhaps we should skip the pretense of a duel, since you're conceding the outcome." Ferrin brandished his sword menacingly. Then he paused. "I'll spare you for good information."

"You'll get none. Go on, coward, strike me down unarmed."

"Fine, take your sword." Ferrin planted it in the ground in front of him.

Corge gritted his teeth. "I would, but my arm—"

"If you had twelve good arms, the result would be the same, and we both know it. I'm in a hurry. Retrieve the sword. Best me, and you're free to go."

Corge snorted. "What about your reputation for justice?"

"This is just. We both have swords. You tried to kill me when you had the advantage. Now I'll try to kill you. Not my fault if I'm better at it."

Aram quietly came up behind Corge and crooked one muscular arm around his neck. The half giant braced his free hand against the back of Corge's head and applied pressure until the conscriptor slumped into unconsciousness. "We don't have time for banter."

"I suppose we can leave him alive," Ferrin sniffed. "He won't have much more to share with our foes than the displacer who fled. Incidentally, Aram, well done back there. You were amazing. Worth every drooma."

"It helped that they fought like fog-bound sheep."

Ferrin laughed. "They had no idea they were racing into combat against a half giant. Next time they may not be so brash. I'm keeping Corge's horse. Are you two happy with your mounts? I noticed a few good ones that Aram didn't butcher."

"You said to fight dirty," Aram reminded him. "Jason and I will retain our steeds. Chancy chose well, and we have no time to spare."

"No argument here," Ferrin agreed, grabbing some gear and mounting Corge's horse.

"Should we scatter the other horses?" Jason asked.

"Not worth the time," Ferrin said. "There are more horses in the village. When reinforcements get here, they'll already be mounted."

Aram maneuvered his horse close to Jason. "You did well back there," he said, placing a large hand on Jason's shoulder.

"Whatever. I should be dead. Thanks for bailing me out."

"You were more effective than I expected with those rocks. And you survived your first swordfight. Many can't say the same."

"Dawn approaches," Ferrin reminded them, kicking his horse into motion.

Aram nodded. "Let's cover some ground before I shrink."

They rode cross-country to the southwest as the eastern sky brightened behind them. As sunrise seemed imminent, Aram brought them to a halt near a small glade, dismounted, and stripped down to his breeches. He packed his armor, sword, and heavy cloak onto his big horse, collected a bundle from his saddle, and started toward the glade.

"Where are you going?" Ferrin asked.

"To get a little privacy," Aram replied.

"Why?" Ferrin pursued.

Aram averted his gaze. "You think I want you watching? It's humiliating!"

"We can turn away," Jason said. "We won't look."

Aram's meaty shoulders sagged. "All right."

"Here comes daybreak," Ferrin announced jovially. "Shall we avert our eyes?"

"We have almost a minute," Aram said. "Sorry to be particular about this. You see, at night I feel like my true self. I don't when I'm Goya or Burt. I hate the thought of people looking at big Aram and picturing some puny—"

Aram uttered a low, involuntary groan.

Ferrin and Jason glanced at each other and turned away.

Behind them, Aram panted and grunted. They waited.

"All right," said a less manly voice.

Jason and Ferrin turned. Aram, face shiny with sweat, pulled a small pair of pants over his skinny legs. His shrunken hands trembled.

Ferrin struggled not to smile. He was unsuccessful.

Ferrin's involuntary grin forced Jason to bite his lip to keep from laughing. Ferrin noticed and began to shake, eyes watering.

Aram hastily pulled on a shirt. Then he folded his arms,

glaring grumpily up at the others. "Go ahead, let it out, have a good laugh."

They did.

Feeding off each other, magnified by the knowledge that the laughter was so inappropriate, their mirth was uncontrollable. Ferrin buried his face, attempting to compose himself. Jason stared at the ground, trying to summon sober thoughts.

"We need to go," Aram said indignantly, clambering up onto his suddenly oversized horse. Atop the huge stallion, he looked like a little jockey.

Jason coughed out a final laugh.

Ferrin shook quietly, wiping tears from flushed cheeks.

"Finished?" Aram asked. "You two are ruthless." He looked down at himself. "I guess it's quite a contrast."

"We don't mean to rub it in," Jason apologized. "We've already seen you both ways. It isn't that big of a deal."

"It doesn't help that you're so shy about it," Ferrin tried to explain. "It was more your expression than anything."

"Let's leave it behind us," Aram said, nudging his horse with his heels. The stallion didn't respond.

Ferrin buried his face in the crook of his arm. Jason ground his teeth.

After Aram flicked the reins and gave a couple of harder kicks, his horse started forward.

CHAPTER 11

FORTAIM

By the time Ferrin, Aram, and Jason had stashed their horses in the woods below the ruined castle of the Blind King, night had fallen. The glow of the waning moon provided the only light as they surveyed the silent hilltop.

"Very quiet," Ferrin whispered, eyes intent on the dark castle from his crouched position behind a bush. "Almost looks abandoned."

"They may be asleep," Aram said.

"Something's different," Jason murmured, his gaze gliding from the crumbling walls to the single tall tower. "I know. There used to be two towers. One that looked ready to collapse. I guess it did."

"Fortaim is in worse repair than on my last visit," Ferrin agreed. "Shameful, really. The stronghold was once formidable."

Staring at the dark windows, Jason bit his lower lip. If imperial troops had beaten them here, Galloran might already have been taken. Or worse. Trying to keep his composure, Jason told himself that they had no actual information yet. Hopefully, there was another explanation.

"Could this be a trap?" Aram asked.

"We're being hunted," Ferrin said. "Our enemies could have

anticipated this destination, particularly if the lurker is still aiding them."

"I haven't noticed the lurker," Jason said.

"That doesn't mean it hasn't been watching," Ferrin said. "No spy is more stealthy. Then again, it had you in an excellent trap back at the ferry. It might have assumed victory and departed."

Ever since sunrise, Ferrin had led them across lonely terrain, passing monstrous oklinder bushes and groves of tall, slender trees. They had glimpsed no other people, friend or foe. Ferrin had allowed only a few short breaks to rest and eat some of the greasy clam fritters prepared by Moira. Aram had acted a little sulky all day, but at sundown his attitude had improved with the return of his intimidating size.

"Do we go in?" Jason asked. They had been watching for several minutes.

Ferrin gave a nod. "I have a plan. If this proves to be an ambush, Aram will kill everyone. And their horses."

"I love strategy," the big man replied.

"Where does the Blind King sleep?" Ferrin asked.

"At the top of the tower," Jason said.

Ferrin stared, as if trying to visually penetrate the castle walls. "If this is an ambush, it's masterful. I haven't seen a sentry. I haven't glimpsed a flame or smelled any smoke. I haven't heard a horse so much as snort."

"No coughs," Aram added. "No conversation. No footfalls."

"Let's have a look," Ferrin said. "Stay ready to run."

The trio slunk forward to a place where the wall had crumbled inward. After listening for a moment, Ferrin gestured for Aram and Jason to wait. Flitting from shadow to shadow, he explored the courtyard, passing out of view. After a few minutes, he returned and waved them in.

Jason and Aram caught up to Ferrin beside a mossy stone block. The displacer was examining a dented helmet. "This belonged to a conscriptor. It hasn't been here long."

Rubble from the fallen tower was strewn across the moonlit courtyard. Several wide, shallow depressions cratered the yard. Moving cautiously, Ferrin squatted beside a blackened pit and sniffed. "Orantium," he murmured. "The explosion was recent."

Jason felt deflated. This was starting to look really bad for the Blind King. He tried to detach from his emotions, but could not help quietly despairing.

Picking their way through the jumbled stones and timbers left by the toppled tower, Ferrin paused to indicate a dusty arm protruding from the rubble. Farther along, near the gates of the great hall adjoining the only remaining tower, they found a corpse pierced by arrows.

Jason recognized her. "She served the Blind King. She was part of the crazy group making up stories in the throne room." Despite the rising nausea, he kept his voice steady.

"Imperial troops only leave enemy corpses behind as a mark of disdain," Ferrin said. "They want the populace to view Fortaim as a monument of shame. I'm afraid the castle is vacant. The troops appear to have moved on."

"Shouldn't we check his room?" Jason asked. "He might have left a message."

"We've come this far," Ferrin said.

The door to the largest, most intact building hung askew on twisted hinges. Inside the great hall, they found the shabby throne overturned and the floor pitted from more orantium detonations. In a corner, Aram spotted a dead hound. Jason noticed dark smears of dried blood on the floor. A broken sword lay near the door granting access to the tower.

Mounting the winding stairs up the tower, they encountered a second cadaver on a landing. "He also served the Blind King," Jason confirmed, examining the mustached face, struggling to keep his emotions clinical.

At the top of the gloomy stairwell, the door had been forced open. Inside the room, a dark, spindly figure crouched on the windowsill, backlit by the moon.

"Who goes there?" Ferrin challenged, drawing his sword.

"I was here first," the figure countered, twisting and coiling as if prepared to leap to his doom. "Who are you?"

"Travelers," Ferrin said. "We seek the Blind King."

"Poor timing," the figure replied, voice anguished.

"What happened here?" Aram asked.

"Did a crow peck out your eyes?" the figure cackled. "There was a massacre."

Jason resisted a vision of Galloran dead alongside the rest of his servants. Stepping around Ferrin, he stared hard at the lanky figure. "Your voice is familiar."

"Jason?" the figure replied doubtfully, his posture changing. "Is that you?"

"Ned?" Jason gasped. "What are you doing here?"

Ned's posture relaxed a degree. "I found him," he said softly. "After all these years, I found him. But I may have lost him again."

"We're looking for him too," Jason said.

Ned's feet came down from the windowsill. He closed the shutters, then twisted a short length of seaweed, which began to emit a purplish glow.

By the violet light, Jason recognized the strange freckled man who had aided him and Rachel months ago in a seaside village. Then, he had worn a sack with holes cut for his arms and head. Now he wore a soiled shirt and trousers. He remained tall and gangly, with disheveled hair. A long knife hung from his belt, as did several pouches. He still wore a glove on one hand.

The luminescent seaweed also revealed a pale corpse on the floor: a wiry old man with a long ragged beard, lying supine. Jugard, from the sea cave.

Jason closed his eyes for a moment. When would this parade of familiar corpses end? Opening his eyes, Jason considered the body once more. It was unmistakably the wily old man from the sea cave.

"That light might be visible from below," Ferrin hissed.

Ned muted the seaweed under his shirt, then glided sideways on the balls of his feet, moving in a slight crouch, as if ready to bolt. "All the windows are shuttered," he replied. "They work, I've checked."

Ferrin, flanked by Aram and Jason, came farther into the room. "Why is Jugard here?" Jason asked.

"I was sent to fetch him from the sea cave."

"By the Blind King?"

"Who else would I obey?"

"How'd he die?"

"He was a corpse when I found him in the sea cave," Ned claimed. "It didn't seem right to leave him there. He'd been stabbed in the back. A lot."

Jason gritted his teeth. "Who did it?"

"No friend of ours."

Jason scowled. "How'd you get past the crab?"

"Didn't. I scaled the cliff with Jugard on my shoulders."

"Climbed a cliff with a corpse in tow?" Aram challenged. "I'm not sure even I could manage that."

"I never claimed you could," Ned muttered.

Ned seemed tense, jittery. Then again, he had always behaved oddly. Ned had given help in the past, but Jason questioned how much to trust him. "You work for the Blind King?"

"Not when I first met you," Ned explained. "I do now. You and Rachel left a trail. I backtracked and found my former master. I hadn't seen him in years." His voice had an edge that suggested he was about to burst into either hysterical cackles or uncontrollable sobs. "Who are your new companions?"

"Ferrin and Aram."

"Are they trustworthy? Loyal to our cause?"

"I think so."

Ned dipped his head. "Pleased to meet you. I'm Nedwin, the Blind King's new squire. And also his former squire." He interlocked his long fingers and rapidly twiddled his thumbs. His unsettling smile showed crooked teeth in the muted purple light.

"Did Tark make it here?" Jason asked.

"Three days ago, filthy and half starved."

"He delivered my message?"

"That was why I was dispatched to retrieve Jugard."

"You returned tonight?"

"Shortly before you three came blundering through the courtyard."

"Blundering?" Ferrin repeated, mildly offended.

"Noisily and sloppily. Mostly the big one, subtle as a church bell rolling down a stairway. You didn't appear imperial, so I allowed you to find me."

"And your backup plan was to leap from the tower window?" Aram asked.

"Maybe," Ned said, one eye twitching.

"He wouldn't have fallen," Jason said. "He can climb like a spider. Ned, do you think the Blind King was captured?"

"I hope not. Sightless or not, he's sly. He always has an escape planned. Those who assaulted Fortaim probably paid sorely for the lives they claimed. The crooked tower was rigged to collapse, and he maintained an impressive stockpile of orantium."

"We noticed the damage," Aram said. "That much orantium would have been worth a fortune."

"Irreplaceable," Ned agreed.

"Do you know where he might be, Ned?" Jason asked.

"I prefer to be called 'Nedwin.' It evokes happier times." Nedwin motioned Jason toward him. "A private word?"

Jason glanced at Ferrin and Aram. They shrugged.

Jason walked over to Nedwin, who leaned in close and whispered softly, "You're really with these two?"

"Yeah," Jason whispered back.

"If you're in trouble, I can get us out of here."

"I'm good."

"All right. If you're sure." Nedwin straightened up to his full height, nearly half a head taller than Jason, though unimpressive when measured against Aram. "This room is smaller than it should be," he announced.

"What?" Jason asked.

Nedwin turned, gesturing. "After viewing the tower from without, the observer would expect more space over here. Instead we have a premature wall."

"Secret passage?" Ferrin asked.

Nedwin was already running his palms over the snugly mortared blocks. Behind a tapestry, he found a trigger that opened a small door constructed to blend with the masonry of the wall. "This way."

Nedwin turned and dragged Jugard's body into the secret space, leaving him on his back against the far wall. The others followed Nedwin into a cramped hall almost too low and narrow for Aram.

Nedwin closed the hidden door and then removed the glowing seaweed from his shirt. He led the way, and Aram brought up the rear, moving in an awkward, sideways crouch. Curving around the perimeter of the round room, the claustrophobic hall became a narrow stairway that spiraled down directly below the regular stairwell.

They descended until emerging into musty tunnels in the bowels of the castle. Jason heard rats chittering and scampering beyond the violet glow of the seaweed. Nedwin navigated down several passageways, doubling back from empty rooms, dead ends, and collapsed corridors. At last they reached a cluttered storeroom.

"Ah," Nedwin said. "Feel the draft?"

"Now that you mention it," Aram said, licking a finger and holding it up.

Nedwin's freckled hand glided over the surface of a bare wall. Before long he tripped a mechanism that revealed a secret closet. On the floor of the closet awaited a trapdoor. Nedwin crouched and opened it.

"Who trespasses here?" inquired a gruff voice from the darkness below.

"Nedwin and Lord Jason," Nedwin answered. "Accompanied by two friends."

"You may pass." The dark hole filled with light. Jason judged that it was a twenty-foot drop. Buttressed by heavy beams, the dirt walls and floor beyond the trapdoor lacked the masonry of the finished corridors above.

Nedwin signaled for Jason to descend a rope ladder. Jason had some trouble getting started, backing hesitantly through the trapdoor, but climbed down easily once his hands and feet found purchase. Ferrin and Aram came after, and finally Nedwin, who closed the trapdoor and sped down the ladder, dropping the final eight feet.

The voice down the hole had belonged to the gatekeeper who had first admitted Jason to the ruined castle of the Blind King. Laying aside a crossbow and a halberd, he greeted Jason heartily, then turned a wary eye to Ferrin and Aram.

"Who are these two?"

"Ferrin and Aram," Jason answered. "My friends. I wouldn't be alive without their help."

"I'm Vernon," the gatekeeper said.

"We must consult with His Majesty," Nedwin said.

"Follow me," Vernon said, leading them along the subterranean passage.

"Is Tark here?" Aram asked.

"Yes," Vernon said. "Would you like to see him?"

"A superb idea," Nedwin interjected. "Vernon, see that Ferrin and Aram get to greet Tark after you deliver us to the king."

Vernon stopped at a sturdy door built into a crudely excavated wall of natural dirt and stone. As he lifted a fist to knock, the portal opened. There stood the Blind King, his hair and beard long and gray, a dingy rag binding his eyes, a grimy robe hanging from his broad shoulders.

Before Jason had last met the Blind King, he had never heard the name Galloran. As a newcomer to Lyrian, he'd failed to grasp the significance of the grubby king's secret identity. He hadn't known how many still reverenced him as the greatest hero in Lyrian. Without any flashy pretense, here stood the true heir to Trensicourt, the strongest human kingdom not directly controlled by Maldor. Jason felt honored and relieved to be back in his presence.

"Did I hear Nedwin?" Galloran rasped with his damaged voice.

"And Lord Jason," Nedwin said.

The king's mouth spread into a wide grin, forming deep creases in the whiskerless skin around his eyes and cheeks. "Is that so?"

"Yes, Your Majesty," Jason said. "Along with two new friends."

"Wonderful, come inside." Galloran backed away from the door.

"You may want to first talk with Jason and me in private," Nedwin suggested. "His friends are anxious to greet Tark."

"By all means, go find him," the king grated.

Jason shared a glance with Ferrin. He could sense that the displacer resented Nedwin not wanting him in the room. Vernon closed the door, leaving Jason and Nedwin with Galloran.

Dorsio, a slender man with a shiny scar down the side of his face, sat unobtrusively in one corner. Jason knew that Dorsio, unable to speak, communicated with Galloran through touch and a system of snaps and claps.

The underground chamber was more storage room than sitting room, but had a cot, a wooden bench, a table, and a couple of chairs. The rest of the space was taken up by stacked barrels, crates, and sacks. Galloran sat on the cot, motioning for the others to sit on the bench.

"You two are well?" Galloran asked.

"Yes," they both responded.

"What of Jugard?" Galloran asked.

"I found his corpse," Nedwin replied. "He was stabbed to death no more than a day before my arrival." Jason noticed that Nedwin suddenly seemed calmer and more coherent.

Galloran pounded a fist against his palm. "I feared as much. Jason unraveled the deception, and word of the false quest is now spreading, so Maldor is retaliating with violence. Did you have to slip past soldiers to get in here?"

"No," Nedwin said. "They've abandoned Fortaim."

"Then it was recently," Galloran said. "They've been scouring the area for the past two days, trying to figure out how we slipped away. The time to act is upon us. Perhaps we can still save some of the other guardians: Trivett, Malar, the Pythoness and . . ." The king paused, unable to continue.

"Corinne," Nedwin supplied.

Galloran nodded silently, his chin briefly trembling with emotion. "How could I have forgotten her for so long?" he rasped softly.

"What matters is that you have remembered."

"You have your memories back?" Jason asked.

"Many of them, thanks to Nedwin."

"I've been giving him small doses of a peculiar variety of snake venom," Nedwin explained. "Comes from a canopy cobra, a furtive species found high in the trees. I've spent the last few years collecting rare specimens from the southern jungle. Too solitary and dangerous a job for most, but perfect for a man with keen senses and a defective personality. The right plant extract or spider poison can fetch a princely sum."

"The cobra venom is sometimes employed by Maldor to extract information," Galloran added.

"They used it on me!" Jason said. "Blue and purple snake?"

Nedwin bobbed his head. "That's the one. I routinely kept some of the more interesting samples I gathered." He patted the pouches at his belt. "I recalled how the canopy cobras were used inside of Felrook. When I captured one in the jungle, I milked a vial for my own use."

"Nedwin talks to me about my past while administering doses of varying strengths," Galloran said. "After the effect of the venom wanes, he reminds me of all we discussed, adding details that he personally recalls. In a matter of weeks, most of my mental barriers have been torn down."

"You mentioned Corinne," Jason prompted.

"Yes." Anxiety colored his words. "You must have met her."

"I did," Jason said. "I can't remember her directly. The weird round mushrooms in her tree blocked our memories. But she was alive. The Pythoness was Corinne's mother, right?"

"The Pythoness was her great-aunt," Galloran said. "Inside the tree, she raised Corinne as her own. Outside of the tree, Corinne understood the reality of the relationship."

"We promised Corinne we'd return if we found the Word."

"It may be too late," Galloran said, striving to sound detached. "Jugard's death proves that Maldor is moving against the syllable guardians. Thanks to protective spells woven into their sanctuaries, the emperor can't use magic against them, nor can he send wizardborn races like displacers or manglers. But I'm not sure much besides secrecy ever guarded them from simple human assassins. The thought of Maldor sending troops to harm her . . ." Veins stood out on the back of his fists.

"It sounds like you know Corinne well," Jason said, trying to fill the silence.

"She is my daughter," Galloran answered, his voice hollow. "My last living child."

"What?" Jason exclaimed.

"Maldor went to great lengths to target the royal family of Trensicourt. He slew my brothers, my son, my wife. In her youth, I hid Corinne with her great-aunt for her protection. After all these years, that decision may have fatally exposed her."

"We'll rescue her," Nedwin vowed. "We'll hurriedly recover all the remaining guardians."

"We needn't fret for the Prophetess of Mianamon," Galloran said. "She has enough protection until Maldor triumphs in the east. And I do not expect Maldor would target the loremaster Bridonus, given his attitude and connections."

"He's Copernum's father," Jason remembered.

"And Damak's son," Nedwin added.

"Damak?" Jason said. "The torture guy?"

"Bridonus lacks their ruthlessness, but he is essentially a puppet of the emperor," Galloran said. "The three other remaining guardians must be rescued."

"I'll see to it," Nedwin said.

Galloran nodded slowly, placing his palms together at his lips. "Trivett on the Isle of Weir will be the hardest to reach. Perhaps we'll dispatch Vernon."

"Have you heard anything about Rachel?" Jason asked, internally crossing his fingers.

"Tark related how he left her with Drake," Galloran said. "He is a seedman of no small reputation, though by my day he had already withdrawn from the rebellion against Maldor. I have heard no tidings regarding Rachel, but if Drake meant to disappear with her into the wilderness, the lack of information is encouraging."

"I have to find her," Jason said.

"We'll make every effort," Galloran promised. "Nedwin, have you anything else to report?"

"Not at present, sire. You'll want to interview the men Jason brought."

"Naturally. Begin preparations for us to depart in the morning. We will all require horses. I wish to converse with Lord Jason in private."

"Certainly, sire." Nedwin rose and exited the room.

"I never expected to see Ned again," Jason said once the door had closed. "When I first met him, he took my knife and threatened me."

"He related your first encounter," Galloran said. "Nedwin is doing his best to cope with deep scars."

"He used to be your servant?" Jason asked.

"My squire. When I was blinded and captured by the conscriptor Grollis, Nedwin was apprehended as well. He was a bright, sensitive young man with enormous potential. That was about fourteen years ago. After six years of torture I was released—a blind, enfeebled mockery of my former self. During the first few years of my incarceration, I was near Nedwin on occasion. He had an unconquerable will and remained fiercely loyal to me even after I was reduced to a babbling wretch. Because of his strength, the tormentors pushed the limits with Nedwin, experimenting with untried toxins and procedures.

"After I was released, I assumed Nedwin had perished. His fate remained a mystery until he located me by following your trail. I've learned that he remained imprisoned more than five years longer than I, enduring excruciating reconditioning the entire time. When he first arrived here, wearing only a coarse sack and a glove, he seemed beyond the brink of madness. But in a short while he has come a long way. Once he was the clever and articulate younger brother of the Earl of Geer. Maldor's tormentors shattered him, deformed his mind, but he is battling his way back toward sanity. Never have I witnessed a more valiant spirit."

"I had no idea," Jason said.

Galloran rubbed the side of his cot. "I know firsthand how thoroughly the tormentors can annihilate a person. Even disregarding my eyes, I do not yet feel like the man I was. It has been an arduous process of long, anonymous years, gradually overcoming fears and frailties to reassemble my identity. My memories regarding the Word were the hardest to recapture, though I've finally enjoyed major breakthroughs of late." Galloran sniffed, adjusting his blindfold. "The time to reconstruct myself has now passed. The hour to act has arrived. Do you intend to continue with us in this cause?"

"That's why I'm here."

Galloran sighed. "Difficult times have befallen us. You've already endured many hardships."

"I'm lucky to be alive."

"Luck only carries any of us so far. You've achieved much more than mere luck would allow. You've made smart choices, forged strategic relationships. Tell me about when you used the Word. Are you certain you said it to Maldor in person?"

"Yes," Jason said. "He didn't know I had the whole thing, so he admitted me to his throne room with a big crowd there. The Word vanished from my mind when I spoke it, but it didn't bother Maldor. He later explained that it was actually the Word to destroy some other wizard named Orruck."

"Orruck?" Galloran repeated, stroking his beard. "Intriguing."

"Maldor told me that years ago you spoke the Word to him in person. Since you were blind, he pretended you were talking to a decoy."

Galloran steepled his fingers. "I only recently remembered that episode with help from Nedwin. So I was actually in the presence of the emperor." A small, sad smile appeared on his lips. "He is a truly gifted liar. Thank you for the vital knowledge that the Word itself is fraudulent. It sickens me to consider how much time and effort has been misdirected. The knowledge you sent with Tark taught me that I remain capable of outrage. As soon as I learned of the elaborate deception, I sent Nedwin to retrieve Jugard from his pointless guardianship, and then I began concocting a plan."

"Can you tell me?"

"It continues to evolve, but centers on uniting all who continue to oppose Maldor in a desperate gambit. It was a course of action I considered long ago, but Kadara still imagined itself untouchable, and too many kingdoms denied the urgency of the situation, preferring to pretend they could somehow appease Maldor and avoid war, so I elected to hunt the Word instead. Hopefully, it is not too late to atone for my folly."

"I'll help if I can," Jason said.

"That would be most appreciated," Galloran said. "Tark told me that you escaped from Felrook. How did you manage such a feat?"

"A displacer rescued me and then forced me to return to the Beyond."

"A displacer?"

"Yeah. When I first arrived here, I had no idea that displacers served Maldor. A displacer befriended me and Rachel to observe our actions, but we sent him away once we learned he worked for the emperor. He must have taken some genuine interest in me, because he smuggled me out of Felrook after the Word failed against Maldor and I was captured."

"He returned you to the Beyond?"

"Yes, using a gateway near Felrook. He only released me from Felrook on the condition that I would go directly home. Despite my promise, I tried to escape, so I could warn you that the Word is a fraud. But he overpowered me and sent me away."

"And you came back to Lyrian?" Galloran said in disbelief.

"Believe it or not, I came through the same hippopotamus that brought me here the first time. Jumped into the tank on purpose. I wanted to keep others from wasting their time pursuing the Word. And I couldn't just ditch Rachel."

Galloran smiled. "Truly, you are possessed by that species of madness that begets heroism. You have performed an invaluable service. Tell me about your new companions."

"One is a mercenary named Aram."

"Aram the smuggler? A mountainous man?"

"Yes."

"I know of him. He has never displayed any willingness to resist the emperor. How did you retain his services?"

"Tark recommended him to me, then I got in good with his mother, and she convinced him. I'm not sure whether he's fully committed yet. He's getting there. You should see him fight!"

"That might prove difficult."

"Whoops, I meant—"

"I'm jesting. Who is the other?"

"Ferrin the displacer."

Even with most of his face concealed behind a blindfold and a beard, Galloran looked alarmed. "He has a deadly reputation. A foe most devious and capable. Young for a displacer, he was just rising to prominence back when I was completing the Word. My sources have followed his career. If his character were less capricious and his methods more orthodox, he would already be a candidate to lead the displacers. This is the displacer who freed you?"

"Yes. According to him, Maldor discovered his participation in my rescue, and he now wants to join our side."

"How convinced are you of his sincerity?"

"Not completely certain. He's been really helpful so far. And he's already passed up a bunch of chances to betray me. Without his help, I doubt I'd be here."

Galloran took a deep breath. "Giving him our trust could prove ruinous. I've learned never to underestimate the deceptive abilities of our enemies. Malar is the only displacer I've ever met who truly joined our cause, though plenty have pretended. Summon your new comrades, and we'll see what I can discern."

As Jason rose from the bench, Dorsio crossed the room and opened the door. Down the hall, Aram and Ferrin stood conversing with Tark. When the short musician saw Jason, he broke off the conversation and sprinted down the passageway. "Lord Jason!" he cried. "I'm sorry I was unable to meet you at Potsug." He looked distressed.

"It worked out," Jason said. "You recommended a good bodyguard."

"All they wanted was you. Our enemies, I mean. Soon after you left me, a group of soldiers began hunting me in earnest, ready to dispose of me after I had led them to their true quarry. It was quite a chase. I killed a few of them. It took me longer than I had anticipated to work my way here."

"I'm glad you made it. I was worried about you."

Tark beamed, then scowled. "The evening I arrived, the castle came under assault. I feel like a token of foul luck. All around me suffer."

"It had to be the information you carried," Jason said. "They must have found out what I told you."

"I revealed nothing until I arrived here!" Tark swore.

"They may have guessed. Maldor knows what secrets I carry. Or the lurker could have overheard us." Jason turned to Aram and Ferrin. "Galloran wants to talk to all of us."

"Galloran is here?" Tark exclaimed.

"He didn't tell you?" Jason said. "Come with us."

The four of them entered the room with Galloran. Dorsio closed the door, remaining inside.

"Do you mind if Tark joins us?" Jason asked.

"Not at all," Galloran said.

Jason sat on a chair off to the side. Ferrin, Aram, and Tark sat on the bench.

"You're Galloran?" Tark asked in awe.

The Blind King snorted. "Is this becoming common knowledge?"

"I know how you feel," grumbled Aram.

"Ferrin deduced it long before we got here," Jason said.

"Ah, yes, the master spy," Galloran said. "I have heard frightening reports about you from my sources."

"Likewise," Ferrin said.

Galloran chuckled. "I'm sure the gossip about me was terrifying. Were you warned that I was a blind pauper serving as an arbiter in a ruined castle?"

"You've only been lionized into the greatest hero of our time," Ferrin responded. "I expect the reputation is well deserved."

Galloran appeared thoughtful. "An inflated reputation can be useful when inciting a revolution. Aram, am I to understand you have enlisted in our cause?"

The others all looked to the big man. He swallowed. "Do we have a chance of success?"

Galloran crinkled his brow pensively. "A succinct and important question. The situation is dire. Our first order of business will be to investigate our assets. Without some key alliances, we have no chance. Even if we manage to unite the remaining free citizens of Lyrian, it may be too little, too late. But this effort will certainly represent our last opportunity to prevent an age of tyranny that will endure for many generations. I will not give up the cause until I am sure we cannot prevail."

"Then I will join you until the cause proves unwinnable," Aram said.

"You're a mercenary. I have little to offer you at present. Should we succeed, you will receive a barony."

"You'd make a fine baron," Tark encouraged.

Smirking self-consciously, the big man looked around the small, dusty room. "We can discuss payment once you've been restored to your throne."

"Fair enough."

Aram cleared his throat. "I may as well tell you, since the secret is out: I'm half giant. My usefulness fades each morning at sunrise and does not recommence until dusk."

"Half giant?" Galloran said. "How did you come to be?"

Tark gaped at Aram in astonishment.

"My mother is human; my father, a giant."

"No magic?"

"Just nature."

"Fascinating. Welcome, Aram." Galloran turned his head, as if looking at Ferrin. "Back to the matter of the famed Ferrin, son of Baldor. Am I to believe you honestly mean to join our rebellion?"

"I do," Ferrin replied. His voice and expression seemed relaxed, but Jason sensed a nervous tension underneath.

"You desire this alliance because your impulsive rescue of Lord Jason offended Maldor?"

"And he must know I've learned about the fraudulent Word," Ferrin added. "Maldor has irrevocably become my enemy."

Galloran frowned. "A common enemy is not necessarily a reliable basis for friendship."

"The circumstances have compelled me to take a step I have long contemplated. Even when I served him, I quietly yearned to see the emperor overthrown."

"You did not believe it was possible," Galloran said flatly.

"I still have my doubts, but I'm willing to try. I know much that could be of service."

"Undoubtedly. How can I know you will not betray us?"

"I could give you my word."

"You're a displacer! Your people have sworn fealty to Maldor. You have personally vowed to defend and uphold his rule. Your presence here makes you a traitor to your kind and an oath breaker to your liege. A tarnished word is of little value."

Ferrin had grown rigid. "Your honor is renowned, and you're right that mine is blemished. Perhaps the truest pledge I can offer is that I understand how the emperor functions."

"Do you?"

"Maldor never forgives treachery. Especially from a steward of my rank. Regardless of how substantially I might aid him in the future by subverting your efforts, I know I can never regain his confidence. He would gladly reap the reward of any betrayal I enacted, but regardless of any good I do for him, death and worse await if ever I come within his reach."

"You speak the truth. But do you realize it?"

"Maldor is my eternal enemy, because no matter what I do, I am his."

Galloran leaned forward. "But what if Maldor already forgave your indiscretion? Or even planned it? What if you are not a fugitive as you claim? What if this is an elaborate scheme?"

All eyes regarded Ferrin.

"Has the emperor orchestrated more subtle and complicated intrigues than you are describing? Absolutely. But if I were a spy, I would not know my trade had I waited until now to act. An hour ago, while exploring Fortaim, I had enough distance between myself and my comrades to easily slip away and lead an army to your doorstep."

"The emperor is patient," Galloran replied. "The emperor treasures information. The emperor might want to investigate how far our budding conspiracy reaches. He might want to root out everyone involved, not just snatch Jason or me. I have some well-placed sources, and I have heard nothing about a manhunt for you, Ferrin. Not a word about your defection."

Ferrin shook his head. "If it could be avoided, Maldor would never announce that a high-ranking displacer had betrayed his cause. He has kept the search for me quiet. But keep your ears open. After my treasonous activities early this morning, in front of imperial witnesses, my defection will become common knowledge. I'll be nearly as wanted as Jason."

"What about the betrayal of your people?" Galloran wondered. "The displacers are well acquainted with the price of failure in wartime. If Maldor falls, the displacers fall with him. You can live with that?"

"I detest the idea of hindering my kind," Ferrin admitted. "We've dealt with more than our rightful share of persecution. But displacers are already doomed. Fearful of natural humans losing dominance, all of the wizards who founded races included safe-guards to limit breeding. As you're aware, when displacers were first created, the odds of having a male child were five times greater than a female. That disparity has increased over time. Today not even one in thirty displacers born is female. Yes, our race lives longer than regular humans, but our ultimate fate is sealed. We were condemned by our founder. We'll cease to exist within three or four generations."

"So why not rise up against the apprentice of your founder?" Galloran summarized skeptically. "Punish him for the sins of his master?"

"It wouldn't have been my first choice," Ferrin said frankly. "However deranged Zokar may have been, or how oppressive Maldor could prove, at least they were on our side. They didn't hunt us. They never openly despised us. Not as a people. My per-sonal story is different. I'm being hunted by Maldor. I've earned his enmity. In return, he has earned mine. I wouldn't be here if not for extenuating circumstances. But I'm at peace with my decision. I am wholeheartedly committed. I would be happy to do whatever you'd like to prove myself."

Galloran let a pregnant silence draw out. All eyes watched him intently. "Two requirements. First, you will take credit for all the harm we do as we make our way across Lyrian. 'Ferrin, son of Baldor, was here.' You get the idea."

"Make my betrayal public knowledge. Defy Maldor openly to ensure that he could never take me back."

Galloran nodded. "And I will need you to detach a small segment from your neck. The divot must include part of your carotid artery. Dorsio will keep it safe."

Ferrin grinned darkly. "You could use the piece of my neck to poison me at will. If I choose to let go of the connection, I bleed to death."

"I harbor hope that you are sincere," Galloran said. "If I didn't, I would execute you. Tonight we stand at the outset of the last serious rebellion against the emperor. At present it is desperately fragile, little more than an idea. Without great care and effort, it will amount to nothing. I would welcome your help, Ferrin, but I will not risk treachery. Accept my conditions, and I will extend my trust."

Ferrin pulled a chunk from his neck and handed it to Dorsio, who studied it and snapped three times.

"I'll spread word of my involvement at every opportunity," Ferrin said. "I pledge my abilities, my knowledge, my resources, and my life to the cause of deposing Maldor. My allegiance is to rebellion."

"Welcome," Galloran said. "We can use your expertise. If you prove faithful, you will have my everlasting support and protection when this conflict ends. I need information. How closely were you followed?"

"We seem to have distanced ourselves from our pursuers," Ferrin said. "The majority of those chasing us came from north of the river, and we sabotaged both ferries at Potsug."

"Good news," Galloran said.

"What about the lurker?" Jason asked.

"Tark mentioned that a torivor might be involved," Galloran said grimly. "You've had contact?"

"Yes," Ferrin said. "We saw the torivor last night. It has been trailing Jason since he parted from Tark."

"Lurkers have not ventured abroad in years," Galloran said.

"Not since you were captured," Ferrin agreed. "The creature may have returned to Felrook. After spotting us, it prepared a trap that should have resulted in our capture. Once we dodged the trap, the chase became sloppy, making me wonder whether the lurker remained involved. It taxes Maldor greatly to keep them abroad."

"There is no lurker currently in the vicinity," Galloran said with confidence. "My family has a history of Edomic aptitude and other unusual mental faculties. I am no wizard, but as much as torivors can sense our minds, I can sense theirs."

"Fascinating," Ferrin said. "Can you hear their thoughts?"

"It depends. I can discern certain types of thoughts more clearly than others. But I can always sense their presence. For now, we have no lurkers in the area."

"That's a comfort," Aram said. "But we do have a large force of more conventional enemies in pursuit."

"All the more reason we must depart in the morning," Galloran said. "Rest while you may. Tark, you told me you had sworn fealty to Lord Jason."

"I am his man," the musician replied solemnly.

"Then I have acquired four unexpected allies of diverse talents. There is little I can bring to our venture at the moment save knowledge and connections. Hopefully, in time, I will regain my kingdom and bring its resources to bear. We must first journey north, to the Sunken Lands, on our way to the Seven Vales. At the Sunken

Lands, we will try to rescue my daughter and supply ourselves from a lost stockpile of orantium. At the Seven Vales, we will strive to enlist the Amar Kabal in our rebellion, the most powerful fighting force yet untouched by the emperor. Without their participation, our insurrection will lack any real promise."

"You think you can rouse the People of the Seed?" Ferrin asked.

"We shall see," Galloran replied. "Our first obstacle will be crossing the river. I recommend we make for the bridge a day east of Potsug. The troops pursuing Jason from the north will probably cross that bridge tonight and head west. If we move in stealth, we should miss one another."

"The bridge will be heavily guarded," Ferrin warned.

"We have a capable team," Galloran said. "And some orantium remains. Do you recommend an alternate route?"

Ferrin considered the question before answering. "The bridge will be quickest. No crossing will stand unguarded."

"The bridge it is," Galloran said. "Eat your fill tonight. We have far more food stored here than we can carry. Sleep all you can. We depart at dawn."

CHAPTER 12

RENDEZVOUS

Rachel awoke in the chill of night, bundled in her blankets, the stars blazing more brilliantly than she had ever witnessed. The moon had set, the night was clear, and no overhanging trees impeded her view. In the gaps between the brighter stars, where darkness should have provided background, lesser stars glimmered, faint and plentiful, twinkling specks of dust. She lay on her back, high atop a tall ridge, gazing at the magnificent heavens.

Could any of those pinpricks of light be Earth's sun? If not, were any of those endless stars at least visible from Earth? Maybe with a powerful telescope? Or was this an entirely different universe altogether, inhabiting some alternate dimension? She didn't recognize any constellations.

Rachel looked over at the charm woman. They hadn't built a fire tonight, but the stars shed enough light for her to see that Elaine was gone, her blankets rumpled and empty.

Rachel sat up, scared and alert. Why had Elaine snuck away? They had just arrived at the ridge this evening after many consecutive days in the saddle. Elaine's donkey was not swift, but it was tireless. They had started at the first hint of dawn every morning and plodded onward until twilight dwindled.

Low, mumbling voices reached Rachel's ears, a single hushed conversation. Listening intently, she could distinguish between a man and a woman speaking. "Elaine?" Rachel called.

"Here, child. We're coming. Drake has found us."

"Elaine?" Drake asked, his voice scarcely audible. "Is that your name?"

"At present," she answered softly. Two starlit figures walked into view. Elaine raised her voice again. "My charms detected an intruder approaching. I knew it wasn't a lurker. I hoped it was Drake."

"You made good time," Drake remarked. "I expected to beat you here. I had to cover much more ground, but of course Mandibar is extraordinary."

"We only arrived earlier tonight," Rachel said.

"I'm glad we found you awake," Elaine said. "It means my inner ring of charms is working."

"I don't get it," Rachel said.

"The outer ring was rigged to awaken me," Elaine said. "When Drake crossed the inner boundary, you woke up."

Upon quick reflection, Rachel realized that usually when she awoke in the night, she rolled over and went on sleeping. Tonight she had awakened alert, her mind active and inquisitive.

"I didn't set up any violent or distractive enchantments, because I wanted him to find us," Elaine explained.

"I have news," Drake said.

"Tell us," Rachel urged.

"Jason is free."

At first she felt stunned. It took a moment to really process the words. Then such a surge of joy and relief overcame her that

Rachel abruptly realized how much of her had never expected to see Jason again. She had faithfully wished for his safety. She had dreamed of an eventual rescue. But deep down, some realistic part of her had known the odds were against it. "Where is he?"

"Our enemies aren't sure," Drake said. "Which bodes well for him, but may make him difficult for us to locate."

"How'd you learn this?" Rachel wondered.

"I set the doll adrift in the Purga River, to create the illusion that you remained in motion. After that I never saw the lurker again, so I assume it took the bait. I traveled north fast enough that I knew I had to be well ahead of you, so I took a side trip to Trensicourt to do some reconnaissance. I still have a few contacts there from bygone years, although they're looking old.

"Once I learned that Jason was supposedly at large, I did some investigating of my own. First, I captured and interrogated a regular imperial soldier, then a displacer."

"You got a displacer to talk?" Elaine asked dubiously.

"It took some finesse," Drake explained. "I pretended to be a bounty hunter, seeking to collect a reward for the capture of Lord Jason. The displacer might not have spilled information to the enemy regardless of the pressure I brought to bear, but he showed only minor resistance to divulging some secrets to an enterprising free agent working with the imperials. I dropped some names and had him convinced."

"What did you learn?" Rachel asked.

"You must understand that our enemies use certain displacers to relay information," Drake explained. "By exchanging ears, they can communicate over vast distances. Their latest reports suggest that Jason is here in the west, south of the Telkron River, accompanied by a dangerous mercenary and a traitorous displacer."

"A displacer?" Rachel exclaimed. "Ferrin?"

"That was the name," Drake confirmed.

"When did you learn all of this?" Elaine asked.

"This afternoon." Drake studied Rachel. "I take it this alters your plans."

Rachel looked apologetically at Elaine. At minimum, this would mean a postponement of her training. "We have to find him."

"We're in the right part of the world," Elaine observed. "Any idea where he might be headed?"

"They came south from Ithilum and crossed the Telkron at Potsug," Drake related. "Most of the forces in the region are being mobilized to track him down. Based on the resources involved, the effort feels more like a war than a manhunt."

"Which will make finding him hazardous for fellow fugitives," Elaine said. Her face scrunched in thought. After a moment her expression brightened. "Have you any items Jason owned?"

Drake cocked his head. "He left me with some items before he entered Felrook. I have his signet rings—one pertaining to Caberton, the other to the chancellorship. Let me fetch my horse."

Elaine held up a hand to stop him. "Rachel. Call Mandibar."

"Can I do that?" she asked. "How far away is he?"

"Visualize the horse. Speak the summons."

As they had ridden to the ridge, Elaine had drilled Rachel on issuing suggestions to animals. It was a tricky art. When dealing with matter or energy, you demanded obedience. When dealing with animals, you asked for compliance. If you tried to compel the animal to obey, natural defenses would engage and the suggestion would fail, stunning the speaker, riling the animal, or worse. If you suggested too gently, the animal might simply ignore the recommendation. The suggestion worked best when supported by enough will to make it convincing, while leaving the actual decision to the animal.

Rachel had practiced mostly with her own horse. After erring often by suggesting too softly, she had eventually found the right amount of insistence to employ. She could now confidently convince her mount to stop, go, slow down, speed up, come, neigh, stomp, rear, buck, calm down, and eat. She had also issued several similar suggestions to Elaine's donkey with routine success. But she had never called out to Mandibar with Edomic, and she had never tried speaking to an animal out of view.

"Okay," Rachel said. Closing her eyes, she imagined Mandibar: his size, his musculature, the sheen of his fur, his name printed on the saddle in neat black letters. She called his name and asked him to come.

Hoofbeats answered her effort of will, and the stallion soon loped into view, slowed to a trot, and plodded over to Rachel, nudging her with his nose. She felt an excited flutter at the prompt success of her summons.

Drake whistled softly. "What can't she do?" He paced over to Mandibar, opened a saddlebag, and pawed through it. He came away with a pair of rings and handed them to Elaine.

She cupped one in each palm, hands bobbing gently, as if weighing them, then gave one back. She held up the other between her thumb and forefinger. "This ring has the stronger connection to him."

"That makes sense," Drake replied. "He had the Caberton ring longer, and has an undisputed claim to ownership."

Elaine held the ring to her ear and closed her eyes, as if listening to secret music. "I can use this to find him. It will take until an hour past dawn to ready the charm."

"I'd call that quick work," Drake replied.

"We're going to find Jason?" Rachel asked, hardly daring to believe it.

Drake tousled her hair. "At least we'll soon know where to look."

The first rays of sunrise shimmered on countless dewdrops as eight riders emerged from a camouflaged portal, well beyond the damaged walls of the crumbling castle. A gentle breeze stole fluffy particles from tall dandelions, scattering airborne seeds across the hillside. Warbling bird calls twittered back and forth in the treetops. One unseen bird hooted like a slide whistle.

Ferrin and Nedwin galloped away from the others to scout the country ahead. Nedwin had already spent the hours before dawn confirming the absence of enemies and collecting the necessary mounts.

Looking undersized, Aram rode the big stallion that had carried him since fleeing Ithilum. Jason rode the same horse that had brought him to Fortaim. Galloran rode beside Dorsio, the silent servant holding a lead, leaving plenty of slack. Tark brought up the rear, riding alongside Chandra, the cook—a rawboned woman with sun-damaged skin who Jason had never seen smile.

Some of Galloran's associates had not joined them. Vernon had been left with the assignment to book passage to the Isle of Weir and warn a guardian named Trivett that the Word was a fraud. Jason wondered how Trivett would feel to know that the syllable he had guarded had been inscribed on the wall of the lorevault at Trensicourt. Brin the Gamester was ordered to find his brother, Nicholas, in Trensicourt and tell him about the burgeoning rebellion. A few others whom Jason had not known well were told to scatter and lie low.

Jouncing along on his horse, Jason patted one of his saddlebags. Crystal globes containing chunks of orantium had been dispersed among the riders, with Nedwin and Dorsio carrying the most.

Jason had three in his saddlebag, each bundled in cloth. If the crystal casing cracked, exposing the mineral inside to air or water, the orantium would explode violently. Ever since receiving the spheres, Jason had treated them gingerly, unable to erase visions of Jasher being blasted to pieces in the field near Harthenham. Aram had refused to accept any of the spheres, for fear of an accidental detonation.

Jason kept a hand near his saddlebag. Despite the dangers of carrying orantium, he knew how effective the combustible globes could be in a fight. Riding away from Fortaim, he felt most on edge for the first mile or two. Out in the wilderness, he trusted the expertise of Ferrin and Nedwin to steer them away from trouble. Of course, if the lurker crashed the party, that would change everything. But Galloran hadn't sensed one and seemed confident about his ability to do so.

They kept to obscure trails through woodlands and wild fields, and hours glided past without incident. Ferrin and Nedwin checked in at intervals, describing the topography ahead and suggesting the safest routes. The party stopped twice to eat. By evening they reached a hillside where they could survey the bridge spanning the Telkron River from a wooded vantage.

Three huge arches supported the wide stone bridge. At either end stood a guardhouse, each manned by several soldiers and a trio of manglers. Jason had partly forgotten how intimidating the manglers looked—perfectly designed to shred enemies into confetti, the bulky, insectile creatures had shell-like armor and a wicked variety of blades at the end of their six arms.

"They really mean to catch us," Ferrin said. "Six manglers to guard a single bridge? That's uncommon. They must have significant assets in motion."

"Could we swim the river?" Jason asked. "Or build a raft?"

"Steal a raft?" Nedwin mused.

"The current here is deceptively swift and treacherous," Aram said, having regained his full size half an hour before. "The river doesn't slow down until you near Potsug. Hence the bridge."

"We need our horses and our gear," Galloran said. "If we can find a raft big enough, we could risk the current. But we can't afford the time to build one. And we can't lose time exploring other crossings. Barring unforeseeable opportunities, we'll assail the bridge in the small hours of the morning. Surprise them with orantium. Perhaps send a couple of our party stealthily across to harass those on the far side. Until then, we should rest. We'll have to ride hard later."

"Once we're over the bridge, I'll take a detour to Whitelake," Nedwin said. "Fetch Malar."

Galloran nodded his approval. "You can manage the lake?"

"Yes."

"Where could we meet?"

"Just south of Three Peaks," Nedwin answered.

"So be it," Galloran confirmed.

"I'll scout for rafts," Ferrin offered.

Dorsio snapped and motioned that he would join Ferrin.

Tark offered to take the first watch, and everyone dispersed, some to sleep, some to reconnoiter. While fetching blankets from his saddle, Jason found himself alone with Nedwin. The redhead was sorting through a variety of metal vials that hung from his neck by thin leather cords.

"What do you have there?" Jason asked.

"Some of the substances I've collected," he said. "I have a powder that can bother any animals attempting to track us. I thought I'd scatter some here, then more after we cross."

"How'd you learn so much about herbs and snakes and everything?"

Nedwin's cheek twitched. "When I was imprisoned at Felrook,

I kept my ears and eyes open. Quietly I learned to prepare many of the concoctions administered to me. When I was finally released, it became an obsession to gather the materials they had used. By immersing myself in the endeavor, I continued to learn." He held up some vials, one at a time. "This induces sleep; this causes gut-wrenching nausea; this opens the mind to suggestion; this increases sensitivity to pain."

"Increases pain?"

Nedwin kept that vial in his long hand, stroking it with his thumb. "A mixture of tarantula poison and juice distilled from a certain carnivorous plant. After a tiny dose, pressure feels like pain, and pain flares into an otherwise impossible agony."

"You experienced it?"

Nedwin gave a bitter chuckle. His somber smile bespoke dark memories. "Endlessly. They probed the limits of my toler-ance. Under the influence of the substance, a finger pressed to my shoulder felt like it was boring into me, searing my flesh. But they wouldn't stop there. They would slap me, or cut me, eliciting over-whelming surges of anguish. Then they would drill my teeth."

Jason winced and clapped a hand over his mouth, experiencing phantom pain just hearing the description.

"Copernum was the worst of them," Nedwin muttered resent-fully.

"Chancellor Copernum?"

Nedwin nodded, wringing his freckled hand with his gloved hand. "He was my chief tormentor for the final years of my confine-ment. I had been transported to the small dungeon of his manor at Trensicourt. He had a grudge against my family. He won our title from my elder brother. Once I had been reduced to a gibbering lunatic, he finally released me. He was liberal with nervesong, the pain enhancer. It had some ancillary effects. Along with amplifying pain, it quickened my other senses: hearing, sight, smell. Under its influence, I overheard many conversations not intended for my ears. Over time, the enhancement of my senses began to linger. And my ability to feel pain vanished."

"Really?"

"To this day." Eyes glazed, he fingered the vial of nervesong. "I can still sense pressure. But physical discomfort has become a distant memory. Unless fate betrays me, one day Copernum will drink from this vial and learn of the pain he inflicted so casually." Nedwin shook his head, returning to the present.

"I hope you pull it off," Jason said. "Did you know Copernum tried to kill me?"

"I'm not surprised, considering how you humiliated the scoundrel. When I heard about your battle of wits, I laughed all day. If you had no other virtues, I would love you forever for the embarrassment you caused him."

"It felt good to beat him," Jason said. "I'm sorry to hear about your suffering."

Nedwin shrugged, staring uncomfortably at the ground. "We all have misery to bear. I'm off to cover our tracks." He swung up onto his horse and rode away.

After spreading out his blankets, Jason curled up on the ground. He tried not to dwell on all Nedwin had suffered. How could a person cope with so much torture? Jason thought about his own time at Felrook, locked within an iron shell fitted to his body. The memory made him sweat. How long could he have lasted? What else would have been in store? Thankfully, he had escaped before the worst ensued. He hoped he would never have to sample nervesong. Of course, if he were ever captured again, that might be exactly what he would have to face. Grim concerns slowed his ability to sleep.

* * *

A soft hand jostled Jason's shoulder. "Wake up, sleepyhead," said a familiar voice.

Startled awake, Jason blinked and squinted. By the light of the setting moon, he saw a pretty face hovering over his own, dark hair hanging a bit longer than he remembered. The face matched the voice. But how could Rachel be here? He scooted away from her, messing up his blankets. His first instinct was that the lurker must have caught up to him and invaded his dreams. Propped up on his elbows, he focused on her eyes. They weren't black. "Is that really you?" he asked in wonder.

She smiled and sat back. "Surprise."

He lunged forward, throwing his arms around her, partly to make sure she was real, partly out of sheer joy. She hugged him back. Holding her made her presence tangible. "I can't believe it!" he exclaimed. "Who found you?"

Several voices chuckled. Jason released the embrace, noticing for the first time the presence of Drake, Galloran, Dorsio, Aram, and Tark, all standing in a loose circle around where he had been sleeping. The unexpected audience made him awkwardly conscious of the exuberant hug.

"Drake and I found you guys," Rachel explained. She held up a little string. From the end of it dangled the Caberton signet ring.

"My ring," Jason said, reaching out a hand.

"Just a second," Rachel chided. "Notice anything unusual?"

He did. As she held the top of the string, the ring didn't hang straight down. The string hung at a slant, as if the ring were being magnetically drawn toward him. Not dramatically, but unmistakably.

"What?" Jason said, looking up at Galloran. "Is this some kind of homing ring?"

"It is now," Rachel said. "We met a lady who makes charms,

and Drake had your ring, so she enchanted it to help us find you. It led us straight here."

"Wow! Did the lady come with you?"

Rachel shook her head. "She's a wanderer. Sort of a hermit. She would have let me wander with her, but she had no intention of joining us." Rachel produced a necklace of bead and bone and a few small feathers. "She gave me this for you. It should prevent lurkers from reaching out to your mind. She tailored a couple specifically for me and Drake. This one is more generic, but she thought it would work."

"Does yours work?" Jason asked.

"We ditched a lurker right after we started using them. It had been after us for weeks."

"I know of this charm woman," Galloran said. "She has a true gift."

Jason gazed at Rachel, still trying to accept that she was real. "How long have you been here?"

"Not long," Rachel replied. "I could have let you sleep a little more. We're not attacking the bridge until the moon sets. But I couldn't wait."

"Let's give them a chance to talk," Galloran suggested. "They have been apart for some time."

He and the others moved away, not too far, but far enough for Jason and Rachel to speak unobserved. Jason stared at Rachel, the pretty missing girl with photos all over the Internet.

"So the Word didn't work," Rachel said softly.

"They already filled you in?"

"A little. You really made it home? Then came back?"

Jason started folding up his blankets, brushing off leaves and dirt as best he could. "I couldn't stay there knowing you were here and that the Word was a fake. I know a way home now, in a cave near Felrook. It would be tricky to find it alone, but Ferrin could lead us straight there."

"Did you check on my parents?" Rachel asked. "Did you let them know I'm alive?"

"Your parents have turned you into a national celebrity," Jason said. "You've been all over the news, the Internet—you name it. Your mom and dad are anxiously looking for you. They've offered a big reward. But I couldn't contact them. I'd mysteriously vanished the same day as you. I would have instantly become a suspect."

Rachel fretted at her lower lip. "That makes sense. I knew they'd be so worried. I'm glad they're looking. It means they still have hope. I've been gone so long."

"It's a little worse than you think," Jason said. "The rate that time passes in our worlds doesn't match up. It's not way off, but when I got home, a few more weeks had gone by than I would have expected. And when I came back, less time had passed here than there."

"So time goes by faster back home," Rachel summarized.

"Seems like it," Jason said.

"Then they think I've been gone even longer than I'd realized," she said, rubbing her forehead. "I guess it'll make the reunion that much sweeter when I make it back. Ferrin really rescued you?"

"Yeah. I guess they filled you in on that, too. Was he around when you got here?"

"He went with Nedwin and Chandra across the river. They stole a canoe. Galloran made it sound like you guys have him on some kind of leash."

"Ferrin joined us voluntarily," Jason said. "And he willingly gave Galloran a piece of his neck with an artery in it. He seems to have really joined our side."

A little line appeared between Rachel's eyebrows. "You think it's for real?"

Jason shrugged. "My instincts say yes. He did everything Galloran asked, and had plenty of chances before that to turn me in."

"We're heading for the Sunken Lands?"

"Yep, then on to the Seven Vales to see if the Amar Kabal will help Galloran fight Maldor."

Rachel nodded quietly. "You and Ferrin know a way home?"

"Yeah."

"Have you thought about maybe . . . I don't know . . ."

"Ditching everyone and having Ferrin take us to the cave?"

She shrugged.

Jason considered the idea. He had found Rachel. He had informed Galloran that the Word was phony. What more could he achieve by remaining in Lyrian? He was no warrior. This might be a smart time to bow out and let the experts run the rebellion.

Then again, he had a hard time picturing himself back home with so much left undone in Lyrian. He had managed to be useful so far. What if he could still make a difference here? Wouldn't he always wonder how it all turned out?

"We'd have to fully trust Ferrin," he said. "The way home is deep in enemy territory. We'd be at his mercy. Believe me, we don't want to get caught."

Rachel nodded. "I'm not saying we should try it. I'm mostly just glad to hear there's a way. We can stress about it later. Looks like crossing this bridge has to come before anything." She stood and offered Jason a hand. He accepted it, and she helped him rise, his blankets tucked under one arm.

"I'm glad you found us," Jason said. "I was so worried."

"You were worried?" she replied, hitting him on the arm. "I thought you were being tortured inside of Felrook this whole time!"

Jason chuckled. "Since we split up, I've mostly been watching movies, playing video games, and reffing Little League."

She swatted him again.

"Hey!" he complained, backing away. "It wasn't my fault! I got back as soon as I could."

Hands on her hips, her expression softened. "You did come back for me."

By her tone of voice, he could tell she was thanking him. "What are friends for?" He wanted to pick her up and spin her around, he felt so relieved.

Tark came tromping over to them. "We're going to start moving into position."

"What's the plan?" Jason asked.

"You, Rachel, and I will ride with Galloran and Dorsio. We're in charge of the horses. We'll each lead one."

"Even Galloran?" Rachel asked.

"He'll stay toward the rear during the charge," Tark explained. "He'll trust his horse to stay on the road and follow the others. He may be blind, but he's an experienced rider."

"We're riding up along the road?" Jason asked.

"Drake and Aram will hit the bridge on this side, first with orantium, then with sword and bow. Nedwin, Ferrin, and Chandra will do the same on the far side of the bridge. If all goes as planned, the fight should be over by the time we reach the bridge."

"We're just the getaway," Rachel said.

Tark nodded.

"Can we blow the bridge after we cross?" Jason asked. "You know, mess up the pursuit?"

"Chandra asked the same thing," Tark said. "The bridge was built to last. I agree with Aram and Ferrin that the orantium explosives aren't strong enough to bring it down, at least not without some prep work. Give me three days and some tools, it might be a different story."

"How do we know when to move?" Jason asked.

"The others will strike right after the moon sets," Tark related. "We start for the bridge when we hear the first explosion. If needed, we'll help mop up when we get there."

Tark led them over to the horses. Dorsio and Galloran sat astride their mounts, each holding a lead to another horse.

"Crazy about Aram," Rachel said.

"The giant thing?" Jason checked.

"Makes me wonder what else we don't know about the types of people in this world."

Jason nodded. "After the lurkers, I think I've learned enough."

"Shall we move into position?" Galloran asked.

Jason, Tark, and Rachel mounted up. Tark explained which horse each of them would be taking, giving the appropriate lead to Jason and to Rachel. Jason had Chandra's horse. Dorsio led the way at a cautious pace, Galloran near him. Tark brought up the rear. By the time they reached a clearing beside a wide road, the moon was about to touch the horizon.

Galloran shifted on his horse beside Jason. "If all goes as planned," Galloran said, "six orantium spheres should detonate simultaneously, demolishing the manglers. Each attacker will throw one, and Drake will throw two. If our attackers shield their eyes correctly, the blinded guardsmen will be left vulnerable. A second volley of orantium should wipe out most of the remaining defenders. The rest will fall by more conventional means."

Jason visualized the scenario. "Sounds airtight."

"It doesn't take a genius to plan a perfect assault," Galloran said. "The trouble tends to show up during the execution."

The waning moon was halfway below the horizon and slowly melting from sight. Dorsio led them onto the road. The bridge was visible less than a mile away, a pair of large cressets burning at either end. As a group, the horses started walking toward the bridge.

Jason felt butterflies inside his stomach. He tried to tell himself that his part in this was simple. Follow Dorsio to the bridge. What could go wrong? Well, they could get to the bridge, find Aram and Drake dead and manglers waiting to chop them into taco meat while guards shot arrows from covered positions. Jason debated whether he should get out an orantium sphere of his own. He decided against it, since he would have his hands full trying to steer his own horse and lead another. The last thing he needed was to drop a sphere and blow himself up. Sometimes the best offense was avoiding self-destruction.

The moon disappeared below the horizon. Up ahead, white flashes blazed at either end of the bridge, the thunder of the explosions following a few seconds later. Jason's horse sidestepped and whinnied, but thankfully didn't go berserk.

Dorsio spurred his horse to a canter. Jason flicked the reins, and his horse followed. He kept a firm hand on the lead of Chandra's horse. A second round of detonations strobed on the bridge, a little less simultaneous this time, the fiery whiteness reflecting off rising clouds of smoke. The resultant booming sounded like three or four cannons, fired in rapid succession.

Jason focused on staying with Dorsio and keeping his horses under control. If Galloran could do it blind, he had no excuse to mess up.

The bridge passed out of sight, obscured by trees. As the road rounded the trees, the near side of the bridge came back into view, one of the cressets still burning. Aram and Drake stood off to one side of the road. Tark and Rachel slowed up to pass the men their horses.

Staying with Galloran and Dorsio, Jason rode onto the bridge.

He smelled charred stone and metal and flesh. The twisted husks of manglers lay in smoldering ruins, along with several fallen guardsmen. Jason felt a pang of regret at the sight of the slain soldiers. At the same time, he knew that they supported an evil cause. Given the chance, none of them would have hesitated to kill him or his friends.

Jason loped across the bridge. Both cressets still burned on the far side. More demolished manglers and slaughtered soldiers lay in disarray, along with fragments of metal and blackened stone. Nedwin, Ferrin, and Chandra awaited them at the side of the road beyond the bridge. Jason slowed beside Chandra, who sprang onto her horse with wiry skill.

"I'll grant Galloran one thing," Ferrin said cheerily. "The man knows how to throw a party." He was the only person who had not yet mounted his horse. He walked it over to the guardhouse, took the dagger from a fallen guardsman, and used it to tack a piece of parchment to the door.

"What does it say?" Jason asked.

"'Down with Maldor, down with his puppets, down with his empire,'" Nedwin recited. "'Warmest regards, Ferrin, son of Baldor.'"

"I composed it myself," Ferrin said. "Best I could manage on short notice. With more time, I might have devised a rhyme." He mounted his horse as Tark, Rachel, Aram, and Drake rode up.

"The village?" Galloran asked.

"Looks quiet for now," Nedwin replied. "I drugged the horses at the garrison, as well as many of the privately owned mounts on this side of the river. We should enjoy an advantageous head start."

"Well done, everyone," Galloran said, holding out the lead for his own horse until Dorsio took it. "Off we go."

Jason nudged his horse forward, riding between Tark and Rachel. The excitement of the decisive victory and the promise of vengeful imperial pursuers left his senses thrillingly alert. As their horses pounded through the night, he gazed up at the countless stars overhead, so numerous that it looked impossible to create constellations in all the clutter.

"I'll rejoin you at Three Peaks," Nedwin called, veering off the road to the right.

Jason and the others stayed on the road for perhaps ten minutes before turning off into a field. Ferrin had the lead. Aram brought up the rear.

As Jason cantered beside Rachel, he could hardly believe that against all odds they were together again. Rocking in time with his horse, cool wind on his face, he squinted ahead at Dorsio and Galloran, then back at Tark and Aram, dim shapes in the starlight. He doubted whether he and Rachel would be safer anywhere in Lyrian. They rode with cunning adventurers who knew how to fight and forage, who could probably survive for as long as necessary on the run. Racing through the night, in spite of his hardships, Jason felt gratitude and relief. A mighty emperor might be hunting him, but at least he wasn't alone.

·✦✦✦ CHAPTER 13 ✦✦✦·
HUNTED

oward the end of the second day after fleeing from the bridge, deep in rugged, hilly country, Jason rode his horse over the lip of a roundish valley. A lake filled the bottom of the depression, the water interrupted by a large, wooded island crudely shaped like a horseshoe.

Drake led the way down to the edge of the lake, then rode out onto the water. Instead of becoming immersed, the horse never sank deep enough for the water to touch Drake's boots.

"Shallow lake?" Jason asked Ferrin.

"I've never been here," Ferrin replied, "but Drake was telling me there are three ways to the island: broad way, narrow way, and crooked way. The rest of the lake is quite deep, but three submerged ridges allow access from the shore to anyone who knows the secret and doesn't mind wading."

Jason and Ferrin found themselves at the rear of the group, following the other riders out onto the lake. Looking down, Jason noticed that the water was a murky green. He couldn't see far below the surface.

"A wizard once called this island home," Galloran commented

over his shoulder, apparently having overheard the conversation. "The valley is difficult to find unless you know the way."

The nine riders reached the island and trotted inland from the shore. Toward the center of the island, Drake brought them to a clearing ringed by tall pines with scaly bark. A large stone cottage and a few smaller outbuildings stood in various stages of disrepair. The cottage lacked a door and had lost most of one wall. The windows had no glass. Part of the roof remained. A pair of young trees grew out of the roofless portion.

"After dark we can build a fire in the cottage," Drake said. "We could all use a full night's rest and some hot food."

"Couldn't we get cornered here?" Aram asked.

"I know all three ways off this island," Drake said. "We've seen no sign of anyone tracking us, and this valley is isolated and elusive."

"Good enough for me," Aram replied, dismounting.

Nobody else raised objections.

While Jason was unpacking his blankets, Rachel came over. She placed a hand on his shoulder and whispered, "I want to show you something."

Curious, he followed her over to one of the crumbling outbuildings. Little more than a pair of adjacent walls remained. Rachel led Jason to the corner where the two walls met, shielding them from view.

"Check this out," Rachel said, taking a candle from her pocket. She held it up and mumbled a short phrase, and a flame came to life. She shielded the fire with her hand.

"How'd you do that?" Jason asked, impressed. He hadn't recognized the words she spoke, yet somehow he instinctively understood they pertained to gathering heat.

"Edomic," she replied. "I can teach you."

"Who taught you?"

"Drake showed me how to light fires. Then the charm lady taught me some other things. It isn't too hard once you get the hang of it."

Jason blew out the candle. "Do it again."

She mumbled the phrase, and the flame returned.

"You just say the words?" Jason verified.

"Partly. The words ask heat to gather. But you have to put your will behind the words and sort of force the heat to obey."

Jason held out a hand. "Let me try."

She blew out the flame and handed him the candle, then slowly and clearly told him the words.

"It sounds like you're singing them," Jason said.

"You don't have to be loud about it," Rachel said. "But the pitch does matter. The charm woman said some wizards used to get results just by speaking the words in their minds. But you still need to pronounce everything correctly."

They repeated the words back and forth. Rachel made little corrections in his inflections. "This seems a lot harder than saying the Word."

"It is," Rachel said. "The charm woman explained it to me. The Word was as close to nonsense as Edomic gets. It was just a password, a trigger, to set a prearranged enchantment into motion. It was deliberately simple. Many Edomic words can't be written with English phonetics. She said the only complicated part would have been designing the Word to erase itself from memory."

Jason kept working to perfect the phrase to summon heat. Finally Rachel approved. He repeated the phrase a few times.

"You've got it," Rachel said. "Now focus on the candle, say the words, and demand them to be fulfilled."

Jason stared at the candle. He imagined the flame flickering to life, spoke the phrase, and focused on the wick, willing it to burn. After a prolonged mental effort, nothing happened. His gaze switched to Rachel. "What did I do wrong?"

"I don't know," she replied, a crease forming between her eyebrows. "Make sure you imagine the heat responding and gathering. It's sort of like making a wish. Have you ever wished for something so hard that it's almost like you're trying to force it to come true?"

"Sure," he said.

"It's kind of like that, except this actually works. Speak the command, then back it up with mental effort. Make the heat fulfill your words."

He tried several more times with no effect. "Am I pronouncing the words right?"

"Sounds right to me. And the meaning is coming through."

"Weird how I don't know the words, but I can feel the meaning."

"Edomic is like that. It's very exact. Everything understands it intuitively. But knowing the words to speak isn't intuitive. You have to learn them."

Jason spoke the phrase again, putting emotion into his voice, then throwing all his mental energy at the wick, as if he truly believed that pure desire could start a fire. As before, he didn't get a single spark or a wisp of smoke. "You do it again," he said.

Rachel spoke the words, and the flame came to life.

Jason looked around suspiciously. "Is this some kind of trick?"

"No way. How would I make a candle spontaneously light itself?"

"I don't know. It just feels like a trick. How long did it take you to learn this?"

"I lit the candle on my first try, after Drake described how. I'd seen him do it several times. My first time, it took a few seconds of pushing to get it right. Now it seems effortless."

"Drake can do this too?" Jason asked.

"Yes. Although I'm already at least as good as him. And I can do some other things that he can't. The charm woman said I'm a natural."

"You truly have a gift," said Chandra, stepping around from the other side of the wall. "I could feel the power in your words."

"How long were you listening?" Jason challenged, embarrassed about his many failed attempts.

"I don't make it a habit to eavesdrop on comrades," she apologized. "Galloran felt Rachel speaking Edomic and sent me to watch. Drake told him about your talent, and he's most intrigued."

This was the most Jason had ever heard Chandra speak. "What do you mean he felt her speaking?"

"He could feel the effect of her words," Chandra said. "The change her words were causing, the power she was mustering with her will. To a lesser extent I could sense it as well."

"Do you speak Edomic too?" Rachel asked.

"A smattering," Chandra replied. "I mostly know how to move things."

"Like telling animals to move?" Rachel asked.

"No, I've never grasped the nuances of suggestion. I can't work with intellects. I mean physically moving objects by command."

"Show us," Jason invited.

Chandra scanned the ground. "This place amplifies Edomic commands. You can almost taste it. The charged atmosphere, rich with energy. It must be why the old wizard chose to live here. You were tapping into a lot of power, Rachel, although you used only a small portion." She extended her hand toward a stone block that probably would have been too heavy for anyone but Aram to lift. She sang a quick phrase, and it shuddered. She repeated the effort, and it rocked. Her face contorted with effort, and on the third try, her words tipped it onto its side.

"Cool!" Jason said.

"It's normally hard to budge anything bigger than you can move with your muscles," Chandra said. "I can feel that my Edomic has more clout than usual here." She extended an arm forward and issued a command, and a stone the size of a hockey puck leaped into her callused hand.

"You spoke directly to the stone," Rachel noted. "You didn't call a force to push it. You just told it where to go."

"Observant," Chandra said. "I name the object or the material I mean to move, then tell it where to move by speaking a command and visualizing a trajectory. I can't tell you why it works. My mother had the same knack, as did her mother as well. I've been doing it since childhood."

"Can I try?" Rachel said.

"Be my guest," Chandra replied, folding her thin, sinewy arms. "Do you need me to repeat the phrase?"

"I think I have it," Rachel said.

"Then try to push something." Based on her stance and expression, Jason thought that Chandra expected Rachel to have trouble.

Rachel extended her hand toward the same stone block Chandra had tipped, focused on it, and said the words. The block flipped end over end, tumbling heavily across the grassy ground, crashing against irregularities in the terrain before wobbling to a rest twenty yards away.

Chandra gasped, wide eyes darting from the block to Rachel and then back. "You were having sport with me. You've done this before."

Rachel smiled self-consciously, clearly pleased and embarrassed. "I've been practicing other types of Edomic," she explained. "But I've never done this. I pushed as hard as I could, because the block seemed so heavy."

"Even in an ideal location such as this," Galloran said, coming around from behind one of the walls, feeling his way with a walking stick, "you mustered significant power."

"How could you tell?" Rachel asked.

"I didn't see the stone, but I could sense the energy you brought to bear and perceive the force that shoved it. And I heard it roll. How long have you been practicing Edomic?"

"Maybe five weeks."

Chandra huffed. "Unbelievable."

"She hasn't been in our world more than a few months," Galloran reminded the cook. "Rachel, I understand you can call fire with considerable aptitude."

"And I can give directions to animals. And I helped the charm woman enchant a decoy doll to fool the lurker."

Galloran rubbed his lips. "I take it you have not encountered an Edomic phrase that you could not employ."

"Not yet," Rachel agreed. "There are limits to what I can do with any phrase."

Galloran smiled. "We have a true adept in our midst. Rachel, your natural gift is the material from which wizards are made."

"The charm woman thought so too. She wanted me to be her apprentice."

Galloran nodded. "She could have taught you many things. Ideally, you would be apprenticed to a true wizard—one who could school you in the finer points of Edomic. Sadly, with Maldor representing the last of his order, no such teacher remains. Rachel, an innate faculty for Edomic is so rare that we may have found why the oracle wanted you here. Simply by mastering the limited phrases that have survived as a kind of folk magic, through practice, you could become formidable."

"Why do you think I'm here?" Jason asked.

Galloran chuckled. "We already have our proof through your deeds, Lord Jason. You discovered that the Word is a fraud. That act alone makes your contribution incalculable."

"Does that mean my part is done?" he wondered.

Galloran pondered the question. "You want to know if you can go home?"

"No," Jason said reflexively, ashamed to look like a coward in front of a man like Galloran. "I mean, well, we had thought about it."

"Ferrin knows a way to the Beyond," Rachel said.

Galloran nodded. "As I have expressed before, I wouldn't blame either of you for going home if you find a way. Nor would I have blamed you for staying there, Jason, had you done so."

"I couldn't help overhearing," Ferrin said, approaching the conversation. "We know a way to the Beyond, but Maldor is aware that we know. In my efforts to ferret out what Maldor suspects, I learned that the investigation surrounding your escape led trackers to the cave. The entrance will now be sealed and guarded. There will be walls and locks and numerous redundancies. Maldor knows the secret is out, which means that from now on he will rely on strength to protect his gateway to your world. The cave lies in the shadow of Felrook, where he can access nearly limitless resources to protect it. The day may come when we could go there, but it would require significant reconnaissance and preparation. Otherwise we'll march straight into captivity."

Jason felt some of his hopes wither. Ferrin was right. As the most wanted criminals in Lyrian, they couldn't hastily travel to the center of Maldor's power and expect to access a heavily guarded location. Glancing at Rachel, Jason could tell she had reached the same conclusion.

"Don't lose heart," Galloran said. "I vow that when the time is right, I will do everything in my power to get you both back to the

Beyond. In truth, the biggest obstacle was finding a way. The only remaining hurdle will be formulating a workable strategy."

"If our rebellion succeeds," Chandra said, "they would have easy access."

"Perhaps even before then," Galloran said. "For now, we will try to survive until we reach the Seven Vales. One crisis at a time. Chandra, I want you and Rachel to spend every waking moment together. Teach her all you know about Edomic. Help her continue to develop, and make sure she understands the danger of failed commands."

"It will be done," Chandra said.

"Jason, I want you to start learning to use that sword. You are surrounded by superior tutors."

"I'd like that," Jason said.

"I'll mentor him," Ferrin pledged.

"Off to it then," Galloran said. "Let the others set up camp."

The next morning, not long after the nine riders left the valley, Nedwin found them. Ferrin had been scouting ahead, and he returned to the group with the lanky redhead riding close behind.

"Nedwin!" Galloran welcomed. "I thought we were to meet at Three Peaks."

"I came south from there, hoping to intercept you," Nedwin replied. "A massive ambush awaits near Three Peaks, staged across all four southern valleys."

"You made it to Whitelake?" Galloran asked.

"Yes. The lake was taxing, but I crossed."

"Malar?"

"I discovered his lifeless head in a pool of cold water. He had been drowned. He would have been defenseless. I doubt he died more than a day or two before my arrival."

Galloran's expression tightened painfully. "Tell me more about the ambush. Were you spotted?"

"I avoided detection. They had a massive host entrenched, cunningly disguised, as if certain of our imminent arrival. Archers, manglers, cavalry—you name it."

"We would have arrived by late afternoon," Galloran said numbly.

Holding a finger to his lips, Ferrin guided his horse over to Galloran. "A lurker must have been eavesdropping. We'll loop around to the west. We may want to consider revising our entire strategy. Who knows what plans have been compromised?" He reached out and squeezed Galloran's shoulder.

"Very well," Galloran said decisively. "I'll need some time to strategize. Perhaps we can make for Port Hamblin, try to solicit allies in Meridon. We'll still want to send some messengers elsewhere. Give me time to mull this over."

Ferrin dismounted, a finger still to his lips, and tugged Galloran's sleeve. Galloran dismounted and accompanied Ferrin. Dorsio followed them silently. They moved into the trees out of earshot, and did not return for several minutes.

When they came back, Ferrin motioned for Jason to join him. The displacer kept a finger to his lips. Jason remained silent.

Once they were separated from the group, Ferrin combed probing fingers through Jason's hair, then meticulously inspected his face. Ferrin pulled Jason's eyelids uncomfortably open and peered into his mouth. After miming for Jason to take off his shirt, Ferrin closely and carefully examined his body, like a doctor giving a physical.

"You're not the problem," Ferrin finally said.

"Can we talk now?" Jason asked, putting his shirt back on.

"I inspected Galloran and Dorsio," Ferrin said. "Neither of them had invasive graftings either."

"Graftings?"

"Meaning that no displacers had attached unwelcome body parts to them. Replaced an eye. Added an ear. There is a risk that any prisoner of Maldor could end up with a secret grafting. If a displacer's eye were exchanged for one of yours while you were unconscious, the eye would function and feel just like your own. Except the displacer would see through it as well."

"It might not be a grafting," Jason said. "You may have been right about a lurker overhearing us."

"Galloran can sense lurkers," Ferrin replied. "After I checked him for graftings, he confirmed that none have come near us. Besides, lurkers aren't known for sharing detailed information. Either somebody has a grafting, or we have a deliberate traitor among us."

"Nedwin was imprisoned at Felrook."

"Galloran just told me Nedwin has a grafting. An eye on his hand, under the glove. Supposedly the glove has not been removed since he first met you. But he could always have another."

So that was what Nedwin had kept hidden under his glove! A grafted eye. "Tark?" Jason said.

"Doubtful. He was only imprisoned at Harthenham. Nobody would have expected him to leave, so a grafting would probably not be wasted on him. But I'll check everyone to be sure."

"I'm clean?"

"Yes," Ferrin said. "I'll check Nedwin next. Keep quiet about all of this for now."

"I will."

Jason returned to the group, and Ferrin led away Nedwin. Ferrin returned alone and consulted quietly with Galloran. One by one, Ferrin led away the others, and one by one they came back. At the end, Ferrin gave Rachel a cursory exam without leading her away. Nedwin still had not returned.

"Nedwin has a false ear," Ferrin reported at last. "It's an almost perfect match in shape, size, and skin tone. Terrific work. Anything less than a thorough exam by a trained eye would miss it."

"It explains much," Galloran said. "The grafted ear must be how Maldor learned what information Tark had brought us from Jason. Also why the emperor moved against Jugard and Malar shortly before Nedwin arrived to retrieve them. Not to mention why our foes have put their recent efforts into the ambush."

"Which would have succeeded had Nedwin not discovered it," Ferrin said.

"Can you take off the ear?" Tark asked.

"I can. It shouldn't even be too hard. As is common with ears, the grafting is shallow. The inner workings of the ear still belong to Nedwin."

"Then how can the displacer hear with it?" Jason asked.

"The external portion of the ear gathers the sound vibrations," Ferrin said. "While sharing the same outer ear, the inner ear of the displacer receives the same vibrations as Nedwin's inner ear. When we remove the ear, Nedwin should manage to retain much of his hearing on that side."

Rachel winced.

Jason rubbed his ear, trying not to wonder how it would feel to have it cut off.

"But we'll wait to remove the ear," Galloran said.

"We'll keep Nedwin away from any serious discussions," Ferrin said. "And we'll do our best to stage planning sessions full of misinformation."

"You two already started," Rachel said.

"Right," Ferrin said. "Thankfully Galloran followed my lead."

"Then we'll be looping around Three Peaks to the east," Aram said.

"And going nowhere near Port Hamblin," Ferrin confirmed. "We'll still proceed with caution, in case the displacer realizes that we've caught on."

"You've done us a great service, Ferrin," Galloran said. "Had that ear gone undetected, it could have undone us. Thank you."

"Just doing my job," Ferrin replied. "I've already explained the situation to Nedwin by whispering in his authentic ear. He's been serving as a scout, and he should simply continue in that role. It will keep him far from our more delicate conversations."

"We'll proceed to the Sunken Lands as previously planned," Galloran said. "But we'll mask our movements with a persistent flow of misleading conversations. We should get underway. Given the forces awaiting us, we're closer to Three Peaks than I would prefer."

Several days later, Jason stood before Ferrin, gripping his sword in a sweaty palm. They faced each other in a clearing encompassed by tall trees. Daylight was waning. While he worked with Ferrin, and Rachel practiced with Chandra, the others were setting up camp.

"You really want me to attack?" Jason asked.

So far their sparring sessions had entailed Jason learning footwork while defending himself against a blunted practice sword Galloran had lent to Ferrin. The dummy blades were made of metal, and it hurt when Ferrin poked or clipped him.

"You've been waiting for this," Ferrin said, swishing his practice sword. "Attack me with all you have. Give no thought to defense. I won't bruise you. Mark me if you can."

Unlike previous practices, today Jason held his real sword. Ferrin had insisted that as a displacer, he could avoid serious wounds from an edged weapon.

Implementing the stance Ferrin had taught him, Jason balanced himself, knees slightly bent, ready to move in any direction. "I just come at you?"

"With everything you have. You've been asking me to let you attack. Here's your opportunity."

"Lop off his head, Jason!" Aram called.

Jason edged forward warily.

"I'm on the defensive," Ferrin reminded him. "You must bring the fight to me."

Jason nervously chewed the lining of his mouth. He wished Aram weren't watching. He began tentatively, somewhat concerned about injuring his teacher.

"This is embarrassing," Ferrin goaded, slapping Jason's sword aside.

Jason put more power into his swings, and his sword began to clash with Ferrin's, the blades ringing through the clearing.

"Attack *me*, not my sword," Ferrin said.

That proved tricky, since the sword was always in the way.

"Don't fret about a counterattack," Ferrin encouraged. "Take advantage of the situation. Use reckless abandon. I will not strike at you."

Jason pressed in closer, hacking wildly. The displacer stood his ground, deflecting blows directed at his neck, chest, and legs. Jason broke his rhythm of chopping and suddenly lunged forward, stabbing at Ferrin's heart. The displacer casually parried the thrust.

"Better," Ferrin said. "Now show me some real vigor."

Jason charged, his blade hissing through the air. Instead of intercepting the blow with his sword, the displacer dodged away. Jason stayed after him. Relying on clever footwork and feinting, Ferrin evaded every swing without using his sword. Jason began to tire.

"Are you appreciating the beauty of defensive footwork?" Ferrin asked.

Jason nodded, brushing sweaty strands of hair away from his eyes.

"Had enough?" Ferrin inquired. "This may be the only time I allow you to engage me recklessly."

Forgetting all caution, ignoring proper footwork, Jason rushed the displacer, getting so close before swinging that he could not imagine the displacer merely dodging the blow. But Ferrin ducked and spun away. Jason kept after him, grunting as he wielded his sword like a baseball bat, swinging relentlessly.

Finally compelled to use his sword again, Ferrin deflected the mighty strokes. "You have strength," the displacer conceded. "Issue blows like that, and an unprepared opponent might drop his weapon."

Jason kept coming. Eluding an overzealous swing, the displacer patted Jason on the shoulder. "Of course, swinging too hard can also leave you defenseless."

After a final energetic onslaught, Jason stepped back, panting. "I'm done."

"You showed tenacity," Ferrin said.

"You were impossible to touch."

"I was entirely on the defensive. I could have held you off all night. Or slain you any number of times. The best openings often occur when an opponent is on the offensive. Go practice footwork."

Jason felt silly, dancing around alone with his sword, going through all the drills Ferrin had taught him. He took some relief in the fact that Lyrian had no video recorders or Internet connections.

It had been fun attacking Ferrin. Jason wished he could have surprised him by penetrating his defenses, but consoled himself that his inability to do so was evidence that he was learning from the best. The displacer really was a great teacher: patient, direct, specific, and very knowledgeable. Drake and Aram had provided pointers as well, but Ferrin had proved to be the most thorough and methodical instructor and had supervised most of the tutoring.

While working in solitude on his swordsmanship, Jason glanced over to where Rachel and Chandra were using Edomic to break dead tree limbs. Before going to sleep at night, Jason privately kept trying to ignite dry twigs or leaves with the phrase Rachel had taught him, but had never even made anything warm. He had temporarily worried that perhaps the Word had failed against Maldor due to his lack of ability, but then he remembered that all of the syllables had vanished from memory after he spoke them together, so he must have said it well enough.

Sweaty and tired, Jason finally quit his exercises, joining the others around a small fire. Drake, Ferrin, and Nedwin had proved so adept at steering the group away from enemies that Jason often forgot they were on the run.

Aram sat, meticulously honing his sword. Dorsio reclined beside Galloran, the two of them eating dried meat and dense bread. Ferrin warmed a skewer of vegetables over the fire. Scowling, Tark whittled, cross-legged on a blanket. Drake leaned against a tree, eyes half closed, irises sliding eerily back and forth. From experience, Jason knew that the trancelike state was as close as seedmen came to sleeping. Nedwin was away scouting. Rachel and Chandra had yet to stop practicing.

After rummaging through a bag for food, Jason plopped down beside Tark, chewing salty meat. Tark held up a mangled block of wood. "It was going to be a duck. I may have to settle for a cube."

"Or a headless duck," Jason said, "without legs or wings."

Tark dropped the wood in disgust. "I wish I had my sousalax."

"You're the only one," Ferrin chuckled.

"I'll second Tark's wish," Aram said, sliding a stone along his blade. "He could give me more lessons."

"Lessons?" Ferrin groaned, covering his ears.

"I was getting good," Aram protested. "Tell him, Tark."

Tark chose his words carefully. "You were . . . one of the few men I have met with the capacity to sound the instrument."

"I wasn't good?"

"Good takes practice."

"I was loud."

"True," Tark said. "I revoke my wish."

"Not many men can blow a sousalax," Ferrin said. "How did you get started?"

Tark grinned. "In my youth I worked as a diver at Ithilum. The job strengthened my lungs." Tark puffed out his chest, pounding his ribs.

"I'm certain our enemies would gladly furnish any of us with an instrument," Galloran said. "We've been hard to find."

On a muggy morning, below an overcast sky, the ten riders reached boggy terrain. They had approached the Sunken Lands from a different direction than Jason had previously used with Jasher and Rachel, but the soupy marshland looked equally dreary.

Drake called a halt. Nedwin walked out of earshot as Drake explained that the horses would not be able to continue.

"Let's strip any necessary gear," Galloran suggested. "We won't be back this way. Our path will take us beyond the Sunken Lands to the Seven Vales."

"Maybe I could talk to the horses," Rachel offered. "Try to send them around to the other side."

Galloran dismounted. "We're approaching the Sunken Lands from the southwest and intend to exit from the northwest. But the horses can't go around to the west. They will find the mountains as impassable as the marshland. I suppose they could try to loop around to the east. It will amount to a long journey through dangerous country."

"What if a couple of us herd the horses around?" Chandra said. "We might be glad to have them on the far side."

Galloran shook his head. "I don't want to risk losing anyone. Even by horseback, the journey will probably take too long. The horses would have to circumnavigate three quarters of the swamp in the time it takes us to cut across part of it. Besides, Maldor has strongholds east of the marshlands."

"The western gate to the Seven Vales does not lie far north of the swamp," Drake said. "On foot the journey will cost us only two days."

"If we're not sending anyone with them," Rachel proposed, "I might as well try to convince the horses to loop around and meet us."

"What if an enemy follows them?" Chandra asked.

"Nobody would suspect the riderless horses had a destination," Ferrin said. "Any who find them will just try to take possession of them."

"Very well," Galloran said. "Give it a try, Rachel."

"Put some extra effort into telling Mandibar," Drake said. "I'd hate to lose him."

Jason sidled over to Rachel as the others transferred gear. "Can you do that?" he asked quietly. "Tell them to come?"

"I don't know," she whispered back. "I know how to ask the horses to meet me. I'd have more confidence if I could accurately visualize our destination. But I've never been there. I'm going to picture us crossing the swamp by boat, and the horses running around to the east, and them finding us on the northwest side. We'll see what happens."

Jason watched Rachel move from horse to horse, stroking them and speaking to each one individually. When all of the desired gear was unpacked, she made a general declaration to all of the horses. Jason sensed that she was telling them to run eastward. Moving in a group, they galloped in the correct direction.

"What about Nedwin?" Ferrin asked. "There are many distinctive sounds in the swamp that may reveal our location. Has the time come to lose his ear?"

"I think so," Galloran said. "Can you manage it?"

"Among his ingredients, Nedwin has salves for burns and infections," Ferrin said. "He claims to feel no pain, so I'll use a hot knife. We'll poke out the eye on his hand while we're at it. I'll pretend like I'm just discovering the ear, in hopes they might continue to trust the nonsense he's been hearing lately."

Galloran nodded silently.

Jason felt chills as Ferrin strode away, drawing a knife. He was glad he wouldn't have to watch.

Ferrin and Nedwin returned perhaps an hour later. A bandage around Nedwin's hand had replaced his glove, and he also wore a bandage tied to the side of his head. He smiled, revealing hideous teeth. Jason realized his teeth must have been deliberately damaged while he was a prisoner.

"I injected nervesong into the eye and the ear just before the surgery," Nedwin reported. "It meant I felt some pain when Ferrin cut and burned me, but not nearly what the displacers felt on their end."

"Once the ear was amputated, I administered poison to it," Ferrin said. "The displacer severed his connection. Hard to say whether he did it in time."

Nedwin could not stop grinning. "At the very least, a pair of spies just had very bad days."

CHAPTER 14

GRULLIONS

Perched atop a boulder at the edge of the swamp, Rachel watched for snakes. She had seen far too many as she and her companions had squelched across the marsh for the last two days. Big ones and small ones, fat ones and thin ones, light ones and dark ones, striped ones and solid ones and patterned ones. A poisonous snake had struck Dorsio's boot twice, the fangs failing to penetrate. A nonpoisonous snake had bitten Nedwin on the wrist. Drake had killed at least three venomous snakes as they slithered into camp while the group slept.

At the moment, the only way for a snake to reach her would be to climb across a steep expanse of bare stone. She had a long stick ready, just in case.

Her current vantage point commanded a depressing view of the muddy shore where the sucking marshland gave way to the black water of the swamp. A miasmic haze had muted the recent sunrise. Tall trees grew up out of the water, widespread branches interlocking like great umbrellas. Bedraggled foliage hung in long streamers from trunks and limbs. In the distance a ponderous slug, longer than her arm, slurped across an island of mulch, eyestalks stretching grotesquely.

If Rachel had been allowed to pick one place in Lyrian never to revisit, without pause she would have selected the Sunken Lands. Only poisonous, diseased, disgusting threats lurked in the gloom ahead, including predatory slime, supersized insects, stealthy serpents, and elephantine frogs.

Two crafts awaited on the shore. The sleek skiff looked large enough to accommodate six. The wide canoe could carry no more than three. There was no way to proceed without boats, but fortunately the Amar Kabal routinely hid vessels along the shore of the swamp. Drake had found one, Nedwin the other. Assisted by Ferrin and Dorsio, both were currently off seeking a third craft.

Rachel wished she could have stayed with the horses. No soldiers would have caught her. In an emergency, she could have transferred to Mandibar. With her ability to issue Edomic instructions, she felt certain she could have led them safely around the swamp. After weeks of riding, she had formed a connection with her mare, and hated the possibility of never seeing her again.

Jason came traipsing toward her boulder, boots cumbersome with mud, one hand on the hilt of his sword. She had noticed that as he kept practicing, he seemed increasingly proud of the weapon. He looked up at her. "You might be safe from snakes, but you're going to fall and break your neck."

The boulder was steep on all sides. Climbing it had required some effort. "I was trying to get away from the smell." After sucking gel from orchid buds, her body odor had been magnified, transforming her into human insect repellant. But that was nothing compared to how terrible the others stank.

"Not a bad reason," Jason conceded. "Nedwin is heading this way with another canoe. We're going to leave soon."

Looking over, Rachel saw Galloran and the others gathering near the watercrafts. Nedwin and Dorsio glided into view, paddling a canoe and leaving a V-shaped wake across the murky water.

"Think Corinne is all right?" Rachel wondered.

Jason glanced toward Galloran. "I don't know. Two of the syllable guardians are already dead. It looks bad. I can tell Galloran is worried."

"The mushrooms should give her some protection. It's got to be hard to kill somebody when you can't remember why you're there."

"Let's hope so."

Rachel turned around and carefully lowered herself down the least sheer side of the boulder. Jason waited for her, and they walked over to the muddy bank.

"We're here," Jason said as Nedwin and Dorsio brought the canoe ashore. All of the others had already gathered.

Galloran raised both hands. "This is a hazardous time of year to enter the swamp. The fungi will be in full bloom, disease will be rampant, and the insects are multiplying. Within a few weeks, the swamp will be utterly impassable for more than a month, during the height of insect season."

"Bind your noses and mouths with rags to filter the air," Drake said, passing out lengths of fabric. "Never inhale without them. At this time of year, airborne spores will readily infect unprotected lungs."

"They should add that to the travel brochure," Jason murmured to Rachel while wrapping fabric over his nose and mouth. "Who doesn't want some tasty lung fungus?"

"Fun for the whole family," she muttered back.

Galloran assigned Tark and Chandra to one canoe, and Ferrin and Drake to the other, leaving everyone else to fill the skiff. Drake, Nedwin, Ferrin, and Tark helped push the vessels into the water. Each canoe had two paddles. In the skiff, Dorsio and Nedwin manned the oars. Aram placed a hand on the tiller. Jason and Rachel sat in the prow to scout for slime.

The skiff surged ahead, pushing ripples across the dark water. Before long, Rachel began to notice dull orange masses of fungus, clinging to the tree trunks like wasp hives, giving them an ailing appearance. Cylindrical piles of spongy fungi thrived on decaying islands of muck. Slick puddles of slime rippled across the surface of the water or oozed over obstacles. Jason and Rachel gave directions when necessary to help the skiff avoid the carnivorous slime.

From above and to one side, Rachel heard a startling gasp. The inhalation was followed by a sharp hiss, like air expelled from a blowhole, and a plume of maroon gas jetted from a bloated clump of yellowish fungus, high on a tree.

"Avoid the spores," Galloran cautioned, as if he could see the powdery cloud spreading above them.

Fumbling momentarily, Nedwin and Dorsio turned the skiff and propelled it away from the drifting spray. The canoes also paddled away from the descending spores.

As they progressed deeper into the swamp, the trees grew taller, lifting the tangled canopy ever higher. The gasp-hiss of fungi excreting spores became frequent. Rachel began to glimpse snakes gliding through the water.

Rachel did her best to ignore the multitudes of spiders, slugs, snakes, and flying insects as she scanned for slime. Her efforts did not keep her from noticing slender dragonflies as long as her forearm, prowling snakes with heads the size of footballs, gooey slugs big enough to wear saddles, and hairy spiders large enough to prey on housecats.

Aram grew at sunset, limbs lengthening and thickening. Since she knew it embarrassed him, Rachel tried not to stare, but it was hard not to peek at something so unusual. After he finished growing, the skiff floated noticeably lower with his added weight. He took both of the oars, and the skiff whooshed forward faster than ever. When the canoes floundered behind, unable to equal the energetic pace, Aram slowed.

"Watch for a place to camp," Galloran said.

"Why not go all night?" Aram suggested.

"The swamp slumbers during the day. Dangerous creatures patrol the waters after dark. We'll increase our chances of survival if we spend the night in our boats, up on an island."

As the swamp dimmed, they pulled the boats up on one of the largest islands they had seen all day, arranging the crafts close together. In the fading light, luminous thumb-size slugs became visible on the trees.

Jason commented on the slugs.

"This portion of the swamp glows all night," Nedwin confirmed. "By tomorrow evening, we should reach the section of the swamp controlled by the frogs. Few slugs survive there."

Nedwin handed out orchid buds. Rachel eagerly consumed the flavorless gel inside. Her horrible odor was much better than stings or bites from prehistoric insects.

The clamor of the swamp began as Rachel curled up in the bottom of the skiff, uncomfortable but exhausted. Crickets chirped so noisily, the skiff seemed full of them. From up in the trees came warbling hoots and staccato bursts of clacking. Occasionally she heard long, low moans in the distance. But without the barking croaks of the huge frogs, the night was not quite so uproarious as her previous experience in the swamp.

As always, Drake took watch, since he never truly slept. The slugs seemed ever brighter as the rest of the swamp faded to true darkness.

With predawn light filtering through the canopy, Nedwin jostled the others awake. They intended to set off early to take advantage of Aram at the oars.

Rachel helped shove the skiff into the water, slipping and planting one hand deep in the mud. She jumped aboard the skiff as it drifted away from the island, dipping her hand in the lukewarm water to wash off the worst of the clinging muck. While wiping the black mud from her fingers, Rachel discovered a leech attached to the back of her hand. She ground her teeth to suppress a shriek.

"I think I picked up a leech," she said, trying to keep her voice steady as hysteria welled up inside.

"Translucent?" Galloran asked.

Rachel inspected the membranous creature. "Yeah, almost transparent." Jason stared at it over her shoulder.

"A jelly leech," Galloran said. "What size?"

"No bigger than my pinkie."

"Do not seek to detach it," Galloran warned. "Such action will provoke the injection of a most irritating venom."

"What do I do?" Rachel felt painful suction and stared as her blood began to flow into the translucent leech, a spreading red stain inside the rubbery body. "It's sucking!" She bit her lower lip, trying not to scream.

"The creature will detach when sated. Be grateful it is so small."

Jason rubbed her shoulders. "You'll be okay," he encouraged.

Rachel watched in disgust as the creature reddened, bulging with the inflow of blood. Just when she thought the leech looked ready to burst, it detached and fell to the bottom of the skiff.

"It finished," Jason said.

"Throw it overboard," Galloran said. "As far as you can. We must keep away from the scent of blood."

Jason tweezed the leech between thumb and forefinger, stood, and tossed it away with a motion that rocked the skiff. The red leech landed on a little island strewn with messy webs. Rachel rubbed the back of her hand, where a purple bruise was forming.

With Aram at the oars, and the canoes keeping up, they made rapid progress. The trees became spaced farther apart, and the trunks seemed thicker. Off to one side of the boat was an open area with no trees.

"I see some open water," Aram grunted softly.

"Keep away," Galloran advised. "We do not want to trifle with the great beasts who inhabit the deep places of the swamp."

"What are they?" Jason asked quietly.

"Winari," Galloran said. "Some of the oldest and largest organisms in the world. Theirs are the groaning calls we heard in the night. We would all perish if one caught us. They're typically dormant during the day, but we'll avoid the risk."

As they rowed onward, the swollen masses of fungus became more plentiful on the tree trunks, in dreary shades of yellow and orange. Towering fungal columns rose from muddy islands, stretching toward the leafy canopy above, swaying away from the boats when they came near.

They were rowing through a grove of colossal, widespread trees with no muddy islands in sight when Galloran whispered, "Too quiet."

"What?" Aram asked.

Galloran lifted a cautionary hand. "Something is amiss."

Rachel peered around. With dawn approaching, the still waterscape looked almost bright. The daytime noises of the swamp did not rival the nighttime cacophony. But there always seemed to be some hooting in the trees, or buzzing wings, or little clicks, or faint chittering, or distant splashes. With the paddles out of the water, Rachel heard nothing.

To one side, Rachel heard the gentle slosh of disturbed water. Twisting, she saw a translucent snake wriggling up and over the side of the skiff.

"Snake!" she cried.

"Leech!" Jason corrected, drawing his sword.

As Rachel scrunched away from it, Jason's blade hacked through the membranous body. Part of the leech withdrew into the water, but about two feet of it was left squirming in the bottom of the skiff. Aram scooped an oar underneath it and catapulted the gelatinous segment overboard.

Splashing up from the water, another serpentine jelly leech hung poised in the air before whipping at Jason. Swinging his sword defensively, Jason saw the flat of the blade slap the leech aside before he toppled backward into Rachel, who steadied him. As the leech stretched toward Dorsio, knives flashed in his hands, slicing off the tip of the leech and then two more segments. What remained of the leech reared away, rising even higher out of the water. Only then did Rachel realize that the leech was actually a tentacle.

"Grullions!" Nedwin shouted.

A new tentacle seized the skiff at the stern, making the vessel buck and spin. The sudden motion jolted Rachel down to a seated position. Jason dropped to his knees. Diving, Nedwin slashed the tentacle with a long knife, severing several feet of it. The rest withdrew over the gunwale. Nedwin skewered the squirming section and flipped it into the water.

As the boat rotated slowly, Rachel drew her knife. It felt way too small. Aram, standing at the center of the skiff with his enormous sword in hand, hauled Jason to his feet.

"Foul luck," Galloran spat, squatting beside Aram.

Looking over at the canoe containing Ferrin and Drake, Rachel saw the displacer standing back-to-back with the seedman, swords sweeping relentlessly to repel a writhing onslaught of tentacles. On the other side of the skiff, one of the grullions lurched onto the canoe with Tark and Chandra, heaving up a fountain of dull water. Its bulbous body was roughly the size and shape of a sea lion, with a pair of flippers, two pairs of tentacles, and a spoon-shape tail.

Tark plunged his saw-toothed knife into the body of the beast as the canoe tilted precariously. Crouching low, Chandra used a dagger to deftly fend off thrashing tentacles while keeping her free hand splayed over the center of the canoe. Her lips moved in a chant, and Rachel realized she was using Edomic to prevent the canoe from overturning. Tark slid his knife along the length of the semitransparent body, opening a deep seam. Tentacles wound around the wide canoe, the tail whipped up and down, Chandra lost her balance, and the craft capsized.

Rachel screamed. Chandra surfaced briefly, only to disappear below the water as if tugged downward. Tark didn't surface at all.

Tentacles seethed from the water at either side of the skiff. Rachel swung her knife wildly, striking nothing. Something slammed the skiff from below, and Aram and Jason fell, their bodies thumping heavily. Nedwin slashed a length of tentacle out of the air. Dorsio intercepted a tentacle reaching for Galloran, slitting it open lengthwise with one knife before severing it crossways with the other.

As Aram arose, a tentacle lashed at him, twining around his muscular sword arm. The heavy blade fell to the bottom of the skiff. Bracing himself, Aram resisted the pull of the elastic tentacle, veins standing out as his bulky muscles clenched and strained. The skiff slid speedily across the water. Blood began to course away from Aram's arm through the transparent tentacle, red mist that soon thickened into a more liquid flow. He bellowed, peeling at the tentacle with his free hand.

"Sorry," Nedwin yelled, his long knife tearing through the sanguineous tentacle, releasing a gruesome spray.

Parted from the grullion, the portion of the tentacle fastened about Aram's arm tensed and vibrated, and the half giant let loose an involuntary roar. He collapsed, his back arched in anguish, his free hand clawing at the crimson parasite.

A pair of tentacles flopped over the side of the skiff near Rachel, and the craft tipped alarmingly. She found herself staring into the face of a grullion, which consisted of a circular mouth wreathed by fluttering flagella. Almost tackling her, Jason brought his sword down in an overhand stroke, cleaving through the head, down to the gaping maw. Sticky juice squirted in their faces. The grullion jerked away and disappeared, and the skiff leveled out.

Rachel heard Galloran chanting. On his knees, head bowed, he was calling heat to the water, specifying one particular area at a time. Borrowing his words, Rachel began summoning heat to the water as well, visualizing roughly a cubic meter of liquid and pouring her will and desperation into the effort. She felt the heat answer her call, then started commanding heat into a different section of water.

Behind her, Aram growled. Recovering his sword, the juicy red tentacle still attached to his arm, the half giant rose to his knees to slice through a squirming forest of rubbery tentacles. He spun and slashed, his long blade lopping off multiple tentacles with each swipe. Nedwin and Jason crouched below him, using their weapons to hastily pitch the severed tentacles out of the skiff. Dorsio stayed close to Galloran, fending off any tentacles that escaped Aram's blade.

Ferrin and Drake were no longer under attack. Drake was calling heat to the water as well, and Ferrin paddled the canoe closer to the skiff.

The skiff shuddered as a grullion tried to climb aboard, injured tentacles of varying length flailing. From the corner of her eye, Rachel saw Aram split the creature with a violent horizontal slash. Galloran gruffly continued his Edomic chant.

Gasping, Tark emerged from the water, one hand gripping the gunwale of the skiff. As he pulled himself up, something jolted the underside of the craft, and the side of the vessel bashed Tark in the mouth. Jason and Nedwin helped haul the musician over the side. He was still clutching his knife.

There was no sign of Chandra.

Tears in her eyes, Rachel kept calling heat to the water. She scanned the surface in all directions, hoping to see her friend.

The last tentacles receded. Everything became still. A sinister silence enfolded them. Galloran and Rachel continued chanting, and the water around the skiff began to simmer, radiating heat and shedding steam. Drake and Ferrin maneuvered over to reclaim the capsized canoe.

Galloran ceased chanting and started to cough raggedly, perspiration shining on his brow. Drake and Ferrin righted the empty canoe.

"Enough heat?" Rachel asked.

Galloran nodded, still coughing persistently.

"What about Chandra?" Rachel asked, eyes sweeping the surrounding water.

"She's gone," Tark said. "She saved me."

"Gone?"

"They dragged us deep," Tark said, red wetness dripping from his lips. "One had my leg, but I cut free with my knife. It never latched onto my skin. My trousers protected me. They were all around us. Scores of them. Chandra started pushing the water with Edomic. How she spoke underwater, I have no idea. But she created strong currents and used them to shove the creatures away and to help me avoid them. Even as they wrapped her up and started draining her, she sent water to push me upward. The water was hot near the surface. The leech monsters kept away from the heat."

Rachel nodded numbly, her insides twisting as she heard the account. How could Chandra be gone? Just like that? No warning, no good-bye. Rachel resisted acceptance as the simmering water around the skiff quieted.

Hands trembling, Aram snatched up the oars. "We have to go."

In the aftermath of the battle, the entire swamp seemed to be holding its breath. But the silence was shattered when a mighty voice bellowed a deafening blast comparable to a foghorn. Recoiling, they all clapped their hands over their ears.

A powerful jet of water streamed through the trees from off to one side, grazing the skiff and setting it spinning. A direct hit would have flipped them. A second explosive roar followed, after which a second high-pressure stream churned the water nearby, as if sprayed by a giant fire hose. From the direction the water came, through the huge trees, Rachel saw what looked like a hill made of brown, folded blubber. The top of it, presumably the head, was screened by leafy limbs and vines.

"It's vast," Aram murmured.

"A winaro," Nedwin whispered.

"The other canoe is ready," Ferrin announced. He and Drake had towed it alongside the skiff.

"Tark, Nedwin, get in," Galloran croaked.

When the deafening bellow repeated, Rachel noticed that she could feel the skiff vibrating. Tark and Nedwin transferred to the righted canoe, accepting the paddles retrieved by Drake and Ferrin. With water spouting behind them, they paddled away from the mountainous brown creature.

While Aram rowed vigorously, the blood-glutted segment of tentacle finally dropped from his beefy arm, hitting the bottom of the craft with a wet slap. A thick spiral of black bruises mottled his skin from wrist to shoulder. Dorsio used his knives to heave the gruesome tentacle overboard.

The trees stopped looking quite so enormous and widely spaced. Some of the natural chatter of the swamp resumed overhead in the canopy. Rachel noticed a fist-size spider scaling a trunk.

Aram grunted, shivering and sweating, and his body shriveled, deflating into a miniature version of himself. The corkscrew bruise shrank as his arm thinned. Sunrise had finally come, muted by the foliage overhead.

Dorsio took one oar, Jason the other. Rachel moved to the tiller. Aram crawled to the bow. He was still shivering, his face ruddy and damp.

"We were near one of the deep places," Galloran whispered. "The resident winaro did not take kindly to us heating the water. Grullions tend to dwell near winari, living as parasites. A foul turn of events. Chandra was faithful and capable. A survivor. It's a grievous loss."

"I can't believe she's . . ." Rachel couldn't finish the thought. They were moving on, and Chandra was not with them. Rachel was left to face the irreparable reality that her friend was gone.

"The Sunken Lands are lethal," Galloran rasped. "Too many exotic predators. We were fortunate. We could have all perished."

Rachel stared at Galloran, his broad shoulders hunched, his expression unreadable behind his ragged blindfold and the fabric masking his nose and mouth. How many of his friends had been killed over the years? How many close relatives? Agonizing loss was a major presence in his life. Did it even surprise him anymore? "You never mentioned you spoke Edomic."

"I have a few hidden talents," he replied. "You already possess a wider variety of practical skills than I do. I could never grasp how to push objects like Chandra. Your help heating the water was invaluable, Rachel. It saved lives."

"Aram doesn't look well," Jason pointed out.

"I'm fine." Sweating and trembling, the shrunken half giant was clenching his jaw and rubbing the wide bruise coiled around his arm.

"He was heavily poisoned," Galloran said. "When the tentacle was severed, it injected him with venom. A lesser man would not be conscious." Galloran raised his hoarse voice. "Nedwin, Aram needs quimbi bark, and anything else that might relieve his fever and help neutralize the venom."

Nedwin and Tark paddled their canoe over to the skiff. Nedwin hopped aboard, already rummaging through his pouches as he crouched beside Aram.

"Let Dorsio administer the remedies," Nedwin said. "I want to look around. I'm afraid we've been veering off course."

"Very well," Galloran agreed.

Nedwin issued some instructions to Dorsio, left him with ingredients, and climbed back into the canoe. He and Tark stroked over to the trunk of an enormous tree. Leaping from the canoe, Nedwin shinnied up the bare trunk like a monkey, avoiding clumps of fungus where possible, tearing them off when they got in his way, indifferent to the vibrant puffs of spores.

Rachel watched from below, astonished at how swiftly and confidently he found handholds where none seemed to exist. Before long, Nedwin reached the height where the first long limbs extended out from the trunk, and he vanished into the leafy canopy. Faintly, Rachel heard foliage rustle.

As Dorsio tended to Aram, the others stared upward. All was

silent for a time, then there came a sudden snapping of limbs, and Nedwin fell into view through the leaves and vines, a gauzy sheet of web flapping behind him like a cape. Adjusting his body as he plummeted, he hit the water, straight as a spear, a few yards from the skiff.

Tark paddled toward him. Nedwin's head emerged from the murky water, and he boosted himself into the canoe, making the vessel rock. He had lost the fabric masking his face. He shook his head briskly, wiping scum from his wet hair. "Spiders," he spat.

"Spiders?" Tark echoed.

"Up in the branches. Big ones. Hordes of them. Good trap. I was surrounded. I had to jump."

Grabbing a waterskin, Nedwin dumped fresh water in his mouth, swished it around, and spat over the side. "That swamp water tastes worse than we smell."

"Impossible," Jason mumbled.

"I saw the tree," Nedwin said. "The monarch where Corinne lives. We're bearing too far to the north. We need to head that way." He confidently indicated a line diagonal to their current heading. "We were veering toward the Drowned City."

"Another eventual destination," Galloran mused.

"We should separate," Nedwin said. "Let me and Drake take a canoe to Corinne. We'll get there faster. Then we can reunite at the Drowned City. It will require some time for you to take care of business there."

Galloran rubbed his blindfold, his lips pressed tight. "Show Dorsio the heading to the Drowned City."

Nedwin pointed slightly to the left of where the boats currently faced. "That way."

"Can you get us there?" Galloran asked.

Dorsio snapped.

"If that's the proper heading, I can help keep us on course," Ferrin added.

Galloran ground a fist against his palm. "I would prefer to fetch my daughter personally. But the quicker we reach her, the better. We should spend no more time in this swamp than we must. Every minute brings new threats. Find her, Nedwin. Keep her safe. Bring her to me."

"We'll get her," Nedwin vowed.

Tark joined Ferrin in his canoe, and Drake joined Nedwin.

"Bring back lots of those gassy mushrooms," Rachel recommended. "The ones that block your memories. They'll help keep the swamp animals away."

"Will do," Drake replied. "Safe journey."

CHAPTER 15

THE DROWNED CITY

I see the top of a tower," Ferrin called back from the canoe. "Correction, a pair of towers."

"The watchtowers above the main gate of Darvis Kur," Galloran said. "Guide us close. We'll pause to confer in their shadow."

Projecting maybe twenty feet above the water level, the time-worn structures were constructed from stone blocks the size of refrigerators. Trapezoidal battlements crowned the watchtowers. Faces had been carved into the stone, just below the crenellations, the finer details mostly eroded. Moss, slime, fungi, and creeping vines smothered the stone, patiently merging the ancient fortifications with the rest of the swamp.

Rachel surveyed the vicinity uneasily. Only big trees grew here, gloomy giants dripping with foul vegetation, widely spaced, like back where the grullions had attacked. Recalling the grullions helped her realize that the swamp seemed too silent.

"It's gone quiet again," Rachel said.

"Very observant," Galloran congratulated. "Elsewhere in the swamp I would be alarmed. Here it is expected. Not many living things venture near the Drowned City."

"Lucky us," Jason said dryly. "We get to be the exceptions."

"What keeps the animals away?" Rachel asked.

"The most dangerous predator in the Sunken Lands dwells here," Galloran explained.

"I was wondering when we'd finally see some action," Jason muttered. "So far this place has been a petting zoo."

Galloran rubbed his hands together. "I don't trespass here eagerly. I had hoped to never again cross the borders of Darvis Kur."

The skiff and the canoe came to a halt beside one of the towers. Galloran stood, moving the fabric away from his mouth and raising his raspy voice as best he could. "The Drowned City is one of the most hazardous destinations in all of Lyrian. A singular threat lurks here, a powerful being of considerable intelligence. Once, long ago, this being aided me, and I intend to solicit assistance again."

"What assistance justifies the risk?" Ferrin asked.

"This is where I acquired my supply of orantium globes. As most of you may recall, the mountain where orantium was once mined has been lost for ages, as has the procedure for extracting and storing the volatile mineral. A handful of orantium globes survive as curiosities in the treasuries of the mightiest kingdoms. Maldor probably has some in reserve, but certainly not many. As a lad, I knew that the lorevault at Trensicourt contained three."

"Most consider orantium so valuable, they would never detonate a globe," Aram said. His eyes were closed, his face glossy with sweat, but apparently he had been listening along with the others. "The spheres we shattered back at the bridge could have purchased a minor kingdom."

"I will use any weapon at my disposal to combat the emperor," Galloran said. "Orantium globes may have become scarce across the rest of Lyrian, but they are no rarity in the Drowned City. The spheres could certainly help us directly: stopping manglers, disrupting cavalry charges, threatening strongholds. But acquiring a significant stockpile of orantium may benefit us even more politically. Mere possession of the explosives will provide an added reason for potential allies to regard us seriously."

"How did you find this place?" Ferrin asked. "I trade in information. Naturally I have heard of Darvis Kur, the Drowned City. I know it is perilous. But I have heard no rumor of orantium here, or of the powerful entity you mentioned."

"My suspicions of an orantium stockpile arose through research," Galloran said. "Material in the lorevault at Trensicourt gave me clues, and I pursued further knowledge at the Repository of Learning and elsewhere. The shadow of the emperor already loomed very large. I was desperate for any possible advantage."

"Considerable orantium remains?" Ferrin asked.

"Much more than I took," Galloran said. "I was given a hundred spheres. Hundreds more survive here, maybe thousands."

"The creature gave them to you?" Rachel asked.

"He was a man once," Galloran said softly. "A wizard. After incurring the wrath of his master, he was cursed—imprisoned here, his body altered, set on a course to mutate into something like a winaro."

"You can't mean Orruck," Ferrin said.

Galloran nodded, the ghost of a smile on his lips. "I had no idea. I doubt anyone knew that Orruck survived in Darvis Kur. It was a secret Zokar took to his grave. Orruck can no longer speak, but I have long been able to discern the thoughts of those with sufficient mental ability. He meant to slay me on sight, but when I sensed his mind, I called out to him. He hadn't communicated with anyone for centuries. When he learned that Maldor had risen to power, he aided me with orantium to harm his former rival."

"Unbelievable," Ferrin murmured.

"Do you think he'll help you again?" Rachel asked.

"Possibly," Galloran said. "If I came to him alone and blind, he might view me as a failure who had squandered his previous gift. But we have two advantages. First, Rachel, I will present you as an adept with the potential to rival Maldor. Your native talent should intrigue and impress Orruck. And second, we carry with us the secret of Orruck's unmaking."

"The Word," Jason realized.

Galloran dipped his chin. "We may not possess the key word designed to undo Maldor. But Maldor informed Jason that he had used a true key word as bait for the false quest, in hopes that an actual key word would better withstand careful scrutiny. He used the word crafted to destroy Orruck. As soon as Jason relayed that secret, I knew we had to pursue the orantium hoard."

"Maldor could have lied," Ferrin pointed out.

"I do not believe that Maldor or anyone else suspects that Orruck survives. After years of listening, I have heard no hint of such a rumor. Still, we can't rule out the possibility that Maldor had less fathomable reasons to lie about the origin of the Word. Nor can we ignore the chance that Orruck has been so thoroughly transformed that the Word will no longer touch him."

"You may not need to actually use the Word," Aram said. "The threat might suffice. A bluff with some teeth behind it."

"Uttering the Word would be a last resort," Galloran agreed.

"Who will join you?" Ferrin asked.

"Rachel, do you recall the Word?" Galloran asked.

"Yes."

Galloran adjusted the fabric over his face. "After the influence of Nedwin's memory enhancer, I recall it as well. I shared it with him, syllable by syllable, while under the spell of the venom."

"Do we really need to show Rachel's abilities to Orruck?" Jason asked. "Can't we just use the Word as leverage?"

"Wizards cannot resist respecting her kind of talent," Galloran answered. "Not only is her innate Edomic aptitude rare and precious, it reflects the abilities Orruck most admired about himself. Her Edomic skill will add legitimacy to our cause in his eyes. It could help us secure what we need without having to test the efficacy of the Word."

"I'll go," Rachel said.

"I don't like it," Jason replied. "Just tell me the syllables. I'll go hit him with the Word."

"It might not work," Rachel countered. "I know you're just being protective, but it doesn't make sense here. If the Word fails, you die and we lose the globes. This orantium might make a huge difference for the rebellion. The safest bet is for me and Galloran to go."

"We'll bring Dorsio," Galloran said. "The rest of you should wait here in the skiff. Dorsio has some globes. If we fail, we'll make sure to detonate some orantium as a signal. If you hear an explosion, get away from here."

"Not that I lack confidence in the outcome," Ferrin said, "but would you consider entrusting the piece of my neck to somebody who is not about to confront one of the most deadly beings in the world?"

"Fair enough," Galloran said. "Dorsio, please lend the fragment to Jason."

After the chunk of flesh changed hands, Ferrin and Tark came aboard the skiff while Galloran, Dorsio, and Rachel moved to the canoe. She and Dorsio used the paddles to propel the canoe beyond the towers. Galloran raised a hand in farewell. "If we do not return by nightfall, we will not return."

Rachel glanced back at Jason. He looked worried. She understood how he must feel. He had risked everything to come protect her, and now she was heading into danger, leaving him behind. She tried to concentrate on paddling. Only a few sparse trees projected from the water up ahead. There were plentiful lily pads the size of tabletops, many supporting basket-shaped fungi. For the first time since entering the swamp, branches were not constantly interlaced overhead. Even screened by the hazy atmosphere, it was nice to be under sunlight. "How do we know where to go?" she asked.

"The water is deep in this part of the city," Galloran said. "We'll cross the empty parts and watch for a round tower, the top of a graven obelisk, or the head of a tremendous statue."

"What happened here?" Rachel asked. "Who would build a city in a swamp?"

"These lands were not always sunken," Galloran said. "Darvis Kur was once the oldest continually inhabited city in all of Lyrian. And arguably the most splendid. Many wizards made their homes here. The great wizards of Darvis Kur belonged to an order called the Custodians of the Mended Chain. They incurred the wrath of a rival order known as the Twenty Magi.

"The Twenty Magi attacked Darvis Kur, and the battle went poorly for the Custodians. They sought help from a wizard hermit known as Pothan the Slow. He seldom came into Darvis Kur, preferring the solitude of the surrounding wilderness. He was described as large and bald and somewhat misshapen, slow of speech and odd of manner. But when the Custodians of the Mended Chain begged him to help save their city, he answered the call.

"Eldrin and Zokar are considered the greatest masters of Edomic. But perhaps no wizard in history could rival Pothan the Slow when it came to sheer power. By the might of his Edomic, Pothan singlehandedly crushed the Twenty Magi. None survived to carry the order forward. The tale tells that they were swallowed by the earth.

"The Custodians were frightened when they discovered just how much power this peculiar wanderer wielded. After his impressive victory, they invited him to become an honorary member of their order, and then tried to poison him."

"How awful!" Rachel said. "After he saved them."

"How foolish," Galloran said. "They succeeded in poisoning him, but not in slaying him. Furious after the betrayal, Pothan sank this entire region, forcing it downward by the devastating might of his Edomic, while raising hills and mountains round about. Surrounding lakes and rivers drained into this realm in an unprecedented flood. The monumental effort cost Pothan his life and created the Sunken Lands. Tens of thousands perished."

"Wow," Rachel said. "What a story."

"Interestingly, the wizard Orruck was a young member of the Custodians of the Mended Chain at the time, one of the few to survive. Centuries later, Zokar chose to make his boyhood home into his nightmare prison."

Rachel and Dorsio piloted the boat around a stone spire jutting up from the water. A few grimy patches of gold suggested it once was gilded. The slime on the stonework glistened more than the precious metal.

"Is Orruck still a person?"

"He looks nothing like a man. His mutation left him speechless, and his mind has grown clouded. With each passing year, he becomes less human. When I last saw him, he retained enough self-possession to hold a mental conversation . . . and to crave vengeance against a former rival."

"Do you think he'll still be human enough to communicate?" Rachel asked.

"He has existed in this state for centuries," Galloran said. "It has hardly been twenty years since I met him. Barring dreadful luck, Orruck should be in a similar state to when I last encountered him."

Dorsio pointed diagonally.

Following the line he had indicated, Rachel saw the merlons of an ancient wall protruding from the water, like broken teeth. Behind the partially exposed battlements rose a rounded tower scaled with lichen, empty windows and loopholes offering glimpses of the darkness inside.

Rachel described the tower.

"Bear to the left," Galloran said. "We are nearing our destination."

"Why does Orruck hold a grudge against Maldor?" Rachel mused. "It was Zokar who did this to him."

"The apprentices of Zokar each desired to replace him one day," Galloran said. "Only one could have survived to do so. Orruck and Maldor would have slighted and betrayed each other whenever possible over the years. Zokar is no more. But Orruck has never forgotten his rivalry with Maldor. Hateful emotions consume him as he patrols the Drowned City, unable to exact revenge on his old adversaries, incapable of wielding the Edomic power he once controlled. As long as he believes he can use us to harm Maldor, we stand a good chance of winning his aid."

Across a broad span of water, a marble head rose above the surface of the swamp. Part of one nostril had broken away, deep cracks diverged across the chin, and one ear was netted with webs, but the imperfections could not disguise the artistic quality of the regal countenance. Some distance from the enormous head, a stone fist broke the surface of the water, positioned as if it had once gripped a weapon.

"We found the big statue," Rachel said.

"Which way is it facing?"

"Toward us, more or less."

"Proceed in the direction opposite the way the figure is facing, and before long you will behold our destination."

"There are a bunch of trees that way."

"Good. The swamp is less deep around the shrine."

Leaving behind the misty rays of the afternoon sun, Rachel and Dorsio guided the boat under the shadow of tall trees bulging with fungal growths. Only the paddles lapping against the murky water disturbed the silence. There was no peace in the quietness, Rachel thought. Only tension.

Carved pillars and stone roofs began to protrude from the water in abundance. Through the trees and man-made obstacles, Rachel glimpsed the elaborate stonework of an immense structure. More details became apparent as the canoe drew nearer. Crowned by six spiraling steeples, the walls of the edifice were ornamented with crumbling stone tracery. Weatherworn stringcourses underscored rows of narrow lancet windows. Leering gargoyles clung to the building like huge stone geckos. The overall impression was that of a partially submerged cathedral.

A yawning hole in one wall allowed water into the structure. The opening was irregular, as if created by brute force.

"It's gigantic," Rachel said. "I see a big hole in the wall."

"Take us inside," Galloran instructed. "Orruck awaits."

"How do you know he'll be here?" Rachel asked, running a hand across the goose bumps on her arm.

"Like most predators in the Sunken Lands, Orruck is nocturnal," Galloran whispered. "This is his lair. He has excavated extensive tunnels in the bedrock beneath the shrine. During the day, he'll be here."

Rachel and Dorsio stroked toward the opening in the wall, a lopsided arch of broken stone wide enough for several canoes to enter at once. Senses alert, Rachel helped paddle through the uneven gap.

The interior of the shrine contained a single vast chamber. Haze-softened sunlight slanted through the western windows, repeating elongated versions of the window shapes on the surface of the foul water. Deteriorating galleries and balconies projected from the walls, sufficient to hold hundreds of onlookers. Craning her neck, Rachel gazed up at the vaulted ceiling, absorbing the intricate details of the cracked, faded frescoes. She wondered how deep the water was in here. Including the underwater floor space, this cavernous room must have held thousands, which made the silent emptiness all the more disquieting.

In a corner of the room obscured by shadow, on a jumbled island of stone slabs, a flicker of movement summoned Rachel's attention. Turning to study the haphazard pile of rubble, she clumsily thumped her paddle against the side of the canoe.

"See something?" Galloran guessed.

"A movement in the corner of the room."

"Take us in that direction."

While Rachel and Dorsio paddled, Galloran stood and cried out in his raspy voice, speaking Edomic. On the island, a bulky form shifted when Galloran commenced speaking. Though the individual words were unfamiliar, Rachel intuited that Galloran was offering a humble greeting and describing peaceful intentions.

As they drew closer, Rachel observed that the creature Galloran was addressing looked something like a huge walrus, minus the tusks. The corpulent beast reclined on a long slab, fat tail in the water. The creature was about twenty feet long, not counting however much of the tail was hidden by the water. Given the size of the lair, she had expected Orruck to be bigger. Still, it was bizarre to think that the bloated, blubbery creature had once been human. Shifting again, the creature emitted a deep, wet sound, like a cross between a sneeze and a dozen bass fiddles.

"I have returned, Great One," Galloran said, reverting to English.

Rachel heard no reply, but Galloran nodded as if listening.

"I have lost my sight," he said. "I brought two companions: my bodyguard, Dorsio, and a Beyonder called Rachel, the most promising Edomic adept Lyrian has seen in many years."

The creature raised itself off the slab, the bulky body supported entirely by the tail as it moved across the water toward the canoe. "Orruck wishes to commune with you," Galloran said to Rachel. "If any being can awaken your mind to telepathy, he can. See if you can sense his words."

Rachel closed her eyes, concentrating. Nothing touched her awareness. "Is it like I hear something?" she asked. "Or maybe just feelings?"

"Think of how you force matter to obey Edomic commands," Galloran suggested. "Try to listen with similar effort."

She exerted herself, and suddenly words filled her mind, as clearly as if she had heard them. *Most who show real Edomic promise can commune mind to mind.* She knew the words had come from Orruck.

The girl only awakened to her abilities scant weeks ago, Galloran replied. *She has come a long way over a short time.*

A little farther now, Rachel added mentally.

Very good, Orruck responded. *This is your first experience speaking in silence?*

Yes.

You only began speaking Edomic recently?

261

I've only really been practicing for a couple of months.

I can feel the validity of your words, Orruck conveyed. *I would appreciate a demonstration of your abilities. But first, Galloran, have you held to your end of our bargain?*

Rachel opened her eyes. The deformed body hovered in front of the canoe, still supported by the tail. Rachel counted at least eight murky eyes spaced around the body, along with several breathing slits. She couldn't identify a mouth.

Galloran replied soundlessly. *Alas, I have not yet disposed of Maldor, though I have been a thorn in his palm. The orantium you entrusted to me has been used exclusively to harm his interests. You will recall that when last we met, my hopes resided in a key word I hoped to recover. In the years since, with the aid of another Beyonder, I have learned that the Word was a fraud.*

The creature reared up and bellowed. The entire brown body spread open, not up and down, but side to side, revealing a tremendous mouth fringed with rows of daggerlike teeth. Rachel finally recognized that what she had mistaken for the body was merely the head. What she had taken for the tail was the neck. The impossibly deep roar seemed to proceed from multiple voice boxes bellowing at different pitches. The exhalation carried a humid stench of decay, and the noise reverberated throughout the cavernous chamber.

Why have you returned? Orruck accused forcefully.

Subterfuge has failed. Open warfare is the remaining option. Maldor increases in power every day. I have come to solicit aid in a final attempt to thwart his schemes. I intend to unite the remaining free peoples of Lyrian in a last stand against his tyranny. This strategy represents our final chance to prevent an uncontested reign such as Lyrian has never witnessed. I do not see how we can succeed without more orantium. Mighty Orruck, will you grant me enough orantium to wage war against your enemy?

Orruck raised his obese head toward the ceiling, horizontal jaws gaping, and let out another bellow, more terrible than the first. Telepathic words hit almost like physical blows. *Why should I trust you to succeed? The original gift should have sufficed! I have no desire to sponsor a losing cause!*

Galloran held up a hand. *My former strategy was flawed. This new plan is sound. Plus, we now have an Edomic adept on our side. Her powers will only grow.*

If I let her live! Orruck expressed sharply. *Show me your ability, Rachel. Turn my rock walls to steel. Take on a new form. Call forth lightning.*

I only know a few phrases, Rachel apologized. *I can summon heat. I can push objects. I can make suggestions to animals.*

No doubt Maldor trembles with fear, Orruck conveyed scornfully. *Protect yourself.* The blubbery head disappeared under the water with a splash.

"Get ready to push," Galloran murmured.

Before the ripples of the splash reached the island of slabs in the corner of the room, the head surfaced there and gripped a tombstone-size rock in its jaws. Tossing his head, Orruck flung the slab toward the canoe. Rachel shouted in Edomic and willed the projectile sideways. The slab did not change course dramatically, but she altered the trajectory enough that it missed the canoe by several yards.

Orruck hurled another slab. And another. Rachel shoved one down to make it fall a little short, then pushed up on the next so it went long. The fourth slab Orruck seized was the size of a mattress and required real effort for him to fling it. Rachel pushed it sideways with everything she had, and the hefty slab barely missed the canoe, drenching the occupants with the splash.

Impressive, for one so new to her power, Orruck conceded.

Galloran patted her on the arm.

I'm eager to improve, Rachel sent.

Very well, Orruck replied. *Try a simple transmutation.* Edomic words reached her mind. She understood that they ordered stone to change into glass. Orruck gripped a slab in his jaws no larger than a dinner tray.

Rachel focused on the slab, mustered her will, and demanded that the stone transform. The slab took on a slicker sheen and a smokier color. Whipping his head sideways, Orruck hurled the slab into a wall, where it shattered.

Excellent, Orruck enthused. *You are curious why I cannot use Edomic if I can speak in silence and I still know the proper words.*

Rachel had not deliberately transmitted the question, but the thought had crossed her mind.

An ingenious physiological modification wrought by Zokar, he shared. *My will can't focus in the manner necessary to issue Edomic mandates. If I try, I experience tremendous pain, together with a host of other distracting sensations. I have managed to work around the obstacle enough to preserve my identity, but even the simplest Edomic commands have become impossible to execute. Show me the spell you will use to jolt Maldor.* Once again he shared an Edomic command.

"No," Galloran said, mentally and verbally. "Lightning requires too much finesse."

She has the strength.

"But not the control," Galloran said. "Don't do it, Rachel. If you mean to slay us, Orruck, do it outright. Without a rebellion to halt Maldor, see how fondly he remembers you after his will dominates this continent."

Orruck glided toward the canoe, neck cutting through the water like a shark fin. *Is that a threat?* The telepathic words had become dangerously silky.

"It's the reality of the situation," Galloran said. "The three of us would make a meager meal for one so grand. But we could serve you well in harming a common enemy."

Could you help me reach beyond my borders and strike down one who spurned me? Orruck scoffed. *Is the orantium useless here in my treasure hoard? Will you see it employed to dethrone my archrival? Will you become instruments of my will, bringing me the vengeance I rightfully deserve? I have heard your arguments before, trickster. Do you expect to fool me again?*

Galloran's raspy voice held steady. "You have little to gain from our demise, but much to gain should you send us abroad. Even if we fail, you strike an unlikely blow against an enemy."

I perceive that you are my enemy, Orruck answered. *I perceive that if I do not comply with your demands, you mean to coerce me. You believe the key word you obtained is destined to destroy me. I can feel that hope behind your words, behind your thoughts. You as well as the girl. Did you come here to threaten me? Do you imagine that a paltry Edomic expression from my days as a groveling apprentice could possibly bother the monstrosity I have become?*

"I imagine that your master knew his trade," Galloran replied. "This can still end peacefully. Give us orantium. I presume you still have it? We will use it against Maldor."

Please, Rachel added.

The head sank out of sight.

"Where's he going?" Rachel whispered.

"Fetching globes," Galloran murmured. "The negotiation is precarious. Stand ready."

Rachel wrung water from her shirt, her nervous hands anxious to be active. Was Orruck really fetching globes? Or was he preparing to attack?

The head returned and hung over the island of slabs. The great jaws unfolded gently, spilling dozens of tinkling orantium globes onto the island. Several rolled into the water, clinking against the stone. Rachel tensed, half expecting the globes to detonate in his face.

I have more orantium than you could carry away, Orruck conveyed. *This is a humble sample.*

"I understood that you guarded an impressive supply," Galloran said.

I set the terms here, Orruck insisted, leaving the island and coming closer to the canoe. *How dare you consider threatening me? I should crush you for entertaining the possibility. Here are my conditions. Since I have lost faith in Galloran, Rachel, scorch my ceiling with lightning, and you will depart with my orantium.*

Galloran and Dorsio, too? she verified.

Perhaps. Scorch the ceiling and we will negotiate. The Edomic command for lightning repeated in her mind.

Rachel looked to Galloran for guidance. She saw his face tense up before he drew his sword and lunged into her, tackling her out of the canoe. Dorsio dove the opposite way. As they hit the water, an enormous claw surged up from beneath the canoe, tossing the craft into the air. Rachel tried to tread water, and Galloran pushed her away with both legs, holding up his gleaming sword so that it impaled the claw as it swiped down and pushed him underwater.

Neck arching, fierce jaws gaping, Orruck snaked forward to swallow Rachel.

"Arimfexendrapuse," she gasped, nasty water lapping into her mouth.

Orruck's head rocked back, blubber fluttering wildly, his great mouth clamping shut. All of his eyes closed, and with a brilliant flare of searing light, he was reduced to a cloud of black ash. For an instant the ash held to his shape, a brief afterimage of his existence, and then the sooty particles began to disperse as they drifted downward.

Galloran surfaced beside Rachel, gasping for breath. *Well done,* he transmitted mentally.

She stared in astonished relief at the floating ash. She tried to recall the word she had uttered, but not a syllable remained. *I'm just glad it worked,* she replied. *He was about to eat me. How did you know he was going to attack?*

Dorsio righted the canoe and began to swim it toward Rachel and Galloran.

The same way he figured out we had the word to unmake him, Galloran explained. *I sensed his intent just before he moved to swipe the canoe. He was afraid. He hoped to crush us before we could try the Word. Showing us orantium and then challenging you to summon lightning were simply distractions. He did a fine job burying his intentions until the last instant.*

And you stabbed his claw the same way?

I felt it coming.

"Are you all right?" Rachel asked out loud.

"The blow dislocated my shoulder," Galloran said. "At least I kept hold of the sword."

Dorsio helped Galloran into the canoe. Rachel stared at the sword in his hand, the lustrous blade gleaming.

"It's a beautiful sword," she said.

"Unequalled craftsmanship," Galloran agreed. "Dorsio, please force my shoulder back into place. We'll have to fetch the others. With all the roaring, they may fear we perished. Plus, we'll need help transporting the orantium. We'll want to scour the area for all we can find."

Dorsio placed one hand against Galloran's back, the other

on his upper arm, and reset his shoulder with a measured jerk. Galloran gave a soft grunt.

"There's a bunch of orantium in view," Rachel said.

"And more beneath the surface," Galloran said. "It should help open doors for us."

CHAPTER 16

GLOBES AND MUSHROOMS

D oing his best to count one second at a time, Jason had reached two hundred and eighteen before Tark surfaced. Since Jason had reached one hundred and seventy during the previous dive, he was concerned but not yet panicked. Tark had proven that he could hold his breath for a very long time.

"Look what I found," Tark said, breathing deeply but not desperately, one hand clutching the side of the skiff while the other held up a crystal globe the size of a soccer ball.

"Is that orantium?" Rachel asked.

"Looks like it," Tark replied.

"It's huge," Jason said.

"How huge?" Galloran asked.

"The rock inside is bigger than my fist," Jason said.

Galloran chuckled with boyish excitement. "A gatecrasher. None are supposed to remain. I have certainly never seen one. They were intended to bombard heavy fortifications. Did you see any more?"

"At least twenty," Tark replied. "Along with plenty of regular globes, all crowded into a deep chamber."

"Twenty gatecrashers," Galloran enthused. "This surpasses my most optimistic expectations."

"All right," Ferrin huffed, "I'll help. But if I catch some horrible disease, I'll be coughing on all of you."

"I can get them," Tark said. "The water isn't cold. And the globes weigh little underwater. They almost float. I could keep this up for hours."

Ferrin pulled off his nose and handed it to Jason. "I've felt guilty this entire time. This last dive kept you under for too long."

"It's a deep chamber," Tark said, "but I can reach it."

"It isn't fair for the one of us who can breathe underwater to relax while you do dangerous work. A find like those gatecrashers pushes me over the edge. I'll make sure the deepest recesses are investigated. Jason, don't let the fabric completely block my breathing." He stepped off the skiff.

"I'm not sure how much more we can carry," Jason said. The skiff and the canoe were both already heavily laden with orantium spheres. They had transferred all the globes from the island of stone slabs, and Tark had already salvaged dozens more from below the water.

"Something tells me we could make room for more gatecrashers," Ferrin said, his face unsightly without a nose. He glanced at Tark. "Show me where to go."

The displacer and Tark both vanished below the murky surface, using the last of the luminous kelp to light their way. The glowing seaweed passed out of sight before long.

Jason, Rachel, Dorsio, and Galloran waited together on the skiff. Aram, still small, lay sleeping in the bow.

"Look!" Rachel said.

Jason turned and found Drake and Nedwin rowing through the gap in the wall. They piloted a vessel not quite as large as the skiff, but significantly bigger than the canoe. The young woman who accompanied them had long blond hair. Like the others, her face was covered with fabric, but her expressive green eyes sparkled with excitement.

"Father!" Corinne cried.

A quiet sob shook Galloran before he pulled the fabric from his face and called out, "Corinne?"

"Your daughter lives!" Nedwin exclaimed triumphantly.

Galloran's smile crinkled the exposed portions of his bearded face into happy lines. He pressed a hand to his chest. Drake and Nedwin swiftly rowed nearer.

Corinne leaped lightly to the skiff. She wore brown traveling clothes and notably feminine boots. A sword hung from her trim waist in a long sheath. Jason was surprised to find she was not much shorter than him. As she pulled the fabric from her face to greet her father with a kiss, Jason noticed generous lips, flawless skin, and elegantly sculpted features. She looked to be in her late teens, and abruptly struck him as the most beautiful girl he had ever seen!

Tark and Ferrin surfaced, each holding a pair of large orantium globes.

"Who's this?" Ferrin asked. "How long were we under?"

"They found Corinne," Rachel supplied.

"Why the blindfold?" Corinne asked Galloran. "What happened to your eyes?"

"I lost my sight," he replied.

"Oh no!"

"It was long ago. Tell me what happened to your great-aunt."

"I don't recall the specifics," Corinne said. "I wrote myself a note that said 'natural causes.' You'll have to check my other set of memories for specifics." She slipped a hand into the satchel that hung from her shoulder and retrieved a round mushroom. When she squeezed gently, spores the color of brown mustard puffed out. Corinne inhaled deliberately.

Even with the fabric over his nose and mouth, Jason added the protection of his hand. He knew the spores would block out all memories except those experienced while breathing the mushroom gas.

"Why can't I see?" Galloran asked in alarm, pulling the blindfold from his empty eye sockets. Jason flinched at the sight. "What has happened to my voice? Where am I?"

"Galloran!" Corinne exclaimed, taking one of his hands.

"Is that you, Corinne?"

"Yes. I'm away from the tree! You sent two men to free me. Drake and Nedwin. You've been blinded since we last met. You look older."

"So it seems. You've grown. You sound like a woman." Galloran grimaced. "How long has it been?"

"Galloran," Jason said. "You may want to cover your face. The gas from the mushrooms is messing up your memories."

"Who speaks?" Galloran challenged, his hand straying to the hilt of his sword.

"I'm a friend," Jason replied. "We're traveling together in the swamp to rescue Corinne."

"Lord Jason!" Corinne greeted warmly, her gaze alighting on him. "Thank you for coming. The others told me the Word did not work."

"What?" Galloran gasped. "The Word failed?"

"You'll feel less confused if you cover your face," Corinne insisted.

Nodding he pulled the fabric into place and backed away. "What happened to my blindfold?" he asked after a moment, pulling it back into place.

"The spores addled you," Drake said.

"What news of the Pythoness?" Galloran asked.

Corinne quietly recited how her mother had passed away, clutching her chest. Jason thought Corinne seemed a little more soft-spoken in her tree persona. She didn't seem to realize that Galloran was her father. Inside the tree she had apparently believed that the Pythoness was her mother and Galloran a friend.

"Where did the new boat come from?" Jason asked.

"Servants of Maldor," Corinne replied. "Four strangers arrived a few days ago. In my youth, Galloran, you taught me to recognize the armor worn by conscriptors, and three of my visitors were outfitted as you had described. The fourth was a displacer. They entered the tree bearing weapons, but forgot their purpose. I could only assume they had come to slay me. I was a perfect hostess. I fed them. They undressed and went to bed. I poisoned them while they slept."

"Well done," Galloran said.

"There were no corpses," Drake said. "She had dumped them in the swamp. I'm relieved that she believed we were there to help her."

"I was nervous," Corinne admitted. "But you bore the proper tokens."

"Good girl," Galloran said. "I'm sorry you had to face such a grim predicament, but I'm proud that you did what was necessary. You still have the sword?"

Corinne drew a magnificent blade, so sleek and shiny that it looked too valuable to actually use.

"It's just like yours," Rachel said to Galloran.

"Great prongs of Dendalus!" Ferrin gasped. His eyes flicked to Corinne and Rachel. "Pardon the expression. Is that sword what I think it is?"

Galloran unsheathed his weapon. "The companion blade to mine."

"They're really torivorian?" Ferrin breathed, his hesitant voice full of wonder.

"Wait," Jason said. "Torivorian? As in made by lurkers?"

"The dueling weapons of the torivor," Galloran confirmed.

"The lurker who followed me didn't carry a sword," Jason said.

Ferrin snorted. "If your lurker had a sword, you wouldn't be here."

"Why not?"

"Maldor can send out lurkers in two ways," Ferrin explained. "To scout or to duel. He very rarely sends them at all, and much less often to duel, because he can only send each torivor to duel once. After the duel is accomplished, the torivor goes free."

"The torivor appears bearing a pair of swords," Galloran said. "Most weapons could not scratch a lurker, but when a torivor comes to duel, it brings a sword that can."

"It is the only time a torivor will initiate an attack," Ferrin said. "Otherwise they simply retaliate. But if you have the swords, Galloran . . ."

"He bested a torivor," Nedwin bragged.

"What?" Jason exclaimed. "You killed a lurker in a duel?"

"It required all of my skill at the height of my strength," Galloran said. "Maldor meant to remove me."

"I knew that, historically, lurkers had been sent out to dispatch enemies on occasion," Ferrin said in awe, "but I have never heard a whisper of a torivor losing."

"There were few witnesses," Galloran replied.

"When did this happen?" Ferrin asked.

"Years ago, not too long before I was taken. It was the fight of my life."

"You have long been reputed as the finest swordsman in Lyrian," Drake said. "But word of this deed never got out. You should be renowned as the greatest swordsman of all time."

Galloran waved a dismissive hand, sheathing his sword. "I am no longer the same man. Boasts of past deeds will defeat no new enemies. Besides, I may have gotten lucky."

Ferrin laughed. "Lucky? Against a lurker? Preposterous. Absent the swords, I wouldn't believe your victory possible. But the weapons are unmistakable."

"Are you holding a gatecrasher?" Drake asked Ferrin.

"Two, actually," he replied, displaying them.

"It's a day for the unbelievable," Drake said. Glancing around furtively, he lowered his voice. "What of the menace?"

"The menace?" Rachel asked.

"The guardian of the Drowned City," Drake explained. "My people venture into the Sunken Lands on occasion, but never here. You negotiated with it?"

"They destroyed it," Jason said.

Drake's jaw dropped.

"Your menace was the wizard Orruck," Galloran explained. "The word Jason and Rachel obtained had the power to unmake him."

"We trusted the message you left back at the watchtowers," Drake said, "but I did not imagine that you had actually vanquished the menace. To any of my people, that feat will sound even less likely than outdueling a torivor."

"Congratulate Rachel," Galloran said. "She uttered the Word just in time to preserve our lives."

"After Galloran drew Orruck's attention," Rachel said modestly. "I had the easy part."

"Corinne," Galloran said. "Put aside the mushroom."

She sheathed her sword and returned the fungus to the satchel. Corinne blinked rapidly and rubbed her forehead.

"Are you back?" Galloran asked.

"Yes," she replied.

"Have you spent sufficient time outside of the tree?" Galloran asked.

"A few hours a day," Corinne replied. "Just as we discussed. Talking with my great-aunt. Reading. Performing exercises with my sword. Waiting." There was an edge of bitterness to the final word.

"I'm so sorry," Galloran said. "I didn't mean to fail. I left you in the safest place I felt I could take you. Mianamon would have been preferable, but there was war in the south at the time. I retrieved you as soon as I was able."

"I understand," Corinne said. Her eyes swept over the group. "Thank you all for coming for me."

"You have been through an ordeal," Galloran said. "The years in hiding were for your good, but it was nonetheless a dismal prison."

"It was hardest after Great-Aunt Madeline died. The solitude felt endless. I would write myself notes from inside the tree. I'm ready to start living. My only memories of an actual life are the blurry recollections of childhood. All I have besides that is what happened day after day on a short stretch of muddy island."

"I'll do my best to make it up to you," Galloran promised. "Sadly, for the present, we have led you from solitude into peril. But it could not be avoided. Maldor is moving against the guardians of the syllables. Already some have perished. You would not have thwarted assassination attempts forever."

"What now?" Drake inquired.

"We load up as much orantium as we can reasonably carry," Galloran said. "We'll spend the night here. The day is waning, and the Drowned City is the last place anyone would look for us.

It should take some time for the denizens of the swamp to realize Orruck is gone. Corinne's mushrooms should also help dissuade bothersome visitors. Then, with the first light of dawn, we'll hurry away from the Sunken Lands."

Standing on muddy ground at the edge of the swamp, Jason peered northward at an imposing wall of mountains. A progression of rugged plateaus climbed from the perimeter of the Sunken Lands to eventually surge skyward in a magnificent upheaval of stone. Somewhere among those sheer faces and lofty crags, an unseen pass granted access to the western gate of the Seven Vales. In the foreground, a lone hawk wheeled and plunged, illuminated by the setting sun.

Behind and above Jason, a branch snapped. Turning, he looked up to where Nedwin, Ferrin, and Drake advanced along a thick bough, returning from hiding the boats and their cargo of orantium. Thanks to the puffball mushrooms, their trek from the Drowned City to the outskirts of the swamp had been relatively uneventful. Stashing the boats in the swamp had been the last unfinished detail.

Ferrin held a branch that had broken off in his hand. He released it, and the rotten limb fell to the water, sending ripples across the surface scum. Nedwin reached the top of a nearby tree and started down. Drake and Ferrin followed.

Jason, Rachel, Corinne, Tark, and little Aram met them at the bottom of the tree. "Everything go all right?" Jason asked.

"No complications," Drake reported.

"Unless you count Nedwin using the vines to attempt some dangerous swings," Ferrin muttered.

"I only fell twice," Nedwin said. "Water is forgiving."

The group walked over to Dorsio and Galloran, who sat on

opposite sides of a modest pile of orantium globes. Most were the regular sort, no larger than baseballs, but three were the larger gatecrashers.

"We're all assembled?" Galloran checked.

"Yes, sire," Nedwin replied.

"Who gets to carry the big ones?" Rachel asked.

Galloran laid a hand on one of the larger globes. "Dorsio will hold them. The Amar Kabal are a reclusive people. Once I was welcome in their land. But times have changed. Should all else fail, I hope to bribe our way in. In these perilous times, I can think of no currency more valuable than orantium."

"They'll admit you without a gift," Drake said firmly. "I don't believe my people hold any living human in higher regard."

"I hope you're right," Galloran responded. "There are influential voices among your people who may not appreciate what my presence could represent in these uncertain times. The boats are hidden?"

"They're well disguised on an obscure little island," Drake said.

"Further guarded by the puffball mushrooms," Ferrin added.

"Then we should start our journey," Galloran said. "The sooner we are behind West Gate, the sooner we can rest. I would be surprised if Maldor did not try to apprehend us between here and there. By now he should have anticipated the Seven Vales as our most likely destination."

"The territory between the Sunken Lands and our gates remains uninhabited by treaty," Drake said. "Imperial troops are only supposed to enter with our permission."

"Maldor understands the stakes," Galloran argued. "By heading us off, he can suppress a possible rebellion. He has reason to expect that the Amar Kabal won't risk a sortie to enforce the treaty."

"There was a day when he wouldn't have chanced it," Drake murmured darkly.

"Your people have grown even more withdrawn while you've been absent," Galloran said. "They refuse to risk hostilities with Felrook. Their emphasis has been to fortify the Vales for a defensive stand. They display little interest in events beyond their gates."

Drake frowned. "I won't be much use in persuading them otherwise. I never expected to return. I may find myself even less welcome than Ferrin. By accepting the invitation to Harthenham, I shamed my people. I expect they will vote to exile me."

"If so, you will be in good company," Galloran said. "The finest seedman I know is an exile."

"I don't need their approval," Drake said. "I just wish I were in a better position to advocate your cause."

"First, we need to get there," Galloran observed. "No sign of the horses?"

"I've been calling," Rachel said. "I'll keep trying."

"I know many routes from here to West Gate," Drake said. "By foot or by horse, with a little caution we should be able to cross unobserved."

Aram came clinking over to join the group. He had slipped off to transform as the sun set, and now wore his sword, cloak, and armor.

Galloran turned to him, having heard his approach. "How are you feeling, Aram?"

"Good as new," he said, rubbing the corkscrew bruise, which had faded slightly, going greenish along the edges. "I won't slow us down tonight. But without horses, my gear could pose a problem by morning."

"We carried the sword and mail through the marsh," Tark pointed out.

"For which I'm grateful," Aram said. "But speed was not essential there."

"We'll manage," Tark vowed stoutly. "I'll lug the sword myself."

"I'll see to your armor," Ferrin said. "I don't want to leave you any excuses for not protecting our hides."

"It's appreciated," Aram said. "I would make my way to the gate at my own pace before I would leave them."

Galloran arose. "When it comes to hampering our speed while traveling afoot, I will be our biggest liability. We had best not tarry. Drake will lead the way. Ferrin and Nedwin will assist with scouting. I'm afraid there is no rest for the weary. Let's cover as much ground as possible by sunrise."

CHAPTER 17

WEST GATE

The night was dark and breezy when Drake called for a halt. Holding a finger to his lips, his stance showed concern. Listening in silence, Rachel heard distant hoofbeats. Everyone scattered, reaching for their weapons while searching for some degree of cover.

"All clear," Nedwin called from an unseen vantage. "They're ours."

Rachel spoke softly in Edomic, calling to the animals. Within a minute or two, three horses came trotting up to her, bathed in soft moonlight. She recognized her mare, the huge stallion Aram had ridden, and Mandibar.

"You made it!" Rachel exclaimed, hugging and stroking each of the mounts.

"Do they know where the other horses are?" Jason asked.

"I'm not Dr. Doolittle," Rachel replied. "I can send out instructions, but we don't have conversations."

Hopping down off a tall boulder, Nedwin rejoined the group. "There's no sign of the other mounts."

"This is very impressive," Galloran said. "Rachel obviously

issued effective instructions. I did not expect to encounter any of these horses again. I'm afraid they brought some trouble with them."

"Trouble?" Jason asked.

"I sensed a lurker trailing them," Galloran said. "Its presence only touched my awareness for a moment. The torivor came near enough to identify us, then immediately fled. Already it has moved beyond the reach of my perceptions."

"If it ran, there must be soldiers within range," Drake said.

"Then it's a race," Aram said heavily.

"Oh no," Rachel said. "If I had known—"

"Not your fault," Galloran interrupted. "If torivors were hunting us, it was only a matter of time before they made contact. Only three of our minds are shielded by charms. The horses will help us increase our pace. This may have worked out for the best."

"Galloran should ride," Drake said. "Aram's horse can carry double. I'll use Mandibar to scout."

"If it comes to it," Aram said, "we can send Galloran, Jason, Corinne, and Rachel ahead on the three horses."

"I'd prefer we all survived," Galloran said, mounting Rachel's mare.

"Rachel, Corinne," Drake said, swinging astride Mandibar. "You should conserve energy by mounting up as well. You'll be no burden to Aram's horse."

Rachel climbed the strapping steed. The back felt ridiculously broad. Corinne mounted behind her. "It has been a long time," she murmured to Rachel.

"You rode as a child?" Rachel asked.

"I have fond memories of the activity," Corinne said. "On this big stallion, I almost feel like a child again."

"You and me both," Rachel said.

As they got moving, the pace increased dramatically. Aram

kept hold of his horse, and Dorsio led the mare. Rachel felt sorry for Jason and all the men as they jogged along. While Drake scouted on Mandibar, Nedwin led the group, and Ferrin roved nearby.

The moon often vanished behind clouds, making it hard to keep track of the surrounding terrain. Sometimes they progressed across level ground. Other times they weaved among boulders and crags. Occasionally they advanced along the floor of a ravine or followed winding paths up rocky slopes.

As the night wore on, Tark began to cough. What started as an occasional clearing of his throat grew into deep hacking. For much of the night his coughing would subside when they paused for a break. But as sunrise drew near, they stopped beside a wide stream, and he fell to his hands and knees, coughing and gagging until he hawked up a dark-green wad of phlegm. Rachel turned away from the disgusting mass, wishing she hadn't glimpsed it.

"What does his mouth look like?" Galloran inquired.

Jason stood nearest to him. Tark opened his mouth and flattened his tongue. Jason winced. "His throat looks full of mold. The whole back of his mouth is coated by purplish fuzz."

Aram peered over Jason's shoulder. "Quite a garden you have in there."

Rachel resisted the bile rising in her throat at the descriptions. Her hand involuntarily strayed to her neck.

"Lungrot," Galloran declared. "Corinne and Rachel should walk for a time. I had hoped to avoid fungal illnesses. Tark will require the horse."

"I'm fine," the musician protested. "Let the ladies ride."

Rachel had already slid off to the ground. "It'll feel good to stretch my legs," she insisted.

Corinne followed her example. "I was getting awfully cramped in that saddle."

Tark was already hacking miserably again. The fit culminated with a noisy bout of dry heaving.

"Will he be all right?" Jason asked.

"The Amar Kabal have skilled healers for such maladies," Galloran said. "Much will depend on how swiftly we can get him there. Drink, refill your waterskins, and then we should move on."

Jason and Rachel went to a slate shelf where water fell in a transparent curtain. Cool water splashed Rachel's wrists as she disrupted the smooth cascade with her waterskin. The horses drank from the mossy pool below.

"You look tired," Rachel told Jason.

"I wish I could jog and sleep at the same time."

"Can't you?" Ferrin asked, joining them at the little cascade. "I always imagined that you could sleep rolling down a mountainside in a barrel."

"I probably could today," Jason conceded.

"How's it look out there?" Rachel asked. She hadn't seen Ferrin in more than an hour.

"Quiet," Ferrin replied. "I haven't heard Drake in some time. He must have roamed far."

"There goes Nedwin," Aram said, pointing.

Nedwin was scaling a vertical finger of rock to get a view of the broken countryside. He ascended without hesitation, despite an apparent lack of handholds.

"How does he do that?" Corinne asked.

"I'm not sure," Ferrin muttered.

Tark erupted in another fit of coughing. His face turned red, veins stood out in his neck, and he began to vomit. Rachel covered her ears until he finished.

Aram came up to Ferrin. "Do you know which way we're heading? I thought I might run ahead while I have my size."

Rachel glanced at the light gathering on the cloudy horizon. The sun would appear within an hour.

Ferrin turned to face the craggy mountains. They loomed much closer than they had at dusk, but a broken succession of bluffs and ridges still separated the group from the feet of the real slopes.

"See the ridge with the notch?"

"The one above that really square edge?"

"Exactly. We're heading around the right side of it, then along a ravine."

"Understood. See you there." Aram took off almost at a sprint, ring mail jangling.

"All of us should hurry," Galloran prompted.

Jason looked up to where Nedwin was descending the spire of rock.

"Nedwin will catch up," Ferrin said, patting Jason on the arm. "Why don't you lead Aram's horse?"

They started moving again, with Ferrin in front and Dorsio and Jason guiding the horses. Corinne and Rachel fell into step beside each other.

"You and Jason both hail from the Beyond?" Corinne asked.

"We didn't know each other there," Rachel replied. "We're from different areas. But yes, we're Beyonders."

"You seem close."

"We've been through a lot together."

"You seem rather young to be involved with my father."

"We didn't have a lot of choice in the matter," Rachel said. "It just worked out this way. We can't be too much younger than you."

"I'm nineteen."

"How long were you in that tree?"

"Since I was four."

Rachel tried to imagine what it would be like if her only real memories of the world came from age four or younger. "This must all feel really new."

Corinne gave a brief laugh, emphasizing the understatement. "I'm not used to company. Or danger. Or changes of scenery. I have vivid, distant memories of my childhood—a nursemaid, a playroom full of wonderful toys, a bed with lacy covers, delicious bowls of chilled fruit floating in cream—culminating with my father smuggling me away in the night. He brought me to a tree in the swamp to visit my great-aunt Madeline. The rest of my life happened somewhere beyond the opening to that tree. Every memory begins when I exit the tree and ends when I enter it. I remember some conversations with my father from my younger days. Then he stopped visiting. I remember conversing with my great-aunt. One memory begins with me dragging her lifeless body out of the tree. I didn't even know how she had died, until I found the note I had written to myself. Thereafter my only memories pertain to performing exercises with my sword and reading books."

"I can barely imagine," Rachel said.

"I dreamed of escaping for years," Corinne sighed. "Now that I'm free, I can hardly believe it. Part of me had begun to suspect I would grow old and die on that muddy little island. Everything has changed so quickly. I barely know how to feel. This might sound silly, but I somehow expected that when I finally did leave the swamp, it would mean the end of my troubles. Father would take me home to a happier, more meaningful life—the hard-earned reward for my patience. I never expected this."

"If it's any consolation," Rachel said, "I never expected anything like this either."

They picked their way across a rugged stretch; then the route became smoother and their pace increased. Rachel found herself perspiring and breathing hard. How had the others done this all night? No wonder Jason had looked so tired.

When the sun came up, Rachel paused to stare at the glorious horizon. Beams of sunlight shot through the clouds at dramatic angles, throwing dazzling highlights over the landscape. "Is it always so beautiful?" Corinne asked.

Rachel realized that the vegetation in the swamp would have blocked out sunrises and sunsets. "It's an extra-good one," Rachel replied. "But they're usually pretty nice."

They hurried onward. After hiking through a long, shallow ravine, they found Aram waiting for them, his ring-mail shirt and heavy cloak bundled with his sword. Ferrin called for a halt, perhaps because he had noticed that Corinne looked ready to faint. Rachel felt bad for her. No matter how much Corinne had practiced with her sword and otherwise tried to stay active, it would be tough to get much cardio when trapped on a tiny island.

While they rested in the shade of an outcrop, drinking from waterskins and catching their breath, Nedwin shouted from a distance that Drake was returning. Within a few minutes, they could hear the horse, and soon Drake rode up on Mandibar.

"I've spotted our enemies," Drake said, urgency in his tone. "At least forty horsemen riding hard, and another large company of riders coming from farther off."

"How close are they?" Galloran asked gravely.

"We're much closer to the pass," Drake said. "I could only spy them from a high lookout miles from here. But in shameless defiance of the treaty, they're on the main road and riding hard. They're trying to beat us to West Gate."

"We have to get there first," Galloran said.

"That or hide in these foothills," Drake said. "I know the region well."

Galloran shook his head. "If they block us from the pass, with a lurker after us and with Maldor adding more soldiers to the hunt, we'll not stay hidden long."

Drake scowled thoughtfully. "You really think the Amar Kabal will remain idle if Maldor brings a major force to their doorstep?"

"They may complain," Galloran said. "But given their recent behavior, I would be shocked if they intervened directly. Maldor has lulled your people into a very cautious state."

"Mandibar could take two riders if we keep a moderate pace," Aram said. "So can my horse. Do we send five of us ahead?"

"Galloran, Tark, Rachel, Corinne, and Jason," Ferrin said. "If they make it to safety, I don't expect Maldor will risk provoking the Amar Kabal just to harass the rest of us. He'd have to commit too many resources."

"Could we find the right way to go?" Rachel asked. "Seems like Drake, Nedwin, and Ferrin are the people who can navigate these ridges."

"Leave me," Tark panted. "Let Drake take my place. I might be done for anyway."

"What do you mean?" Jason said. "You've been sounding better lately."

"He lacks the breath to cough," Galloran said. "I've been listening to him wheeze. The lungrot is advancing swiftly."

Tark climbed down off the horse.

Galloran lowered his eyebrows when Tark's feet hit the ground. "I didn't mean for you to dismount. I just meant that your condition is most serious. You could survive, but if you don't reach the Amar Kabal soon, the illness will take you. Mount up, Tark. Drake, what are the chances of us beating the horsemen to West Gate if we stay together?"

"Despite our huge lead, they're moving very fast on a good

road. It could be close. I rigged three orantium traps along the road. That's what took me so long. When a hoof hits the wrong spot, an orantium globe will send up an unmistakable signal. The explosion might also confuse and slow them, if they think they're under attack."

"There's a thought," Ferrin said. "We have plenty of orantium. A pair of us could set up an ambush along the main road and slow them, buy time for the others. If we can find a favorable spot, we might even defeat them."

Galloran frowned. "If we stay together, can we beat the horsemen to the mouth of the pass?"

"To the mouth?" Drake repeated. "Almost certainly. We're perhaps three hours from the start of the pass. If we exert ourselves, our pursuers couldn't get there before us. But even hurrying, it will require more than an hour to make it up the pass to the gate. They could very well ride us down in the meanwhile."

"Is there a better bottleneck than the pass for an ambush?" Galloran asked.

Drake shook his head. "West Gate was placed in that pass because the way becomes so narrow."

"Let's race them," Galloran said. "If it comes to it, the tight confines of the pass should allow an ambush to wreak havoc on them with orantium."

Drake folded his arms, his expression brooding. "Once in the pass, there will be no fleeing except through West Gate. If our enemies catch up, or if we're denied admittance, there will be nowhere to hide."

"I am an honorary citizen of the Seven Vales by ceremony," Galloran said. "If the Amar Kabal look on while I'm slaughtered outside their gates, our cause is already beyond hopeless."

"Corinne's tired," Rachel blurted.

"We'll put her on Mandibar," Drake said, dismounting. "I have little reason to scout between here and the pass."

"This is our final sprint," Galloran said. "We'll take turns riding as needed to keep the best possible pace. We're running for more than our lives. The future of Lyrian depends on our success."

The pace did not feel enough like a sprint to Rachel. Then again, an actual sprint over rough terrain for several miles after so much exertion might not have been realistic. Still, they went faster than ever, and before long the pace seemed plenty quick. Rachel eventually rode again for a while, and Jason mounted up behind Tark for a time. Corinne took another turn jogging so that Aram could ride behind Rachel.

The sun rose higher. Rachel returned to jogging once she felt rested. She had always been in good shape, and roaming the wilderness for weeks on end had her in the best shape of her life. But still she found herself flagging. She tried to draw strength from Nedwin, Drake, Ferrin, and Dorsio, who could apparently press forward forever without respite.

At length they came into view of the road. Drake led them down a gentle slope until they intersected the wide, dirt lane.

"I take it there are no orantium traps ahead of us," Aram said.

"All are behind," Drake assured him. "In fact, it's a favorable sign that the first has not yet exploded."

"Could they have missed it?" Jason asked.

"I rigged each sphere so that a reasonably broad area of road would trigger the detonation. One rider might miss it, but forty will surely spring each of the traps."

"On level ground I can walk as fast as any of you," Galloran said. "Let others take my mount."

Tark coughed weakly—a hitching, reedy wheeze, as if his airway were mostly plugged. He rode with his head bowed and his eyes closed. Rachel, Corinne, and Aram rode as well.

The pass came into view ahead, a deep gorge that wound up into the imposing mountains. On the level road, they made their best time yet. Rachel hoped that after so many miles at high speeds, the horses chasing them would become tired.

They were not yet to the mouth of the pass when a distant boom reached their ears. Mandibar whickered in response.

"The first trap," Drake said. "We have a chance, but it will be close. Ideally, we should quicken our pace, but the grade up the pass will make that easier said than done."

"Onward," urged Galloran, increasing the speed of his shuffling jog.

They advanced into the shadow of the gorge, steep walls of rock rising to impressive heights on either side. The road steepened. Everyone on foot panted harder.

Suddenly Galloran stopped and held up a hand. The group halted. He craned his neck, tilting his head from side to side. "I sense a presence."

"There," Drake said, a finger stabbing upward.

Rachel followed the line on his arm up to a distant silhouette atop one wall of the gorge. Just as her eyes found the figure, it jumped, arms and legs spread wide, and fell hundreds of feet as if fully committed to a suicidal belly flop. An instant before impact, the hurtling lurker changed position, landing in a crouch on the road. Although it seemed to land with tremendous speed, Rachel heard no sound.

The dark, featureless figure stood upright, spreading its arms. Rachel dimly sensed a command directed at their mounts.

In unison, the horses reared. Rachel and Corinne slid backward off Aram's big stallion. Rachel landed hard. Croaking for breath, she lunged for the reins of the horse as it bolted away. She fell short, sprawled in the dirt, one hand inches from getting crushed by a rear hoof.

Raising her head, Rachel saw Aram clinging to the side of Mandibar's saddle. Tearing free a bundle of gear, the little man skidded into the dirt, bouncing and rolling, embracing the rescued equipment. Tark had fallen with a foot snagged in a stirrup, and was dragged dozens of yards down the road, spewing a dusty contrail before wrenching his leg free.

All three riderless horses galloped away down the pass.

Rachel called out to the horses in Edomic, asking them to return. It was tricky to tell if they even heard her.

"Whatever happens," Galloran commanded in his perpetually hoarse voice, "take no aggressive action involving the lurker." Drawing his beautiful sword, he strode directly toward the dark figure blocking the road, as if he could see it.

"Servant of evil," Galloran announced. "Stand your ground and meet your ruin, for I have dispatched others of your kind with this blade."

"No," Jason whispered.

Sword held ready, Galloran advanced without hesitation. Rachel held her breath. When the lurker was almost within reach, the creature crouched and sprang up against the wall of the gorge, then with another tremendous leap, soared over Galloran to land in a sprint. A dark blur, the figure dashed down the road faster than the horses had run.

Rachel gaped at the inhuman speed of the lurker. Turning, she saw Jason regarding Galloran with astonishment.

"How did you do that?" Jason asked.

"The torivor knew I spoke the truth," Galloran said, sheathing his sword. "Unarmed, it would have fallen."

"But you're blind," Jason said.

"I could feel the mind of the lurker," Galloran replied. "I knew where it stood. It knew that I knew. Also, it had nothing more to accomplish here. It succeeded in slowing us, and now hastens to urge our pursuers to increase their pace. The complexion of our race has taken an awful turn."

"Tark is injured," Ferrin called, crouching beside the short musician in the road. He had not moved since twisting free of the stirrup.

"Is he conscious?" Galloran asked.

"No."

Galloran sighed. "Rachel, any chance of calling the horses back?"

"I'm trying," she replied.

"I can try to fetch one," Nedwin offered.

Galloran shook his head. "It will cost too much time. Who will carry Tark?"

"Where is my size when I need it?" Aram lamented. His clothes were torn and filthy from his fall, but he seemed unhurt beyond cuts and scrapes.

"I'll carry him," Drake said, trotting over to him. Ferrin helped Drake situate Tark over his shoulder. Dust billowed from Tark's cloak. His hair was caked with dirt and blood.

"Is that your gear?" Ferrin asked Aram.

"Leave me with it. Give me ten spheres of orantium, and I'll buy you some time."

"Give me the sword," Ferrin said.

"I'll carry the armored shirt," Nedwin offered.

Eyes closed, Rachel kept calling the horses. She could envision them clearly. Why wouldn't they come? Had the lurker struck some primal chord of panic within them? Or maybe the torivor was blocking their return?

In the distance, she heard another explosion, closer than before. "Second trap," Drake said. "They're gaining too fast."

"Why don't they get off the road?" Jason asked. "You know, run parallel. How many mines does it take?"

"Most of the terrain off the road is rugged," Drake said. "If they leave the road, they won't catch us."

"Are we ready to proceed?" Galloran asked.

Nedwin draped the ring mail across his shoulders and rubbed his chest absently. "Ready."

As they continued up the pass, Rachel kept calling the horses. She repeatedly instructed them to be calm, combined with the request to come to her. The incline of the road soon became torturous to Rachel's fatigued muscles. She and her companions were basted in sweat. The way twisted and turned, preventing them from seeing far ahead or behind. The weary group shambled forward, failing to go much faster than a brisk walk. Corinne seemed on the brink of collapse. Rachel plodded forward in an exhausted haze, cresting a rise only to find the pass winding onward and upward with no end in sight.

Hoofs pounded behind them. Rachel felt a brief jolt of panic, but the emotion turned to relief when her mare and Mandibar loped into view. Drake hastily draped Tark over Mandibar's saddle and had Corinne mount up to stabilize him. Galloran climbed onto the mare, and they hurriedly packed Aram's gear onto Mandibar.

With the help of the horses, they managed to pick up the pace. The effects of sleeplessness and relentless exertion were impacting Rachel. Her eyes itched, her legs ached, and her throat felt raw. Jason kept his head down and wore a constant grimace.

When the third explosion rumbled behind them, Rachel cringed. It sounded nearer than the previous blasts.

"That one wasn't far behind where we joined the road," Drake said. "They've ridden hard to close this quickly. The horses may tire."

"No," Galloran warned. "The lurker will be behind them, driving them forward. Only death will slow those steeds."

"Then they may beat us to the gate," Drake said.

"I can climb the wall of the gorge," Nedwin said. "I see a position where orantium could provoke a rockslide. And I'll be out of their reach. I'll need globes."

"Include a gatecrasher with his supply," Galloran said.

Dorsio rapidly prepared a knapsack of orantium spheres, including one of the larger globes.

"There will be negotiations at the gate to gain admittance," Drake said. "Galloran should ride ahead."

"Tark, Rachel, and Corinne will join me," Galloran decided. "The rest of you make sure you have orantium ready."

Nedwin was already heading up the side of the gorge, climbing deftly. Dorsio checked that everyone had some orantium globes.

"Sit in front of me so you can guide the horse," Galloran told Rachel.

"We're not leaving them to make a last stand?" Rachel checked as she mounted.

"We're trying to get everyone to safety," Galloran said. "But they need to be prepared for the worst contingencies."

The horses sped up. Rachel encouraged them with Edomic. Drake had ridden Mandibar hard earlier, and even though the mare had not traveled quickly, she had covered rough terrain nonstop all night and for part of a day. And who knew how hard the horses had run to make it around the Sunken Lands? Even so, both horses managed a loping gait that swiftly took Rachel beyond view of her friends.

The way steepened, twisting ever higher into the mountains.

Rachel tried not to think of Jason and the others having to cover all of the same ground on foot with a cavalry in pursuit.

They rounded a bend, and an enormous fortification finally came into view at the top of the pass, spanning the gorge like a dam. A raised drawbridge made the imposing wall even less inviting.

As they rode forward, further details became apparent. Soldiers could be seen among the battlements atop the gate. A pair of maroon banners, emblazoned with golden peaks, hung from the top of the massive granite wall. Scores of holes lined the sides of the pass above the gate. Rachel glimpsed faces peering from some of the holes and concluded that the apertures allowed defenders to fire arrows from tunnels in the mountainside.

Rachel slowed her mare as they reached the base of the wall. Corinne drew up beside her. It had to be more than fifty feet high, and in front of the base ran a deep trench with spikes bristling along the bottom.

"Are we near enough to address the gate wardens?" Galloran asked.

"If you shout," Rachel guessed.

Galloran dismounted and raised his voice. "Hail, children of Eldrin! Could one of you fetch your captain?"

"I am Halak, High Captain of West Gate," a tall figure answered from above. "We have not been ignorant of your approach, traveler. Why have you brought bloodshed to our doorstep when we make it no secret that this gate is sealed to outsiders?"

"Will it not open for an honorary kinsman?"

"Who am I addressing?"

"I am Galloran, heir to the throne of Trensicourt and sworn ally of the Amar Kabal."

The captain paused. "If you speak truth, what errand brings you to the borders of our land unannounced?"

"If I speak truth?" Galloran repeated incredulously. He tore the rag from his eyes, revealing his scarred sockets. "I once frequented these vales. The years have not been generous, and I now wear a beard, but does no man upon the wall recognize my face?"

"My apologies," Halak answered. "Why do you seek entry into our land?"

"By ceremony, I am a friend of the Amar Kabal. I wish to invoke my right to bring a proposal before the Conclave."

"So you are not seeking passage through this gate to evade imperial pursuit?"

"The riders who pursue us are a consequence of my visit, not the motivation. We set out from Fortaim many days ago with this destination in mind."

"Regardless of your intent, given the circumstances, admitting you could jeopardize our tenuous relations with Felrook."

Galloran replaced his blindfold. "Dozens of imperial soldiers have invaded the neutral territory between your gate and the Sunken Lands to hunt my companions and me. The emperor is in open violation of your treaty already. His horsemen are chasing us up the gorge. Given the opportunity, they will cut us down outside your very gates."

"We're aware of their movements," Halak replied carefully.

"We come bearing a tribute of more than fifty orantium spheres, including two of the large globes known as gatecrashers. I imagine you would not relish the idea of these explosives falling into enemy hands."

"A bribe and a threat in the same breath. Which should I heed?"

"Neither. I am conversant with your laws. Until my friendship status is revoked, it remains my right to pass through this gate at will. My status can only be revoked by a majority decision of the

Conclave, at a hearing where I am afforded the opportunity to speak in my defense."

"I cannot refute your claim. But your privileged status does not extend to your comrades."

"I can vouch for each of my nine companions. When I last visited your realm, my word would have been more than sufficient to secure a welcome. I recognize that times are changing. I do not visit to abuse my privileges. I do not seek prolonged sanctuary for myself or my companions. Grant us admittance for a week, so I can bring vital information before your Conclave. Complain to Felrook that I invoked my legal rights, according to your laws. We will voluntarily depart after I conduct my affairs with your elders. If your leaders so choose, you can turn us over to the minions of the emperor at that time. No harm will befall your delicate treaty."

"Who are your companions? I only count three."

"This is Tark, former musician with the Giddy Nine, who requires urgent treatment for lungrot and who recently returned the seed of Jasher to the guards at East Gate. Forgive his unconsciousness. He rides with my daughter, Corinne. And we're also joined by a Beyonder named Rachel, a promising Edomic adept."

"And the others?"

"Only two of our horses remain with us. The rest of my comrades straggle behind us on foot. My bodyguard, Dorsio, is not present; nor is my assistant, Nedwin, formerly of the House of Geer; nor is Ferrin, my chief scout. We also travel with Aram, a smuggler from Ithilum; Lord Jason of Caberton, a Beyonder who has joined the fight against Maldor; and Drake of the Amar Kabal."

"Drake, the son of Hessit?" Halak exclaimed. "He accepted an invitation to Harthenham!"

"And recently fought his way free," Galloran added.

"Very well," Halak responded. "You are a man of no small reputation, Galloran. I will admit you and your companions. You will have your hearing before the Conclave. Be forewarned: It is possible that you are merely stalling your capture rather than evading it."

"We understand."

Halak gave a signal, and the iron-plated drawbridge clattered open, spanning the trench at the base of the wall. Galloran climbed back onto the horse with Rachel. As the group crossed the bridge, Rachel glanced down into the trench at the thicket of spikes.

The wall was quite thick, with a pair of raised portcullises, and a huge gate standing open at the far side. In the paved yard beyond, many soldiers stood at attention, mostly clad in leather armor. A group of at least twenty sat astride horses. The men were mainly armed with swords and spears. Several women held longbows. They all had a portion of their hair rolled up at the nape of their necks. Jasher had once explained that the style helped conceal and protect their seeds.

A succession of blasts came thundering up from lower in the gorge. Rachel looked back in distress. Rumbling echoes muddied the cannonade. After a few trailing blasts, the explosive clamor ended.

Halak quickly descended a stone staircase, one hand resting on the hilt of a sword at his waist. A tall man with dramatic eyebrows, he strode over to the horses as Galloran dismounted.

"Trouble follows you up the pass," Halak said.

Galloran faced him, speaking calmly. "Captain Halak, would you send riders to escort my friends who travel afoot?"

"We've monitored the progress of your pursuers," Halak replied. "If we sally forth, it could spawn a major confrontation."

"If you hesitate, imperial forces will murder friendly visitors in the pass outside of your gates. I understand that relations with Felrook are strained, but we both know that Maldor is no respecter of weakness. You will find little resistance. Not more than twenty foemen would have survived the ambush you just heard deployed."

Halak gave a signal, then helped lead the two mounts bearing Rachel, Corinne, and Tark away from the gate. Twenty riders galloped out of the gate and across the drawbridge.

Halak drew near to Galloran, speaking for his ears only. Rachel made an effort to overhear. "We kept a very close watch of your movements across the neutral territory and up the pass. I have sentries along the rim of the gorge. We have an efficient system of signaling that has kept me informed minute by minute. I would have sent help earlier had intervention become necessary. Our riders will reach your friends before the enemy, all save the lone man who scaled the wall of the gorge. His chief threat at present is his precarious climb."

"You have my deepest gratitude," Galloran said. "It took planning to have those riders standing ready."

"My discourteous welcome on the wall was a shameful political necessity. There are isolationist proponents in our midst who must be appeased. By appealing to the fearful, they wield enough clout to create serious trouble."

"I appreciate your explanation," Galloran replied. "Believe me that I grasp the all-too-frequent need for careful political maneuvering."

"Many eyes observed how I greeted you. I am grateful you withstood my disrespectful reception and offered such convincing reasons for me to grant admittance to you and your comrades. Your persuasiveness freed me to perform my duty correctly."

Halak strode over to Tark, parting the musician's lips with his thumbs. "Your comrade is sorely afflicted."

"The illness has evolved quickly, aggravated by strenuous travel," Galloran said.

"Trust him to our care." Halak helped Corinne down, then

handed Mandibar's reins to a woman, who led the horse away. A second woman kept a steadying hand on Tark. "Can I make the rest of you more comfortable?"

"The young women, perhaps," Galloran said. "I would rather wait until the others are safe."

"I'll wait too," Rachel put in.

"Me too," Corinne agreed.

"Very well," Halak said. "I'll be back shortly."

Rachel listened intently. The next round of explosions would come when the enemy horsemen engaged Jason and the others. She waited in agony.

The longer we hear nothing, the more likely we'll hear nothing, Galloran conveyed mentally.

Did you just read my thoughts? Rachel asked.

Once you learned to speak in silence, your mind became much more open to mine, Galloran explained.

You can't just read anyone's thought?

Only other beings who can speak in silence, like wizards or torivors. For example, I can't hear Nedwin's thoughts, nor can he hear mine, no matter how intensely I try to transmit them.

Rachel considered the idea. *But you read my mind even though I wasn't trying to speak to you.*

An ability that sets me apart from many. Of those who can hear your thoughts, most will only recognize those impressions you deliberately send.

Rachel glanced at Corinne. *We're sort of leaving your daughter out of the conversation.*

I can hear you as well, Corinne conveyed.

Yes, Galloran shared. *Corinne and I have held mental conversations ever since exiting the swamp together. Had you exerted yourself, you could have listened in.*

I frequently spoke this way with Great-Aunt Madeline, Corinne explained. *She told me this type of gift is often hereditary.*

Do you speak Edomic? Rachel asked.

Not with much power, Corinne replied. *On a good day, with a lot of effort, I can ignite a small fire. I can't do much else. But speaking in silence comes naturally.*

Halak returned. "I've had news. That was a good man you sent up the mountainside. He created enough of a rockslide to block the pass. The imperial soldiers took heavy losses. The horses couldn't cross the rubble, so those who survived tried to proceed on foot, but retreated when challenged by our horsemen."

"How is the man who scaled the wall?" Galloran asked.

"Most of our riders are waiting for him."

"Everyone is all right?" Rachel asked.

"Your comrades are on their way," Halak replied warmly.

CHAPTER **18**

THE SEVEN VALES

The soldiers at West Gate resided in tunnels chiseled into the mountainsides. Captain Halak made arrangements for a meal to be served in his personal quarters. The room where Halak escorted Jason and the others held a long, low table surrounded by twelve mats. An elegant, square storage cabinet stood against one wall. Two round windows and a few oil lamps provided light.

The polished table supported woven baskets of bread, cheese, nuts, fruit, and vegetables. Wooden bowls that held soups and sweet confections sat alongside pitchers of juice, milk, and water. After inviting his guests to help themselves, Halak departed.

"Not much furniture," Jason observed.

"The Amar Kabal value simplicity," Galloran said, "which is a powerful endorsement for the principle, considering they have spent many lifetimes determining how best to live."

"I heard they have vast caves full of treasure," Aram said.

"Any chance others are listening?" Ferrin asked.

"Halak assured me a private room," Galloran said. "He understands our need to confer."

Drake opened the cabinet door, snooping around. "That's one explanation for why he left so swiftly. He also may not wish to be accused of consulting with us. I know Halak. Not a bad man, but very careful about his interests."

"He opened the gate," Galloran pointed out.

"As I said," Drake said, closing the cabinet door, "not a bad man."

"Is their treasure a forbidden subject?" Aram asked.

"Unlike most tales of hidden wealth, that one is true," Galloran said. "The Amar Kabal keep enormous stores of food and valuables in secret caverns. They are a prudent people. The Seven Vales were chosen as a homeland, for the highly defendable geography. And fallback strongholds await the seedfolk deep in the mountains."

"Too many of my people obsess about preserving their long lives," Drake griped. "With the threat of Maldor looming, certain shortsighted leaders have preyed on our cautious natures to our detriment. If we continue to avoid confronting the emperor, we may be the last kingdom to fall, but fall we will, and Maldor will burn our seeds."

Galloran sat cross-legged on a mat. "If your people will acknowledge that reality, we might obtain the help we need."

"Good luck," Drake said. "The fruitless debate influenced my decision to stay away."

Jason sat between Rachel and Corinne. After days of grueling travel, the abundance of fresh food nearly brought tears to his eyes. He grabbed a thick slice of dark bread and took a bite. Hearty and dense, the bread was saturated with honey.

"This bread is amazing," Jason said.

"You will find no finer bread or vegetables anywhere," Galloran said.

Jason was very conscious of Corinne eating beside him. Girls that beautiful dated quarterbacks and rock stars. They weren't supposed to inhabit the real world. Despite the eagerness of his hunger, he tried to eat with his best manners.

Aram held up a long, knobby vegetable. Having bitten off the end, he scowled with displeasure. "No meat?"

"Most of my people avoid meat," Drake said. "Some will occasionally serve fish or poultry. I'm fond of a thick steak or a salty ham, but that places me in the minority."

"The Amar Kabal want their bodies lithe and strong," Galloran explained. "They also generally eschew addictive substances, including strong drink."

Aram shook his head, stirring his soup. "I can't fathom the point of living a hundred lifetimes without beef, venison, and mutton."

"I hear you," Ferrin said. "Then again, these cucumbers aren't bad."

Jason finished munching some nuts. "I heard you discussed a conclave?"

"The Amar Kabal value experience," Galloran said. "They are ruled by a gerontocracy. Their governing body, the Conclave, consists of the eldest living member of the Amar Kabal, together with the next two eldest males and the next two eldest females willing to undertake the responsibility."

"Those five leaders will decide whether the Amar Kabal will help us?" Aram checked.

"They get the final word," Drake confirmed. "But they're surrounded by counselors, and any member of the Amar Kabal is free to speak out on any topic. Our leaders listen to the people."

"We need the Amar Kabal," Galloran said. "Their women are the truest archers in Lyrian. Their men are the most proven warriors. Their commanders possess centuries of experience. And perhaps most important, if they join us, it will become much easier to recruit other nations."

"But first they must stop clinging to their neutral status," Corinne said.

"This is our problem," Galloran agreed. "The inert tend to remain inert. Passivity has been the standard for so long, it will be hard to rile the seedmen to action. When last I counseled with Pallas, eldest of the Amar Kabal, he helped me arrive at my decision to try to destroy Maldor by discovering the Key Word. The hope of a simple solution was too tempting to resist. Now the situation has changed. Our only realistic option is a coordinated rebellion against the emperor. I must awaken the Amar Kabal to the reality that their neutral status will only survive as long as it works to Maldor's advantage."

"It will be an uphill battle," Drake said. "Plenty among us have tried to raise the alarm."

"I'm still formulating my strategies," Galloran said. "But I'm in a unique position to promise outside help and to bring a fresh perspective to the discussion. And I can proclaim the Word a fraud, thereby erasing an excuse for waiting."

Drake swallowed a hunk of bread. "You realize that if you fail, there are many among our leadership who would gladly curry favor with Felrook by handing you over."

"I'm aware," Galloran said.

"In which case, we'll let Nedwin shower them with orantium," Ferrin said glibly.

"Nedwin really saved the day," Jason said.

The redhead looked uncomfortable with the praise. He rubbed his knuckles against his chest. "I got fortunate. I gambled by using the gatecrasher to start the rockslide. It blasted away more of the cliff than I could have expected. I threw the globe far, and it fell a fair distance before detonating, but I still barely hung on as the mountain quaked. I may have wasted some of the subsequent globes I threw. A dust cloud hid the bottom of the gorge."

"You gave the guards here a new chore," Drake said. "It will take some time to clear that much rubble. But I'm sure they'll find a use for the stone. We tend to be resourceful that way."

Jason sampled a dark-green fruit topped by a tuft of silky white strands. The tiny fruit tasted sweeter than pure sugar, making him cough in surprise. "What is this?"

Several around the table chuckled. Ferrin grinned. "Qualines are only meant for use as a sweetener."

Jason licked at a bit of the fruit lodged between his teeth. The pulpy fragment continued to secrete sweetness until it came loose, and he swallowed it.

"You used to come here often?" Aram asked Galloran.

"I have visited this realm three times before," Galloran said. "Once I remained for a couple of months. My other stays were shorter."

"Are the Seven Vales big?" Rachel wondered.

"Bigger than an outsider would suppose," Drake said. "The seven main valleys include Broadvale, Crookvale, Longvale, Midvale, Roundvale, Deepvale, and Farvale. There are a score of smaller offshoots from the main valleys, along with several other disconnected vales, higher in the mountains."

Galloran dabbed at his lips with a napkin. "Tomorrow we will travel to Longvale, where the Conclave convenes. The journey will consume most of the day."

"And no meat in sight," Aram grumbled. "What's wrong with these people? Those seeds have corrupted their good sense."

"Didn't you hear what Ferrin said about the delicious cucumbers?" Jason teased.

"I kept my legs moving today with the thought of a hearty roast at the end of the road," Aram sulked.

"I cannot believe you're going on like this in front of the cucumbers," Corinne chided, taking a deliberate bite of the vegetable and sharing a glance with Jason.

"Corinne, was that a joke?" Ferrin said in mock astonishment. "Welcome to the conversation!"

She flushed shyly.

"If we can expect another journey tomorrow, we should secure horses," Ferrin went on. "And if the sun will be shining, perhaps a goat for Aram."

"Keep it up," Aram dared him through clenched teeth.

"Is a goat too large and unruly?" Ferrin asked. "Maybe we could saddle a raccoon."

"Odd how these taunts tend to fade after sundown," Aram growled, taking a large bite of bread.

"But a new day always dawns," Ferrin replied. "And we can all use some entertainment."

Aram glowered. "Then perhaps tonight I should pull you apart and let the others puzzle you back together."

"That's the spirit!" Ferrin applauded. "Taunt back! I get the sense you've seldom had to deal with ridicule."

Aram appeared to be resisting a pleased little smile.

"Halak offered us accommodations for the night," Galloran said. "I suggest we claim some well-earned rest."

"Should I check on Tark?" Jason asked.

"He's in good hands," Galloran said. "And almost certainly unconscious. We'll pay him a visit in the morning."

Everyone stood. Jason stretched. Nedwin staggered, steadied himself, lowered his brow, rubbed his chest, then tipped forward onto the table. He landed without making any effort to stop his fall, his body crushing woven baskets, his face upsetting a wooden bowl of diced fruit slathered with cream.

"What happened?" Galloran asked.

"Nedwin fainted," Rachel said.

Ferrin and Drake were already rolling him off the table and onto the floor.

"Blast!" Galloran exclaimed. "Check his mouth."

Drake was already wiping cream from Nedwin's slack face and pulling his jaws apart. "Advanced lungrot," Drake reported, eyes squinting in disgust. "Worse than Tark."

"I should have known," Galloran muttered. "Somebody fetch Halak. We'll need to get Nedwin immediate treatment. Is he breathing?"

"Barely," Drake said.

"Watch him," Galloran said as Corinne and Aram hurried from the room. "He can't feel pain or many types of discomfort. He probably knew something was wrong, but failed to appreciate the severity. Or maybe he was just being stubborn."

"How could he not feel it?" Drake said. "The disease has almost taken him."

"He was a prisoner at Felrook for years," Jason said. "They experimented on him with pain enhancers. It left him permanently numbed."

A pair of seedmen rushed into the room. One quickly checked Nedwin's mouth and grimaced in revulsion. They picked him up, one supporting him under the shoulders, one by the legs.

"We'll rush him to the sicktent prepared for your comrade," one of the seedmen assured them.

As they exited the room with Nedwin, Corinne entered. "Aram is still looking for Halak. The guards we found seemed helpful."

"You did well," Galloran said. "Let's hope the treatment isn't too late."

* * *

After breakfasting on hot cereal the following morning, Jason accompanied Galloran to visit Tark and Nedwin. An unsociable man in leather armor directed them toward the gate. Unrushed, Jason got a better look at the people. They were mostly tall and serious, wearing light armor, if any. There was a tendency toward dark hair and light eyes. Some wore the unrolled portion of their hair in braids, while others let it hang free.

A few people nodded at Jason. Most went about their business: unloading provisions from a wagon, adjusting the mechanisms of a huge catapult, standing watch on the wall or on the crenellated balconies projecting from the mountainside. No one approached Jason or Galloran to make conversation.

"Why didn't we ever hear Nedwin coughing?" Jason wondered.

"I doubt he ever felt the urge," Galloran said. "Felrook left his senses damaged. He must have noticed a shortness of breath, but Nedwin is the sort to silently push through such inconveniences."

Not far from the gate, they found a small, domed tent of stitched animal hides. A flap on the tent lifted as a skinny middle-aged woman emerged, along with a billow of fumes.

"Is Tark inside?" Jason asked.

She blinked repeatedly, wringing tears from her red-rimmed eyes. "Nedwin as well. Both should recover." She spoke with a heavy accent, slurring her words. "Nedwin's fate remained questionable until after the moon set. Tark should be able to quit the treatment by tonight, Nedwin by the next day. The wounds to Tark's head were superficial. For both men, the lungrot is in full reversal."

"May we go inside?" Galloran asked.

"If you like." She smiled, showing small teeth. "You might consider holding your breath."

"Are they contagious?" Jason asked.

Galloran shook his head. "The treatment is unpleasant."

Jason raised the flap and followed Galloran into the tent, ducking through the entrance. The low ceiling forced them to remain crouched. Tark and Nedwin lay on mats spread across wooden pallets that took up most of the floor space. Jason and Galloran squatted between them. Pungent vapors swirled up from clay vessels. Tark leaned up on one elbow and smiled, both of his eyes horribly bloodshot. "Kind of you to remember me," he said before launching into a fit of coughing. He hawked up phlegm and spat into a pail.

"Good to hear you coughing again," Galloran said.

"I feel loads better," Tark agreed. "My eyes sting, though. And my mouth feels packed with cotton." He fingered his chapped lips.

Nedwin remained on his side, his breath quick and shallow, his eyes closed.

"You should be back on your feet by tomorrow night," Galloran said.

"So they tell me."

"We ride to Longvale today. I have preparations to make. A guide will bring you and Nedwin to us once you're both whole. Obey whatever instructions your caregiver offers."

"You wouldn't believe some of the remedies I've had to drink," Tark confided with a shudder.

Galloran scratched his beard. "I would. I was treated for lungrot here myself once. Do yourself the kindness of not inquiring about the ingredients."

Tark grimaced. "The treatment almost seems more violent than the ailment." He coughed again.

"Such is the price one must pay to evict airborne parasites. Has Nedwin awakened?"

"Several times," Tark said. "He's been in and out all morning."

Galloran touched Nedwin's shoulder. The freckled man sat up, red eyes blinking. "Sire, am I needed?"

"I just came to bid you adieu," Galloran said. "I'm overjoyed to hear you will recover."

"It will take more than fungi to vanquish me, sire."

"I believe it. You appear to be in competent hands. Farewell until we meet again in Longvale."

"Hope you feel better," Jason gasped. Since his first inhalation inside the tent, he had struggled to limit his breathing. Every whiff of the potent vapors made his eyes burn and the lining of his mouth tingle uncomfortably.

While Tark croaked a reply, Jason stooped out of the tent. Gulping fresh air, he held the flap aside for Galloran. The brief exposure to the heady atmosphere already had his legs feeling unsteady. He wiped tears from his cheeks.

"Back to the others?"

Galloran nodded.

Half an hour later, Jason and his companions rode down the pass on borrowed mounts into Broadvale. The expansive valley was sectioned into a patchwork of farmland nourished by an extensive irrigation system. Crops even flourished on the terraced slopes enclosing the valley, the tiered plots buttressed by retaining walls.

Cornstalks overburdened with ears rose higher than Jason as he sat astride his horse. Workers labored amid countless acres of wheat, binding the harvest into golden sheaves. Fragrant trees were assembled in long rows, limbs laden with bounteous fruitage. One field contained white pumpkins the size of Volkswagen Beetles, and huge yellow squashes contorted like bizarre, bloated sculptures.

Most of the buildings Jason observed were squat dwellings roofed with floral gardens. He also identified several windowless storage facilities. Beside a waterfall on the near side of the valley stood an enormous structure connected to a massive waterwheel.

Jason wondered if he had ever felt this refreshed. Yesterday, death had only been a few minutes behind them. Today they rode at a leisurely pace through the safest nation in Lyrian. The mat he had slept on had not been soft, but it had done the job. He had slumbered long and deep.

Beneath the warm sun, the group traversed the fertile valley at a relaxed pace. They passed a field smothered by tangled, leafy vines.

"What crop is that?" Jason asked.

"Describe it," Galloran said.

"A bunch of vines that look like they belong in a jungle."

"Those are kathoras, the most essential of all crops here. The fruit draws impurities from the soil. The vines hoard nutrients. Once the vines mature, the fruit is discarded, and the rest is plowed into the soil. Humankind has yet to discover a superior fertilizer."

The road began snaking up a rise at the far end of the valley. When they topped the slope, another spacious valley spread out before them, running a long way to the east before it seemed to turn a corner. Like Broadvale, all available land was being culti-vated, but this deeper valley also featured a large lake that mir-rored the blue sky. Fishing vessels drifted on the water, the distance reducing them to miniatures.

One switchback below Jason and his companions, a pair of riders were ascending out of Crookvale. The riders looked up. One was a young man who bore an uncanny resemblance to Jasher, except he wore a neatly trimmed beard along his jawline and had darker hair. The other was a lovely woman, her striking eyes a frosty blue.

"Galloran?" the woman called.

"Is that Farfalee?"

"You have sharp ears." She urged her mount to lope up the final switchback, and dismounted.

Galloran dropped to the ground, his broad grin creating a pair of dimples. "I did not expect to greet you until we reached Longvale."

"I couldn't wait," Farfalee said. She walked to Galloran and embraced him. Tall and slender, she was nearly his height. Her thick black hair was pulled back in intricate braids, and she wore earth-toned clothing, with an elk-hide shawl draped across her shoulders. The days of young womanhood were behind her, but her beauty had yet to fade.

"Greetings, Galloran," the young man said from astride his piebald mount.

"Could that be Lodan?"

"Yes, sir."

"He sounds like a man!"

"His First Death ceremony is only weeks away," Farfalee said. "You should attend."

"His First Death? Has it been so long? When I last saw Lodan, he came no higher than my waist."

Farfalee placed a hand on Galloran's arm. "It has been too many years." She looked up at the others in the group. "I understand one of you brought my husband's seed to East Gate."

"That would be Tark," Drake said. "He and one other of our number remain at West Gate undergoing treatment for lungrot."

Farfalee regarded Drake coolly. "Why must those who least deserve misfortune suffer the most?"

Drake gave her a wink. "What? No welcome for me?"

"I'm saving my enthusiasm for your departure," she said.

Drake shrugged. "Maybe I'll stay."

"Until you're exiled. Shouldn't take long. It's really just a formality."

"Don't fret, Failie," he said, turning and raising the hair at the nape of his neck. "You'll be rid of me soon enough."

Farfalee gasped, her hands covering her mouth. "Your amar!"

"Karma has spoken," Drake said simply.

Tears shimmered in her eyes. "Oh, Drake. I had no idea."

"What happened to it?" Lodan asked, brow steepled in concern.

"My seed failed to form correctly the last time I was reborn," Drake said. "This will be my final lifetime. I'm at peace with the notion. I'm not sure any lesser incentive could have convinced me to rejoin the living."

Farfalee plucked uncomfortably at her shawl. "Under the circumstances, I imagine I can persuade the Conclave to defer any—"

Drake laughed harshly. "You think I care how the Conclave rules about me? I'd wear exile like a badge of honor. My only concern would be if they tried to keep me here. Save your influence for cajoling those old windbags into letting our people survive."

Farfalee sighed tolerantly. "Your charm never ceases to amaze."

Jason looked at Lodan. "Jasher is your father?"

Drake slapped his forehead. "We've skipped introductions! Lodan is the son of Farfalee and Jasher. Farfalee is my eldest sister." Drake went on to introduce Jason and the others. "It was Lord Jason who helped me find the will to forsake Harthenham," he finished.

"You changed his mind about something?" Farfalee exclaimed. "Surely you must be a sorcerer."

"All I did was provide an opportunity," Jason replied. "Without Drake, we wouldn't have fought our way free."

"My brother has always been handy in a fight," Farfalee said. "The question tends to be whether he'll see it through to the end. Galloran, is it true you seek audience with the Conclave?"

"I come to discuss matters of great significance."

"Were you aware that I now sit as an elder?"

"You're one of the windbags?" Drake gasped.

She raised her eyebrows. "Jeneva abandoned the Vales, Prizette refuses to serve, and Lubella is in the ground. I have fixed your hearing for tomorrow."

"So soon?" Galloran said.

"Your arrival made waves," Farfalee explained. "We've already received a formal complaint from the emperor. To hear him tell it, you're wanted criminals who murdered a dozen guards on a bridge. Apparently we interfered with the arrest of nefarious fugitives. The message even cited a signed confession by a member of your party. A displacer, no less."

"All distortions," Galloran said. "Maldor drew first blood when he attacked my home and slew a number of my people."

Farfalee held up a hand. "Nobody gives any real credence to the charges. You and the emperor are at war. What concerns some is that the emperor is behaving as though he now has a grievance with us."

"Absurd!" Drake blustered. "The emperor was indisputably in the wrong sending troops up our pass!"

Farfalee eyed her brother. "I'm certain you can imagine his arguments. It was a small force, obviously not meant to invade the Vales, but rather to bring murderous criminals to justice. Outlaws whom we protected with our troops and whom we are now harboring. Modest imperial forces are currently encamped outside the passes to both gates. Maldor demands we turn all of you over to his representatives immediately."

"Or what?" Drake scoffed. "He'll invade? With what army? The bulk of his forces are tied up besieging Kadara! Even with the full strength of his armies behind the endeavor, he wouldn't dare attack us until the rest of Lyrian has been thoroughly cowed. He's acquainted with our defenses at the gates and along the rims of both gorges, and he can't lay siege to a self-sufficient kingdom."

"But he can openly seek to burn our seeds," Farfalee responded. "He can stop pretending to respect our strength and formally declare war."

Drake shook his head. "That day is inevitable. Why hide from it? Why not commence hostilities while his forces are divided and we might actually have a chance to harm him?"

"You know the concerns," Farfalee sighed. "The longer we have to prepare, the more likely we can endure the eventual assault. Our warriors would be much more vulnerable on offense than on defense. If the emperor wants a fight with us, he'll have to best us on a familiar battleground that we've been prepping for centuries."

Drake chuckled cynically. "The only catch being that if we have no offense, we'll never *win*."

"I wholeheartedly agree," Farfalee said. "You know I'm with you on this issue. But many among us would rather delay the confrontation for as long as possible. They imagine that our defenses could prove so strong that Maldor will ignore the Vales and content himself with governing the rest of the continent."

"Lunacy," Galloran grunted.

"Agreed," Farfalee said. "Maldor's ambition knows no bounds. He will never be content so long as the greatest threat to his rule survives."

Galloran spoke gravely. "Let him finish with the other kingdoms of Lyrian, give him time to marshal his forces, time to craft the attack of his choosing, and these Vales will burn."

Farfalee arched an eyebrow. "I take it this will be the subject of the Conclave?"

Galloran gave a nod. "After imparting some news, I intend

to argue that the Amar Kabal should terminate their treaty with Maldor and actively rebel against him."

Farfalee placed a hand on his shoulder. "Should your motion fail, your opponents among my people will seek to turn you over to the emperor."

"I understand the stakes. What are the chances of success?"

Farfalee frowned. "Unfavorable. The climate here grows ever more cautious. None wish to acknowledge the threat the emperor could pose in fifty years. Some are talking of flight."

"Preposterous!" Drake blurted. "Where would they flee? The northern hinterlands?"

"Some have suggested as much. Others have spoken of exploring the far reaches of the western ocean."

"Why not a ladder to the moon?" Drake proposed.

"Who currently serves on the Conclave?" Galloran asked.

"Pallas, Dregan, Naman, Ilestra, and myself. Be forewarned, Naman has gained serious influence, and no argument will quiet his skepticism. A majority of our citizens currently side with him. In these uncertain times, when the other kingdoms of Lyrian are either subdued or under siege, our people prefer the idea of defending familiar territory rather than sacrificing themselves abroad on a hopeless offensive."

Galloran cleared his throat. "If an offensive is indeed hopeless, such sentiments would be justified. I will endeavor to demonstrate otherwise."

"May you succeed where others have failed," Farfalee said earnestly. "An unflinching examination of how best to oppose the rising power of Felrook is long overdue."

Galloran reached for his horse. "If the Conclave intends to hear me on the morrow, we ought to keep riding."

Farfalee and Galloran returned to their mounts. As they

descended the looping path, Lodan fell in beside Jason. Once Jason explained his friendship with Jasher, Lodan insisted Jason recount all that he could remember about their time together. Jason told how the seedman had rescued him from an ambush of manglers and conscriptors. He related their travels through the Sunken Lands, including Jasher's courage battling giant toads. His tale culminated by detailing how Jasher had sacrificed his life to enable an escape from Harthenham.

Lodan absorbed the information, obviously grateful for any anecdote about the father he had not seen for years. "I envy you," he admitted once Jason had finished. "I've longed to be abroad with my father on adventures like the ones you describe."

"His seed is in the ground?"

"It was the only way he could have reentered the Vales. He should be with us in a week or so. I can hardly wait! Of course, after his rebirth, he'll be expelled again. His banishment remains in force."

"So you haven't . . . died yet?"

"This is my first lifetime. There aren't many others my age. Eldrin designed our race to become less fertile over the years. Hardly any of our women can have babies anymore."

"Farfalee mentioned your First Death," Jason said. "How does that work?"

"When I die for the first time, the physical condition of my body will become permanently sealed to my amar. Thereafter I will be reborn at exactly the same age as when I first experienced death. My memories will continue to accumulate, but my body will look the same every time. There's a big ceremony involved. I've lived nearly twenty years, the age at which most of my people choose to embrace the First Death. I've been working to build up my strength and endurance, so that ever after I'll be born in good health."

"Wow. So they'll kill you?"

"Just this body. I'll be reborn into an identical one, which will age until I perish and my seed is replanted. The First Death is necessary. It would defeat the purpose of having an amar if I lived a long life only to be reborn over and over as an old man on my deathbed."

"Makes sense," Jason said. "Do you know how much you look like your father?"

"I hear that often, especially from my mother."

They continued in silence. Jason tried to absorb the beauty around him—the smell of ripe crops in fertile soil, the splashing of a lively brook, the way cloud shadows gradually slid across the wheat fields.

They stopped for lunch at the edge of the lake. Jason sat on a rock near the water, chewing on a hunk of pumpkin bread. Corinne came and sat beside him, picking at a muffin.

"Good muffin?" Jason asked.

"I like the nuts. I can still hardly believe we made it here."

"It looked bleak." Jason motioned toward the lake with his bread. "This sure beats angry soldiers trying to kill you."

"I would take the soldiers over the swamp," Corinne said, brushing hair back from her eyes. "Even when I was exhausted and frightened we were going to die, part of me kept insisting how pleasant it was to be actually doing something."

Jason raised his eyebrows. "You must have had a serious case of boredom."

"It may sound ridiculous, but I truly felt that way." She sighed. "After all the loneliness followed by the danger, these vales feel even more heavenly."

"I'll agree with that." Jason stared at the water, groping for something winning to say. "You did well. I was impressed you could keep up."

"Why?" She seemed mildly offended.

"Because I was worn out, and I can't imagine you've had much exercise in a long time."

"More than you might think. The exercises father prescribed for me were quite rigorous, and I performed them every day."

"With your sword?"

"Mainly. Jumping, lunging, rolling, footwork patterns. You'd weep for me if you knew how much I've swung my sword at nothing. I am quite the specialist at dispatching imaginary villains."

"I bet. Show me your routine."

Her cheeks flushed as she looked over her shoulder at where the others were eating. "Not here in front of everyone."

"Why not?"

"Would you want to?"

"Good point."

"Ask me later, when I won't make such a spectacle."

"Ferrin sometimes trains me in swordplay. He's really good. You should join us."

"I'd like that."

Jason swallowed his last bite of pumpkin bread, pleased to have made a connection with Corinne. He found a flat rock and winged it sidearm out onto the water, where it took three good skips and a few small ones. Corinne grabbed a rock and imitated his throw. The stone skipped twice before plopping out of view.

Rachel came up behind them. "I vote we stay in the Seven Vales. I have a feeling I could get used to it here."

"I agree," Corinne said wistfully. "Maybe we can convince father to argue for us all to be made honorary seed people."

Jason pondered the possibility of remaining in the Seven Vales. He considered the lake, the mountains, the farmland. This was the nicest place he'd visited in Lyrian. If Galloran successfully convinced the Amar Kabal to resist Maldor, what would Jason really have to contribute? He was no general, no warrior, not even a wannabe wizard like Rachel. His role in the rebellion might be ending. If the talks went well, he, Rachel, and Corinne really could win the opportunity to wait out the war here in paradise.

"Let's hope your dad makes a good case," Jason said. "Otherwise we might get kicked out of heaven and sent straight to the alternative."

CHAPTER 19

THE
CONCLAVE

The home of Farfalee and Lodan consisted of three squat, round buildings connected by a pair of arched hallways. Bright flowers adorned the conical roofs, and grapevines thrived atop the halls.

When they had arrived the night before, Jason had missed most of the details in the darkness. He had noticed that part of the reason the buildings looked squat was because they were half underground. After following Lodan to a sleeping mat made from a corklike substance, Jason had stretched out and promptly fallen asleep.

Today, with the sun rising, Jason waited beside an irrigation trench to one side of the house. Freestanding trellises laced with leafy limbs stood around the yard in unusual formations, some cylindrical, others boxy, a few shaped like thick crosses, and a couple curving into spheres. They all bore fruit of varying shapes and sizes.

Lodan had roused him early, asking if he wanted to train. Secretly Jason had wanted more sleep, and was worried that Lodan would easily outclass him sparring with swords, but pride had prevented him from expressing either of those concerns. So here he stood.

Lodan came into view pulling a handcart. Ferrin and Corinne trailed behind him. The foursome gathered in a recently cleared field, and Lodan produced four wooden practice swords, balanced to perfection. They all put on padded tunics, thick gloves, and leather helmets affixed to wire masks. Jason felt both excited and intimidated to try mock combat with the elaborate practice gear.

"Jason tells me you have been performing exercises with your sword for years," Ferrin said to Corinne. "Show us an example."

Corinne shot Jason a vengeful glance. She assumed a stance on the balls of her feet, holding the wooden sword poised, then began an elaborate routine, springing forward, shuffling back, wielding the weapon defensively and offensively, darting laterally, and occasionally rolling only to spring back into a balanced stance. Jason was impressed, especially considering she was wearing a lot of unfamiliar gear that should have disrupted her equilibrium.

She finished with a lunging thrust. "That should give you a general idea," she said. "I always vary the combinations and improvise moves of my own."

"I'm impressed," Ferrin said. "You have solid fundamentals. I saw evidence of practiced footwork and graceful balance. You demonstrated a fluid command of your weapon. Your next step is to employ those skills against another combatant."

"I have often wondered how that would feel," she said.

"Let's find out," Ferrin replied. "Come at me. Focus on offense."

She nodded and charged forward, mounting a spirited assault that kept Ferrin moving backward. Slowly retreating, he blocked her blows, and occasionally tapped her tunic with his sword to show where she was leaving herself open.

"Enough," he finally said. "You have never faced an opponent?"

"Only in my imagination."

"You either have a superlative imagination or else swordsmanship is inheritable. I'm curious. Prepare to defend yourself."

Ferrin launched a vigorous attack, and the wooden swords clacked fiercely. Corinne held her ground at first, then faded back. After some time, Ferrin managed to touch the tip of his sword to her chest a couple times. He patted her on the thigh. Suddenly he lunged, and Corinne spun, deflecting his thrust, and whacked him on the side.

Ferrin stepped back, lifting off his helmet. "That was a trap!"

"You were falling into a pattern," she said.

"You shouldn't be this proficient."

Corinne took off her helmet, grinning, her hair matted. "Truly?"

"I have never seen such natural talent," Ferrin said, shaking his head.

"I may not have had opponents," she said, "but my sword has provided my only recreation for years."

Ferrin turned to Lodan. "What did you think?"

"I think she could give me trouble," he replied.

"Work with her while I spar with Jason. You noticed when she was overswinging?"

"Yes."

"And when she was sneaking in too close?"

"And when she was leaving her left side exposed."

"Good eye. Make the corrections, and then have some fun."

Corinne and Lodan moved away.

Ferrin and Jason sparred as the sun rose higher in the sky. The first hour was straight combat. During the second hour, Ferrin showed Jason some dirty tricks desperate opponents might attempt.

Ferrin prepared him for foes who might toss sand, throw a knife, sneak in a kick, or use a number of simple but slippery feints.

By the time Jason finished, his lungs were burning and his clothes were drenched. But he felt more confident about his swordsmanship. The protective gear allowed for a much more authentic combat simulation, and he was beginning to grasp the practical application of many of the drills Ferrin had insisted he endlessly perform.

Lodan appeared with the handcart to collect the gear.

"How'd it go with Corinne?" Jason asked.

"She performed remarkably," Lodan said. "Until Mother saw us. She insisted we quit so Corinne could start getting ready for the Conclave. Between the two of us, I think Mother was more concerned about me bruising a foreign princess with a wooden sword."

"Everybody should get to clobber a princess at least once," Jason said. "What now?"

"Time to wash up."

Rachel sat alone, her back against an earthen storage bunker across the yard from Farfalee's house. From three sides the bunker looked like a grassy hillock, but the side facing away from the house contained a heavy wooden door.

Speaking Edomic, Rachel lifted a stone the size of her head into the air. She held it there for some time, her will and focus constant, occasionally muttering phrases to raise it higher or lower. It was a strengthening exercise Chandra had taught her. This stone was one of the heavier objects she had tried to hold steady, but it felt within her limits.

She was already dressed for the Conclave, her formal robes loose in the arms and legs, but more fitted in the shoulders and waist. Artfully embroidered, the outfit looked fancy while remaining very comfortable. The soft moccasins on her feet were the comfiest footwear she had ever worn.

A phrase made the heavy rock rotate briskly. Another phrase made it stop. A third phrase turned it to glass. A final phrase, accompanied by a fierce jolt of willpower, shattered the vitrified rock, scattering angular shards in a cone-shaped spray. The power she had focused and released left her momentarily breathless.

As the pleasurable rush subsided, Rachel felt quiet contentment at the successful series of commands. She was improving daily—gaining strength, deepening her concentration, and discovering new ways to combine phrases.

The words Orruck had taught her for the summoning of lightning flickered through her mind. She had not yet tried to carry out the command, but she had often repeated the words internally, examining them. The language called for massive opposing charges, which would then become linked by a bolt of lightning. To cast the spell, she would have to pick two objects to charge. She wished she could figure out how to describe minor opposing charges, so she could attempt the spell on a smaller scale.

None of the other phrases she knew described the scope of the desired effect. The fire phrase, for example, just called to heat. It never specified how much heat. The quantity of heat summoned only varied based on what she was trying to accomplish and how much will she put into the effort. She could not figure out how to extract the Edomic equivalent of "massive" from the lightning phrase. For that matter, she couldn't figure out how to add "massive" to the heat-summoning phrase. In Edomic, the words wove together in such a way that they often became difficult to untangle or rephrase. Combining commands was not too hard. Changing the phrasing got very slippery.

"Rachel!" Jason called, interrupting her reverie.

"I'm here!" she answered, standing and walking around the storage bunker. He stood beside an arching trellis of purple fruit, looking handsome in his robes. Apparently he had bathed after banging swords with Ferrin all morning. She crossed toward him.

"What's behind the mound?" Jason asked.

"It's a storage room."

He lowered his voice. "Steal anything good?"

She reached him just in time to punch him on the arm. "Right, I was stealing stuff from our hosts."

"Then what were you doing back there? They have an out-house, you know."

"Ew, sicko. I was practicing Edomic."

"Sure you were," Jason said. "You're just too embarrassed to admit you were playing hide-and-seek all alone. Rachel hiding, nobody seeking."

"You got me," she said. "It's a homeschool thing. We make our own fun."

"They said the meeting starts at noon, and we're riding there in a wagon."

"You mean the conclave?"

"I thought the Conclave was the group."

"The group is called the Conclave, and when they preside over a meeting, it's also called a conclave. I asked Farfalee."

"Lazy," Jason complained. He spoke in a mocking voice. "The Conclave is having a conclave. It should be really conclave." He shook his head. "They should call the meeting something else."

"Like what?"

He shrugged. "A jamboree."

"Slip that one into the suggestion box."

Rachel and Jason found the others waiting in a large, open wagon on the far side of the house. It was the sort of vehicle people back home might have used for hayrides. Rachel felt a little awkward once she saw that the others were ready and waiting. She must have really lost track of time.

"Sorry," Rachel said, climbing into the bed of the wagon.

"No apologies required," Galloran said. "I felt you issuing some potent commands. Such dedication to your talent is commendable. I waited until the last moment to send Jason to fetch you."

Lodan and Farfalee sat up front. Lodan snapped the reins and the team tugged the wagon forward.

They all wore dressy robes. Rachel wondered how they had scrounged enough for everyone. Corinne looked especially gorgeous, her hair woven into elaborate braids. If that girl ever made it to America, she was a supermodel waiting to happen. No surprise that Jason found her so interesting.

"Everyone looks really official," Rachel commented over the clatter of the wagon.

"It was tricky to outfit Aram," Ferrin said. "Fortunately, Farfalee had kept some apparel from Lodan's infancy."

"Keep it up," Aram dared him.

Ferrin grinned. "Or perhaps she borrowed the robes from a doll."

"Do us all a favor and toss your mouth overboard," Aram replied.

"Not bad," Ferrin said. "You just earned a truce."

"Only until the sun goes down," Aram grumbled.

Rachel sat silently, enjoying the cool breeze, the bright sun, and the pleasant countryside. She wondered idly why they didn't see more people on the road. Aside from their wagon, the day seemed very still.

She got her answer when they arrived at their destination. The Conclave met in a large amphitheater between five hills. The oval depression descended one concentric ring at a time, forming a bowl large enough to seat thousands. Not only was the sunken amphitheater crammed with seedfolk, but the surrounding hillsides were thronged as well. Nobody had been on the road, because they were already at the conclave!

"I hope we have reserved seats," Jason said, voicing her thoughts.

"We'll sit up close," Galloran said. "How glad we are to be there will depend on how the Conclave rules."

Lodan remained with the wagon while the others disembarked. Farfalee led them down a long stairway to the bottom of the amphitheater. Galloran kept one hand on Dorsio's shoulder. Rachel watched the crowd, men and women clad in robes, not many of them beyond middle age. She only spotted one possible teenager, a girl with light brown hair. Nobody looked younger.

As members of the crowd took notice of the procession marching down the stairs, they became quiet. Rachel felt the weight of thousands of eyes staring her way.

At the bottom of the huge bowl, three men and one young girl sat at a bulky stone table surrounded by a flat, open area. There was clearly room at the table for a fifth person.

"Who's the little girl?" Jason asked.

"Ilestra, the eldest surviving seedwoman," Farfalee said. "Her First Death happened by accident at age seven. Her latest rebirth occurred only a year ago."

After the stairs ended, Farfalee gestured toward an empty bench situated front and center. Rachel filed over with the others as Farfalee claimed her seat with the Conclave.

A strapping man with his hair twined in a pair of long braids arose off a bench and strode to a position to one side of the stone table. He was meatier than the typical seedman, and spoke in a strident voice.

"By order of the Conclave, five speaking as one, this emergency conclave is now in session. Galloran, son of Dromidus, will be the sole petitioner. Naman of the Conclave has elected to personally serve as rebutter."

A murmur rippled through the onlookers.

The heavyset seedman glanced over his shoulder. The man seated at the center of the table dipped his head. The speaker turned and announced. "The Conclave recognizes Galloran." He withdrew and sat down.

Dorsio guided Galloran to the position vacated by the speaker, then stepped back a few paces. "Forgive my voice," Galloran said, raising it as best he could. "I inhaled an acidic concoction some years back, and it has never been the same."

He sounded plenty loud to Rachel. The audience was silent, and the space seemed to have good acoustics, which helped. Craning her neck to look upward, she figured the crowds on the neighboring hillsides were out of luck.

"I am honored to be back among the Amar Kabal and to stand before this illustrious Conclave," Galloran began.

"We are delighted to see you again," said the seedman in the center, a handsome man with dark-gray eyes and a slightly crooked nose. "Diverse rumors have circulated concerning your fate. We feared you had met your end in the dungeons of Felrook."

"My mind and body were maimed in those dungeons," Galloran said. "But I was eventually released. It has required some time and effort to become functional again."

"What brings you before the Conclave?" the seedman asked.

"I wish for the Amar Kabal to reconsider their current relationship with Maldor. I want to urge your people to support a rebellion."

Murmured reactions percolated through the assemblage. The seedman at the left end of the table stood. Tall and trim with rather wide shoulders, he wore his black hair in a topknot. He had a high forehead, sunken cheeks, and a broad mouth. "We expected this request." He strode around the table to stand opposite Galloran, separated by several paces. "This debate has been settled for some time, unless you have new information to contribute."

"I have a proposal you may not have considered," Galloran said. "And yes, Naman, I also bring new information that could impact your current stance. Pallas, you may recall discussing a particular word with me some years ago."

The seedman seated at the center of the table nodded. "Those specifics may need to remain private."

"No longer," Galloran said. "There has long been a rumor of an Edomic key word that could destroy Maldor. Supposedly the Word had been created by Zokar to keep his dangerous apprentice in check. As it turns out, both myself and my friend Lord Jason, a Beyonder, succeeded in obtaining this key word and speaking it to Maldor. The Word had no effect. It was a fraud."

Garbled commentary arose from the crowd.

"Order!" Pallas called. The onlookers went silent immediately. "No doubt some here have heard of the rumored Word. Most are probably learning of it for the first time. Some, myself included, have harbored a quiet hope that one day this Word would undo the emperor. Is it wise to mention this Word in public?" The question held reprimanding overtones.

"This false Word has diverted the efforts of many," Galloran said. "Some of the best blood in Lyrian has been spilled searching for it. All along, Maldor had been using the quest for the Word to stall traditional opposition and waste the efforts of his most ardent enemies. As soon as Jason confirmed that the Word was fraudulent, Maldor began slaying those who had guarded the individual syllables. Once the emperor made that move, I decided it was time to publicly debunk the myth, lest any more effort be wasted."

"Understandable," Naman said. "This is news, indeed, and you paid a grievous price to secure this information. But consider the reasoning behind our attitude toward Felrook. We have assessed that an offensive against the emperor would be doomed to failure. Therefore, preparing our defenses became the only acceptable policy. If the Word is false, Maldor is even less vulnerable than we had supposed, which only serves to support our current stance."

All eyes at the table turned to Galloran.

"That is one way to interpret the news," Galloran acknowledged. "The main reason most kingdoms have avoided open conflict with Maldor is because they do not believe he can be beaten. Many have surrendered to him without a fight. His conquest of Lyrian has only been slowed by kingdoms like Belaria, Hindor, Meridon, and now Kadara, which have elected to defend their borders. The former three kingdoms I mentioned have all fallen, just as Kadara will fall before next year is through.

"As most of you know, I hail from Trensicourt. My father was king. Like the Amar Kabal, Trensicourt hesitated to go to war with Felrook largely because we did not believe that Maldor could be defeated. Part of the justification for our hesitation derived from the hope that the Word provided. In our highest councils, the Word was viewed as a possible alternative to widespread bloodshed. Had we known the Word was false, we would have accepted that the only remaining course of action would have been to unite the remaining free kingdoms and stand against the emperor."

Naman folded his arms. "We of the Amar Kabal have no intention of kneeling to the emperor. We know that Maldor despises and fears us more than any nation in Lyrian. We understand that there will never be true peace between us. And we realize that our best chance of resisting Maldor is to force him to bring the war to our gates. We continue to fortify our defenses, knowing that only by repelling his armies will we endure as a people."

Galloran frowned. "Do you honestly believe the defenses of the Seven Vales can withstand the emperor once the rest of Lyrian has fallen?"

"I would like to think that with proper planning and vigilance, we could hold out for many lifetimes. This is our best hope."

"You evaded my question," Galloran said. "Consider the history of your enemy. Consider his resources. Consider his motivation. Do you honestly believe that you can indefinitely keep the emperor out of these Vales?"

Naman pressed his large lips together. "Our defenses will eventually fail." Some utterances of dismay arose from the gathered multitude. Naman held up a finger. "But if they must resort to an assault on our homeland, our enemies will pay much more dearly to take our lives than if we participate in a desperate offensive abroad."

"The Vales will eventually fall," Galloran summarized. "Do you suppose that you can run?"

"For a time," Naman replied. "We have fallbacks prepared."

"I agree that you could retreat for a time. Do you imagine that you could run to a place where Maldor will not follow?"

"No," Naman said. "We might prolong our existence for many lifetimes, but in the end, we will perish. Some talk of fleeing over the sea, but within twenty years Maldor will have massive fleets on both coasts."

"*Many lifetimes* suggests a very optimistic time frame," Galloran said. "The emperor will not relent until all of Lyrian is secure. Barring collaborative opposition, you and the drinlings will be the last free people in Lyrian within five years. Rooting out the drinlings will take time, but Maldor will succeed. He will then spend some years mustering his strength, laying plans. By my most optimistic assessment, within twenty years Maldor will attack the Vales from the north and the south simultaneously. In the north he will merely cut off your retreat; from the south he will storm your gates. He will not fight fairly. He will show no mercy. You will die alone and cornered. Some of you will be tortured. Some will be examined. Maldor is curious to study how you were made. In the end, your seeds will burn."

A boisterous outburst from the assemblage made Rachel cover her ears. Apparently the notion of dying permanently did not sit well with the audience. It took Pallas some effort to restore order.

"These are vile prospects to consider," Pallas recognized, once he could be heard, "but such are the times in which we live."

"I have heard your assessment," Naman said reasonably. "I have answered your questions candidly. Now show me equal courtesy. With the present resources the free kingdoms have at their disposal, is it possible to mount an offensive against the emperor with any reasonable expectation of success?"

Galloran straightened. "I don't know."

The crowd reacted raucously. Again Pallas called for silence.

"I find myself wondering why we convened this conclave," Naman said, earning a chuckle from the onlookers.

"I believe there is hope for a successful offensive, or I would not have traveled here," Galloran explained. "Nevertheless, I do not intend to lead the free people of Lyrian to a hasty demise on a hopeless campaign. I do not desire to spend your lives casually. Without a truly viable offensive strategy, I would rather you died defending your homes. My concern is that if we never take the offensive, there is no chance we can win."

"What are you here to propose?" Pallas asked.

"We have a small window of opportunity while the armies of

Maldor toil in the east against Kadara. His forces have simultaneously besieged their three largest cities, which entails a massive
commitment of resources. I am the heir to Trensicourt. I am ready
to regain my kingdom and to lead a rebellion. I have come into
possession of a vast new stockpile of orantium. I cannot divulge
the location publicly, but in private I will share the whereabouts of
hundreds of globes, including a score of the larger spheres known
as gatecrashers."

This earned an excited buzz from the crowd.

"I believe we can also enlist the drinlings. They only fell out
of the war after Kadara abused them. I expect we can also arouse
Meridon. My sources there report that Maldor does not have a
strong enough presence to suppress a revolt."

"Assuming all of this is true," Naman said, "how does it amount
to sufficient power to combat the emperor? He has the resources of
more than twenty kingdoms at his disposal. Not to mention the
displacers, the manglers, the giants, and the torivors."

"I do not imagine we could stand against his full might,"
Galloran said. "We would have to outmaneuver him. Fight the
battles we can win. Earn victory one step at a time."

"Such tactics could yield modest success in the short term,"
Naman allowed. "But once the emperor has dealt with Kadara and
brings his full strength against us, we would fall."

"We could fall," Galloran admitted. "But embracing any other
strategy makes our doom certain."

Naman shook his head. "Not only will we fall just as certainly
if we pursue an offensive like you describe, we will fall sooner than
with any other tactic. Our nation applauds your motives. For years
the citizens of Trensicourt have tacitly followed the orders of imperial puppets. We would welcome them to openly resist the emperor.
And we would rejoice to add orantium to our defensive stores.

But we have no need for that breed of heroism that only hastens destruction."

"You foresee absolutely no hope for a successful offensive," Galloran said. "This is the problem?"

"Correct," Naman replied.

"Do you or any among the Amar Kabal profess the gift of prophecy?"

"Not prophecy. But we have centuries of experience with observation and reason."

"I have a proposal," Galloran stated. "There remains a living oracle in Lyrian. The true gift of prescience survives in the Temple of Mianamon. Why not consult the oracle to see if a combined offensive could succeed? Get a definitive word on the matter? If the oracle foresees no possibility of success, I will wholly support your defensive posture. In fact, I will adopt the same philosophy with Trensicourt."

The amphitheater was silent. All eyes regarded Naman.

"I have no particular objection to consulting the oracle," Naman finally ventured. "Yet you came here with imperial troops in pursuit, Galloran. You have been informed that the emperor has demanded we release you and your comrades into his custody. A cynical man might call your desire to appeal to the oracle an effort to postpone the apprehension of your friends."

Galloran's posture changed, as if getting ready for a fistfight. Even without eyes, his expression hardened. "Would you turn me over to Maldor, Naman? Would you hand him my daughter?"

"We might consider handing over the displacer in your company," Naman replied accusingly.

The crowd gasped.

"The displacer Ferrin betrayed Felrook to join the rebellion," Galloran affirmed. "To prove his sincerity he gave me a chunk of his neck, which I could use to dispose of him at my whim. I heartily vouch for the loyalty of all in my party. Otherwise I would not have brought them here."

"You chose a poor hour to test our hospitality," Naman said. "You knew what signals your presence would send. You knew that our relations with Felrook have never been more tenuous."

"Your relations become more tenous as Maldor fears you less. Obviously, he fears my presence here. Why else would he show such interest? Naman, my understanding is that you control the military."

"I serve as High Commander."

"Then, as a military expert, please demonstrate a single instance when Maldor has respected weakness." Galloran paused, but Naman offered no response. "If you can, name one occasion where bowing to his will forestalled invasion or yielded any measurable benefit?"

"When has provoking the emperor led to prosperity?" Naman countered.

"Ask Drake, or any man in Harthenham," Galloran growled. "I can identify many who have gained respect or reward for defying the emperor. Unless you mean to surrender, it is the only sane course. Those who treat Maldor as an honest and reasonable adversary soon discover that he is neither. If you are so afraid of Felrook that you close your gates to friends and scurry to obey imperial mandates, your cause is already lost. You spoke of Trensicourt as being run by imperial puppets. Who is pulling your strings here in the Vales? Imperial forces defied your treaty by chasing us across forbidden neutral territory, and you react how? With apologies? Those same forces remain camped outside of your passes unchallenged. You lead your military? A cynical man might label you a coward."

Naman stiffened. "No one degrades my honor!" he thundered. "If you had eyes, I would challenge you this instant!"

Galloran faced him silently. The tension of the moment had Rachel wringing her fingers. Galloran drew his sword, the blade gleaming brilliantly in the sunlight. He did not speak loudly. "If naming your deeds sullies your honor, perhaps I'm not the man to blame. I need no eyes to crush a cockroach. I accept your challenge."

Naman looked off-balance. "Don't be ridiculous. Striking down a blind opponent will bring me no satisfaction."

Galloran strode toward him, sword held ready. "When you speak of duels to a king in public, you had best have a weapon ready."

"This is madness," Naman protested, looking to Pallas.

Pallas rose. "Must this escalate to violence?"

Galloran stopped directly in front of the stone table. "I was not the first to mention a challenge."

"Very well," Naman said. "You insist too fervently. If you desire to meet your end with a sword in hand, I will oblige."

"You don't foresee me emerging victorious?" Galloran asked.

"No, and if you expect that outcome, your judgment is far more corrupted than I had suspected."

"We have plenty of witnesses present," Galloran said. "Sufficient space. Have you a sword?"

Naman drew a sword from beneath his robes. "Nothing so fine as yours, but I stand ready." His gray blade looked a little longer than the torivorian weapon.

Drake arose. "Let me stand in for Galloran," he declared. "Even if he had eyes, I would not sit by and allow a man of his stature to cross swords with one of our people."

Naman sized up Drake with a smirk. "I'm willing."

"I am not," Galloran said. "I fight my own duels. There are more senses than sight."

"Please, Your Majesty," Drake implored. "Do me this honor."

"I appreciate the gesture," Galloran said. "Be seated."

Drake plopped down beside Rachel. "Naman is an accomplished swordsman," he muttered. "This can't end well."

Rachel felt words in her mind. *Keep your eyes on the fight, especially on Naman. You must serve as my eyes.*

Galloran assumed a fighting stance. "Would you be so kind, Pallas?"

"Begin," Pallas said solemnly.

Rachel tried not to blink. How well could he use her eyes? Was it possible for Galloran to fight effectively while only viewing himself and his opponent from off to the side? She could not imagine how he would stay oriented.

Focus on opening your mind to me, Galloran conveyed in response. *Corinne will be doing the same.*

Rachel exerted her will, attempting to send everything she saw toward Galloran's mind.

"Win or lose, this duel will not resolve your problems," Naman warned, slowly approaching Galloran. "The current quarrel is between the two of us."

"Should I fall, I trust Lord Jason to speak on behalf of our cause," Galloran said.

Naman extended his sword probingly and Galloran knocked it aside. Naman moved in, slashing aggressively, and the swords clashed, ringing almost musically. Galloran pivoted so that his back was mostly to Rachel, but on a diagonal, so his body didn't impede a view of Naman. Galloran deflected another fierce sequence of blows.

"How are you doing that?" Naman asked, backing off. "Are you truly blind?"

Galloran cast aside his blindfold in reply.

Their blades met again, and Galloran's sword became a blur. Naman paced backward sloppily, struggling to hold off the onslaught. Rachel could see fear and disbelief in Naman's eyes. Then Galloran lopped off his sword hand and impaled the seedman without hesitation.

Galloran withdrew his sword, and Naman fell to his knees, his expression bewildered, one hand over his punctured chest. The seedman tipped onto his side.

Rachel stared up at the crowd. Most faces gaped in astonishment. Some people shifted uncomfortably. The only voices spoke in whispers.

Thank you, Galloran sent to Rachel. *Well done.* She could sense weariness behind his psychic message. There was a slight tremble in his hand as he wiped his sleeve across his forehead. He looked pallid and winded. She realized that the effort of seeing through her eyes must have required much more energy and willpower than mentally exchanging words. She wondered how apparent it was to the other bystanders how greatly the endeavor had taxed him. Galloran was doing his best to disguise his fatigue.

Galloran sheathed his sword. "Dorsio, please fetch his seed and place it on the table." He raised his voice. "As you all know, Naman is not truly gone. He'll be younger and stronger a couple of months from now. I regret the interruption. We'll need a new rebutter."

Drake chuckled softly, covering his grin with one hand. He spoke in hushed wonder. "I've never seen a man fight like that. Such economy of motion. It was over the instant Galloran attacked. Imagine if he could see!"

The four seed people at the stone table conversed privately. Finally Pallas addressed Galloran. "I will rebut. Although not without trepidation."

The crowd laughed uneasily.

Dorsio placed Naman's seed on the table and returned the fallen blindfold to Galloran, who covered his gaping sockets. He already looked more steady than immediately following the duel. Pallas walked to where Naman had stood previously.

"Where were we?" Pallas asked.

"I believe Naman was insinuating we hand over my daughter to the emperor," Galloran said flatly.

"I do not envision us handing anyone over to Maldor," Pallas said. "All other considerations aside, it is true that letting him flout our treaties and issue mandates will only reduce his respect for us. We may have begun to lose sight of that truth. Galloran is a sworn friend of our people. I move that our guests should enjoy our full protection. Unless there are any dissenters?" He looked first to the rest of the Conclave and then scanned the audience. Nobody volunteered a complaint. Rachel felt herself relax a bit.

"Is the vote unanimous?" Pallas asked the Conclave.

Three voices responded, "Aye."

Pallas nodded. "So be it. Galloran, I wish to explore your proposal regarding the prophetess."

"Naman was quick to dismiss the possibility of me besting him in a duel," Galloran said. "Yet there he lies. I imagine that most present would also doubt the feasibility of vanquishing the menace who lurks in the Drowned City."

The suggestion caused an incredulous outburst.

Galloran raised his hands until the overlapping comments subsided. "I can hear the disbelief. Rachel, would you stand up?"

Rachel complied, keeping her eyes on Galloran, trying not to think about the soaring rows of seed people all around her. "This young woman is a Beyonder and an Edomic adept. She slew the menace this week. You will now find the Drowned City deserted."

The subsequent uproar sounded more skeptical than pleased.

"Believe me or not, when you investigate, my words will be confirmed," Galloran said. "My point is that although an offensive would certainly be risky, we would be foolish to utterly ignore the option. Victory has occurred against difficult odds before. In our present circumstances, defense can delay, but it cannot prevail. The oracle at Mianamon has been reliable for centuries. Why not send a delegation to investigate whether an offensive could succeed? If it can, we plan an attack. If it can't, we concentrate with full purpose on prolonging the inevitable."

"This delegation would have to include seedfolk," Pallas said.

"Naturally," Galloran assented. "The delegation should arrive in six or seven weeks. You could start sending eagles to Mianamon for a response at that point."

"It will not be easy for a delegation to reach the destination," Pallas observed.

"The prophetess can only read the futures of those present," Galloran stressed.

"I understand, but how do you propose they get there? The emperor will be watching our passes."

"The emperor has unfinished business with me," Galloran said. "You need to discuss the status of your treaty. We will journey to Felrook together on a diplomatic mission. That should prevent men from accusing me of coming here to hide. It will also help preserve the illusion that your people are willing to bargain with Maldor. Besides, my presence would only hinder the delegation to Mianamon, given the road they must travel."

"And which road is that?" Pallas asked.

"There are other ways out of these Vales besides the passes," Galloran said. "The details should be contemplated in private."

"I'm amenable to this course of action," Pallas said. "Our current strategy is founded on the proposition that an offensive would be ineffective. With our survival in the balance, we would be wise to verify that premise."

"Do you need to add a member to the Conclave for the vote?" Galloran asked.

"Not if three or more agree," Pallas said.

All four approved the proposal.

CHAPTER 20

THE DELEGATION

The following evening, Jason sat between Nedwin and Tark, using flatbread to scoop various mashed preparations from wooden bowls. Since the bowls were communal, everyone tore the dense bread to create one mouthful at a time. Each time he dipped the bread, a twinge of pain reminded Jason that his index finger remained bruised and swollen after a practice duel with Lodan earlier in the day. Tark seemed to eat without enthusiasm, but Nedwin gulped down food, as if the lungrot and his stay in the sicktent had never happened.

"You should try the purple stuff," Jason suggested to Tark. "It's sweet and nutty."

Tark held up a hand. "Ever since the treatment, everything has a foul aftertaste. Even water." He smacked his lips discontentedly. "It's unfortunate."

"I don't mind it," Nedwin said, shoveling a large bite of flatbread and orange mush into his mouth. "Twists the flavor a little."

Tark grimaced. "It's more like a glimpse of how the food would taste after it spoiled."

345

Nedwin shrugged. "I'm not a reliable judge. Nothing has tasted quite right since Felrook—different shades of bland."

"That's too bad," Corinne said. "The food is delicious." She had a smudge of purple goo on the corner of her mouth.

"Renetta told me the aftertaste would fade after a week or so," Tark added.

"I'm surprised how pleasant it is to sample dishes from my homeland again," Drake said, motioning for Corinne to dab her lips. She did so with a blush. "For all the variety represented at Harthenham, we seldom got fare like this."

"I'll wager they fed you meat," Aram grumbled, his voice deep now that the sun was down.

"From the common to the exotic," Drake confirmed. "Have you ever tried ground sloth? Wonchut? Horned shark?"

"Don't torture me," Aram said. "At this point, I'd settle for chipmunk."

"Speaking of the Eternal Feast," Nedwin said, voice halting, eyes remote, "did you ever encounter Tristan, the former Earl of Geer?"

"I remember Tristan well," Drake said, sharing a glance with Jason. Now that Jason thought about it, if Nedwin packed on about eighty pounds, he would look a lot like the husky nobleman who had tried to escape with them.

Nedwin bowed his head, drumming the fingers of one hand against his hairline. "Then the rumors were true. When I was held in Trensicourt, Copernum claimed that my brother had challenged him for the chancellorship and had lost. I sought him after my release, but heard he had accepted an invitation to Harthenham. I never imagined him surrendering."

"He died helping us escape," Jason said softly.

"What?" Nedwin asked, blinking.

"He came with us, but didn't make it. He fell in battle." Jason thought it best not to add that he had been savaged by a pack of fierce dogs.

Nedwin smiled and made a choked sound that was half sob, half laugh. He wiped his eyes. "He met his end bravely?"

"Helped save us all," Drake confirmed. "He died with blood on his sword."

"That's a weight off me," Nedwin said, eyes moist. "Tristan always valued his honor. He taught me the meaning of the word. I'm relieved that he regained some of it before the end. I'm glad I brought it up. I'd been afraid to ask."

Jason found himself clenching his jaw to resist tears. He was thankful the tidings seemed to gladden Nedwin rather than depress him. Nedwin had suffered much more than his fair share.

Wiping her mouth with a napkin, Rachel stood. "Come on," she said to Jason.

"What?" Jason asked.

"Galloran's back," she said. "He needs to speak to us."

A door opened, and Farfalee entered. She, Galloran, and Dorsio had left earlier in the day to confer with Pallas and the other members of the Conclave. "Jason?" Farfalee summoned. "Rachel?"

Jason followed Farfalee and Rachel into an arched hallway.

"I'm thinking of a number," Jason said.

"It doesn't work that way," Rachel sighed.

"Come on. It's between one and five."

"Two?"

"Pi."

Rachel rolled her eyes. "I can only read minds close to my intelligence."

"Oh. Like clams? Inchworms? Bread mold?"

"More like wizards, torivors, and supercomputers."

Farfalee led them to a door and entered with them.

"I didn't mean pie like you eat," Jason explained. "I meant pi like the number."

"I get it," Rachel said. "I was calculating the area of circles in second grade."

"I wasn't," Jason admitted. "I was playing with friends."

Galloran cleared his throat. He sat on a mat behind a table, Dorsio at one side, a grim seedman on the other, his dark hair trimmed rather short except for the roll at the nape of his neck. They all wore robes somewhat dusty from recent travel.

Jason glanced at Rachel. "Galloran says you shouldn't joke about my intellect or it might swallow yours whole."

"Now you're hearing his thoughts too?" Rachel replied.

Jason gave a small shrug. "Galloran says don't be jealous, but we've been using telepathy since our first meeting. Right, Your Majesty?"

"Jason and I share a quieter understanding," Galloran said diplomatically. "Please, sit; we have much to discuss. This is Sakar, a friend of Jasher and Farfalee."

Sakar nodded a greeting.

Jason and Rachel sat on mats across from Galloran. Farfalee occupied a mat at the side of the low table.

"You met with the Conclave?" Rachel asked.

"Indeed," Galloran said. "The delegation to Mianamon will depart the morning after tomorrow."

"You want us to go," Jason said. Why else would Galloran have singled them out for a conversation?

"No," Galloran said. "You have already sacrificed so much for the sake of Lyrian. The trip to Mianamon will be dangerous, and if successful, the journey will only lead to more peril. This request has nothing to do with my wants. Only our need."

"So you need us to go," Rachel said.

Galloran sighed heavily. "My hopes that an offensive could be successful largely rest on the fact that the oracle of Mianamon summoned you from the Beyond to aid our world. She must have seen your involvement making a vital difference. Since you've already contributed more than I could have dreamed, your roles in our struggle might be complete. However, if the oracle truly foresaw a chance for victory, I suspect your involvement may remain integral to our success. The only way to know for certain will be to bring you before her."

"You told Pallas that the oracle can only see the futures of those present," Jason said.

"Those are certainly the futures the oracle can see most clearly," Galloran confirmed. "For that reason, members of the Amar Kabal should be in attendance, as should some drinlings, as well as any others who may play a key role in the rebellion."

"What if we find out that our roles are finished?" Rachel wondered.

"Then I'll do everything in my power to shield you from the upcoming hostilities," Galloran said.

"Won't you need to be there?" Jason asked. "Your role might be the most crucial."

Galloran nodded. "For that reason, after my diplomatic mission to Felrook, I will seek to rejoin you at the Last Inn, the southernmost outpost before the jungle. In case I fail to arrive, Corinne will have to join your delegation, prepared to fill my role in my absence. As the last true heir to Trensicourt, she should be able to rally the kingdom under her leadership, if necessary."

Jason could tell that Galloran didn't relish the thought of that responsibility falling to his daughter. "Why are you going to Felrook at all? It seems too dangerous."

"Partly to satisfy the Amar Kabal," Galloran said. "My presence will reduce the appearance that they are trying to secretly harbor fugitives. I'll share in their diplomatic immunity, and consequently I do not expect Maldor to move openly against me. He does not yet crave a war with the People of the Seed. I believe this will be the safest way for a blind man to escape the Vales. Also, I have some unfinished business of my own with the emperor."

"Sounds risky," Jason muttered.

"We're all out of safe options," Galloran replied.

"I have a question," Rachel said. "If we have to be at Mianamon in order for the oracle to prophesy, how did Tark's friend Simeon learn about how Jason and I could help Lyrian?"

"I'm not sure Simeon ascertained many specifics," Galloran said. "He may have simply learned that you two could make a significant difference and how his own efforts could summon you."

Jason rubbed his hands together anxiously. "With us there, the oracle should be able to fill in the details more clearly?"

"In theory," Galloran said. "Predicting the future is an uncertain endeavor. You can never guarantee how much or how little will be visible to even the most powerful oracle."

"It would be nice to know for sure why we were brought here," Rachel said.

"The price of that knowledge may be high," Galloran warned. "You'll take a precarious northern passage through rugged mountains, until you reach the tundra of the hinterlands. From there you will move eastward, paralleling the mountain chain. You won't be able to go south until you reach Ebera, the Forsaken Kingdom."

"None who enter Ebera are permitted to leave," Farfalee interrupted. "The Forsaken Kingdom lies on the eastern coast of Lyrian, north of Kadara and the fertile hills of the drinlings. The infamous wizard Kel Jerud built his tower there, a stronghold known as the

Black Spire. Before his death, he warned that his abode was protected by nightmarish wards. He was the mightiest wizard of his time. Centuries after his death, a group of treasure hunters finally defied his warning, lured by the promise of unguessable riches. The fortune seekers unleashed a virulent plague that transformed them into the walking dead."

Galloran continued the narrative. "Only the geography of Ebera, accompanied by the swift action of King Linus, ruler of Ebera when the plague broke out, saved all of Lyrian from infection. North of Ebera lies frozen wasteland, west lie the mountains, east lies the ocean, and south lies the Silver River. Linus burned all of his shipyards and ferries, cutting off Ebera from the rest of the continent. When the sickness spread quickly to the various cities of Ebera, he established walled settlements for those not yet infected by the plague, and forbade any citizen of Ebera, healthy or not, from leaving. Linus warned Kadara of the plague, and Kadarians have patrolled the Silver River ever since, to help prevent an infected person from crossing."

"We get to go there?" Jason asked.

"The current state of Ebera is unknown," Sakar said. "Surely the population has dwindled and grown sparse. The drinlings help Kadara patrol the Silver River. I'm not wanted by the emperor. While you go through the mountains and across the tundra, I can take a more direct road to consult with the drinlings. I've dealt with them in the past. Hopefully, they can help us get you across the Silver River and aid you on your way to the Last Inn."

"The way will be hard and fraught with uncertainty," Galloran said, "but that is part of the reason we doubt Maldor or his minions will anticipate this road. We have no surety about what to expect in Ebera. We're hoping that if you stay in the wilderness, you might slip through the Forsaken Kingdom unnoticed. But there is a significant element of risk. None will be compelled to join the delegation, including the two of you."

"The Seven Vales represent the most secure sanctuary in Lyrian," Farfalee said. "Either one of you would be welcome to remain here as guests until the end of your days . . . or for as long as our nation stands."

"Who else will join the delegation to Mianamon?" Jason asked.

"I intend to invite all of our companions besides Dorsio," Galloran said. "There will also be six seedfolk."

"Including me," Farfalee said. "I will represent the Conclave."

"Really?" Rachel asked.

"We all must do our part," Farfalee responded.

"Rachel," Galloran said. "Jason. You've had little choice regarding much of your involvement against Maldor. This time the decision whether to participate is truly yours. As Farfalee said, the Amar Kabal would grant you safe harbor if desired. By staying here, you would have a fair chance of avoiding violence for years to come. I will still do everything in my power to help you get home as soon as that option becomes feasible. Should this rebellion fail, the Seven Vales will almost certainly be the last nation to fall. If you need time to deliberate, you're welcome to respond tomorrow."

"I don't need to wait," Jason said. "I came back to Lyrian on purpose. Our best chance of getting home is to defeat Maldor, and if my help might be important, I want to know. If my help isn't needed, that would also be good to find out."

"I'm with Jason," Rachel said. "You can count on us to go to Mianamon."

Galloran smiled. "The need is great, or else I would not consider this strategy. You will be accompanied by some of the finest warriors in Lyrian. The way will be difficult, but I do not believe it will be impossible, or else I would not involve my daughter."

"Tomorrow evening we'll travel to the trailhead to quietly get an early start," Farfalee said.

"Anything else you would like to know?" Galloran asked.

"What about all of the orantium in the Drowned City?" Jason asked.

"The Conclave sent a message by eagle to a small group of seedfolk who man a permanent observation station in the trees near the northeastern corner of the swamp. They will recover the orantium in the rafts and dive for more at the Drowned City."

"Yesterday you mentioned how we killed the menace," Rachel recalled. "You also talked about finding a large stash of orantium. Some who listened might guess that the orantium was in the Drowned City."

"Which is why we sent the eagle," Galloran said. "We have no reason to believe spies have infiltrated the Amar Kabal, but we can't be too cautious. Pallas is doing everything in his power to quickly and quietly acquire the explosives."

"One more question," Jason said. "Rachel told me you were able to psychically use her eyes to win the duel yesterday. If she stayed with you, couldn't you keep on borrowing her sight?"

"It was a desperate gambit," Galloran said. "Viewing myself and Naman that way required extraordinary mental exertion. You may have noticed, after I maneuvered into position and got used to the perspective, I went for a hasty victory. Had Naman held off my attack, exhaustion would have soon led to my demise. It was a calculated risk, and one that would not be very useful outside of a controlled environment. Could I see through her eyes again? Certainly. Could it ever be useful again? Possibly. Am I willing to bring Rachel to Felrook, even under supposed diplomatic immunity? Given her gift for Edomic and her status as a Beyonder, absolutely not."

"I'd come if you wanted," Rachel said.

"You're brave and loyal. But no, I would honestly prefer you far from Felrook. If Maldor understands your capabilities, he'll be more interested in apprehending you than any of us. Your presence could jeopardize the mission."

"Then I guess I have a final question too," Rachel said. "What can we do to prepare between now and when we leave?"

"Get rest," Farfalee advised. "It will soon be in short supply."

From the southern rim of Highvale, Rachel gazed down at the fat crescent of Northvale, and farther to mist-enshrouded Roundvale. A steep, serpentine path had led up from Roundvale to these smaller, higher valleys, but the way was about to become impassable by horses.

The Amar Kabal had no intention of improving the northward trails. Farfalee had explained that the few routes through the mountains were tricky to find or to follow. The narrow, treacherous windings helped ensure that any attack from the north would come as a trickle rather than a flood. Not that anyone lived north of the Vales. Still, in the warmer months, an invading army could theoretically gain access by crossing the tundra from the ocean.

Rachel glanced to one side, where Drake sat astride a chocolate brown stallion. He had given Mandibar to Galloran for the journey south. She and Drake had wakened early and slipped away from camp. The delegation had ascended to Highvale in the dark, and he had insisted that she shouldn't miss the view from the southern rim. His flat features did not leave the seedman much of a profile as he glowered down at the misty morning.

"I love these valleys," Drake said, apparently feeling her gaze. "So many memories. So many relationships. Years upon years. Lifetimes upon lifetimes. It is strange to ride through here unwelcomed. I wonder if I will ever behold my homeland again."

"It's beautiful," Rachel said. "This is my favorite place in Lyrian."

"I have a cottage deeper in these mountains," Drake said. "Built it myself. I lived there for more than two lifetimes. Not short, reckless lifetimes like at Harthenham. Long ones. Good ones. I had my own valley. Not very big, but much more than I needed. To my knowledge, nobody else has ever found it. There is no easy way to get there. Winters were long. I needed to hoard plenty of wood and food."

"Did you get lonely?" Rachel asked.

"Not for a long time. I grew old alone twice—older than I reached during any other lifetimes. I had patience. I really felt the difference after each rebirth. By the third lifetime, I finally began to itch for something else, so I left. Many of my people depart on their own like that. Some never return. These mountains go on and on, nearly spanning the continent. There are plenty of places to hide away. We've lost some of our best men and women to solitary living. Maybe they're the smart ones."

"Is that what you want to do?" Rachel asked.

He shook his head. "Not now. If I had no responsibilities, possibly. It might enable me to repair my spirit, purge Harthenham from my psyche. But I intend to see this rebellion through. So long as you, Jason, and Galloran stand, I'll stand with you." He took a deep breath, looking around and rubbing the back of his neck. "My people despise me. My lives have run out. I don't belong here anymore. I have no future here. But it still hurts to leave. I miss these vales. I would have liked to see my cottage one last time."

"You still might," Rachel said.

"It's nowhere near our path."

"I mean afterward."

He squinted at her. "A whole lot needs to happen between now and then. Including an improbable amount of me not dying.

I thought I'd bid these valleys farewell once before. I'd rather say good-bye again, then let it be a welcome surprise if I get to return."

Rachel thought about her home. Was she crazy to believe she would make it back there? She had to see her parents again. She couldn't lose faith, whether or not Drake thought their future looked bleak. "Hope isn't bad."

"Depends on the person," Drake replied. "If it works for you, use it. Ready?"

With a brief Edomic phrase, Rachel told her horse to head back to camp. Drake used heels and reins to similarly encourage his mount. She urged the mare to run, and enjoyed the cool wind in her face.

Back at camp, everyone was prepping to hike into the mountains. They all wore the robes of the Amar Kabal and carried heavy winter traveling cloaks. They expected to forage most of their food, but several people still carried packs loaded with nonperishable rations.

Besides Farfalee, five other seed people had joined the delegation. One was a young woman, Delissa, who stood half a head shorter than Farfalee and seldom spoke. The four other men included Nollin, the nephew of Naman, who bore an unmistakable resemblance to his uncle and had served for several lifetimes as his chief advisor. Farfalee had quietly informed Rachel that Nollin was along to help assure that even the most cynical seedfolk would believe the report sent from Mianamon. The other seedmen were named Kerick, Halco, and Andrus, all three reputedly proven warriors and huntsmen.

Galloran no longer accompanied them. He, Dorsio, and their accompanying seedmen had bid the delegation farewell at Roundvale, on their way to East Gate and eventually to Felrook.

"How was the joy ride?" Jason asked as Rachel dismounted.

"There's a beautiful view of Roundvale from here. The valley looked full of whipped cream."

"It's probably better that I didn't look. Chilled berries in cream was my favorite dish here. I already miss it."

"Looks like we're almost ready to go?"

Jason nodded. "Are you going to tell your horse to meet us at the tundra?"

"That might not be very kind," Rachel said, even though she knew he was kidding. "I bet she'd try. She's earned a break in a safe place."

"Too bad we can't say the same," Jason sighed.

Not far from Rachel, Drake was transferring gear from his horse into a backpack. Nollin sauntered over to him, a tall walking stick in hand. "Well-timed arrival," Nollin congratulated. "You managed to skip all of the work."

"I figured you could use the practice," Drake said without looking at him. "It takes more skills than speechwriting to survive in the backcountry."

Nollin's nostrils flared. "I suppose I have much to learn. Perhaps you can instruct me how to secure food and drink by bowing to Maldor?"

Drake straightened, his expression relaxed. "Based on your politics, I assumed he was already paying you handsomely."

Nollin glanced sideways and noticed Rachel and Jason watching. "There is a significant difference between recommending defensive strategies to protect your people and betraying them by kneeling to the emperor."

Drake nodded. "You have a point. I was only killing myself."

"Seedmen have long been recognized as incorruptible," Nollin said. "We are unerringly true to ourselves and our people. No seedman in history ever openly accepted a bribe from the enemy. You tarnished the unblemished reputation of—"

"I wearied of fighting the emperor without the support of my countrymen," Drake shot back, finally losing his temper. The heated discussion was beginning to draw the attention of others in the camp. "How many manglers have you slain? How many con-scriptors? How many displacers? I was invited to Harthenham for a reason. Believe me, our reputation was destroyed long before I dined there. You haven't been abroad in decades. We're known across the continent as the cravens cowering in the mountains."

"The rest of Lyrian suffers while we prosper," Nollin said defensively. "Let them mock. Soon there won't be any scoffers left."

Drake shook his head. "The servants of the emperor scoff the loudest, and with the least fear of reprisal. Make no mistake. Under the policies you've supported, they'll have the last laugh."

"Prudence is not cowardice. If we had declared war against Felrook, we would no longer exist!"

"It's only a benefit to have a long life if it's worth living! If we insist on survival, we could always try winning."

"This from the one seedman who ever surrendered!" Nollin laughed. "The only one who sold his honor to live at Harthenham."

"Who has less virtue—the man who fought until the lack of support killed his spirit or the man who never fought?"

"You're very noble," Nollin mocked. "I'll admit, while you fought, I gave you no support. You had one thing right when you went to Harthenham—nobody is going to stop the emperor! The rest of Lyrian lost the war long ago. The war has been over for years."

"Then why are you here?" Drake growled.

"I'm here to assure an honest report reaches the Conclave. I'm here to watch the oracle confirm what those of us who haven't spent the last thirty years in a stupor already know. There is no hope for a rebellion. Brave words can't change that. Neither can bold actions. Neither can Beyonders or orantium or throneless kings with inflated reputations. This journey will only be worth the trouble in order to finally have the matter settled."

"Don't disrespect better men than you," Drake warned.

"Why not?" Nollin replied. "You do it all the time."

Drake reached for his sword.

"Stop!" Farfalee commanded. "This discussion has limped forward long enough."

Drake left his sword sheathed. Nollin smirked at him. By now the entire delegation had become engrossed by the argument.

"Yes, we have different viewpoints represented among us," she continued. "Yes, we have a displacer in our number, and a half giant, and a seedman who publically disgraced us."

"She's talking about you," Drake muttered to Nollin, loud enough to draw a laugh.

"No, Drake, I'm talking about you," Farfalee corrected. "Nollin's views are shared by many of our people. Nollin never accepted a bribe from Maldor to hide from his problems in a debasing frenzy of self-indulgence."

"It didn't work," Drake said. "The hiding, I mean."

"If you speak again, we will leave you behind," Farfalee threatened.

Drake raised both palms in surrender.

Farfalee smoothed her hands down across her robes. "As I was saying, our delegation represents diverse viewpoints. Some of us have reason to dislike or mistrust one another. But we are all united by a common goal: we want to know what the Prophetess of Mianamon can predict about the outcome of a rebellion. It does no good to speculate about what she will foresee. I think Nollin and

Drake have already debated the possibilities enough for the entire trip. I move we don't discuss the matter again."

"Seconded," Kerick said.

"Any opposed?" Farfalee asked, her intense eyes daring anyone to speak up. Nobody did. "Fair enough. Does any member of this group have a problem with the presence of any other member? Be honest. Speak now, or keep silent hereafter."

"Aram snores," Ferrin said.

Several people, including Rachel, strained to resist laughter.

Farfalee looked exasperated. "Does this seem like a useful time for humor?"

"I'm not joking," Ferrin deadpanned. "It sounds like a bear drowning in a tar pit."

Bursts of laughter escaped several people, including Rachel. Aram really did snore.

"I take no pleasure in traveling with a displacer," Delissa said. The mood suddenly became much more sober. A couple of the other seedmen murmured agreement.

"Galloran entrusted Nedwin with the piece of my neck," Ferrin assured her. "He can slay me at will."

"I just hope it won't be too late," Nollin muttered.

Ferrin folded his arms. "Just as Drake can do little about the cowardly reputation of his people, I can't do much about the untrustworthy reputation of mine."

The statement elicited an outburst from the seedmen. Drake stared at the ground, lips trembling as he resisted laughter.

"Stop!" Farfalee demanded.

"The displacer isn't wrong," Tark said. "The reputation of the Amar Kabal has fallen."

"Very well," Andrus said, drawing his sword. "He's welcome to test himself against me."

"You're missing the point," Ferrin said calmly. "Nobody questions that you're fine warriors. In fact, your prowess only makes you appear more cowardly. No one blames a weakling for hiding from a fight."

"You claim to be tarnished by the reputation of your people," Andrus said, sheathing his blade. "We have scouts, Ferrin. We know about you personally. You're as slippery as any displacer serving the emperor."

"Then your scouts should also know I have irrevocably fallen out of favor with the emperor," Ferrin replied. "I may have been slippery, but until he turned on me, I was always loyal to him. I am now loyal to Jason and Galloran. I have proven that loyalty in every way possible, and will continue to do so. You will likely need my help as we approach the eastern battlefront. There will be considerable imperial traffic to navigate."

"I do not ask any of us to fully trust the displacer," Farfalee said. "But I do ask whether any among us cannot abide his company. If so, speak now, so we may replace you."

"Replace us?" Delissa complained. "For a displacer?"

"For a member of the delegation approved by the Conclave," Farfalee rephrased. "If he were not willing to work with us, he would be left behind. But he appears willing."

"We're willing too," Andrus said.

"Delissa?" Farfalee asked.

"I won't make trouble," she pledged.

"This is no casual exercise," Farfalee said. "We're about to pass the point of no return. This delegation must be united. A difficult road awaits us. We can't afford internal strife."

"May I speak now?" Drake asked, raising a finger.

"I suppose you'll have to resume at some point," Farfalee said.

"Who made you the leader?"

Her jaw tightened. "Take your pick: experience, competence, intelligence, charisma—"

"Also the Conclave agreed to it with Galloran," Kerick interceded.

"Very well," Drake said, clearing his throat theatrically. "Now that we have all of this settled, I move, less talking, more walking."

"Seconded," Nedwin said tiredly.

The motion passed unanimously.

CHAPTER 21

HOWLING
NOTCH

The days began to blur as Jason marched northward into the soaring mountains. At first he had frequently paused to admire the jaw-dropping vistas of rugged cliffs, glittering cascades, chiseled ridgelines, hidden lakes, and craggy peaks. Although he lived in the Rockies and had visited several national parks, he had never witnessed such consistently grand, dramatic terrain.

But eventually the postcard panoramas became so commonplace that he began to lose the ability to view them with fresh eyes. Instead of basking in the beauty, he started to focus on how steep the trail was to the next rise, or how closely the narrow path ran along the brink of the cliff up ahead, or how far the way had to twist and wind to cross a relatively short distance.

There seemed to be no end to the mountains. No matter how high they climbed, when peering ahead or back or off to either side, only more rocky slopes and stony crests remained in view, rank upon rank, a granitic ocean sculpted over eons.

The way became more challenging the deeper they progressed into the maze of canyons and summits. More often the trail became a ledge with a sheer drop on one hand and a steep rise on the other. More often, dizzying crevices were spanned by wobbly rope bridges. More often, carved tunnels or natural caves granted access through otherwise impassible terrain.

Although the sky remained mostly clear, the thinning air gained a chilly bite. Heavy winter cloaks were worn with increasing regularity. Snowy glaciers appeared upon the highest peaks and saddles.

They ate well. Aram reveled in the elk meat prevalent early on the hike, and later in the goat meat featured at the higher altitudes. Jason spotted all sorts of life, especially birds of prey, bighorn sheep, mountain goats, and an unfamiliar breed of shaggy, hopping rodent.

Drake and Nedwin helped scout, but Ferrin invariably remained with the main group. Farfalee and Nollin seldom ranged far ahead or behind, but the other seedfolk spent much of the time away from the delegation, either to hunt or keep watch for trouble.

The demanding trail offered little chance for conversation. Words tended to be limited to instructions about avoiding danger along the treacherous route. They hiked long hours, eating hastily and sleeping greedily. Jason was glad the Amar Kabal required no real sleep, because he never had to stand guard.

Jason had overheard no harsh words since Farfalee had called for cooperation at the trailhead, but he had observed plenty of surly glances.

On the ninth day of their hike, they reached a large stone building at the brink of a yawning chasm. With irregular walls and steep angles to the slate-shingled roof, the weatherworn structure could almost have passed for a natural outgrowth of the mountainside. Three thick ropes curved across the chasm, the thickest for walking on and the other two for handrails, all three connected at intervals by slender lines.

Four seed people manned the remote outpost—two men and two women. The building contained a stockpile of edibles and other goods, along with enough space for the entire delegation to sleep indoors, warmed by a blazing fire.

Farfalee counseled with the head of the outpost, a deep-voiced man named Valero. Jason overheard snatches of advice about weather and cave sloths and news from even more remote watch points.

As they prepared to depart the next morning, Jason found Ferrin reclining in an isolated storeroom, munching on dried fruit. He had specifically sought him out because the displacer hadn't seemed like himself since the trip began.

"You doing all right?" Jason asked directly.

"Never better," Ferrin said, popping what might have been a shriveled apricot into his mouth.

"You haven't joined any of the scouting missions," Jason said.

Ferrin grinned faintly. "I have a keen sense for when my services are unappreciated."

"You have as much right to be here as anyone," Jason assured him.

"In theory, perhaps, thanks to Galloran. Not in practice. Don't fret for me. I'm right at home when most of the people around me wish I were elsewhere. Even among imperial servants, the company of a displacer is undesired."

Jason frowned. "Don't let the seedmen get to you."

"It isn't just the seedmen," Ferrin said without evident resentment. "The rest of you don't trust me to varying degrees. I don't expect Nedwin or Tark would put a hand out to steady me if I teetered on a brink. Drake and Aram could take me or leave me.

Corinne is too innocent to know better. And of course you and Rachel are nursing old wounds. I'm accustomed to this kind of atmosphere. Right now it's time for me to lie low. If I appear happy or helpful, it will only cause irritation and heighten the tension. An unwelcome guest should avoid flaunting his presence."

"I'm trusting you more and more," Jason said, feeling bad for him.

"Which feels much stranger than suspicion," Ferrin said. "When you were new to Lyrian, before you knew anything about displacers, I could rationalize your acceptance as ignorance. I've never had a true friend, Jason. I've used others. I've been used. But a principled person has never knowingly accepted me. When Galloran stood up for me in front of the Conclave? When he vouched for me? That was a new experience. I almost stood and objected."

"Why?" Jason said. "Was he wrong?"

Ferrin compressed his lips. "I want him to be right," he finally said. "Displacers are raised to spy for Maldor. I was taught to scheme since the cradle. I've always had a knack for it. I can't stop noticing how I might take advantage of information. How I might exploit relationships. Among displacers, I took pride in having more honor than most. I often passed up unwholesome opportunities. But next to integrity like I've seen in you and Galloran, I'm entirely unworthy."

"People can change," Jason said.

"I'm trying, Jason. But don't you see? About as honest as I can get is confessing how dishonest I instinctively want to be!"

"That's a start," Jason said. He regarded Ferrin soberly. "What do you feel tempted to do?"

Ferrin stared at the floor. "Part of me muses how difficult it would be for the seedmen to pass judgment on me and my people if they were extinct. Part of me wants to exploit a million flaws I've noticed in their attitudes and defenses. Part of me wants to show you and Galloran that you were fools to trust me, that I don't need your sympathy or protection. Part of me wants that piece of my neck back from Nedwin."

Jason didn't like where this was heading. Had he worried that Ferrin might somehow betray them? Sure. But it was different to hear those words from his lips. Then again, he was just trying to be honest, right?

"You don't know how to respond," Ferrin said. "I'll make it easy. The safest course of action for your young rebellion would be to toss me off the tallest cliff you can find. I have played a perilous game for years—trading secrets, telling lies, finding leverage, earning trust only to betray it. I got away with an eccentric lifestyle among Maldor's elite by hiding much of what I learned and proving myself too valuable to kill. It was a precarious, unforgiving game. When I released you from Felrook, I miscalculated, and I lost. Game over. Bridges burned. But the game is part of my nature. I don't think I can stop playing until I stop breathing."

"You want us to kill you?" Jason said, unconvinced.

Ferrin snickered miserably. "I don't know. Part of me suspects you'd never do that. Part of me thinks my candor will only make you trust me more. Maybe part of me is nobly trying to warn you. Maybe part of me doesn't care anymore. I'm an actor. I've pretended to be too many things to too many people. Cut free from Maldor, having betrayed the only cause I had always upheld, I'm not sure I have an identity."

"Start fresh," Jason urged. "Be true to this. Play your games for us."

Ferrin sighed. "I never chose this cause. Not really. I didn't walk away from Maldor as a matter of principle. I made a mistake and ran away. Am I so inconstant that I then become unswervingly loyal to his enemies?"

"Why were you loyal to him?" Jason asked.

"Partly out of tradition," Ferrin said. "I'm a displacer. All displacers are loyal to Maldor. Mostly for security. He's going to win. Displacers know what happens to the losing side. I was loyal to the future undisputed emperor of all Lyrian."

"What if we can win?" Jason said. "What if the oracle sees a way that Maldor can lose?"

"Oracles see thousands of possible futures," Ferrin said. "Maybe millions. Maybe more. Out of the countless possible futures, is there one where Maldor fails? Probably. Even if this oracle predicts possible victory for a rebellion, I'm willing to wager she'll see many, many more futures where we get crushed. Besides, if that oracle lays eyes on me, she'll probably order me slain on sight."

"Why?" Jason asked.

Ferrin met his gaze. "Because who knows how many of those futures where the rebellion gets crushed will begin with an act of betrayal by me?"

Jason had no words. Ferrin didn't help him. "Should you ask to be imprisoned?"

"What do you think?" Ferrin asked.

"I already told you. I think you should start fresh. I think you should call your old life over. This is a better cause. You said you never had real friends. You're on your way now. I'm one of them. Let that be enough."

Ferrin flicked a piece of fruit into his mouth with his thumb. "I don't know. I think if you lie long enough, often enough, you become a lie. Strip away my pretenses and deceptions, and I'm not sure there'd be anything left."

"You won't fix that problem with more lies," Jason said. "Not by lying to yourself. Not by lying to us. If you're true to this cause, you'll have something left when you strip away the rest—this cause and these friendships."

"You don't get it," Ferrin said. "No matter how hard I try, there's a cynical corner of my mind where everything is an act. People are game pieces. Information is currency. At the same time I portray myself as a rebel displacer loyal to a new cause, I secretly feel like a deeply placed spy worming his way deeper all the time. I've mustered sincerity before. I've almost believed it. I'm an expert at almost believing my lies. How is this different? How can it be?"

"Because we know what you are and we're still giving you a chance."

Ferrin bowed his head. He reached one hand up the sleeve of his robe and withdrew a chunk of flesh.

"What's that?" Jason asked.

"Part of my brachial artery," Ferrin said. "Take it. Consider it an extra fail-safe. I've spent my life backstabbing anyone foolish enough to trust me. Now I'm betraying the one master I've always served. And I'm betraying my people. But I'll try to be true to this rebellion. For the sake of friendship. It's a better reason than I've had before."

Jason accepted it with a nod.

Footsteps approached. Drake poked his head into the store-room. "We're getting ready to move out. Is that dried fruit?"

"They have mountains of it," Ferrin said.

"Bring me a handful," Drake said. He looked back and forth between Jason and Ferrin. "Everything all right?"

"Just peachy," Jason said.

Crossing the three ropes over the chasm was no fun. They jiggled and swayed far more than Jason preferred, and it seemed impossible to avoid looking down at the seemingly infinite fall awaiting him.

Drake explained that these makeshift bridges were easily destroyed, leaving the trail virtually impassable if even lightly defended. The delegation traversed several more of them as the trail zigzagged northeast toward the unseen tundra.

By the twelfth day of the trek, still surrounded by colossal crags and escarpments, Jason began to notice the wind keening ominously in the distance. "We might have some bad weather coming," he commented to Farfalee as they gathered around a campfire below a sheltering overhang.

"Not necessarily," she replied. "You hear Howling Notch. We'll get there tomorrow."

"That's where the fun really begins," Drake said, munching on a strip of dried meat.

"What's Howling Notch?" Rachel asked.

"An unnatural anomaly," Drake said.

"The terrain north of Howling Notch funnels high winds through a narrow gap," Farfalee explained.

Drake prodded the fire with a stick. "The wind is constant and fierce, yet the terrain never changes, the gap never erodes."

"A secretive wizard once made his home in the vicinity," Farfalee added. "He built his stronghold into the living rock, shaping it with Edomic. Many believe the terrain around Howling Notch is under some lingering enchantment."

"I've been through the notch a time or three," Kerick said, stepping up to the fire. "It's demanding, but if you keep your head, it can be done."

The prospect of high winds and steep cliffs made Jason recall a certain nightmare with a torivor involved. "Can we blow off an edge?"

Kerick chuckled knowingly. "It's the deadliest stretch of this trail. In stormy weather, no living thing could drag itself through that gap. We're later in the year than I'd prefer, but the summer weather keeps holding. If you hold tight to the line and follow instructions, we should get you through."

The next morning the wailing wind grew progressively louder. The tempestuous howls seemed incongruent with the blue sky and wispy clouds overhead.

"You'd think we were hiking into a hurricane," Rachel said from behind Jason.

"It's weird," he replied. "I've hardly felt a breeze all morning."

Walking in front of Jason, Drake glanced back. "The same terrain that funnels the gusts through Howling Notch mostly shields the approach. You'll see it just up around this bend."

When Howling Notch came into view, Jason stopped walking. Still some distance ahead, a high saddle of rock connected a pair of towering escarpments. A steep, V-shaped gap split the saddle.

"It's so loud even from here!" Rachel said. Jason could hardly make out her words.

The trail approaching the notch was a narrow ledge chiseled into the mountainside. Jason had begun adapting to the constant threat of falling a thousand feet to his death, but this scant trail was the narrowest they had encountered. No matter how carefully he positioned himself, his feet were never more than six inches from the edge.

Fortunately, a rope ran along the wall of the ledge, staked in place. Without something to hold, Jason wondered if he could have forced himself to proceed. Even with the rope, he tried to focus on Drake's back and ignore the dizzying drop. The wind roared constantly, occasionally falling to a moan or rising to a piercing shriek so intense that Jason could hardly believe he still felt no significant stirring of the air.

The closer they got to Howling Notch, the less Jason could see of it. The trail climbed diagonally from below and to one side. At last the narrow ledge widened into a semicircular shelf spacious enough for the entire group to assemble. Farfalee shouted to be heard over the deafening gale.

"We'll cross through the notch in two groups of five and one of four. Kerick will lead the first group, Halco the next, and Andrus the last. Listen carefully to their instructions." Kerick and Halco each tapped four other members of the delegation. Andrus claimed the remainders. Jason ended up in Halco's group, along with Delissa, Nedwin, and Aram. They huddled together apart from the others.

Halco had spent most of his time away from the delegation, scouting and hunting. Jason had never really conversed with him.

"Three rules," Halco said. "First, hold on to the line. The line will guide us through. Always have a firm grip with at least one hand. You never know when the wind will surge. Second, stay low. If the wind grabs you, it will be a very long time before you hit the ground. It can happen very suddenly. We move through the notch hugging the ground—slithering, not crawling. We don't want to present anything for the wind to seize. Third, move when I move, pause when I pause. We won't be able to hear one another. If somebody gets torn from the line, you can't help them. Raise your head, reach for them, rise up even a little, and you'll join them. Any questions?"

"Can we do this after the sun goes down?" Aram asked.

Halco shook his head. "Your smaller size will probably serve you better than greater strength. Less surface area. Nobody out-muscles the wind in Howling Notch. Besides, the wind tends to blow harder after dusk. Anything else?"

"What order?" Nedwin asked.

"I'll lead, then Jason, you, Aram, and Delissa. Once we're through the notch, the line will guide us to a trench. Only by keeping low in the trench will we be able to descend the far side." He held up little cylinders of cork. "We'll all want these for our ears."

Jason accepted a pair of earplugs and inserted them. Rachel was part of the first group, led by Kerick. After adjusting his pack and his robes, Kerick guided his group beyond the sheltered shelf and out of sight. Jason and the others sat down to wait.

Even with the earplugs, the wind remained plenty noisy. Jason listened to it rise and fall, imagining how it must be whipping at Rachel. Tense with anticipation, it was hard for him to tell whether time was passing slowly or quickly. He could have waited on the shelf all day without growing bored.

Off to one side, Corinne put a hand on Farfalee's shoulder and spoke to her. Farfalee made a motion to Halco, who stood and gestured for his group to rise.

Corinne came over to Jason, and he pulled out an earplug. "The first group made it," she reported. "Rachel says it's worse than we could guess."

"Comforting," Jason replied. "See you on the other side." He replaced his earplug and got into position behind Halco. The seedman led him away from the shelf along a narrow ledge.

They progressed another couple of hundred yards, sheltered from the wind by the wall of rock beside the trail. The wall shrank until it finally ended. Just beyond the end of the wall, a guideline was staked into the gray rock of the ground, proceeding up to the notch.

Halco looked back at the others, holding up his forefinger. The wind screamed unnervingly. Finally, the howl diminished to a strong moan. Flat on his belly, Halco took hold of the line and wormed beyond the sheltering barricade.

Jason followed. Even at a low moan, he could not believe how forcefully the wind washed over him. Air had never felt so tangible. If he had tried to stand, no amount of strength could have kept his hands on the guideline. It felt like he was trying to drag himself upstream through a raging river.

The ground rose at an incline to the notch, overlapping sheets of stone textured by grooves, lumps, and other irregularities. Pulling himself over the sharp-edged terrain was uncomfortable, but Jason figured the jagged unevenness might serve to help disrupt the wind a little if he stayed low. Twenty yards behind him, the incline ended at the brink of a lofty precipice. The cold air smelled like iron, stone, and snow.

The moan rose to a roar. The wind slicing by overhead seemed to have weight, pressing him down. If he raised a finger, he could picture the slipstream tearing it off.

Jason kept moving forward hand over hand. Even below the worst of the wind, and with Halco in front of him bearing the brunt of the gale, it took all of his strength and concentration. Keeping his eyes down, Jason tried to press himself into the mountain.

The wind gusted to an earsplitting shriek, and his head bumped against Halco's moccasins. Jason halted, clinging to the line. The shriek remained steady until long after an opera singer would have passed out. As the scream diminished to a roar, Jason glimpsed Halco squirming forward again.

Foot by foot, inch by inch, Jason gained ground. At intervals he passed the stakes that kept the guideline anchored. He expected he would have bruises all over tomorrow, not from impact, but from merciless pressure on various points of his anatomy, especially his elbows.

Finally they reached the front of the notch. Halco paused. The wind roared like never before. Without earplugs the volume might have done permanent damage. The muscles in Jason's hands and arms burned with exertion. After what felt like forever, the wind ebbed a little, and Halco scrambled hastily forward.

The narrow notch ran straight for about ten yards before it started to widen. Jason felt relief as he slithered across the highest point of the saddle, the ground scraping his face as he tried to keep low. Descending the far side, he peeked ahead at where the guideline vanished into a trench. Twenty more yards.

He heard the wind increase in force before he felt it. Halco froze, flattening himself. The wind rose to a shriek, then to a penetrating whine, like a jet engine. Jason gripped the rope with all of his might. He could feel the guideline shuddering. No matter how low he remained, the blasting air seemed on the verge of taking hold of him. Several times his rope jerked so hard that part of his body left the ground slightly before slamming back down. These new bruises would be from impact. The wind was unbelievable. This was how it would feel to water-ski behind a missile. How fast was the wind going? It had to be hundreds of miles per hour.

Jason glimpsed Halco, still flat, gazing backward, eyes wide. Turning his head slightly, keeping his cheek to the ground, Jason looked back as well. Nedwin clung to the rope behind him, head down. Then Aram. Delissa trailed them, just coming over the highest part of the saddle. Her body looked like a flag in a tornado. Suddenly Jason understood why the rope had twitched so much.

As Jason watched, the relentless wind gusted even harder, and she lost her grip. It looked like Delissa had been shot from a cannon. Her body clipped the side of the notch, setting her spinning as the gale rocketed her away. Despite the low angle of Jason's viewpoint, she stayed within sight for a very long time, shrinking with distance until she dropped out of view.

Horrified, Jason bowed his head, squashing his face against the ground. Closing his eyes, forearms burning, he squeezed the guideline harder than ever. Surely the wind would slacken any moment. If anything, it rose a bit more. Any moment. Any moment.

At last the wind ebbed, becoming a scream, then a roar. Peeking ahead, Jason saw Halco advancing. Jason hurried forward in his wake, not wanting to lose the seedman as a partial wind-break.

The notch widened. Glancing ahead, Jason saw the entire valley spreading outward from the gap, a giant funnel, just as some of the others had described.

The wind weakened even more. Jason kept moving forward until hands helped him down into a deeply cut trench, so perfectly square that it must have been carved by tools. The wind remained noisy, but he no longer felt it. Nedwin dropped in behind him, then Aram.

Jason slouched against the wall, numb and exhausted after the ordeal. Had he really just seen a woman launched into the air, like a blade of grass dropped on the stream of a fire hose? Hitting the side of the notch could have killed her. If not, the fall would definitely have finished the job. He consoled himself that at least she had an amar. Then again, this was rocky country. Would it ever get planted?

Kerick and Halco yelled at each other, trying to be heard. Kerick hurried off down the trench in a crouch, and Jason saw him hollering to Rachel. Time passed. Jason could barely believe he was alive. Rachel had been right. Even with all of the warnings, that had been much worse than he had guessed.

Eventually Farfalee dropped into the trench, followed by Corinne and Drake. Where was Andrus?

Jason had to wait for an explanation. They spent the next hour moving along trenches. On this side of the notch, the wind was much more widespread. The farther they traveled from the notch, the less concentrated the gale became, but even after an hour, the wind still seemed to gust like a hurricane.

The trench eventually led to a cave. Once they were inside, the air seemed eerily still. After they'd advanced for some time, it even began to get quiet. In a tall chamber with undulant flowstone walls and stalactites dripping on stalagmites, Jason removed his earplugs to hear the others.

"Andrus went after Delissa," Farfalee explained. "He didn't want to risk her seed getting stranded on barren rock. Nobody travels the canyon below the notch."

"It will be a tricky climb," Nollin said.

"He's the best climber we have," Kerick said.

"Andrus relayed that if he can find her amar swiftly, he'll try to catch up," Farfalee said.

"Unlikely," Halco grunted. "He'll have to descend thousands of feet. Then find the seed. Then climb back up. It will take days."

"He may kill himself trying," Kerick said. "Either way, rejoining us is wishful thinking."

"Andrus will survive," Halco said. "He'll find her amar. But I agree that he won't be back."

"A foul loss," Nollin uttered bleakly. "Delissa was perhaps the best archer in the Seven Vales. And few swordsmen could outperform Andrus."

"No matter the precautions taken, surviving Howling Notch always involves some luck," Halco said. "Delissa did nothing wrong. She was simply in the wrong place when the wind became most fierce. We're fortunate more of us didn't fly free. It was the harshest crossing I've experienced."

"We can only continue," Farfalee said. "We knew Howling Notch would be our biggest test in the mountains. We're almost through to the tundra. The rest of the way is mostly downhill."

"Straight to the Forsaken Kingdom," Drake muttered. "Delissa and Andrus may be the lucky ones."

CHAPTER 22

THE FORSAKEN KINGDOM

*W*ill this tundra ever end? Rachel thought to Corinne.

It's lovely, Corinne replied. *I like the foxes. And the birds. And the lack of cliffs.*

You need to stop being so positive, Rachel scolded. *You're totally unrelatable. You're going to alienate everyone.*

I'm not sure anything I do will make me relatable, Corinne conveyed. *I grew up in a tree deep inside of a deadly swamp. I'm an exiled princess. And I talk more with my mind than my mouth.*

All the more reason to act grumpier, Rachel affirmed.

The ground here gets too muddy in some places, Corinne complained tentatively.

Very good, Rachel encouraged. *That's a start.*

I can't say I'm fond of the caribou droppings, she added.

Who can? Very relatable. And you're right about the foxes. They couldn't be cuter. At least when they're not chewing on carcasses.

Rachel currently walked at the rear of the delegation, near Farfalee. Corinne was toward the front, closer to Jason. Yet they heard each other perfectly. Their mental link had been very useful back at Howling Notch. They had experimented, and the telepathy

378

worked just fine with hundreds of yards between them. Half a mile apart required a lot of focus. Around a mile apart the communication became too faint to comprehend, like the fading memories of an elusive dream.

From behind, Rachel watched Jason hiking beside Corinne. They leaned together, sharing a laugh. Since reaching the tundra, Jason had made a noticeable effort to hang around her. The flat terrain enabled more socializing than the lofty passes. Rachel supposed it was natural. Not only was Corinne older than him and a total knockout, she also had an innocent sweetness that made her accessible. Rachel plucked a leaf from a shrub and tore it as she walked. Had Jason ever tried this conspicuously to earn her attention? Or was it only conspicuous to her? Why did she bother noticing?

Off to her right loomed the omnipresent mountains, an unbroken chain reaching from horizon to horizon. To the east, west, and north sprawled open tundra, grassy country contoured by hillocks, boulders, tussocks, and low ridges. In the wide-open terrain, almost everyone took turns scouting. As she watched, a twitchy rabbit darted from the shelter of one scraggly bush to another.

We might miss the monotonous tundra when we reach the Forsaken Kingdom, Corinne conveyed.

Nobody seems to know many details about it, Rachel replied.

Ferrin knew more than the Amar Kabal, Corinne agreed. *At least he had heard rumors that the disease was transmitted by worms.*

Ew, I just stepped in a squishy spot, Rachel complained. *You really feel it in these moccasin boots.*

Be glad it's summer, Corinne replied. *Kerick said this whole area is under ice and snow for most of the year.*

We have land like this not too far from where I lived back home.

You lived in an icy place?

Sometimes. Washington was more rainy than snowy. Huge trees, lots of moss.

That I can imagine, Corinne assured her.

I bet. But not too far north from my home there were reindeer and tundra.

Do you think we'll be attacked by the walking dead?

Rachel had been trying to avoid dwelling on it. She considered the question. *We should definitely expect trouble. There has to be a reason nobody goes there. Farfalee told me a small river forms the unofficial northern border of the kingdom, and they've never seen the walking dead on this side of it. We shouldn't have to worry until then.*

How do you kill something that's already dead?

Nobody knows enough about them. Ask Jason. He'll have an opinion.

Wait a moment. Rachel could see Corinne talking to Jason, but they were too far ahead to hear. *He says you chop them up into little pieces.*

But what if that infects you with the disease?

Jason leaned close to answer Corinne quietly. She laughed. *You let Nollin do it.*

Ferrin and Nedwin were the first to spot a walking corpse. Ever since they'd lost Andrus and Delissa, Ferrin had contributed more with the scouting. A few hours after the group had forded the Agwam River, Ferrin and Nedwin returned to the delegation and reported a lone woman limping their way from the south. Rachel had felt uncomfortably alert since crossing the northern boundary of the Forsaken Kingdom. In a way, it was a relief to end the anticipation. Based on the description, the undead woman did not sound like a major threat.

"We should study her," Drake recommended. "Approach her and see if she can listen to reason."

"And when she attacks?" Ferrin asked.

"We see how hard she is to take down," Drake replied. "The information could become extremely relevant."

"The corpse is coming directly toward us?" Farfalee asked.

"She can obviously sense our presence," Nedwin affirmed. "Despite her injured leg, she's hurrying along a perfect line to intercept us."

"He's right," Ferrin agreed.

Kerick folded his arms. "If we'll have to face her sooner or later, might be best to get it over with, confront the abomination on our terms."

"We must neutralize her from a distance," Halco said. "No close combat."

"That still may not sufficiently protect us," Nollin cautioned. He turned to Ferrin. "How certain are you that the disease is transmitted by worms?"

"I heard a rumor. I've never personally been to the Forsaken Kingdom, but Maldor has long taken an interest in the plaguelands. He considers the plague the greatest potential threat to his domination of Lyrian. If it ever spread, the disease could destroy all of the kingdoms on the continent, regardless of their power or politics. Research has been quietly conducted. The rumor is probably credible."

Nollin folded his arms. "Setting aside opinions about rumors, what I hear is that we lack certainty on the matter. This sickness obliterated a mighty realm! We know the condition to be dreadfully contagious. Mere proximity to an afflicted person might spawn infection. For the sake of the mission, some of us should keep well back."

"Like those of us without seeds," Aram muttered.

"We're unsure whether the amar will be immune to the malady," Farfalee said.

"The amar could not regenerate an undead body," Nollin asserted. "But the amar could be incapacitated by the disease. The safest course for an infected member of the Amar Kabal would be a quick death to reduce the risk of exposing the seed."

"What if one of the rest of us becomes infected?" Corinne asked.

A troubled silence settled over the group. Farfalee spoke. "If the disease manifests, we would need to accept that the afflicted person had become a puppet controlled by an illness."

"How will we know if we catch it?" Rachel asked. "Or if the disease has taken hold?"

"A sudden craving for blood and brains?" Jason guessed.

The joke fell flat, earning uneasy smiles instead of laughs.

"You may not be far from the truth," Farfalee said. "I imagine some of the symptoms will be evident. We'll need to remain vigilant—pay attention to how we're feeling, keep a sharp eye on one another. Nollin is right that some of us should go to extreme lengths to keep our distance from the walking dead. That core group needs to include those whose presence we most need at Mianamon, namely Corinne, Rachel, Jason, and Nollin."

"And you, Farfalee," Nollin added.

"Halco and I will do everything in our power to keep the key members of the delegation uncompromised," Kerick asserted.

"Any threat to Jason will have to pass through me first," Tark vowed.

"I am under specific orders to protect Corinne and Rachel," Nedwin said.

"I am here to do whatever is needed," Drake pledged.

Farfalee glanced at her brother, a flash of pain and concern in her eyes. "Unwelcome as such a discussion may be, it does provide a practical hierarchy."

"What of our bold displacer?" Nollin asked.

"He wants everyone to live," Ferrin said tactfully. "Himself included."

"Same with the smuggler," Aram inserted.

"I believe we all understand what needs to happen," Farfalee said. "Five of us have pledged to help ensure the survival of the others by any means necessary. But of course I want all of us to survive this passage through the Forsaken Kingdom. Aside from an examination of this diseased woman, our goal will be evasion. I agree that we need to investigate the effectiveness of projectiles against her. Hopefully, these unfortunate plague victims can be slain from a distance."

Ferrin and Nedwin led the delegation to a hilltop that offered a view of the infected woman coming toward them. It was hard to apprehend details from a distance, but she was clearly limping. Her body was emaciated, her clothes tattered, her hair matted and filthy.

The rest of the delegation waited atop the hill while Kerick and Halco advanced fifty yards down the slope. Kerick carried a bow and Halco brought a sling. As the disheveled woman drew nearer, her hasty limp became more frantic.

"Halt!" Kerick demanded in a clear voice. "We mean you no harm."

The woman continued forward without a response.

Kerick set an arrow to his bowstring and pulled it to his cheek. "Halt or I will be forced to shoot. We only wish to converse."

The woman rasped a moaning reply. Straining her ears and using some imagination, Rachel believed the woman might have said "need." The woman shambled toward Kerick with desperate vigor.

Kerick put an arrow through her chest. The impact made her stumble; then she continued toward him, oblivious to the injury.

Halco loosed a stone from his sling, which knocked her to the ground. Teeth bared angrily, the woman scrambled back to her feet.

"Please, halt," Kerick demanded, retreating a few paces, his bow bent again.

She gave no response.

With rapid efficiency, Kerick began putting arrows through her head. By the third, she collapsed to the ground, finally immobile.

"Not promising," Farfalee murmured. "At least enough arrows stopped her. The disease may control her, but it seems the commandeered body needs some brain function to stay in motion."

"I have considerable experience handling dangerous and exotic substances," Nedwin said. "Do you mind if I examine the corpse?"

"If you're willing to risk the consequences," Farfalee said.

Kerick and Halco withdrew from the fallen woman, and Nedwin approached gingerly, as if expecting that her unconsciousness might be a ruse. Eventually he crouched beside her and used a dagger to prod her in several places. With some effort, he extracted the arrows. After several minutes spent hunched over the inert form, Nedwin returned to the group.

"Worms," Nedwin reported. "Small ones. Gray. Lots of them. No blood. Just skin, sinew, and bone. The worms were already at work repairing her injuries, knitting her flesh back together. They seemed too heavy to be transmitted through the air. I used my knife to dig out a worm. When I placed it on her arm, the little creature immediately burrowed below her skin."

"It seems Ferrin provided accurate intelligence," Farfalee said.

"The walking dead are vehicles governed by parasites," Nollin said. "They aren't people. We don't need to show them any mercy."

"If my corpse becomes animated by maggots," Drake said, "please have mercy. Behead me. Burn me. Whatever it takes."

"You didn't even need to ask," Halco assured him.

Rachel shivered. How would it feel to have worms tunnel into her body and assume command? How would she feel to see it happen to one of her companions? To Jason or Corinne? She might truly lose her mind.

Leaving the plague-savaged woman behind, the delegation marched southward. They passed a dilapidated village overgrown by shrubs and small trees, with most of the structures having collapsed into their foundations. Just after sunset, from a ridgetop, they glimpsed a distant city encompassed by a stone wall, its towers silent and dark in the twilight.

Kerick steered the group away from the quiet city. Rachel tried not to picture bloodthirsty zombies lurking behind those gloomy walls. She failed.

After some discussion, they made camp on high ground and lit a fire. Ferrin had insisted that the limping woman had been drawn to them by some instinct far more powerful than firelight, but hoped the flames might be used to intimidate attackers. Kerick had reasoned that while the high ground exposed them visually and allowed enemies to approach from all sides, it also enabled the group to see their enemies coming and to flee in any direction.

Rachel bedded down near Corinne and Jason. "Do you think we can outrun these things if they're not limping?" Rachel wondered aloud.

"Guess we'll find out," Jason replied. "Let's hope there's a reason they're not called the running dead."

"What do you call the walking dead when you kill them?" Corinne asked.

"Morbid question," Jason approved. "The walking deader? The no-longer-walking dead?"

"The resting dead," Rachel said.

"Rachel wins," Corinne decreed.

"I don't like how that lady was coming straight at us," Jason said. "Makes you wonder how many of them are out there right now, heading our way, walking, or limping, or dragging themselves over—"

"Enough," Rachel said firmly. "I'm already going to have a lousy time sleeping."

"Better to be prepared than surprised," Jason said.

"Imagining zombies in the night doesn't prepare us," Rachel countered. "If we're going to get attacked, better to rest than stay up worrying."

As if in response to their conversation, a shape appeared out of the night at the edge of the firelight, making Rachel gasp until she recognized Nedwin. They hadn't seen him in hours. He came and crouched beside Jason.

"You were gone a while," Jason said.

"I don't like this place," Nedwin whispered. "I found some hoofprints. Feral pigs. Goats. Wild horses. I toured an abandoned town. There was evidence of other members of the walking dead. I expect we'll see trouble tonight."

Jason shot Rachel a significant look. "So what do we do?"

"Try to get some sleep," Nedwin said.

Rachel shot a look back at Jason.

"I better go report to Farfalee," Nedwin said.

"I'm not sure I can sleep," Corinne said. "I've never felt so nervous! Is it like this a lot?"

"This is extra bad," Jason said.

"Horror movie bad," Rachel agreed.

"Horror movie?" Corinne asked.

"Scary stories we have in the Beyond," Rachel clarified.

"With titles like *Attack of the Wormy Zombies*," Jason added. "They tend to be really bloody."

Eyes wide, Corinne sat rigidly. "How do they usually end?"

Jason and Rachel shared a knowing look.

The assault came in the deepest hours of the night. Kerick roused the group with a shouted warning. By the time Rachel was on her feet, she could hear the walking dead stumbling in the darkness. A muffled groan somewhere in the blackness made the hair on her arms stand up. Heart thudding, mind wishing she was dreaming, her first realization was that the attackers seemed to be closing in from all directions.

Clouds muted the moon and blocked much of the starlight, leaving Rachel squinting at vague shapes approaching up the hillside. Farfalee and Kerick began loosing arrows, and some of the shapes staggered. Nedwin appeared beside Rachel. "We're surrounded," he hissed, a dagger in each hand. "Stay near me."

Jason drew his sword. Tark stood at his side, a weighty knife in one hand, a torch in the other.

"Plan?" Drake asked.

"They're on all sides," Halco answered.

"We move as a group," Farfalee said briskly. "Break through their ranks and try to outpace them."

"Which way?" Ferrin asked.

"Hard to say," Kerick responded, releasing another arrow. From multiple directions, infected corpses neared the perimeter of the firelight.

"That way," Nedwin said firmly, extending an arm. "A bit steeper, but fewer enemies."

A husky man with curly hair lumbered into the light, moving in an awkward jog and clutching a heavy stick. One of his eyes was rolled back, showing almost no iris, and he wore no shirt. A pair of arrows to the head dropped him.

Aram brandished his massive sword. "Follow me," he boomed. "I'll open a path." Bearing a sword and a torch, Ferrin advanced beside the half giant in the direction Nedwin had indicated. The group formed up around Rachel, Corinne, and Jason, weapons ready, moving away from the campfire with hurried, shuffling paces. Vicious sweeps of Aram's sword sent enemies sailing.

Glancing back, Rachel saw figures rushing forward from the far side of the campfire. Focusing on the logs, she uttered a command that sent them flying at the undead attackers amid a fiery spray of sparks and embers. The logs launched with terrific force, some of them shattering against bodies, and the assailants recoiled from the blaze with tucked heads and upraised hands.

The use of Edomic brought a euphoric rush utterly incongruent with the fear that had been squeezing Rachel's heart. Suddenly she felt more alert and capable. The logs had taken flight with more force than she had expected, probably because the command had been energized by her panic.

"They don't like fire," Ferrin called, jabbing with his torch before slashing with his sword.

Aram clubbed a sinewy woman with the flat of his sword, the impact sending her into a clumsy cartwheel. Tark swung his torch to ward off an undead teen with a bony body. Kerick released more arrows.

"Faster!" Halco warned from the rear of the group. "They're converging on us."

Peeking over her shoulder, Rachel saw figures hurrying jerkily toward them from all sides of the hill, adjusting their pursuit with alarming coordination. The slope had become steep enough that Rachel was descending sideways with her knees bent, the soles of her moccasins sliding on the dirt.

"Run!" Farfalee ordered.

Aram bullied his way forward even faster, a human wrecking ball who left broken zombies cast aside like groaning heaps of litter. Rachel did not know what they would have done without him to lead the charge. She picked up the pace along with the rest of the group. By the faint moonlight and the unsteady glow of three torches, they raced down the slope, Aram slamming enemies aside with his sword, Ferrin and the others doing their best to cut down the leftovers. The incline helped Rachel reach such great speed that she doubted whether she could stop herself. If she fell, it would be painfully spectacular. Around her the others ran with similar haste, weapons glinting in the torchlight.

As the incline became less steep, Rachel regained some control of her strides. Nollin had tripped on the slope, but Halco had dragged him to his feet speedily enough that the pair of seedmen had not fallen too far behind the others. For the moment the delegation had outdistanced the zombies, although Rachel could hear them crashing recklessly down the hillside.

"What now?" Kerick asked, still running as he spoke.

"Some of us could stand our ground and slow them," Tark offered.

"Too many of them," Farfalee said. "They'd sweep by you. The sacrifice would be meaningless."

"Split up?" Nedwin asked.

"That attack felt planned," Farfalee said, breathing hard. "Sloppy, but with evidence of organization. A group massed around us and came from all sides. If we split up, I expect they will adapt."

"We need to find a narrow place," Kerick said. "A position where a few of us might detain them."

"I saw nothing like that in the area," Nedwin said. "But we need to veer left up here or we'll get boxed in by some steep terrain."

They continued at a sprint, Aram in the front, Halco in the rear, the torches shedding just enough light to allow them to dodge natural obstacles. Behind the group, Rachel could hear their blood-less enemies crashing through bushes and stumbling over rocks. With the delegation running at full speed, the zombies were gradu-ally losing ground. Rachel doubted whether she could sustain this pace for more than a few minutes. She assumed the walking dead could keep charging all night.

"How many were there?" Nollin asked.

"At least forty," Farfalee said.

"At least sixty," Nedwin corrected.

"It will be minutes before they overtake us," Kerick asserted. "Any defensible ground up ahead?"

"A little table of rock," Nedwin said. "Maybe twenty feet above the surrounding land. One side is rather steep; the others are sheer. If we beat them there, they'd have to climb to reach us."

"No escape?" Aram asked.

"We'd only go there to make a stand," Nedwin said. "The inac-cessibility makes it defendable. I don't know of a better option."

"Lead on," Farfalee said.

"Agreed," Drake approved. "If we're caught in the open, we're finished."

"What if a pair of us head off on our own?" Nollin proposed, panting. "A small detachment might avoid detection."

"It's a gamble," Ferrin said. "If the duo gets noticed, they'll be defenseless. Who'd you have in mind?"

"Some key delegates," Nollin said. "Perhaps myself and Aram."

Rachel shook her head. Evidently Nollin had noticed the criti-cal role Aram had played during the escape.

Ferrin laughed openly. "Aram, you've been promoted to essen-tial!"

"I'm generally more appreciated at night," the big man rumbled. "I'm going to the table, Nollin."

"Maybe we should all remain together," Nollin repented.

"How far?" Halco asked.

"Maybe five minutes," Nedwin said. "Beyond this next rise the ground slopes down to a dry creek bed. The little ridge is on the far side."

They were currently running up a gentle incline. By unspoken assent, nobody was moving at a true sprint anymore. Rachel's lungs heaved with the effort to maintain her quick jog. She could clearly hear the worm zombies in pursuit. Aside from scattered moans and snarls, most made their presence known by disturbing rocks and foliage.

"They're gaining," Halco pointed out.

Farfalee increased her pace, and Rachel strained to match it. A stitch burned in her side, and the muscles in her legs protested painfully.

"Some of them are faster than others," Nedwin observed. "We're spreading them out. Many are quite slow."

They topped the rise and the slope tilted downward. Having the incline back in her favor helped Rachel find her second wind.

"Watch out," Aram called from the front. "Thorns!"

Rachel saw the half giant plowing through bushes that reached higher than his waist, which meant they came to her shoulders. Jason ran just ahead of her, and she could see thorny shrubs tearing at his robes as he charged between them. She tried to follow the path he was clearing, but many of the slender limbs whipped back into place after he ripped free. Her robe snagged in dozens of places. Rachel kept her weary legs churning despite the sharp prickers shredding the fabric of her robes and occasionally her skin.

Suppressed expressions of pain surrounded her, aggravated

hisses seasoned with some angry growls and a wounded yelp from Corinne. Aram was trying to whack the irritating vegetation with his sword, but without accomplishing much. There were just too many shrubs with too many wiry little limbs.

"Forward!" Farfalee ordered as their pace flagged.

Rachel pressed ahead, twisting and lunging in an attempt to avoid the thickest tangles. Sharp points raked scratches across much of her body. Occasionally the thorns stabbed deep, forcing her to swallow exclamations of pain. Under the light of day, the group would have doubtlessly looped around these briars, but in the dark, pursued by undead enemies, their only choice was to push agonizingly onward.

At last Rachel tore free from the last of the taller shrubs. Off to one side, she saw Nedwin towing Corinne from a thorny embrace. Rachel realized that she, Nedwin, Halco, and Corinne were now trailing the others in the group by a significant margin. Several paces ahead, Jason and Tark skidded to a halt, looking back. Close behind her, Rachel heard reckless pursuers blundering through the prickly shrubs.

With countless prickers still clinging to her robes and needling her skin, Rachel picked up her pace again. "Go!" she shrieked at Jason.

Corinne and Nedwin raced beside her. Halco followed a step or two behind. A hasty glance back showed Rachel the first of the zombies emerging from the spiny shrubs, threadbare clothes mangled. No matter how tired she felt, the frightening sight was sufficient to spur Rachel to her fastest sprint.

Thirty yards ahead, Aram and Ferrin reached the dry creek, dropping down to the rocky bed. The moon emerged from the clouds, unveiling the stone butte on the far side of the creek, vertical walls with a flat top.

Ahead of Rachel, Jason leaped into the creek bed. The lip of the creek was maybe five feet higher than the bed. When Rachel reached the brink, she slowed a bit and used her hands to help break her fall. Rocks ranging in size from apples to melons littered the floor of the creek, making footing treacherous. But with the worm zombies at her heels, there was no time for caution.

Rachel dashed across the creek bed, a pair of steps behind Corinne and Nedwin, six steps behind Jason. Halco ran at her side, his torch casting a wavering radiance around them. She could hear enemies landing on the stones behind them.

Then a rock shifted beneath Rachel's foot just as she trusted all of her weight to it. She fell hard, unforgiving stones pounding against her, one wrist screaming in pain after she had extended her hands to catch herself.

She was dead. The cold certainty hit her with inarguable clarity. Her injuries meant nothing. She would have no time to really feel them. Her undead enemies were right behind her. Rachel rolled over to her back in time to see the nearest zombie pouncing, grimy hands extended. He had long arms. Dark eyes. Ragged fingernails. A receding hairline.

Reflexively, Rachel raised a protective hand and shouted the Edomic command to push him away. The zombie went flying backward, like he had been hit by an invisible train. His body clipped a couple other undead assailants before he smashed against the low wall of the creek.

Invigorated by the successful command, Rachel beheld the scene with greater lucidity. More enemies were flooding toward her. There were already eight in the creek bed. A dozen more between the creek and the thorny shrubs. Dozens more crashing through the briars.

Halco was using torch and sword to engage a husky man clad in pelts. The combat drew the interest of a few of the nearest attackers. Nedwin and Jason crouched beside Rachel, having returned to help her to her feet. Drake dashed to assist Halco, sword flashing in the torchlight. Knife in hand, Tark placed himself between Rachel and the oncoming zombies.

The zombies were dead, Rachel realized. The worms inside might be alive, but apparently if she focused on the dead flesh, she could use Edomic!

As a desiccated middle-aged woman rushed Tark, Rachel focused on the upper half of her body and spoke the command to gather heat, pouring her panic-fueled will into the effort. The woman burst into flames, and Rachel spoke a fresh command that shoved her backward. Other zombies stumbled away from the blazing woman, eyes squinting away from the brightness. The woman collapsed to the ground, screeching and thrashing.

Halco and Drake had each incapacitated a pair of zombies. Currently a small elderly zombie dangled from Halco's arm, biting his hand. Halco fell as Drake hacked at the undersized attacker. The successful commands coupled with the horrible danger left Rachel feeling abnormally alert. As more zombies charged Drake and Halco, Rachel infused the nearest pair with fire from the waist up and shoved them toward the others.

The effort left her knees weak. While her spirit exulted, her body suddenly felt drained. From her hours of practice, Rachel knew that she was making too many ambitious commands in succession without resting. She could not keep it up much longer.

Each with an arm around her torso, Nedwin and Jason hauled Rachel across the creek bed, her arms draped across their necks, her wrist aching. She tried to help, but her legs felt limp and distant.

Farther back, Drake helped Halco retreat while a fresh wave of zombies dashed forward. "Just the heads," Rachel murmured, looking over her shoulder.

Exerting her will, she began setting the heads of the attackers on fire, one after another, working from the nearest to the farthest. The smaller targets required less effort than igniting the entire upper body, and the result seemed equally effective, leaving the victims writhing in the creek bed. After igniting the fifth head, Rachel felt blackness encroaching at the edge of her vision, and paused. She had a metallic taste in her mouth. Her head pounded.

Flaming bodies lay strewn between the zombies and their prey. The nearest zombies hesitated, baring their teeth to hiss at the fire.

"It got me," Halco huffed to Drake, who had a supportive arm across his shoulders. "I saw worms enter my wrist. Take my amar."

Sheathing his sword, Drake drew a dagger in one hand and cupped the other against the base of Halco's skull, where his seed was located. Rachel glanced away as the dagger moved, but looked back in time to see Drake placing the amar in a pouch as Halco slumped to the stony ground.

Nedwin and Jason dragged Rachel up the far side of the creek bed as the undead attackers rallied, weaving between the burning corpses. The foremost zombies descended on Halco in a frenzy.

Without Halco slowing him, Drake caught up as Rachel, Tark, Nedwin, and Jason reached the base of the rocky butte. The others were already scaling it. The least steep side was still quite a climb, only leaning slightly away from vertical, although it offered abundant handholds.

"Can you manage?" Nedwin asked.

"No strength," Rachel said. She doubted she could walk, let alone scale a steep wall. "Bad wrist."

Aram landed beside Rachel after having dropped the last several feet of the descent. He heaved her over one beefy shoulder, as if she weighed nothing. The others were climbing. Aram started up as well.

Rachel found herself facing an onrushing mob of tattered men and women, old and young, grotesquely eager. Aram was rising, but the mob would reach the butte in time to claw at his boots, perhaps to climb after him and tear him down. She felt angry. These bloodthirsty creatures had attacked without provocation. They had killed Halco. They yearned to kill all of her friends.

Extending a hand, lips moving soundlessly, she focused heat on several in the front, then mentally pushed with all of her might, hurling her will at them with the psychic equivalent of a lunging dive at the end of a hard run. She dimly saw the flames engulfing them and felt the warm rush of heat as she sank into unconsciousness.

CHAPTER 23

THE SENTINELS

Jason peered down from the brink of the huge stone block as Aram climbed below him. He flinched back as the leaders of the oncoming zombies burst into flames, a few of them from head to toe, others along one side, or just the head and shoulders. Several zombies stampeded into their burning comrades, flames spreading as they tumbled to the ground at the base of the butte. Dry wails filled the night. The nearest unburned zombies fell back, snarling impotently.

Apparently Rachel had been eating her Wheaties! Jason knew she had been practicing her Edomic, but had no idea that she had grown so powerful. She had saved them back at the creek bed. Thanks to her, around twenty zombies must have perished.

As Aram reached the top of the butte, the zombies below resurged, dodging around disgusting bonfires to start climbing the little mesa. Drake, Ferrin, Tark, Nedwin, Nollin, and Corinne began hurling rocks gathered from the top of the butte down the side. Jason joined in, discovering that solid throws to the head sent the hideous climbers tumbling.

Aram gently laid Rachel on her back and bent over her. As Jason saw the barrage of stones successfully repelling the climbing zombies, he hurried to her side. She was breathing shallowly, her face pale.

"Wiped herself out," Aram said.

"She wields serious power," Farfalee acknowledged. "If she's breathing, she'll recover. Aram, we need you guarding the edge."

Kerick approached Farfalee. "I see three of the dead standing aloof on the far side of the creek," he reported quietly.

"The masterminds?" Farfalee asked.

"They're the only enemies showing restraint," Kerick said. "I suspect they're coordinating the others."

Jason gazed where Kerick had indicated, and saw the zombies he had mentioned. They stood side-by-side on a mound well back from the creek, still and silent, one quite tall and the other two rather short.

Farfalee set an arrow to the string and bent her bow. Jason wondered if an arrow could reach that far. She tilted the bow upward and released. The projectile curved away into the night, and landed in the head of the tallest zombie. He fell out of sight and the other two hid as well.

"What a shot," Jason said, hardly believing it.

"I've had some practice," Farfalee replied.

"They're pulling back!" Aram called, hurling a stone larger than a bowling ball.

Nedwin approached Farfalee, jutting his chin toward where her arrow had flown. "Those three were the leaders?"

"Appears so," she replied.

"I can get the other two," Nedwin said.

"By all means," she invited.

Dropping flat to the ground, Nedwin crept like a salamander to the opposite side of the butte from where they had ascended, then slunk over the edge.

"Don't watch him," Farfalee murmured, turning away. "If he succeeds, it will be by stealth."

"They're already re-forming," Aram said.

"They might try to send some up one of the steeper faces," Farfalee warned. "Corinne, watch that one. Nollin, the far one. I'll keep an eye on the other."

Corinne moved to watch the designated face. The others were gathering rocks to help repel the next assault.

"Drake," Nollin said. "I'll keep Halco's amar."

"If you prefer," Drake replied, fishing the seed from a pouch. "That should keep the amar away from the fighting."

Nollin grunted. "Some of us have to survive for the good of the mission. Seems like it's chiefly my people laying down their lives on our behalf so far."

"Which is according to plan," Farfalee reminded everyone. "Nollin, please watch the rear approach."

He hustled over to the far side of the butte to stand guard.

Two more attacks came in the next few minutes, both quelled before the zombies gained much ground. Aram could throw large stones with chilling accuracy, leaving undead enemies functionless after a direct hit or two. A pair tried to scale the back side, but failed.

Rachel remained unconscious throughout. Jason checked her breathing and pulse during lulls.

After the first two attacks, the night became still. Eventually Nedwin returned, signaling carefully before climbing the easiest side.

"They've pulled back," he announced after reaching the top. "I dispatched two of the three leaders. They were a little tough to find. I finished the man with the arrow in his head and cut down a short, older man. I left the woman alive after she vowed to withdraw with her remaining forces."

"She could communicate?" Farfalee asked.

"With some exertion, yes. Her mind is far gone. But with her companions disabled and having freshly lost a limb, she made the effort."

"You believe we can trust her?" Nollin challenged.

"Not much," Nedwin replied. "But I wanted to prevent us from getting besieged here. I think we can at least trust her sense of self-preservation. More than half of her followers have been rendered inert. She knows I can get to her whenever I choose. I watched her lead the others away before I returned. I demanded that they go north, away from our route, and they complied."

"You didn't get infected?" Nollin asked.

"I'm uncompromised," Nedwin said.

"We should move," Ferrin urged. "The leader could change her mind. Or she might lose control of her minions. Nedwin is right. We can't afford to get pinned down."

"I agree," Farfalee said. "We'll have to choose our campsites with greater care. Our scouts should range even farther. Had we stopped for the night atop this rock, we might still have Halco with us."

"I'll carry the girl," Aram muttered, picking up Rachel carefully.

Jason found the climb down the little bluff disconcerting. Fleeing up the craggy slope to escape zombies had seemed simple. But while descending, he found it hard to decide where to place his hands and feet. Forced to gaze down in search of handholds, he became disconcertingly aware of the height and the potential fall. Corinne seemed to climb down without much trouble, which motivated him to endure the descent without complaint.

The rest of the night passed quietly, although Jason kept a hand on his sword. He had slashed his way past two zombies during the hurried escape. It had felt like hacking at bundles of dead sticks—they weren't overly heavy or solid, and his blade hadn't cut very deep. He had basically used his sword as a tool to knock them away while he dodged around them.

The group remained in motion until dawn, when Aram shrank and had to lay Rachel down. Nedwin, Kerick, Drake, and Ferrin were off scouting in different directions. Farfalee knelt beside Rachel and wafted a tiny bag of smelling salts beneath her nostrils. Rachel's eyes opened abruptly, and she sat up with a gasp.

Farfalee placed a steadying hand on her shoulder. "We're all right," the seedwoman assured her.

Rachel sagged a bit. "That's good." She narrowed her eyes and rubbed her forehead. "Ow!"

"You overextended yourself," Farfalee said. "I used to see it with wizards of old."

"I burned a lot of those zombies," Rachel said with a smile.

"Yes," Farfalee said. "I was surprised how much power you brought to bear. If you were able to muster much more, you probably would have destroyed yourself along with them. Be grateful you passed out. You must learn to rein in your abilities before they destroy you. It would be shameful to see such promise snuffed out."

"I'll try to be careful," Rachel said, although her expression looked stubborn rather than repentant. "You knew wizards?"

"The eldest of my people remember our father, Eldrin, and the wizards of his time," she said. "And I am among the eldest. Can you stand?"

"I think so." With help Rachel arose, her face scrunched up. "My head is pounding. And my joints feel sore."

"Ideally, I would let you rest," Farfalee apologized. "Unfortunately, we're far from the ideal out here."

"And our biggest asset won't be back until sundown," Jason added.

Farfalee nodded. "Without Aram to force a way past our attackers, we might all have perished. Let's hope we can evade them throughout the day."

It was afternoon when Drake reported the approaching horsemen.

"Three of them," he said, still breathing hard after his sprint to rejoin the group. "Heading right for us."

Farfalee suggested they retreat to the cover of some boulders to help negate any advantage the horses might offer. She got her bow ready. Nedwin and Ferrin returned from scouting before the horsemen came into sight, although Kerick remained abroad.

All three horsemen wore helms and armor. They cantered briskly, eventually bringing their steeds to a halt and saluting from a distance. "Hail, visitors to our land," called the foremost rider. He waved a white handkerchief. "May we approach and confer under a flag of truce?"

"You may," Farfalee invited.

The horsemen rode forward at a walk, stopping several paces shy of the cluster of boulders. "Who is your leader?" asked the rider in front, face hidden by a visor.

"I am," Farfalee answered boldly, striding into view. "Who do you represent?"

"The last remnant of the grand kingdom of Ebera," he replied, removing his helm. The rider looked to be in his twenties, with thick auburn hair, heavy eyebrows, and shaggy sideburns. He had an unhealthy pallor.

"You're not infected?" Farfalee asked, astonished.

He gave a somber smile. "None escaped the plague. Some of us have managed to cling to our reason. You are one of the Amar Kabal?"

"Indeed," Farfalee answered. "Great need has brought us into your realm."

"No doubt you have your reasons," he acknowledged. "You come at a timely hour. Our reasoning citizenry has dwindled. Only a few years ago we had five settlements. Now three remain. We must outlast the mindless ones and the hungry ones."

"We faced many of the walking dead last night," Farfalee said.

The rider nodded. "Many fell. Others have been left vulnerable. Our leaders are strategizing over how best to exploit the opportunity. Come with us. Let us escort you to safe beds and warm food."

"Safe beds?" Farfalee questioned. "Shouldn't we fear contamination?"

"We mean you no harm," the rider assured her. "We are drawn to your blood, but we have learned to curb our thirst. We keep herds within the city walls and sate our urges with the blood of animals. We could use your help, and you need ours. The mindless ones and hungry ones have united into savage tribes. The largest lies to the south and already has your scent."

"How many?" Farfalee asked.

"Several hundred," he replied, "including a multitude of cunning chieftains."

Jason shivered. How could they possibly get past an army of several hundred zombies?

"Perhaps you can aid us," Farfalee allowed. "We have to cross your land and reach the Prophetess of Mianamon to the south."

The rider hesitated before responding. "You're aware that none who enter Ebera are permitted to leave."

"Our need is an exception," Farfalee stated.

His unblinking eyes did not leave hers. "We allow no exceptions. Do you understand the virulence of this condition? A mighty kingdom succumbed within days. We sentinels have stood watch ever since to contain the epidemic. Without our efforts and our fortunate geography, all of Lyrian would share our fate."

"I am Farfalee, daughter of Hessit," Farfalee said calmly. "What is your name?"

"Borial."

"Inform us about the condition, Borial."

"The goma worms inhabit human flesh," Borial said. "We have encountered no other susceptible animal. The worms were perfectly engineered in that respect. They feed on blood, preferably human, but any fresh blood can nourish them. Introduced to a living subject, the worms multiply and consume all internal blood within two days. Once the blood is depleted, the worms keep the body operational and share the desire for more blood with their host."

"How did you resist the urges?" Farfalee asked.

"Strength of will, I suppose," Borial said. "I've always had a deep sense of self and a strong respect for propriety, which is common among those who have resisted. My aptitude for resistance may also be physiological, a consequence of how the worms physically interact with my tissue and my brain. Most could not suppress the urge, which helped the disease spread. Without the blood of animals, the hunger would eventually govern even the strongest of us. As we're injured, or as we age, some among us lose our restraint."

"You appear young," Farfalee observed.

"The worms preserve our bodies at the age we were taken," he said. "They can work remarkable feats of healing. But every injury takes a toll, particularly where the brain is involved."

"Some of the walking dead seem to have lost their humanity," Nedwin observed. "But the leaders among those we faced were still capable of speech."

"Succumbing to the hunger seems to accelerate the decline of the mind," Borial said. "In the end, they become the mindless ones. Some hold on to awareness longer than others. The hungry ones lack restraint but retain some human cunning."

"Why haven't they sought to escape Ebera?" Farfalee asked.

"Some have tried," Borial said. "We don't let them. We have patrolled the borders since we first established any stability. King Linus helped protect the reasoning individuals among the infected and saved Lyrian. He burned the ships, wrecked the ferries, demolished the bridges, and closed the borders. He retained his reason after becoming infected, and helped those of us with self-possession to wall ourselves away from the others.

"The early days were ugliest. An endless massacre on both sides. Entire towns burned. Fire is the best way to ensure the destruction of the worms. They can hibernate for centuries. Over time they can knit broken bodies back into functionality.

"I do not believe Kel Jerud meant to destroy the world if thieves invaded his tower. Just Ebera. For all their adaptability, he designed the worms with several weaknesses. They are not fond of sunlight. They detest extreme heat and cold. They abhor water. And they perish in fire."

"I see," Farfalee said. "The abhorrence of water keeps them off the sea and away from the rivers. The dislike of cold keeps them from scaling the mountains or working their way into the tundra. Their distaste for sunlight further discourages travel. And should all else fail, the reasoning dead hold them in check."

"Correct," Borial confirmed. "I'm not sure Kel Jerud anticipated the reasoning dead. We're actually most important for people like you. Mortals who cross into Ebera and who might exit contaminated actually pose the greatest threat. King Linus still wears the crown, and his incontrovertible edict is that all who enter Ebera must remain. We will attempt to let you dwell among us without contamination for as long as possible. Our settlements are within strong walls, though the largest tribes of hungry ones have found ways to threaten our security of late."

"Did they only recently become organized?" Nedwin asked.

"To this scale, yes," Borial replied. "A startling adaptation. One of our great advantages, despite our limited numbers, has always been our capacity for teamwork. Over the years, we began to realize our dream of hunting the mindless ones into extinction. We bred livestock behind our walls while in the surrounding countryside easy prey had grown scarce. The most devious of the hungry ones kept out of our way, hiding in deep lairs. In recent years they have begun to unite and attract followers. All of us can detect blood from great distances, and the blood of our livestock called to them. Unity was the only way to rob us, so they united, and some of our strongholds have fallen, along with some of our most stalwart warriors. Only the three strongest settlements remain, defended by fewer hands than any of us would prefer."

"And you want our help defending your walls," Farfalee concluded.

"That, and more," Borial acknowledged. "Human blood is irresistible to our foes. They can survive on animal blood, but yours is nectar. The scent of your blood could lure them into folly. If we can finally trap them and burn them, all of Lyrian will be safer."

"We are also on a mission to save Lyrian," Farfalee explained.

"From what threat?" Borial inquired.

"The emperor Maldor," Farfalee said. "The former apprentice to Zokar is poised to bring all of Lyrian under his dominion. Our party represents the last hope for the races of Eldrin and any who oppose darkness, injustice, and tyranny."

"I am willing to accept that your cause is just and good," Borial said. "However our duties as the sentinels of Ebera transcend all matters of politics and personal interest. None who enter Ebera may leave for any reason. We will faithfully uphold that decree until the last of us expires."

"We're not infected," Drake said with some heat in his voice. "If we were compromised, yes, by all means, prevent us from leaving. But since we're whole, why not help us make it through your kingdom without contamination?"

"This plague could destroy all human life in Lyrian," Borial bristled. "The only sure way to contain it is by never making exceptions."

"Exceptions have already been made," Ferrin countered. "Maldor has sent spies into Ebera more than once. He will do so again. If he can use the plague as a weapon, he will. He must be stopped. He represents a much greater threat of contamination than our modest delegation. He is the enemy we seek to dethrone."

"We've been attacked by one group of worm-infested maniacs already," Drake asserted in a steely tone. "Despite your powers of reason, I'm not finding much difference between you and your less civil countrymen, except in numbers."

"Drake," Farfalee cautioned.

"What?" Drake replied coldly. "You see where this is going. It won't end politely, so there's no use in squandering valuable time."

"Does this one speak for all of you?" Borial asked, eyes darting.

"We need horses," Farfalee said. "With horses we could easily cross Ebera without becoming contaminated."

"Perhaps," Borial considered. "We would have to visit the lord of our settlement. If you explain your need in full, he might grant what you ask."

An arrow appeared in Farfalee's hand, ready to fly, her bow suddenly stretched. Jason could not say how she had nocked and pulled it so quickly. "We won't walk into any traps. You cannot imagine the import of our mission. Let us continue on our way, and we will let you return to your duties. You need to dismount now, or your reasoning dead will lose another able warrior."

Borial smirked. "Farfalee, there are many others like me—mounted, well equipped, and ready to do anything to prevent you and your comrades from leaving Ebera. They know where I am. They know when I should return. Listen to reason. Do not act rashly. Lay down your arms. Join us. Trust others to take up your cause. Your road must end here, for the good of all."

"I don't want to harm you," Farfalee said, unflinching. "We need your mounts, and I can't have you warning your fellow sentinels."

Borial did nothing to conceal his outrage. "I have spent more than a hundred years protecting you!" His eyes shifted to Drake. "And you." Then to Nedwin. "And you. Yet you threaten me because you find the precautions necessary to safeguard humankind inconvenient?" He plunged a hand into a satchel and pulled out a heap of little gray balls piled onto his palm. "Hibernating goma worms. Of no threat to me. But potentially quite problematic for you. Should I toss them in your direction, at least half of you will face infection. That might alter the tenor of our conversation."

Jason prepared to dive behind the nearest boulder. The other horsemen had each grabbed their own handful of worms.

"Is there any room for compromise here?" Farfalee asked, her arrow trained on the center of Borial's forehead.

Before Borial could reply, his hand burst into flame. So did the hands of the other two riders. So did all three satchels from which the goma worms had been withdrawn.

"Fly!" Borial cried, face contorted in pain. The three riders wheeled their horses about. Farfalee put futile arrows in two of their backs. Nedwin darted from amid the boulders and tore one rider from the saddle before his horse could pick up speed. Extending a hand, Rachel flung Borial from his saddle with a gesture and a word, then dropped to one knee, one hand pressed to the hollow of her temple, blood leaking from one nostril.

The third rider was getting away, beyond the reach of any in the company—until Kerick leaped out of hiding and tackled him from his saddle. Jason could hear Rachel murmuring Edomic from her kneeling position.

"Knock it off," Jason said. "You're wiped out. You haven't healed."

She glared up at him defiantly, brows knitted in pain. "We need the horses."

Jason noticed that the horses had slowed and were coming back around. "Okay, good point, but we've got it from here." She bowed her head. He knelt beside her, wrapping an arm around her shoulders. "You okay?"

She nodded, eyes squeezed shut. "Ever had an ice cream headache?"

"Sure."

"Picture having a really bad one and then guzzling down a freezing shake."

Jason winced. "I'm sorry."

"Not your fault. Bad luck. I was barely starting to feel a little better. At least the commands worked. Did the zombies get away?"

Jason looked up. "We've got them. And the fires are out. We have the horses, too. Good job."

CHAPTER 24

THE WILD CLAN

The three horses made all the difference. Suddenly Rachel could ride instead of hobble along, one scout could thoroughly explore the territory ahead, and another could effectively monitor the country around them.

Nollin had been loudest in his desire to slay the injured sentinels. Farfalee contended that Borial was indeed engaged in a noble cause and should be given the maximum possible leniency. Nedwin noted that the riders must have ranged far on horseback, and on foot would probably not find their comrades in time to cause harm. Nollin argued that search parties might find Borial in time to mount a pursuit. In the end, they left Borial and his two countrymen alive but without footwear.

For Rachel, the first day on horseback was agony. Her sore, swollen wrist was the least of her problems. It felt like her skull had shattered into irregular fragments and was now only held together by her scalp. Every jolt as her mount plodded forward stabbed painfully throughout her head. Rachel felt Corinne trying to contact her telepathically, but even the simple effort of will that allowed Rachel to understand the messages was too great. She could hardly think through the pain, let alone attempt telepathy.

Nedwin gave her a preparation for the pain, but despite the unfortunate taste and unpleasant medicinal smell, the concoction did nothing to ease her suffering. What if the damage from the overexertion was permanent? What if the pain never subsided? What if the injury was to her mind rather than merely her brain? Worries plagued her as the pain gnawed persistently into the night.

By the next day, her body showed signs of recovery. Her joints were stiff rather than sore, her wrist was less bothersome, her appetite was returning, and the ache in her head had eased to an uncomfortable tenderness that flared less violently than the day before.

Rachel wondered what exactly the magic had done to her body. Were the headaches a side effect of the forces called into action by the Edomic commands or a direct result of overextending her will? Could she expect similar symptoms after overtaxing herself in the future, or would she face a new set of unwelcome consequences? She hoped never to find out.

On the morning of the third day after meeting Borial, while still bundled where she had slept, Rachel heard Farfalee arguing with Ferrin.

"We've approached the wild horses twice," Ferrin said. "They're too skittish. You would be too if every person you met was a zombie intent on draining your blood. Even astride our own horses, we haven't gotten close. If she could just calm them."

"Did you watch her face yesterday?" Farfalee asked. "Have you noticed how she moves like an old woman? I tell you, any exercise of Edomic before she mends puts her at great risk."

"And an army of hundreds of the walking dead puts us all at great risk," Nollin answered. "They can smell us from miles away, and for all we know, they've assembled and are preparing to intercept us as we speak. She's the only one who can do this."

"The mobility more horses would offer could save our lives," Kerick said.

"Once she mends," Farfalee said. "She needs more—"

"I'm mended enough," Rachel interrupted, sitting up. "You found horses?"

Farfalee glared at Ferrin, Kerick, and Nollin before turning to Rachel. "You've been through some heavy trauma," Farfalee said. "You saw what happened when you pushed yourself too hard before recovering."

"It was worse than the first big effort," Rachel admitted. "And that was bad enough. But I'm feeling better now."

"You keep resting," Farfalee insisted. "You could very well develop into our greatest weapon against Maldor."

"I won't develop into anything if we all get eaten by zombies. Besides, influencing horses is more a suggestion than a command. It doesn't take as much effort."

Farfalee sighed. She glanced at Ferrin and Kerick, then back at Rachel. "Very well. Since the need is urgent, I'll defer to your judgment." She turned to Ferrin. "When Drake and Nedwin return, go see what you can find."

Rachel found Corinne and Jason breakfasting on fruit and nuts. Jason met her eyes with a smile. "You look better!"

"Thanks," Rachel said. "It feels like the day after being sick. I'm not all the way back, but so much better than the worst of it." Rachel winked at Corinne. *Good to see you, too!*

Are you sure you can talk like this? Corinne checked worriedly.

Feels natural again, Rachel assured her.

"Are you guys already doing telepathy?" Jason asked. "That was the one good thing about your headache. People using words for a change."

"We still use words," Rachel said.

Jason shook his head regretfully. "It's like everyone is texting, and I don't have a phone."

Rachel ate nuts and fruit with Jason and Corinne. Their camaraderie felt more natural and pleasant than ever, probably because she was no longer imprisoned in her own private cell of anguish.

After Drake and Nedwin returned, Ferrin claimed Nedwin's mount and Rachel climbed onto hers. Drake, Ferrin, and Rachel set out toward where Nedwin had last spotted the wild herd. For everyone to have a horse, they would need eight more. Ferrin and Drake each bore a pair of improvised rope halters.

They rode for the better part of an hour before pausing on a ridge to gaze down on the herd in a valley below. Even from a distance, the wild horses looked considerably mangier than their current mounts.

"Can you reach them from here?" Ferrin asked.

"Maybe," Rachel said. "The chances go up as we get nearer."

"They'll run if we get too near," Drake said. "They've learned to keep away from people."

"As we move closer, I'll keep sending calming messages," Rachel assured them. "What do you guys need to do?"

"I brought some of the sweetleaves that I normally save for tea," Drake said.

"I have fruit," Ferrin said. "If Drake and I can each claim a pair of horses, we'll be halfway to our goal."

"There must be at least thirty," Rachel estimated.

"Seems like plenty," Drake said. "But they're fast, and they're unburdened by riders. So far Ferrin and I haven't managed to get close enough to have any chance of catching one. Kerick knows horses as well and has had no luck either."

"If you can keep them from running," Ferrin said, "we'll do the rest."

From where she sat, Rachel invited the horses to eat and relax. As Drake and Ferrin led her closer, she sent calming Edomic messages. She told the horses that she, Ferrin, and Drake meant no harm. She sent impressions of safety and security. As she pushed hard, Rachel noticed a faint pain blossoming behind her eyes.

By the time they reached the herd, the horses were all grazing tranquilly. Most of the horses appeared scrawnier than the other mounts Rachel had seen in Lyrian. But despite their unkempt coats and rawboned frames, they generally seemed healthy. A few let out gentle whickers to welcome the newcomers. Most paid them no mind.

Ferrin and Drake approached their prospects on foot, petting them and sharing treats before slipping on halters. Rachel spoke peace to the horses, and evidently they listened.

"What other horses would you ideally want?" Rachel asked.

After conferring, Drake and Ferrin pointed out four other mounts. While Ferrin and Drake each led a pair of horses, Rachel called to the other four with her mind. More than ten followed, and then the entire herd.

Rachel had an annoying headache by the time they made it back to camp. The others could not believe the bounteous equine entourage, and set about rigging additional halters. By the time the sun went down, everyone had spent time getting accustomed to their chosen mount. Though wild and presumably never ridden, the horses remained mostly obedient and manageable. Rachel went to sleep with her head throbbing at a tolerable level.

Halco entered camp shortly before sunrise. He approached with his hands up, Nedwin riding behind him, and showed no ire at the bows bent in his direction. Several of the horses let out spirited whinnies, but even those without pickets did not gallop away.

"He claims he hasn't lost his mind," Nedwin explained.

"I haven't," Halco affirmed. "I've lost my amar, and my life, and my looks, but somehow my mind remains."

His robes were soiled and torn, and all visible skin was pale and blemished with puckered scars. The tips of two adjacent fingers were missing, as were some patches of his long hair. And he moved with less grace, favoring one leg slightly.

"I'm full of worms, naturally," he announced. "I checked. But since I retained my sense of self, I decided I might still be of service. I chose to track you. I know I'm little more than a ghost. My real self is in the amar. But I thought I may as well do all I can to help ensure I get planted somewhere far from here."

"Can you . . . smell us?" Nollin asked.

"Your blood? I can, yes. The walking dead apparently feasted on me. I was unconscious. They drained me, and the worms took whatever I had left before I woke. I awoke bloodless. I didn't even have traces on my robes. Your smell made it easier to track you. I could hurry through the night without rest. So far I feel no fatigue. I figured you could give me a clean end when we reach the river."

"You can control your appetite?" Farfalee asked. Her direct tone demanded honesty.

"I believe so," Halco answered without pause. "Considering what I've become, it's odd how unchanged my mind feels. I think I can regulate myself. I feel well inside of my limits. I don't expect to be a threat. I might be a help, though."

"Does it hurt?" Nollin asked hesitantly.

"No pain. My senses have changed. The sun bothers my eyes. My hearing has an irritating echo. While my sense of touch has been dulled, I've grown much more sensitive to smell. I'm still getting accustomed to it."

"If a horse will carry you, please join us," Farfalee invited. "But watch yourself. Keep your distance. No close proximity. It will be the token of your self-control."

"I won't disappoint you."

The wild horses proved sturdy. With three or four mounted scouts roving, and everyone on horseback, the group made rapid progress. Following advice from the scouts, they took a zigzag route to keep well away from the mobs of zombies trying to close in on them. The horses proved much quicker than even the most eager zombies. The vast horde of walking dead to the south had no chance of heading them off once they had been spotted and a detour was devised.

Moving ambitiously during the day allowed the delegation to almost relax at night. Still, they remained vigilant, with a mounted sentry always in motion, and their weapons ready. Halco prowled the darkness on foot, a tireless fail-safe.

Within a few days Rachel could feel no lingering effects from her overexertion earlier in the week. She issued suggestions to the horses at her leisure without adverse reactions and maintained effortless telepathic conversations with Corinne. If anything, she felt more capable than before. Most of the herd had stopped following them, but five riderless stragglers persisted, even after Rachel had gently invited them to leave. In the end, she decided that a few spare mounts wouldn't hurt anything.

The morning they sighted the Silver River glistening in the distance was the same morning Kerick galloped to the group and breathlessly reported a host of more than a hundred riders in hasty pursuit.

"Can we make it to the river?" Farfalee asked.

"Maybe," Kerick answered. "They're coming hard from the southeast. We'll have to veer southwest to have a chance of reaching the water first."

"Of course, crossing the river will be the problem," Aram observed.

Rachel frowned. The Silver River was the main eastern outlet for runoff from the mountains. Farfalee had warned that it averaged more than half a mile across.

"To the southwest," Farfalee urged.

They ran the horses hard for the first time. Until now, the greatest need had been to conserve energy. Rachel enjoyed the wind in her face, and she sent suggestions to the mounts to run quickly and steadily.

As they cantered across the top of a tall ridge, Rachel glanced back and glimpsed their pursuers for the first time, a galloping cavalry small with distance. Kerick had been right. There looked to be at least a hundred of them. A hundred reasoning undead warriors, armored and mounted. Rachel wondered how many of them she would set on fire before she fell. Then she wondered if she should even resist them. After all, they were just trying to keep the world safe from the ravages of a devastating plague. Hiding from the thought, she clung to the small hope that she and her friends might outrun them.

As the glittering expanse of the Silver River drew nearer, a pair of horsemen appeared up ahead, racing toward them. Of the four scouts, only Drake had failed to report back since the undead riders were sighted. One of the two riders was Drake. The other turned out to be Sakar, the emissary to the drinlings, whom Rachel had not seen since the Seven Vales.

"This way," Sakar ordered without explanation.

They followed him west, directly away from the riders, paralleling the river rather than heading toward it. Farfalee rode beside Sakar, but Rachel could not overhear the conversation.

The delegation reached a mounting series of low ridges backed by sizable hills. Atop the first ridge, Sakar pulled his horse to a stop. The brush around him stirred, and several men and women stood up, wrapped in cloaks expertly designed to blend with the wild terrain. Rachel felt her horse prance nervously, and quietly spoke Edomic words of comfort.

"Meet Ul, son of Tha," Sakar said gravely, "chief of the wild clan of drinlings."

A stocky man with a broad nose and heavy jaw nodded curtly. His mouth was firm, but smile lines radiated from his attentive eyes. His golden brown skin had a different tint than any complexion Rachel had seen before, and his irises were coppery, like bright pennies. The coloring seemed shared by the other members of his party.

Ul turned to Sakar and spoke in an indecipherable burst of rapid, clipped syllables.

"He tells me we should fall back and try to keep out of sight," Sakar translated. "He will confer with the sentinels of Ebera on our behalf."

"Thank you," Farfalee said, bowing her head in appreciation.

Ul gave a curt nod and waved her away.

Rachel and the others followed Sakar to a higher ridge. After securing the horses, Sakar led the group to a position where they could observe the plain below unobtrusively from behind a screen of tall brush. Rachel positioned herself near Farfalee and Sakar.

"The wild clan are drinlings?" Rachel asked quietly.

"Correct," Farfalee said. "Evidently, the drinlings are the only race in Lyrian immune to the goma worms. In recent years they have played an increasingly pivotal role patrolling the Silver River."

"I only recently learned this as I explained our need," Sakar said. "The drinlings are divided into forty clans. The wild clan has historically provided many of the finest drinling warriors and has maintained close ties with the Amar Kabal."

"Mind you," Farfalee inserted, "drinlings seldom live more than two years. So for them, it has been many generations since they have worked with Sakar or any of our people."

"But they keep an extensive oral history," Sakar said. "A necessity if they hope to preserve a group identity, in spite of their brief life spans."

The undead horsemen came into view on the far side of the plain, riding hard. As Rachel watched from the top of the ridge, she thought surely there must be many more than a hundred. "What will happen?" Rachel asked, noticing that Jason and Ferrin had drifted over close enough to listen.

"They will talk," Sakar said. "Ul will claim we are all in his custody. He will ask the sentinels of Ebera to leave the matter in his hands."

"And if they refuse?" Rachel asked.

"The wild clan is ready and willing to fight," Sakar said. "The result would be tragic. We need the sentinels of Ebera right where they are, doing just what they're doing."

"The drinlings could win?" Rachel asked.

"Drinlings were made to fight," Farfalee said. "It's like Eldrin somehow compressed eighty years of energy into two. The drinlings are strong, tireless warriors. They don't die easily, and they heal very quickly. They're immune to most sicknesses and toxins. They never sleep, not even in a trance. They can eat and digest almost anything—even soil. They supposedly can also draw energy from the air and the sun."

"And there are more drinlings ready to take the field than a glance would suggest," Sakar added. "Horses or not, the sentinels won't stand a chance."

"Why are the drinlings helping us?" Jason asked.

"The drinlings are not currently avoiding the war because they love Felrook," Sakar answered. "On the contrary, for years the drinlings stood between Maldor and the east coast of Lyrian. They made the kingdom of Kadara untouchable and received aid from Kadara in the form of men and arms.

"As the conflict wore on, and as more kingdoms fell elsewhere, Maldor brought ever greater hosts against the drinlings. Eventually the drinlings' numbers began to dwindle. The king of Kadara withdrew his support from the drinlings, choosing instead to fortify his defenses. Kadara and others had taken the fierce commitment of the drinlings for granted for ages, but in this instance, the drinlings surprised everyone. Instead of sacrificing themselves to buy Kadara more time to prepare, the drinlings quit the fight. They abruptly stopped resisting and turned their efforts to evading. They know the hills south of here like no other people, and eventually the hosts of Maldor gave up trying to chase them. The commanders opted to bypass the drinlings and engage Kadara."

"Kadara definitely had it coming," Ferrin murmured.

"So where do they stand now?" Rachel asked.

"In the years since quitting the fight, the numbers of the drinlings have made a significant recovery," Sakar explained.

"It helps when pregnancy lasts little more than a week, and twins or triplets are common," Farfalee commented.

Sakar nodded. "There has always been a high mortality rate with drinling women during childbirth. That rate is increasing. But they are doing their best. I told Ul about Galloran's return and the possible involvement of the Amar Kabal against Felrook. He knows that once Kadara falls, the drinlings will be encompassed by enemies. If this rebellion comes to fruition, he pledged the involvement of his clan."

"What of the other clans?" Ferrin asked.

"Ul and I will work to convince them," Sakar said. "It may take some time. For now, he has vowed to intervene with the sentinels of Ebera on our behalf. It was he who warned me that the sentinels would never allow you to cross the Silver River. He brought his people across in unprecedented numbers to give you a chance."

On the plain below the ridge, a detachment of riders approached Ul and a party of drinlings. Rachel was much too far away to catch any of the words. At one point, Ul turned and gave a signal with one arm. Hundreds of drinlings stood up along the ridge and on the plain, casting aside their camouflaged cloaks.

The discussion on the plain continued. Eventually, the detachment of riders turned and galloped back to their comrades. Within minutes, the undead horsemen were riding away to the east.

In time, Ul joined Sakar and Farfalee on the ridge. Three others came forward with him—a girl and a boy who looked not much older than Rachel or Jason, and an older man crisscrossed with scars, especially on the left side of his face and body. His left hand was missing, replaced by a sharp metal spike with a small hook affixed to one side.

The girl introduced herself as Nia, the boy as Io. "My father wishes us to speak for him," the girl said in a clear voice with a slight accent. "He has little patience for a language so tedious as yours."

"He means no offense," Io clarified. "Our language, Ji, conveys information much more succinctly, although it lacks the variety and nuances of your tongue." Rachel immediately liked Io. He seemed calm and considerate. And it didn't hurt that he had handsome features—more boy band than rock star, but undeniably cute.

"Father negotiated your freedom," Nia said. "We have a boat waiting to convey you to the south. We keep a few hidden along the river. You will officially remain under our vigilant watch for three days. If any of you have contracted the plague, you will be burned."

Halco cleared his throat. "I'm infected."

A brief patter of syllables flowed from Ul.

"Father says you can either perish by fire or seek to join the sentinels," Io relayed.

Brow lowered, Halco thumbed a jagged scar on the back of one hand. He attempted to answer twice before the words came out. "I might prefer to join the sentinels. My hunger remains manageable, and I suppose they can find a use for every man they can get."

The request was translated, and Ul favored Halco with a nodding smile of acknowledgment. Through Io, he assured Halco that his assistance would be valued.

"My father also desires to relate that my brother and I are intended as gifts to your cause," Nia said. "He was informed that you would need representatives from his people to join you at Mianamon, to allow for a more accurate prophecy. Of all his children, we are the slowest."

"Meaning we are most adept at conversing in your language," Io added. "And we are young, so we still have much life ahead of us."

"We're both in our fifth month," Nia explained. "He's two weeks older."

"I come too," said the heavily scarred man, his accent much thicker.

"He's Raz, our mentor," Io explained. "He killed a mangler while unarmed, to save our mother."

"Tree," said Ul, holding up three fingers. He pointed at Raz, scowling and clenching a fist, as if to suggest he was tough. Then he held a hand out toward the other two and moved the other hand like a jabbering mouth while rolling his eyes.

"Father!" Nia exclaimed, appalled.

"We sometimes talk too much," Io apologized.

Ul spat some chattering syllables.

"We must wait until after dark for the boat," Nia translated. "We should remain here for the present. He will send for some agreeable food."

After many thanks had been expressed to Ul and his clan, the meeting ended. Nia and Io gravitated toward Corinne, Jason, and Rachel—perhaps because they appeared to be of a similar age. The conversation started slowly and politely, with Rachel and Jason explaining that they were Beyonders and Corinne explaining that she used to live in a swamp.

"You have interesting pasts," Nia said. "I have never left these hills, though I've yearned to see the world."

"You speak our language well," Jason said. "Have you had a lot of practice?"

"Chiefly among my people," Nia said. "Many among us endeavor to keep the tradition alive in the hope of future alliances."

"We once met a messenger from Kadara who spoke with us," Io said. "He wanted us to attack the army besieging the city of Highport. Father told him we would send Kadara the same assistance in their hour of need as they sent us when we faced extinction."

"Afterward, Father told us that if there had been any hope of success, he would have attacked," Nia said. "Regardless of our past grievances, none of us are pleased to see Kadara fall and the emperor grow stronger."

"I can't believe you guys are five months old," Jason said. "When I was five months old, I was a bald little baby who couldn't do much more than cry."

Io chuckled. "Our lives move at a different pace. Our parents begin teaching us the moment we are born. We never sleep. Our minds mature faster along with our bodies."

"I was less than a month old when my mother discovered my aptitude for English," Nia said. "It is why I was given such an extravagant name."

"I was the same," Io said. "In Ji, two syllables is a very long word."

"We come from a long-lived line," Nia explained. "We develop a touch slower, but we live longer than many drinlings. Some of our ancestors survived nearly three years."

Rachel looked away.

Io touched her shoulder. "That sounds quick to you."

"A little," Rachel replied, not wanting to emphasize her discomfort. How unfair for them to live so briefly!

"I have heard that some outside our culture feel this way," Io said. "You must understand, our lives feel sufficient to us. Does your life feel long enough? Eighty years?"

"Yeah," she said. "I guess."

Io smiled. He had a smile like his father. "Yet compare yourself to the Amar Kabal. If you tally their many lives, they could endure a hundred times longer than you. Or more. To them, your life seems fleeting. To you, our lives seem short."

"To us, all of you live much too long," Nia joked. "How tedious it must become!"

Rachel forced a smile. "I see what you mean. It's all relative." She still felt the wizard who had devised a two-year life span must have been terribly insensitive.

"Besides," Io said, eyes twinkling, "we have some advantages. We never get ill. And we don't have to wait for food!" He tore up a clump of weeds, put it in his mouth, chewed, and swallowed.

"No way!" Jason said. "That won't make you sick?"

"Our bodies consume a lot of energy," Nia explained. "We need plenty of nourishment." She shoved a palmful of dirt into her mouth.

Rachel winced. "Doesn't it taste bad?"

"Not to us," Io said. "It probably tastes bad to you because your body can't use it."

"Don't you like normal food better?" Jason asked.

"Depends on what you call normal," Nia said, biting off a portion of a dry twig, clearly enjoying how Jason cringed. Rachel could hear the twig snapping as Nia chewed. "Unlike many other cultures, we never cook our food."

Io made a disgusted face. "Talk about ruining flavor."

"The stick doesn't hurt your teeth?" Corinne asked.

"Our teeth are tough," Nia assured her.

"Okay, I'm a little jealous," Jason admitted.

"Just wait a few months until you have to treat us as your elders," Nia replied.

Rachel laughed along with the others, but the thought still made her a little sad.

⊹⊹⊹✦CHAPTER 25 ✦⊹⊹⊹

THE LAST INN

J ason leaned against the side of the ship, staring out at the rolling swells and the coast beyond, blue with distance. The scent of the salt on the air made him thirsty, and he took a sip from his waterskin. He tried not to think of poor Corinne, huddled at the back of the boat, unable to keep any food down.

After dizzying heights, blasting winds, and murderous zombies, the ocean voyage had been just what he needed to get his equilibrium back. He almost regretted that they would reach their destination tonight. He supposed he was relieved for Corinne's sake.

For almost a week this boat had represented the only safety he had really known since departing the Seven Vales. Long and narrow, with a dozen oars on each side and a big square sail, the drinling vessel had outpaced a variety of more elaborate ships manned by Kadarians.

Jason had watched the drinlings in awe that first night. A stocky people, they tended to have more muscle than height; they were broad through the shoulders, with long torsos and sturdy legs. They seemed to put all of their power into each stroke, but still found reserves for another and another and another. They didn't break to rest or to sleep. Only to eat and to drink.

Heaps of black tubers had crowded the boat at the outset of the voyage. Nia had explained that the dense tubers were a favorite among her people, due to their rich nutrients. Inedible to most living things, the rootlike growths flourished beneath the soil among the hills where the drinlings dwelled.

By sunrise on the first morning aboard the longboat, they had already passed beyond the estuary of the Silver River to the open sea. A surprising amount of the black tubers had already been consumed, and the drinlings showed no hesitation about washing them down with seawater. As they rowed, Jason watched the bodies of the drinlings adapt to the work, muscles thickening across backs and along arms, men and women alike. Rather than tiring out over time, the drinling rowers were growing stronger and more able.

The longboat was not designed for as many passengers as it presently carried, but the members of the delegation made the best of it. Sleeping was the worst part, huddled in cramped spaces while the rowers toiled through the night.

They had not been harassed by any imperial ships. Raz and Io had related that although Maldor had built an impressive navy in the western ocean, the emperor had made no effort to dominate the eastern waters. A navy had been essential to conquer the island nation of Meridon off the western coast, but as the eastern ocean held no such spoils, Maldor had opted to attack Kadara strictly by land.

Consequently, the Kadarian navy went unchallenged on the water. Unfortunately, this did little to help their besieged cities, except the capital, Inkala, which had docks shielded by massive city walls.

Ever since the drinlings had stopped fighting the emperor, the

Kadarians had shown no love for them. But the Kadarian ships the delegation had encountered only made token efforts to harass them. Evidently the Kadarians had bigger problems on their hands.

Now, for the first time in five days, the prow of the boat turned diagonally toward the shoreline. Tark joined Jason, hairy forearms resting on the gunwale. "Back to land," he said in his gravelly voice. "No more fish."

"I had no idea you were such a fisherman," Jason remarked, glancing down at his friend. "You caught twice as many as anyone aboard."

"I worked the sea for a time," Tark answered simply.

"What haven't you done?" Jason asked. "You were a fisherman, a diver, a miner, a musician. What am I missing?"

"Cook," Tark said. "Soldier. Tradesman. Hedonist. Traitor. Those are the main ones."

"You need to go easier on yourself," Jason said.

"I've gone plenty easy often enough," Tark replied. "I appreciate the sentiment, Lord Jason, but I'll decide when my penance is done for turning my back on good causes. I've got too many comrades reprimanding me from their watery graves."

"What do you think we'll find back on land?" Jason asked.

"Nothing so terrible as what we faced in the Forsaken Kingdom, I hope," Tark said, hawking up phlegm and spitting over the side. "That business was the worst I ever want to see."

"I hear you," Jason agreed. "Thanks for watching my back through all of that."

"Thank Rachel," Tark said.

"Good point."

"I wouldn't mind some bread," Tark mused. "Been some time since we had any bread. We were spoiled in the Vales."

"Will the Last Inn have good food?" Jason asked.

428

Tark rubbed his hands together. "Don't torture me. I've never made it there, but the Last Inn has a reputation that spans Lyrian. That doesn't happen without desirable fare."

"How far from the Durnese River to the inn?"

"Just a day or two on foot, according to Raz."

"Think Galloran will be there?"

"Hard thing to guess. I sure hope so. He's had some time. Thanks to the speed of this ship, we'll arrive more or less on schedule."

Under the cover of darkness, the longboat entered the wide, slow Durnese River. Jason swatted at biting insects as he watched the banks glide by, grateful to be in motion without any personal effort. To either side of the vessel, beyond the flat water, bobbing fireflies twinkled amid ferny shrubs. The lukewarm air tasted humid, as if poised to condense into a rain cloud all around him, although the starry sky above was mostly clear.

At length, the longboat ran aground against a level bank of firm mud interspersed with puddles. Raz and other drinlings helped the delegation disembark. After nearly a week of backbreaking labor, the drinling rowers had swelled up like bodybuilders.

Without ceremony, Raz aided the drinlings as they shoved the longboat back into the water. The few vessels secreted near the Silver River were among the drinlings' favorite assets, and the experienced crew wanted to reach the safety of the open sea by sunrise.

"This nearest of river to Last Inn," Raz explained in uncertain English. "We have fresh legs. We walk."

So Jason, Rachel, Farfalee, Nollin, Kerick, Drake, Ferrin, Tark, Nedwin, Aram, Nia, Io, and Raz hiked away from the river and soon came to a road. Aram cradled Corinne in his strong arms, as she remained too nauseated to walk. He seemed relieved to be on dry land. The half giant had patiently endured growing and shrinking aboard the longboat for all to see.

"This is a remote corner of Lyrian," Ferrin said, falling into step beside Jason. "I've only made it this way once, and then simply out of curiosity."

"You've been to the Last Inn?" Jason asked.

Ferrin nodded. "A massive structure. Maldor technically occupies this part of Lyrian, the former kingdoms of Durna and Hintop. But the area is sparsely populated, and since the emperor has not yet elected to engage any of the settlements within the southern jungle, little heed is paid to this southeastern portion of the continent."

"How far is the Temple of Mianamon into the jungle?" Jason asked.

"Far enough to keep the emperor away for now," Ferrin replied. "I've never entered the jungle. I'm not sure Lyrian has more perilous terrain. Forget the venomous snakes, poisonous plants, deadly insects, and impenetrable foliage. The wizard Certius left behind some ferocious races that Maldor has opted to leave unchallenged."

"Certius was part of the big war with Zokar and Eldrin," Jason said, remembering his lessons in history from the Repository of Learning.

"Good memory," Ferrin said. "Zokar attacked Certius first, and suffered horrible losses to gain victory. Certius was killed, his races scattered, but the forces of Zokar never recovered sufficiently to stand up to Eldrin. None really know how much the races of Certius have recuperated. Certius and his creations never showed interest in venturing beyond the jungle. Historians believe that Zokar lost the war by engaging Certius prematurely. Had Zokar initially bested Eldrin instead, strategists argue he could have rebuilt his forces at his leisure before attacking Certius. Maldor participated in that conflict, and is a devoted student of history."

"So you think Maldor will leave the southern jungle alone?" Jason asked.

"From what I've managed to gather, I believe the southern jungle is Maldor's last priority, even after the Seven Vales. Which is why I never went there. The region was not particularly relevant, and unquestionably dangerous."

"But some people visit the Temple of Mianamon," Jason said. "Galloran went there."

Ferrin nodded. "Formerly, many pilgrims went to Mianamon for advice from the oracles. A wide, stone road cut through the jungle, and the inhabitants of Mianamon welcomed visitors. The Last Inn thrived in those days.

"After the war with Zokar, none went to Mianamon for years. Word had it that the oracles had dwindled in number and in power. The jungle reclaimed the road. Only a few intrepid explorers, like Galloran, have ventured there since. The Last Inn became a curiosity mostly frequented by locals rather than the gateway to a mysterious society."

"Well, you'll finally get to see the jungle," Jason said.

Ferrin rolled his eyes. "If I stick with you, there won't be a deadly destination in Lyrian without my footprints."

By sunrise, Corinne was able to walk. Raz kept them moving at a brisk pace. To amuse himself, Jason invented a game called Will Nia Eat It? The answer to the question was typically yes. She generally said no only to stone and metal. Mud, bugs, rags, leaves, rope, leather, dead mice, pinecones, hair, and thorny stems were all proven edible.

The Last Inn came into sight just after sundown, situated by a crossroads outside the palisade of a modest village. Portions of the sprawling inn reached five stories tall. Built of wood and stone, the huge structure featured endless gables and turrets, united by swooping sections of roof that came together at unusual angles. Plentiful balconies and rooftop terraces added layers to the rambling inn, and a variety of chimney pots, cupolas, and weather vanes provided character. Large stables adjoined one side of the building, next to a working smithy.

"Looks like you could fit more people in the inn than the village," Corinne said in wonder.

"Once, you certainly could," Farfalee said. "Now much of the inn is permanently vacant. The Last Inn has been owned by the same family for generations. During the good years, they put much of their income toward adding to it."

They entered the common room through a great set of double doors. The cavernous space was three stories high, with thick rafters and an assortment of magnificent trophy heads on the walls. Fires blazed in multiple hearths. Dozens of patrons sat at long tables, dining on a variety of fragrant foods, yet the room was barely filled to a quarter of its capacity. A long marble bar against one wall blocked access to the two largest mirrors Jason had ever seen, set inside elaborate frames. A thin man in the corner sawed at his fiddle, to the approval of those seated nearby.

Jason smiled. Despite the exaggerated size, the room felt warm and lively, and the prospect of hot food boosted his spirits. Several curious heads turned as the delegation entered, and a stout woman in a frilly white cap approached hurriedly, wiping her hands on her apron.

"Welcome, travelers," she gushed. "I'm Angela; call me Angie. I don't believe I've seen many of these faces before! Welcome, leave your cares at the door, and come inside for food and drink! Do you have horses?"

"No horses," Nedwin said. "We were told to ask for Clayton."

Her face fell. "Clayton, the owner, of course. I'm sorry you missed him. He rarely ventures abroad, but he is gone for the next several days. Many apologies if you are friends of his."

"You have rooms?" Farfalee asked.

"Rooms? We have more rooms than we know what to do with!"

"We'd like to stay together," Nedwin said.

"Easily arranged," she replied cheerily.

"Has anyone asked after a group from the north," Farfalee wondered. "Perhaps a blind traveler?"

Angie scowled and placed her hands on her hips. "Travelers we still get, but no blind ones of late. From the north, you say? I'll keep vigilant."

Jason let his attention wander from the conversation as Farfalee and Nedwin discussed the arrangements. They had brought plenty of money from the Seven Vales, so cost would not be an issue. They had planned to be ready to completely outfit themselves here if necessary before heading into the jungle.

"Big inn," Rachel commented beside Jason.

"Congratulations," he replied. "You just won the understatement award."

"Think about it from the outside," Rachel said. "It covers more ground than a city block."

He leaned close to her. "I hope they use a lot of chlorine in the pool. Have you looked around? Some of these other customers don't look very sanitary."

She swatted him with the back of her hand. "It's just nice to see people. Normal people having a good time."

"You'll take that over dead people trying to eat us?"

"Just this once."

The delegation sat together along opposing benches at a long table. A parade of toasty, wholesome food kept them busy. Nothing seemed particularly fancy, but everything tasted hearty and good. Tark saluted Jason with a dark hunk of bread slathered with melting butter. Even Corinne managed to eat with enthusiasm.

The weight of the meal magnified Jason's weariness exponentially. He could hardly drag himself up the stairs with the others when the time came. He ended up sharing a room with Nedwin and Ferrin, and hastily claimed one of the three cots by flopping down unceremoniously.

The room was a bit cramped, but clean and solid, with a single window looking out at a slanted section of roof. The simple cot felt heavenly after days of sleeping on the ground or huddled on the creaking boards of a longboat. Stomach full, muscles weary, he contentedly settled in for a delicious slumber. He felt truly happy and comfortable for the first time in weeks.

In retrospect, he probably should have guessed it was a trap.

The soldiers burst into his room at dawn. Jason barely had time to awaken before he was flung to the floor beside Ferrin. He felt cheated of any opportunity to react as the sole of a boot pressed his head against the floorboards and a heavy knee weighed on his back. Within moments, biting cords bound his wrists together.

As Jason staggered to his feet with help from a conscriptor, he noticed that Nedwin was gone. The cot beside the window had no bedding on it. He deliberately avoided staring at the inexplicably empty cot. While other soldiers continued to bind Ferrin, the conscriptor brusquely steered Jason out into the hallway, where other soldiers awaited.

Two doors down, Raz burst from a room, the spike at the end of his arm buried in a soldier. Other soldiers mobbed the scarred warrior. With swift, lethal movements, Raz slashed open another soldier, and a third, before succumbing to multiple stab wounds.

The soldiers brutally made sure that Raz would never rise again.

"Move," the conscriptor growled at Jason, tugging him toward the stairs. Kerick lay on his side in the hall, body pierced by arrows, an empty socket gaping at the base of his skull. Jason stumbled along on numb feet, shocked to see other members of the delegation being escorted from their rooms, hands bound behind their backs. Nollin. Tark. Tiny Aram. Had the soldiers moved in before daybreak, they would have had a much different Aram to deal with. Perhaps they had known that.

The conscriptor manhandled Jason down the stairs to the huge common room, which stood empty now except for uniformed soldiers. Dozens of them. Too many.

Jason knelt between Nollin and Drake. He watched Corinne being led down the stairs, then Io, then Farfalee. Rachel entered the room gagged. Ferrin had to be carried because he had been bound inside of a sack that covered all but his head.

Jason tried to make sense of Nedwin's absence. Why was his bedding gone? Had he slipped out much earlier? Did he get away, or had he been the traitor?

After the entire delegation—minus Kerick, Nedwin, and Raz— had been assembled on the common room floor, kneeling in two rows, Duke Conrad entered the room. Jason felt an instant jolt of recognition and surprise. He looked much like Jason remembered him from Harthenham, except his prominent nose had clearly been reset imperfectly after Jason had broken it, and he was perhaps a tad leaner. Otherwise his skin was deeply tanned, his posture erect, his hair slicked back, his princely uniform impeccable, boots polished, medals gleaming. He wore a controlled expression of bemused disdain, as if this moment had been inevitable, and he was quietly pleased to watch his enemies arriving at that realization.

"This did not prove half so troublesome as I had been led to believe," he finally said, pacing before his prisoners. "You have led many others on a merry chase across the continent. While some asked where you were, and others wondered where you would be next, I stopped and asked myself where you would ultimately go. And I went there. And I waited." He grinned, showing his teeth. "And here we are."

"And you can release me at once," Ferrin said.

"Can I?" Conrad asked politely. "I understood that you were wanted along with the rest."

"It's what I do," Ferrin responded tiredly. "I infiltrate the enemy. You know that. This interrupts the operation for me. Ideally I would have prolonged the arrangement until after Mianamon, but perhaps this is for the best. They have been creating quite a stir."

"You have been spying all along," Conrad said, unconvinced. "The manhunt for you was a ruse."

"Check with the emperor," Ferrin replied coolly.

For the first time in a while, Jason doubted Ferrin. He suddenly examined the displacer through new eyes. Could Ferrin be trying to fool Conrad? Or had Ferrin expertly fooled the rest of them all along? *A lie twice believed is self-deceived.* The thought stirred a smoldering anger deep inside.

"That will not take long," said a man in the corner, studiously picking at a fingernail with a small knife. He raised his head, wavy gray hair framing his pallid face. He wore a long coat of brown leather.

"Torvic!" Ferrin called, the exuberance hollow. "I hadn't seen you over there. Still in touch directly with Felrook? You know, to come clean, I haven't brought Maldor in on my plan yet, so it might be of little use to bother him at this juncture."

"We'll be in touch with the emperor soon enough," Conrad

assured him. "Keep talking, traitor, and every word will cost you." Conrad swept his eyes over the group, then let his gaze linger on Jason.

"Want to go two out of three?" Jason asked, unable to resist. Conrad's eyes and jaw hardened at the insolence. The posture of his body suggested he was about to lash out. It was fun to see the words elicit a reaction. "There has to be a billiard table somewhere in a place this big."

"I am no longer a gentleman of rank and title," Conrad murmured, the soft words laced with hatred. "We common soldiers have different methods for settling grievances."

"You were stripped of your office?" Drake asked. "Well, I suppose you *did* botch the easiest job in the empire. I see the emperor let you keep your medals."

Conrad turned slowly to face Drake. "I see a seedman without a seed. A pathetic laughingstock who will suffer enough for all his other lifetimes combined before his fading spark is finally extinguished. I am ecstatic that we have crossed paths again."

"But not half so glad as you should be to see Lord Jason," Drake insisted congenially. "You never got to thank him for sparing your life after he defeated you."

Conrad bowed stiffly, a vein throbbing in his forehead, then turned to Jason. "You lured me into an absurd duel, bested me, and spared me. It was no kindness. I lost everything. Through the triumph of this day, I shall regain all I lost, and more. I expected no mercy from you, and you should expect none from me. You and your companions will promptly be delivered to Felrook."

"You spared him?" Io blurted incredulously, looking to Jason.

Conrad regarded Io and Nia with a sneer. "Drinlings should not attract attention. You vermin should be summarily executed. It's the only way to deal with inhuman pests. But the emperor requested that as many of this party be taken alive as possible, and I have no intention of tarnishing the glory of my victory."

"The Amar Kabal will not stand for this," Nollin warned, no confidence backing his words.

Conrad shifted his attention to Farfalee and Nollin. "It is the emperor who will not stand for your open involvement against him, in direct defiance of his treaty with your people. Have the two of you considered that you could be prisoners of Felrook forever, lifetime after lifetime, awakening after each death with a fresh body ready for new torments? I have." He sneered, eyes roving. "Does anyone else wish to speak? The exiled princess of Trensicourt, perhaps? The diminutive giant? The ridiculous little musician?"

Rachel tried to mumble something through her gag.

Conrad grinned. "Ah, yes, the Beyonder witch. Do not fear, the emperor is most intrigued with you. He will have many questions." He snapped his fingers. "But the Beyonder Jason will have the honor of the first private conversation. Torvic?"

The gray-haired displacer came forward, casually using a cane. A pair of soldiers hauled Jason to his feet and escorted him from the common room, through the quiet kitchen to a small storage area where three wooden chairs awaited. The soldiers departed, leaving Jason alone with Conrad and Torvic.

"Are you contacting him?" Conrad asked.

"This may require some time," Torvic answered, closing his eyes.

Jason stared at Conrad. "How did you know we would come here?"

"It might be best for you to keep silent until spoken to," Conrad murmured.

"Come on, you got us, it's over—how'd you know?"

Conrad narrowed his eyes. "I didn't know. Not for certain. In truth, I was beginning to doubt my instincts, it took you so long.

I had to beg for involvement in the hunt, to atone for my errors. I was tempted to chase you like the others. In the end I merely put myself in your position. To really incite rebellion this late in the war, you would need hope, and authority, and guidance, so sooner or later you would seek the oracle."

"You just came here and waited," Jason said.

"The inn boasts plenty of space," Conrad said. "We occupied a rearward wing. I took the innkeeper hostage. Clayton's family became very cooperative afterward. I brought fifty men. I lost three. Many others with more resources could not match my accomplishment. But I'm a soldier and a hunter. I rose to my former position on merit, as I shall rise again, and continue to rise."

"What's taking Torvic so long?" Jason asked.

"The emperor is a busy man," Conrad said dryly. "Torvic has kept me in touch with Felrook. We learned much before Nedwin discovered his ear. It is how I knew to attack at dawn and avoid the half giant. We waited outside your hall all night, poised to strike. You were weary. You rested past sunrise. A lone seedman stood guard in the hall. How we missed Nedwin, I'm not sure. He somehow slipped away. We're looking; we'll find him. But he is a small matter compared to the big game we acquired."

"I have Maldor," Torvic said abruptly. "I am his eyes, ears, and mouth. I speak his words. Congratulations, Conrad."

"Thank you, sire," Conrad said, bowing his head.

"Torvic informed me who you apprehended. Bring them to Felrook and not only will all of your holdings and titles be reinstated, you will select your next assignment."

"You are too generous, sire," Conrad said. "We'll add troops from the nearest garrison. The prisoners will travel to Felrook with an army as escort."

"I am pleased." Torvic turned to regard Jason. "Lord Jason."

"Can you see me?" Jason asked.

"I can."

"How? You're not a displacer."

"No."

"But Torvic shares parts with a displacer."

"Torvic exchanged an eye and an ear with a displacer called Gobrick. And I can read Gobrick's mind, borrowing his sight and hearing." Torvic turned to Conrad. "Leave us."

Conrad exited the room.

"You were a fool to return," Maldor said through Torvic.

"Return?" Jason asked as if confused.

"I know you made it home to the Beyond," Maldor said. "I know Ferrin aided you. There is nothing for you here. You were free."

"I left somebody behind."

"Rachel. You have character, Jason. Tell me about her abilities."

Jason scrunched his eyebrows. "Let's see. She has heat vision and super speed and bulletproof skin and ESP and a lasso that makes you tell the truth and—"

"Do you really believe this is a wise time for flippancy? If you do not value your own welfare, consider your companions. I have little interest in many of them."

"Sorry," Jason said, fear for his friends making his stomach drop.

"I am not going to extend another offer for you to join me."

"Then why are we talking?"

"Mostly I wanted to see your face. You have been elusive. I wanted to be sure. Also, I thought you might be interested to know that Galloran has finally knelt to me. He is now my creature. With your capture, the rebellion is officially over."

Jason scowled. Galloran had knelt to Maldor? What did that mean exactly?

"Alas, we will not speak again," Maldor went on. "I am much more interested in Rachel. Congratulations on causing me more trouble than I expected. Unfortunately, your return to Lyrian was inevitably a return to my dungeons. So much for high ideals. So much for character. You may depart. Tell Conrad to fetch the girl."

CHAPTER 26

FOREIGN EYES

Conrad sat Rachel down across from Torvic and remained beside her. Rachel disliked the close confines of the cluttered little storeroom.

"Rachel," Maldor said through Torvic with a fatherly smile. "I have longed to meet you. I wish we could speak in person, but all in due time. Please trust that I can see you clearly and hear every word. I understand through my agents that you possess some talent with Edomic. If we remove the gag, we will trust you to hold a civilized conversation. Should you betray that trust, three of your comrades will immediately perish. Do you understand?"

She nodded. Torvic glanced at Conrad, who removed the gag and then ducked out of the storeroom.

"Better?" Maldor asked.

"I guess." She tried to calm down and think. When Conrad had returned Jason to the common room and separated her from the others, Rachel had demanded bravery from herself. But now, seated across from a displacer who was speaking the words of a distant emperor, she wasn't sure what bravery required. Did bravery demand she ignore him? Would the bravest plan be to deny

442

whatever he asked? Or was bravery doing whatever she felt would best protect her friends? Could bravery mean pretending she would cooperate with him? "What now?"

"Tell me how you came to Lyrian," Maldor prompted through his puppet.

Rachel glared at him. Even though this wasn't really Maldor, she felt tempted to command objects in the storeroom to sail at his head. She didn't want to reveal anything to him. He didn't deserve to know her story.

"Come now," he said. "I understand you feel cross with me. I don't blame you. But I will only remain cordial to an extent. I won't harm you just yet. Think of your friends. Talk to me."

Boiling inside, she told about the butterfly and the stone archway. She explained about meeting the Blind King and Jason. She related some of her adventures, all the while trying to avoid incriminating her friends.

"You never chose to come here," Maldor eventually summarized. "You never even really chose to resist me. Yet here we sit, enemies by circumstance. I imagine you would like to see your parents again."

"More than anything," Rachel confessed. Was it wrong to reveal that? It might make him sympathize with her. Was he capable of sympathy?

"Tell me how you discovered your aptitude for Edomic," Maldor invited.

She paused. This was a dangerous subject. He didn't want anyone using Edomic. She could get people in trouble. What did he want to hear?

"I know you have skill with Edomic," Maldor said. "Be forthright. If we can come to an understanding, you may save your friends a great deal of suffering."

Rachel explained how she first learned to ignite fires. Instead of naming Drake, she claimed she had learned from a stranger in the woods. She told how Chandra had taught her to move objects, because Chandra was dead and Maldor couldn't harm her. Rachel admitted that the more she practiced, the more will she could force into her commands.

"How do you feel when you execute an Edomic command?" Maldor asked, the eyes of his puppet watching her intently.

"Good," she said. He watched in silence. "Really good. More alive. It's hard to describe."

"No description necessary," Maldor said. "I know precisely what you mean." He regarded her quietly. "I have wavered of late in my opinion of Edomic adepts. Someday, perhaps far in the future, I may regret not having an heir. Do I really wish to see my knowledge perish with me? Show me what you can do. Move something in the room."

Rachel hesitated, trying to strategize. Should she downplay her abilities? She could try to make a tiny Edomic command seem challenging. Or would it be more advantageous if Maldor thought she had real potential? If he was looking for a possible heir, the latter might be the case. Then again, he might only have mentioned an heir to fool her.

"Just use your talent," Maldor encouraged. "Show me. You've been captured. Your friends have been captured. Your only leverage is my interest in you. If you have a gift for speaking Edomic, I assure you that my interest will increase."

She looked around the room. A wooden cask roughly the size of a watermelon caught her eye. She issued a terse command that sent it crashing up into the ceiling. The cask fell heavily back to the floor, cracking without fully rupturing.

Conrad burst into the room, sword in hand. Torvic held up a

palm to stop him. "I asked for a demonstration of her Edomic abilities," Maldor explained. Conrad nodded and withdrew.

The displacer puppet turned his attention back to Rachel. "Impressive. The cask did not appear light, and you handled it with ease. You have come a long way in a short while. Tell me, how large of a fire can you ignite spontaneously?"

"At least the size of a person," Rachel answered.

"Interesting. What else can you do? I know you spent time with the charm woman."

"I can influence animals."

"Many accomplished wizards never master that ability. I would like you to try an exercise." He shared with her the Edomic command to summon water out of the air, and the command to hold it in the form of the sphere. "Then you can call heat to make the water boil. Try it, please."

Rachel asked him to repeat the commands, which he did. Mustering her willpower, she spoke the first command, trying to envision the water particles all around her, an invisible mist. As she felt the water responding, she spoke the second command, visualizing where she wanted the water to gather. Soon a sphere of water just smaller than a racquetball hovered between her and Torvic. While using her will to hold the sphere in place, she summoned heat until the water steamed and boiled. Once the water reached a boil, it became indefinably slippery, fell, and splattered against the floor.

When the water hit the floor, Rachel let out an exhausted breath. It had taken all of her focus to hold the water together. She felt like she had set down a heavy weight.

"I am very impressed," Maldor said. "You have never gathered water from the air before?"

Rachel shook her head. "Never."

"You have real promise," Maldor mused. "Beguiling potential. Of course, it would require centuries of extensive tutelage and hard work if you were to approach that potential. But over time you could develop into a sorceress of formidable abilities. How would you like to live for a thousand years and uncover secrets mortal man has never known to wonder about?"

"That sounds interesting," she said, partly intrigued, mostly trying not to offend.

"The secrets of Edomic are lost to Lyrian," Maldor said. "I am the last custodian of that knowledge. I am the only one left who can teach you. And you may be the most worthy student I will ever encounter. You could be a terrible threat to me. My survival instincts warn me to crush you in your infancy. To help you develop would be to repeat the tragic folly of wizards past. Yet how awful to lose all of that promise! Adepts have become so rare. You are young and innocent. If we could strike the proper arrangement, complete with certain safeguards, this could evolve into a mutually beneficial relationship. How determined are you to return home?"

"I really want to," Rachel said frankly. "I worry about my parents. They probably think I'm dead."

"Would you walk away from the potential to become a wizard of universal renown, profound knowledge, and unfathomable power simply to see your parents? Would you walk away from centuries of meaningful life for decades of mediocrity? I know firsthand that Edomic does not function in the Beyond. Here you could be extraordinary. There you won't be nearly so exceptional."

Rachel considered the question. Maldor was evil, so to learn from him might mean forsaking everything she was. But what if the alternative was death? And what if she could strike a bargain to save her friends? Did part of her want to use the excuse of saving her friends as an excuse to gain knowledge and power?

"You've been to the Beyond?" Rachel asked, hoping to stall.

"I have. Among other things, it is where I hid after Zokar fell."

"Really? How long were you there?"

"Lyrian and the Beyond are growing apart," Maldor said. "They have been for millennia. Eventually there will be no way left to cross from one to the other. It is impossible to ascertain when that day will come. The passage of time does not always correspond between our realities. A year here might be ten there. A year there might be a hundred here. The ratio is inconstant. You may go home and find yourself wandering your world decades before you were born, or a thousand years in the future. I once spent a few days in the Beyond, and hundreds of years passed here in the interim."

"But Jason went home and came back pretty close in time," Rachel said.

"As I mentioned, the passage of time between our realities is inconstant," Maldor said. "On my first excursion to the Beyond, the passage of time matched up precisely."

"I might never see my parents again," Rachel realized with despair that seemed to sink into her bones. "Even if I get home, it might not be home anymore."

"Whereas here you could become an ageless sorceress of incomprehensible power. You could make Lyrian into your personal paradise. You could make it a paradise for all who live here. But to do so, you would need to stay. And you would need to learn."

Rachel stared away from the gray-haired puppet speaking for Maldor. This new information changed everything. Could he be lying? What if he wasn't? What if she went home to a future where pollution had wiped out all life? What if she went home to a past where she would be mistreated? What if home became even more foreign than Lyrian? How would it feel to give a simple Edomic command and get no response? Here she had made friends. Here she was discovering powers.

Her eyes returned to Torvic, her mind to Maldor. "What about my friends?"

"Everything would depend on our arrangement," Maldor replied. "I have never truly negotiated with the weak or the foolish. You are neither. I have given you much to consider. Take some time. If you do not join me, I will not torture you. I will not keep you imprisoned. You are too dangerous. I will kill you. Your friends I will torture, unless you, perhaps, intervene. Consider your fate. Ponder theirs. Be wise. This is no game. Lives and destinies are at stake. We will converse in person soon enough. Please tell Conrad that I would like to speak with Farfalee."

And the conversation was over.

The gray-haired man stood and opened the storeroom door. Rachel overheard him relaying that Maldor wished to speak to Farfalee. He was no longer speaking as Maldor. He was Torvic again.

Conrad replaced her gag and led her with a hand on her elbow. Rachel felt dazed as she returned to the others in the common room. Jason looked concerned. She tried to smile. Something about the attempt only made him look more concerned.

Are you all right? Corinne inquired tentatively.

Not really, Rachel conveyed. *I think I will be. We'll see.*

When Jason had been captured, Maldor had offered him a job. There had been strings attached, of course. Jason had denied him, although it had meant imprisonment and torture.

But would Jason have made the same choice if he hadn't been captured alone? What if by accepting the offer, he could have saved his friends?

Rachel did not want to die. She didn't want her friends to suffer and die. But she didn't want to become evil either. She didn't want to work for a monster.

What could Maldor teach her? How powerful could she become? What if she learned enough to betray Maldor and free her friends? What if she bided her time and eventually overthrew him? Was that wishful thinking?

She tried not to picture her parents. Since arriving in Lyrian, the hope of finding a way home had kept her going. Now she knew that even if she found a way home, it might not get her back to her family. She might end up trapped in the wrong time. She might wish she had never left Lyrian. She would probably have no way back.

Rachel tried to be pragmatic. Eventually she would have grown up and left the nest. She would have become busy with college and work. She probably would have started her own family at some point. Maybe coming to Lyrian was like leaving the nest a little early. With less visitation. What if Maldor didn't exist? Could she build a life here?

But of course Maldor was part of the equation. How long would it take to reach Felrook? She would soon be faced with the toughest choice of her life. A choice that could end her life and the lives of her friends. A choice that could ruin her life, maybe even her soul. She wished none of this were happening. She wished she could stop thinking.

After a time, Farfalee returned to the common room, and Ferrin departed with Conrad for an interview. Rachel sat in silence, watching as the grim-faced soldiers tried to ignore their prisoners while also watching over them.

Words intruded on her thoughts without warning. *I need your eyes. Look around the room. Concentrate on sending the details to me.*

Galloran?

We'll get you out. It has to be now. Maldor will send more guards. He knows that to take you will end the war. Who is left?

Rachel tried to keep her expression casual as she glanced around the common room. The cavernous space comfortably accommodated dozens of guards. So many! She focused on sending everything she saw to Galloran's mind. *They killed Kerick. And Raz, one of the three drinlings who joined us. And Nedwin disappeared.*

I see what you're sending. You're all bound. Stay low. Keep your head. This will have to be messy.

She felt a small surge of hope. *How many are with you?*

Three. See you inside.

And Galloran was no longer in her mind. Rachel's eyes roved the room. Three besides Galloran? How could such a small group take on fifty? She should warn the others. But she was gagged.

Corinne?

He's coming, Corinne answered. *He doesn't want me to say anything until it starts. He says the attack needs to be a complete surprise.*

The front door to the common room opened slowly. A stooped old man in a cloak toddled inside, tapping his way with a cane. A grimy rag bound his eyes.

"Inn's closed," said a soldier near the door. "Who let you in?"

"I always eat here midmorning," replied a raspy voice belligerently. "They give me fish."

The soldier who had spoken walked toward the hunched figure. "Not today, codger. Imperial business. Out you go."

The old man tore the blindfold away, dropped the walking stick, and drew a sleek sword that gleamed like a mirror. The same motion that produced the blade delivered a lethal slash to the unprepared soldier.

Rachel started with a gasp, partly because of the sudden attack, partly because Galloran had eyes: one brown, the other blue. Three soldiers died before anyone had weapons ready. Once the soldiers reacted, it made little difference.

Rachel had never seen anyone move like Galloran. He tended to dodge attacks rather than deflect them. He did not duck or twist an inch more than necessary to make his adversary miss. After each errant blow, Galloran ended the opponent with a quick stroke and moved on. His subtle feints were just enough to prompt lethal mistakes. His expression of quiet certainty was much more intimidating than ferocious scowls or shouted threats. When it was necessary to redirect a sword or spear, he expended just enough effort to frustrate the strike, and then hastily dispatched the attacker. Every thrust, every stride, every parry was measured and precise. No effort was wasted. Somehow he managed to avoid most of the fighting and skip straight to the killing blows.

It was a hypnotizing dance. Rachel had never imagined such concise and deadly motion, such calm focus amid turmoil. Neither had Galloran's enemies. All who drew near were slain with ruthless efficiency. No armor could slow the gleaming blade. Helmets parted. Chain mail was pierced. Galloran never paused. Every moment of combat seemed choreographed in his favor. And he was not alone.

Dorsio burst through the door with a crossbow in each hand, just after Galloran drew his sword. The nimble bodyguard produced a second pair of smaller crossbows after dropping guards near the prisoners. Once those quarrels had been launched, he went to work near Galloran, a knife in each hand. Whenever he threw one, a replacement instantly materialized, pulled from within his cloak.

When a seedman burst through a nearby window, Rachel thought it was Lodan at first. After a moment, she recognized that it was Jasher, looking much younger than she remembered. He didn't enter with crossbows.

He brought orantium.

Jasher hurled the first sphere across the room to a corner where a group of soldiers had previously stood huddled in conversation. They now had weapons out, but seemed uncertain about where to employ them. The mineral gleamed a blinding white before a deafening explosion thundered through the room. Soldiers took flight, splintered chairs and tables filled the air, and heat washed over Rachel.

The second sphere landed near the bar with similar results. Other explosions boomed upstairs and outside, accompanied by hoarse shouts and the shattering of glass.

Guards who had been initially frozen with disbelief now seemed overwhelmed by the sudden devastation. Swords were raised uncertainly as confused soldiers sought to assess the greatest threat. To an extent their numbers worked against them. Most men seemed to expect another to solve the problem, but nobody was getting the job done. Those who rushed Galloran were cut down by an expertise that rendered their best efforts woefully incompetent. Those who hung back or sought cover became targets for orantium. Jasher seemed to have an endless supply.

The same initial shock that had temporarily incapacitated many of the guards had also frozen Rachel. She suddenly noticed that her companions were huddling together, trying to keep out of the way. Corinne had knocked over a long table that offered some shelter. Rachel mouthed some words against her gag, speaking more with her mind than her voice. The command tipped four tables and dragged them into position to form a crude fort around the bound captives.

Nedwin vaulted down the stairs, a long knife in one hand, a sphere of orantium in the other. Apparently he had been responsible for the repeated explosions above. A gash on his forehead sheeted his face with blood, but his eyes were alert. He threw the orantium sphere and raced to the fort of tables, deftly cutting his way past a pair of conscriptors to get there.

He went straight to Rachel, parting her gag without slicing her skin, then freeing her wrists with a second quick movement. He moved to Drake next. Rachel dimly realized she had been freed first because Nedwin felt she could make the biggest difference.

She scanned the room. By necessity, Jasher was now defending himself with his sword rather than hurling orantium. She had seen him fight before, and he had seemed incredible, and he was fighting well today, but compared to Galloran he appeared inefficient. Three guards had taken up a position behind the bar and were getting ready to use their crossbows. A sharp command from Rachel brought one of the huge mirrors down on top of them.

On the other side of the room, not far from the entrance, many of the remaining soldiers were pressing toward Galloran and Dorsio. Galloran fought with the same skill and exuberance as when he had first entered the room, but Dorsio had an arrow in his back and a gruesome wound in his side. As he stood between Galloran and two enemies, Rachel watched a sword skewer the silent bodyguard.

Fury flooded through her, and with a shouted command, a nearby table flipped sideways and rammed the two assailants into the wall. With a fresh Edomic command she set the entire table aflame and then sent it hurtling across the room, crashing against soldiers like a demonic bulldozer.

Rachel felt a thrill as the ambitious commands worked, but the exertion left her feeling like she had sprinted a mile uphill. She fell to one knee and tried to stay conscious.

The flaming table had helped break the soldiers. Drake had joined the fight now, and Tark, Farfalee, Jason, Io, and Aram seized weapons from fallen enemies as soon as Nedwin cut them free. The soldiers were no longer trying to win. They were trying to escape.

Rachel crouched behind an overturned table, trying to get her breath back, trying to stop the room from spinning, hoping that some scurrying soldier wouldn't stumble across her in this weakened state. She smelled burning wood. She was unsure how much time had passed when Nedwin helped her to her feet, the wound on his forehead bound with her former gag. She began to cough. Smoke billowed everywhere. The inn was on fire. Nedwin hurriedly escorted her to the road. Most of the others were already outside.

Drake and Ferrin exited the inn, their swords to the backs of Conrad and Torvic. A few other soldiers, who had apparently surrendered, knelt in the street, minded by Tark, Jasher, and Farfalee. Rachel overheard Drake telling Nedwin that he had found Ferrin in the storeroom, restraining Conrad with his arms and Torvic with his legs. Ferrin explained that he had quietly unbound himself inside the sack and then attacked his interviewers when he heard the commotion. Drake took Kerick's seed from Conrad.

Galloran strode out of the inn, cradling Dorsio in his arms. He laid the lifeless body gently on the street. It was still morning. Flames leaped from several of the upper windows of the inn. Smoke leaked into the otherwise clear sky.

Galloran came to stand before the new prisoners, regarding them stormily. Rachel realized that the mismatched eyes had been a deliberate insult. The glaring discrepancy emphasized that his vision had been restored by displacers. "Do you surrender to us?" Galloran asked.

The prisoners responded in the affirmative. Except for Conrad.

"I will not surrender," Conrad said stiffly. "I was disgracefully withheld from combat. It was my right to face my adversaries. I must have satisfaction."

"Let me," Drake said.

"Galloran," Conrad demanded. "I challenge Galloran to a duel."

"Swords?" Galloran asked.

"Naturally."

"Now?"

"Immediately," Conrad responded.

"Very well," Galloran said.

"No!" Farfalee protested.

"He's not a duke anymore," Jason complained.

"He has a reputation with a sword," Ferrin warned.

"Let me have him," Jasher begged.

"He accepted," Conrad insisted.

"I did," Galloran said. "Arm him."

"I have his sword," Ferrin said. Galloran nodded, and Ferrin reluctantly handed the weapon to Conrad.

"If I best you, I go free," Conrad stipulated.

"Agreed," Galloran said. "You lost a duel to Lord Jason. He left you with your life. I will show no such kindness."

"I have won eleven mortal duels," Conrad said. "The one I lost was a farce fought with billiard balls. I have heard tales of your prowess with a blade. In my experience, most tales grow with the telling."

Rachel overheard Jason murmuring to Jasher. "Conrad hasn't seen him fight."

Galloran backed away into the street, and Conrad stepped toward him. Galloran drew his sword.

"A remarkable blade," Conrad conceded.

"Begin?" Galloran asked.

"Begin." Conrad edged forward, sword ready.

Their blades touched twice before Conrad was impaled. Galloran withdrew his sword and wiped it clean while Conrad expired in the road, a stain spreading across his white uniform. Rachel could not suppress a quick, involuntary laugh of relief. She heard beams collapsing inside the inn. Sparks gusted from some of the windows.

Then Galloran became very still. He slowly turned to look down the road. Rachel felt no premonition of her own, but the expression on Galloran's face gave her chills. She followed his gaze. A figure was approaching, still a long distance away. A black silhouette bearing a shining sword in each hand. A living shadow defying the morning light. A torivor.

"This adversary has come for me," Galloran said, his voice heavy and resigned. "I believe it followed me from Felrook. I did not know it had brought swords. Keep back. Unless you attack, it can only claim one victim like this. If I fall, proceed to the Temple of Mianamon with haste."

They watched in silence as the torivor drew near. It did not hurry. The swords it carried matched Galloran's perfectly, superbly crafted, chromium bright.

"We do not have to cross swords!" Galloran called throatily. "I have no quarrel with your kind. Depart in peace."

The lurker showed no indication of having heard. The steady tread did not falter until the creature stopped ten paces from Galloran. The torivor tossed one of the swords. Galloran caught it by the hilt. He now held an identical sword in each hand.

"Very well," Galloran said, perhaps answering words the others could not hear. Rachel could vaguely sense communication. She strained her mind to understand, but could catch nothing. She fingered the necklace the charm woman had given her, realizing that it must be causing interference.

Galloran waited placidly. The lurker stood still as well. Until it rushed forward with otherworldly speed and its sword scythed outward in a hissing arc. Galloran narrowly blocked the attack, and the next stroke, and the next.

The blades did not clash or clang as they connected—they chimed musically, beautifully, like a battle fought with expensive tuning forks. Rachel could almost feel the vibrations.

It did not take Rachel long to see that Galloran would lose this fight. The torivor was clearly quicker and stronger. Only by moving with flawless economy was Galloran able to deflect the relentless blows. Rachel suddenly understood where Galloran had learned to fight so efficiently. It was the only way he could have previously survived combat with an opponent such as this.

Rachel held her breath. Any moment Galloran would make a tiny mistake and lose his life. Even with two swords—one used primarily to protect himself, the other to attack—he was only barely staying ahead of the lurker. No thrust or slash from Galloran came close to touching the tenebrous surface of the torivor. The only question seemed to be how long Galloran would last.

The blades flashed in the sunlight. Heat radiated from the burning inn. Galloran slowly retreated, his breathing becoming labored. Any moment the torivor's sword would slip past his defenses. Except it didn't.

Rachel had never envisioned such virtuosity with a weapon. It was like watching a concert pianist play an impossible piece of music, fingers flying to strike mind-boggling patterns of notes and to pound sprawling chords. No, it was more than that. It was like watching that pianist play an impossible piece with dynamite strapped to his back, rigged to detonate if he touched a wrong note.

The frantic blur of motion was almost too quick to follow. Before Rachel could feel nervous about any particular blow, it had been blocked, a counterstroke had been parried, and the blades chimed on.

Galloran was no longer giving ground. The combatants slowly circled each other, swords ringing relentlessly. Galloran looked determined, his eyes fierce with concentration. The lurker fell into a pattern of swinging high, forcing Galloran to defend his head, then lashing out with a shadowy leg to kick Galloran in the side.

A blade blurred down and took the black leg off just below the knee. The severed portion disappeared with a brilliant flash. Whiteness gleamed from the stump, as if the torivor were bleeding light. The fight continued, with the torivor clearly wavering. A moment later, Galloran cast aside one of his swords.

Single sword against single sword, the blades met over and over. Perfectly balanced on its remaining leg, the torivor was now defending as often as attacking. Galloran's face was red and perspiring. They seemed to be standing too close together. And then Galloran's blade sliced through the torivor's midsection, and the creature vanished with a blinding flash.

As Rachel blinked away the dazzling afterimage, she saw Galloran stagger back and drop to his knees. He bowed his head forward, hands on his thighs. Had he been wounded at the end? Had she missed it?

Nedwin hurried forward and helped Galloran to his feet.

"I'm not as young as I once was," Galloran muttered, wiping a sleeve against his glossy forehead. "I am thankful that the fiend grew impatient and tried that kick."

"That was unbelievable," Ferrin mumbled humbly to no one in particular. "I've never . . . if I hadn't seen . . ."

"I've lived a long time," Jasher told him. "Nobody handles a sword like Galloran."

"You mean to defy me," Torvic said flatly, the comment unsolicited. The words did not belong to Torvic. Everyone looked his way. The displacer sat with his legs crossed, staring blandly.

Galloran faced Torvic, still panting. He was uninjured, but clearly exhausted. "You offered the eyes long ago. I finally came to claim them. I pledged no fealty."

"After all the futile suffering, after all the fruitless effort, after the countless disgraced followers, you persist in returning to your folly. I can see through those eyes, Galloran. You are mine. I will watch your every move."

"Then you will watch me dismantle your empire piece by piece," Galloran said. "When you see anything, it will be the cowardly criminals you employ perishing by my blade. Come for me if you can. I will be waiting."

And with that he replaced the blindfold.

CHAPTER 27

THE ORACLE

As a furry snake, longer than a shower rod, rippled across his path, Jason decided that he liked the jungle even less than the Sunken Lands. The tropical chaos of ferns, fronds, vines, and towering trees was much hotter than the swamp and just as poisonous, and the journey was taking much longer.

They followed the remnants of an ancient stone road that survived mostly as a jumbled mess overgrown with shrubs and creeping plants. For much of the way, the broken paving stones seemed more likely to turn an ankle than to provide solid footing. But the vanishing roadway still provided access through dense portions of steaming jungle that appeared otherwise impenetrable. And according to Galloran, the archaic thoroughfare led directly to the Temple of Mianamon.

Galloran had not removed his blindfold since the battle at the Last Inn. He shuffled forward with one hand on Corinne's shoulder, the other using a walking stick to tap the ground ahead. Drake had tried to convince him to abandon the blindfold during the journey, stressing that Maldor must have already assumed where they were headed, and that views of the surrounding vegetation would reveal little if anything. But Galloran had maintained that he wanted his enemies to see as little as possible, whether or not the view was considered consequential.

Nedwin led the way, using a bright torivorian sword as a machete to hack through the worst of the verdure. He had commented several times about how the edge never seemed to dull no matter how many obstacles he slashed. Galloran had lent the other captured sword to Jasher.

Jason had spent time in conversation with Jasher as they walked the jungle road. Jasher had been reborn in time to witness Lodan's First Death, and then had tracked Galloran and the diplomats from the Seven Vales to Felrook. The Amar Kabal had reached a peaceful settlement with the emperor, and Galloran had claimed the eyes that Maldor had offered years before. Following the grafting, the emperor had let him depart with no argument.

Once Galloran and Dorsio left Felrook, Jasher had joined them and traveled southeast until meeting Nedwin in the wilderness near the Last Inn. Apparently, Nedwin had heard a disturbance in the hall and slipped out the window with his bedding an instant before the soldiers had entered his room. He had stealthily made his way across the rooftops in order to sneak away and go for help.

Jasher looked younger, but his mannerisms were the same as ever. Jason felt grateful to be back in the company of the first seedman he had met in Lyrian, but he could tell he was not nearly as grateful as Farfalee.

Murky clouds had threatened overhead all morning. From off to one side of the road came the familiar patter of raindrops on leaves. A moment later, rain came bucketing down, soaking Jason's hair in seconds.

Downpours tended to come and go quickly in the jungle, but the wetness inevitably lingered. The air was too humid for clothes to really dry, so Jason generally ranged between drenched and damp. He felt certain they would all end up reeking of mold before the tropical trek was complete.

He saw a parrot with feathers like flower petals roosting on a nearby limb, head tucked to hide from the deluge. Thanks to his interest in animals, the staggering variety of wildlife in the jungle had been one of Jason's compensations for the heat and the danger. Bright frogs, exotic birds, vivid lizards, vibrant insects, and numberless serpents contributed to the local fauna. Nedwin had pointed out a constrictor longer than a school bus, slithering among high limbs in a sinuous series of loops and curves.

Jason's favorites were the monkeys. The diversity seemed limitless—short black hair; long golden hair; striped hair; tiny round ears; huge pointed ears; two arms; four arms; slender tails; bushy tails; stubby tails; colorful ridges; spurs on the ankles or wrists to aid in climbing—all ranging from the size of squirrels to the size of toddlers.

The plants exhibited comparable variety. Broad fanlike leaves; limp streamers; ferny fronds; corkscrewing tendrils; slim, pointed greenery; clusters of minute leaflets; and seemingly every other conceivable manner of foliage decorated the shrubs and trees. Jason had never pictured flowers of such striking hues—metallic, fluorescent, iridescent. Nor had he imagined such an assortment of carnivorous flora—grasping vines, clutching leaves, sucking tubes, stalks affixed to mouthlike pods, stinging bowls of sweet nectar, and sticky mats that folded around unsuspecting prey.

The pelting rain persisted until puddles had formed at frequent intervals along the ancient road. By the time the rain relented, the delegation had been thoroughly soaked. Even with all the wetness, Jason didn't feel chilled. Nor did he feel refreshed. The air was too hot and sticky to feel much besides uncomfortable.

Galloran slipped and splashed to his knees in a brown puddle. He did not arise any wetter, but he was certainly muddier. His face remained composed, but Jason noticed one hand clenched into a fist, veins standing out on the back.

"You could take off the blindfold, Father," Corinne said.

"It is better this way," Galloran replied in his raspy voice. "My borrowed sight comes at a price. I must never rely too much on these eyes. They are a last resort."

Jason felt a sting on his neck, like the bite of an insect. The tropical bugs had not bothered them so far, thanks to a lotion Nedwin had devised. Slapping the sting, Jason found a small dart, little more than a feathered needle.

Soft hisses came from the surrounding foliage. "Blowguns!" Nedwin called. "We're under attack."

Galloran tore the blindfold from his eyes and drew his sword. The others sprang into action as well. Nedwin and Ferrin raced to one side of the path, pushing through tall stalks of reddish wood similar to bamboo. Drake, Jasher, Tark, and Aram ran the other way, slashing foliage when necessary. Farfalee set an arrow to the string of her bow, as did Nollin. Io, Nia, Corinne, Rachel, and Jason all drew weapons, positioned near Galloran on the road.

As part of the group plunged into the jungle and the others scanned high and low, there came no more whispers of blowguns. Nor was there any sight or sound of enemies fleeing. After passing out of view for a few minutes, all of the delegation besides Nedwin returned to the road.

"They moved like ghosts," Ferrin said. "Nedwin kept after them."

The group remained alert as more time passed. No further attacks came, and eventually Nedwin returned. "I glimpsed green figures, apparently clad in ivy. They were too swift. Few can outmaneuver me across difficult terrain, but these folk were my superiors. They fled through the trees like monkeys and across the ground like wildcats. I was fortunate to catch sight of them from a distance. I had no hope of reaching them. I was hit by three darts but can perceive no effects."

"A dart pricked me on the hand," Galloran said.

Jason, Corinne, Tark, Io, and Drake had all been hit on their skin. Several of the others had little darts sticking to their clothes. Nobody was feeling adverse reactions.

"What were the darts for?" Jason asked.

Galloran inspected the tiny pinprick on his hand, sniffing it and tapping it. "When last I visited Mianamon, I heard tales of treefolk who dwelled deep in the jungle. I never saw them, nor heard of any this far north. But times change."

"One of the races of Certius?" Ferrin asked.

"Most likely," Galloran agreed.

"Would they have used a slow-acting venom?" Ferrin asked.

"I sense no irritation," Galloran said, perplexed, flexing his hand. "None at all. Why risk drawing near and firing darts? We'll have to watch these injuries."

Two days later, the first short tufts of moss appeared around the spots where the darts had pierced skin. The dense green growth looked as though it could be carelessly plucked away, but was actually anchored deeper in the flesh than a first glance could discern. A sharp knife could scrape away some of the moss, but it became apparent that a deep incision would be required to root it out. Of all who had been hit, only Io remained unaffected.

Showing no indication of pain, Nedwin rooted out the tiny patch of moss just above his wrist. By the next day, it had not only grown back, but the greenery had spread. Moss that had been trimmed the day before had also returned and multiplied. The untouched patches had spread as well.

The moss inflicted no pain. When Jason stroked the fuzzy circle on his neck, the moss seemed to belong there as much as the surrounding hairs. But who knew what would happen as it continued to spread? At best, he would become a mossy freak. At worst, the moss would overwhelm his body, causing harm or death.

A couple of days later, Jason watched Nia munching on a large, glossy leaf as she walked. Scarcely a few weeks had passed since meeting her, but as promised, she already looked older. When they had met she had looked thirteen or fourteen. Now she looked sixteen or seventeen. She was a few inches taller, having surpassed both Rachel and Tark.

For the past week, the delegation had mostly eaten unusual fruit and vegetables foraged by Nedwin. But Io and Nia claimed food whenever they wanted it. "This jungle must look like one big salad to you," Jason said.

"I'm a growing girl," she replied, taking another bite. "Think I'll pass you up?"

"I doubt it, since your dad was shorter than me." He unconsciously rubbed his hand against the lush moss now covering most of the side and back of his neck. It had become a habit.

"How much does the moss bother you?" she asked.

"I kind of like the texture," he admitted, realizing that he had been stroking it again. "But it's gross how it keeps spreading. It's really weird to think of it covering my face."

"There must be a way to stop it," Nia said.

Jason shrugged. "Nedwin knows more about these jungles than just about anyone. He has no idea what this moss is or what might cure it. I just hope it doesn't start controlling us, like the goma worms."

"What would moss want you to do?" Nia giggled. "Go sit on a rock by a stream?"

"What if I turn into a plant?" Jason asked, trying to keep his voice casual, although he was voicing a deep concern.

"I'll make sure you get sunlight and water," Nia said.

Jason tried to smile at the joke.

"It only seems to coat the surface," Nia pointed out, her tone more consoling.

"After it covers everything, the moss might grow inward."

"Hopefully, we can get help at the temple," Drake said from behind. A dart had hit the side of his jaw, and the resultant greenery had spread into half a mossy beard. "The oracle and her people have dwelled in the jungle for a long time."

They continued in silence for some time.

"Too bad Io couldn't grow any moss," Nia said. "He'd have a portable snack."

Jason forced a chuckle. She was trying to lighten the mood. The effort made him think of her adaptability. She no longer had an accent, and had picked up on the nuances of how he and Rachel spoke and kidded. Under other circumstances, her comments would have amused him more. But the worry of parasitic moss slowly claiming his body was hard to shake. Still, she was trying, so he might as well meet her halfway. "He can always have some of my surplus."

Nia scrunched her nose. "This jungle gets hot. What if your moss inherits your body odor?"

"You guys eat dead rats," Jason said.

"We have to draw the line somewhere."

At the front of the group, Nedwin raised a hand. "Hear that?" he asked.

"What?" Galloran replied.

"A high whine," Nedwin described. "Perhaps a whistle. Faint. At the edge of hearing."

Jason heard nothing. But he noticed the vines at his feet had begun to writhe. The entire forest floor came to life at once, inert vines suddenly thrashing like bullwhips. With alarming speed and accuracy, the vines began to curl around legs, arms, and torsos. A strange smell suffused the air, and the ground suddenly seemed to tilt and undulate.

Jason tried to draw his sword, but was too late. He was already on the ground, arms pinioned to his sides. From his position on the ground, Jason watched Galloran, blindfold discarded, slicing vines with his torivorian blade. The vines lashed at him from all directions, but he pivoted and slashed with flawless skill and timing, slowly carving a path away from the road.

Jason felt like the ground was rocking and spinning. Galloran began to stagger drunkenly, not from the onslaught of vines, but apparently in reaction to whatever odor had made Jason unsteady. Finally the tendrils caught hold of Galloran and dragged him down.

Jason struggled against the vines. They tightened painfully as he resisted, then slackened a degree when he relaxed.

"Rachel?" Farfalee asked.

"I can't," she replied. "I tried. Edomic won't work. The commands won't stick."

Jason closed his eyes. He had never felt this dizzy. It was like the ground was whirling on multiple axes, not just spinning but flipping and rocking in every possible combination. Eyes open or closed made no difference. The sensation made him nauseated, but before he could throw up, Jason lost consciousness.

Jason awoke, dangling from a horizontal pole by his arms and legs. The pole was in motion, probably being carried between two people. He was bound in place at his wrists, elbows, knees, and ankles. The position was neither comfortable nor intolerable. His eyes were blindfolded.

"Hello?" Jason called.

A blunt object, probably a stick, thumped painfully against his side. Apparently he wasn't supposed to speak.

"We're here," answered Drake. Jason heard a few meaty thumps, presumably the punishment for the reply.

Jason dangled in silence for some time. At least he wasn't dizzy, and at least he wasn't dead. They had been captured, probably by the same guys who had shot them with darts. Jason supposed it was better than being strangled and devoured by vines.

How long had he been out? It was impossible to tell. He could feel the sun shining. It could be the same day or a different day. The air felt hot and humid as usual. Whoever carried them moved silently and smoothly.

Where could they be going? Jungles and blowguns made his mind wander to cannibalism and shrunken heads. Would he and his friends become the ingredients to a tribal soup?

Surely Ferrin could escape these bonds. Detach arms and legs, reattach, and he would be free. The poles were not living wood, so Rachel should be able to split them. Perhaps they were waiting for the right moment. Telepathy would be useful right now. He supposed Galloran, Corinne, and Rachel were all engaged in mental conversation. Assuming they had survived the vines.

After a long time, Jason was set down. He could feel plants and roots beneath his body. Fingers crammed paste into his mouth. It didn't taste too bad, vaguely fruity. He drank from a wooden cup pressed to his lips. After a few minutes, the pole rose into the air, and he moved onward.

After another break, Jason began to sense the light of day

fading. What would happen at sunset, when Aram grew?

Jason never got to find out. His pole tilted to a steep angle, as if his bearers were climbing a steep hill. The pole leveled for a short while. Then he was set on a floor of smooth stone tiles.

"Release them," said a female voice with a casual air of command. "These are the wayfarers we have expected. Please forgive the impolite reception, good travelers. There are many from outside the boundaries of the jungle who mean us harm."

Nimble fingers unbound Jason's wrists and feet. He rose to his knees and pulled off his blindfold, finding himself surrounded by his friends at the center of a strange assemblage.

Some of the hundreds of beings around them looked like regular humans clad in fine robes, hoods cast back to reveal curious faces. Most of the figures were humanoids enshrouded by vegetation. Shaggy moss covered the majority, but ivy coated a great number as well. A few were draped so heavily in dark vines that they lost most of their shape and looked more like tall heaps of seaweed than living beings. Another minority were encased by twisted black wood bristling with huge thorns. None of the vegetated people wore clothes, but the plants kept them perfectly modest.

Among the crowd stood tall, white apes with fur-fringed faces and round eyes. With their slender bodies and long limbs, Jason thought they looked like gibbons, although they were much too large. The snowy primates watched the proceedings sedately, a few clutching slim rods.

They were all gathered within an immense room composed of dark gray stone. The walls slanted together at odd angles overhead, forming the inside of an irregular pyramid. The room had several openings. Through one Jason could see the sun poised to set, red rays caressing miles of exotic treetops.

"I should not remove my blindfold," Galloran said, pushing away the hands of a robed figure who had been trying to unbind his eyes. "I am Galloran, son of Dromidus. My eyes belong to our common enemy. Have we reached Mianamon?"

"You have," replied the woman who had ordered their release. Short and slight, the speaker wore a silky robe the color of storm clouds. A circlet of purple blossoms adorned her brow. "I am Ulani, daughter of Hispa."

"Does the prophetess still abide here?" Galloran asked.

"She does," Ulani answered. "Her Eminence told us weeks ago to expect you, otherwise you would have been slain long before now. Of late we seldom offer hospitality to outlanders."

"Several of us have been infected by peculiar vegetation," Galloran said.

"We can reverse the process," Ulani assured him. "Attar of regent orchids will expel the invasive moss. Please forgive the inconvenience. Such measures are meant to warn and dissuade imprudent pilgrims."

"I have been here before," Galloran said. "When I came here last, I beheld no treefolk among you."

"You behold them now?" Ulani asked, amused.

Galloran touched his blindfold. "I saw them coming for us when we were held fast by vines. They carried us here."

"The people of the jungle have united against the threat of Maldor," Ulani said. "The oracle administers to them and offers our services. In return we enjoy their cooperation and protection. Old wounds strain relations between the various tribes of treefolk, but they have agreed to consider the temple neutral ground and to stand together against the pupil of their ancient enemy from the north."

"This is bracing news," Galloran said. "We have traveled far at great cost in search of guidance regarding how to resist the enemy you have named."

Ulani inclined her head slightly. "The oracle is aware of your intent. She has spent weeks preparing for her greatest prophecy. Tomorrow you will have your answer. Today she wishes to meet with you, one by one. Follow me."

The conversation had afforded Jason some time to massage feeling back into his tingling hands. He walked with the others up some broad steps, and then into a corridor. They arrived in a trapezoidal room where tilted walls rose to a flat ceiling. Abundant furniture upholstered with the pelts of jungle cats awaited in clusters across the wide floor.

Ulani passed through a door set back in an alcove. She returned accompanied by an elderly woman. The woman wore a white robe with gold trim. Wrinkles lined her angular features. The visible tendons and bones on the back of her spotted hands made them appear fragile. Golden charms hung from sagging earlobes.

Despite her age, the woman held herself erect and walked with no difficulty. She came and stood before Jason. "I would converse with you first."

"Me?" Jason asked.

The woman gave no reply. She pointed to Ferrin next, then Tark, Nedwin, Drake, Aram, Jasher, Nia, Farfalee, Io, Nollin, and then Corinne. She indicated Rachel second to last, and finally Galloran.

Without another word, the aged woman withdrew from the chamber through the same portal she had entered.

"Go," Ulani told Jason, gesturing toward the recessed door.

"Okay," Jason said. He went to the portal and found the door ajar. He opened it further, stepped inside, and shut it behind him. Incense burned in sculpted vessels around the room.

The elderly woman sat on a cushioned chair that looked like a curving length of ribbon. She gazed at Jason with fathomless eyes, her expression neither kind nor hostile. "Come take my hand," she invited.

"Are you the oracle?" Jason asked.

"I am. Give me your hand and relax your mind."

Jason crossed to her and gently grasped her bony hand. She clasped his hand in both of hers and closed her eyes. Jason sensed no otherworldly powers at play. If anything, he felt a little awkward.

She released his hand and looked up at him. "Sit down."

He sat on a low, round, cushioned stool. It might have been an ottoman.

"What do you wish to ask me?" she invited.

"You can see the future?"

"At my best."

"How?"

She smiled. "You wish to understand. Do you think of time as sequential?"

"One thing happening after another? I guess so."

"Do you consider space that way?"

"Space? As sequential? Not really."

"Yet when you gaze upon the stars, you see them as they were, not as they are."

"Okay," Jason said, trying to make sense of the statement using some of what he knew about astronomy. "The light travels through space. The farther the light has come, the older it is. Some of the light we see tonight could be from stars that have died long ago. It just took the light a long time to get here. So we're seeing back in time."

She smacked her lips. "In the Beyond, you have those who gaze deep into space through lenses, who gather light and sound and particles as they seek to understand their place in the universe."

"We have astronomers."

"I am like an astronomer." She said it as if she had fully explained herself.

"You have a telescope that sees through time?"

"In a sense. Time is more like space than you appreciate. You recognize time as sequence only. Beginning and end. Before and after. We dwell in a temporary state, and so this is natural. Your current state began. Your current state will end. But that which is eternal views time differently."

This wasn't making sense. "You're eternal?"

"I try to touch the eternal. You and I move through time like a flame on a string. The ashes behind are the past, consumed, unreachable. The string ahead is the future. But the only moment we inhabit, the only moment where we can act, is the present, the point where the flame burns, the point where time touches eternity."

Jason nodded. "All right."

"To the eternal mind, the entire string is ever present, ever burning. No point is out of reach."

"Are you trying to break my brain?"

She grinned. "Try simpler terms. Before making a particular choice, have you ever endeavored to anticipate the consequences?"

Jason thought about the dungeon at Felrook. Maldor had offered to free him in return for servitude. Jason had known that to deny him would mean long days and weeks and months of torture. He had glimpsed his future. He had also guessed what serving Maldor would mean and how it might change him.

Jason had experienced this same kind of foresight for simpler choices throughout his life. He knew generally what a bike ride with Matt would bring versus a day volunteering at the zoo. "Yes.

Is that what you do? Guess at the consequences of decisions? Try to visualize them?"

"It is similar to what I do," the oracle explained. "Like you, I am a temporal being. I was born. I will die. I am caught up in what feels like the stream of time, my body gradually aging, the seasons changing, each breath keeping me alive. But I am trying to see beyond the present, into the future and the past. I am trying to see beyond the point I currently inhabit in space and time to the infinite points I do not inhabit."

"How?"

"By tapping into senses beyond the five most obvious," she replied. "By striving to access the eternal mind. Viewing the future is more difficult than seeing the past. The past is singular, definite. The future is also singular. Something definite will happen. But since what will happen shifts with every choice made, there are kaleidoscopic possibilities when the future is viewed from the present. Instead of looking for truth through a telescope, try a kaleidoscope. It is a challenge. The farther you dare to look, the more destinies involved, the more difficult it becomes."

"So you make educated guesses," Jason said.

She shrugged. "Some forecasts are more certain than others. Maldor's rise has eclipsed most possible futures. Sometimes we oracles try to see the future in order to influence it. We do our best to nudge the coming years toward prosperity and away from disaster. I searched for many years to find some way to avoid Maldor's dominion. In all those years, scouring every reality open to my awareness, I only glimpsed a single path that might lead to his premature downfall."

Jason felt chills. "That's why I'm here."

"That's why you're here."

He swallowed dryly. "Have I already played my part?"

"I believe we are on the proper path. I knew that you, Rachel, and Galloran would need to come here for success to be possible. I will be sure tomorrow."

"Why me?" Jason asked.

"Imagine standing on a mountaintop. Imagine stones scattered at your feet. Imagine you have been tasked with selecting a stone or two and then throwing them for the purpose of causing an avalanche that will devastate the surrounding wilderness.

"Simeon of the Giddy Nine came to me. I considered all of the possible stones. I elected to throw him at you and Rachel. You both impacted Galloran. I hoped that you three would in turn collide with other key targets in precisely the right way. I believe that your arrival here means I selected good stones and estimated correct trajectories. But the avalanche is just beginning. Tomorrow I will know more about the possibilities."

"How did you find us?" Jason wondered.

"I'm aware of the Beyond," she said. "Yours is not the only other reality besides this one. Of everywhere I looked, only bringing you and Rachel here allowed me to glimpse success. Not probable success. But possible."

"So now I wait until tomorrow?"

"I will meet the others. Then I will entomb myself in clay. To prophesy I must consume substances harmful to my health. This time I will heavily poison myself with fumes and liquids and minerals, and exert myself to touch the eternal as never before. I will search for the path to depose Maldor and share all the insight I can acquire."

"Poison yourself? Will this kill you?"

"Not until after I deliver the prophecy."

Rachel sat beside Galloran, lost in thought. After the others had communed with the oracle, they were escorted elsewhere. Some had remained with her for a long time. Rachel assumed the oracle was reading their futures. Should she ask to know her future? Should she ask whether she would ever return home?

Corinne had been with the oracle for some time. Rachel had considered asking her a telepathic question, but had worried that it might cause some sort of psychic interference.

She glanced at Galloran, blindfold over his eyes, arms folded, head bowed, mouth frowning. Could he be asleep?

I am awake, he conveyed. *You would not be able to communicate with Corinne from here. That room is shielded from prying minds.*

You've talked to the oracle before. Should I be nervous?

Do not be afraid of her. She means to help. If you are nervous regarding what future she will see, you are not alone.

Rachel laughed softly. *I can't picture you nervous.*

Good.

Rachel laughed again. *I've wanted to ask you something.*

Go ahead.

Rachel hesitated. *How did you defeat that torivor? I mean, I know you're a great swordsman, but that seemed impossible.*

His lips bent into a smile. *Can you keep a secret?*

Sure.

I'm not sure that the secret must be kept. But I want it kept just in case.

I'll never tell anyone. I swear.

Galloran shifted in his seat. *I wouldn't tell you, unless I thought the information could become relevant for you someday.*

Okay.

You know that I can hear your mind, even thoughts you do not intentionally send.

Yes. You did it a moment ago.

To an extent, I can do that with torivors.

She thought about the implications. The realization hit her hard. *You know what they're going to do before they do it!*

He nodded. *When we fight, I watch what they are about to do. I'm moving to counter them before they are moving to strike. I watch how they adjust, and I adjust accordingly. It requires focus and expertise with a sword. Even knowing each movement in advance, one small miscalculation would destroy me. I have always been a student of the sword, but fighting my first lurker was how I learned to fight as I do. I saw the duel as the lurker saw the duel, and learned to fight as it fought.*

Rachel stared at the faint scars on his strong hands. *I noticed that you seemed to know shortcuts or something. You defeat people so easily.*

I have now bested three lurkers. Each battle has been easier than the one before. That is not to say that the fourth won't kill me. But I have learned much. I learned during this fight that I can engage a lurker more effectively with a single sword than with a pair.

You can't read just any mind, Rachel sent.

I can't read most minds. Sometimes I'll catch unpredictable glimpses of what an opponent means to do. But if I couldn't reliably spy on the minds of lurkers, the first one who came for me years ago would have slain me in an instant.

Corinne emerged from the portal that led to the oracle. Ulani gestured to a servant, who led Corinne away. "Come," Ulani told Rachel, motioning toward the door.

See you later, Rachel conveyed. *I'll keep your secret.*

You're the first to know it, Galloran replied.

Rachel entered the room, and the oracle asked her to sit. The woman stared at her in silence for an uncomfortable length of time. Rachel wondered if the oracle was looking into her future.

Are we going to talk? Rachel conveyed.

"Not that way, child. I must conserve all of my strength. Let me have your hand."

"Are you going to read my future?"

"I just need to get a clearer sense of you. Information to use when I do try to penetrate the future."

The oracle took one hand in both of hers. She closed her eyes, nodding faintly, her whole body rocking slightly, then let the hand fall. The oracle kept her eyes closed. Her upper lip quivered.

"I've waited my whole life for one who could replace me," the oracle said.

"What do you mean?" Rachel asked.

"None of my acolytes have sufficient talent. Ulani is the closest, but she will never be more than a shadow of me, as I am but a shadow of the greatest seers. You, however, could surpass me."

"You know I've been practicing Edomic?"

"Even when you were far away, in the Beyond, I could sense potential in you. I gave Erinda the task of drawing you here for that reason. Potential is not always realized, but, Rachel, you are more than I expected. I can feel the power in you. You have come a long way very quickly. Many options will be open to you."

Rachel braced herself. She didn't want to ask the question. The words escaped as a whisper. "Will I ever get home?"

"Do you still wish to go home, child? Consider all you could do here. All you could be."

"I want to help Galloran. I want to stop Maldor. But if we succeed, I want to go home."

The oracle considered her. "Part of me wishes to keep you here, whether you choose it or not. I don't mean here in Lyrian. I mean here in this temple. Under my guidance, your skills would grow.

You would learn how to gain the knowledge needed to guide this world."

"But you won't keep me here?"

"Galloran needs you. And I need Galloran. Should he fail, Lyrian will fall. Despite the best efforts of the children of Certius, this temple will be overrun. Darkness will reign from the northernmost tundra to the southernmost jungle."

"The treefolk were made by Certius, right?"

"As was this temple," the oracle said. "Certius built two strongholds in the jungle: Mianamon in the north, and Paggatar to the southwest, in the heart. He shaped these walls with his words, raised them with his will. At Mianamon he established my order and taught us how to enhance our sight. He lived and worked at Paggatar. But Zokar came and destroyed him, much as Maldor seeks to come here and destroy us, the descendants of those who escaped the prior invasion."

"Can we stop him?"

"I will know more tomorrow. You must continue to increase your abilities. Some here can assist you. Learn all you can while you remain with us."

"Okay," Rachel said.

"You want to know if you will go home. I have spent considerable time studying our respective realities. Five years and nine weeks from tomorrow our realities will be properly synchronized. I cannot speak for any other time. If you survive, and if you so choose, that would be the day I recommend for your return."

Rachel felt a violent surge of relief. Five years might be a long time to wait, but it was much preferable to uncertainty and despair. Tears sprung to her eyes. She had not expected this particular hope to resurface. "If I go home on that day, I should be able to find my parents?"

"It should get you close to your proper time. Now leave me. I must speak with Galloran."

"Thank you so much."

The oracle gave her a sad smile. "My dear girl, please do not thank me yet."

CHAPTER 28

THE PROPHECY

The next morning, Jason and Rachel walked down a long stairway deep below the temple. Ulani led the way, flanked by a pair of hooded acolytes bearing torches. The entire delegation followed. Nobody spoke.

At the bottom of the stairs, cowled figures hauled open a pair of ornate doors, granting access to a shadowy chamber. Melting candles partially illuminated a variety of ancient carvings. A disgustingly sweet smell saturated the air.

The delegation walked toward the circular pool on the far side of the room. A scaffold over the pool allowed a group of hooded figures to raise a slick gray slab from the fragrant fluid. When the upright slab hung suspended, the acolytes departed.

The face of the oracle was visible in the center of the upper half of the slab. Her eyes were closed, her wrinkled face composed.

The ornate doors closed. The slab dripped. Fumes rose from the aromatic pool.

The eyes of the oracle opened, made iridescent by a creamy film. Those eyes did not make contact with anyone present. They seemed to stare inward or, perhaps, far beyond the confines of the room.

"All paths but one lead to Maldor's dominion," the oracle intoned. Her voice did not sound much like it had the day before. She spoke with a remote certainty. "A single precarious lane leads to his premature demise, encompassed by failure, littered with corpses."

"What should we do?" Galloran asked.

The eyes showed no flicker of recognition. "Two quests. Galloran must rouse Trensicourt. The Amar Kabal must join him, as must the drinlings. Together the free people of Lyrian must march on Felrook in the coming spring. The host will be insufficient, yet Felrook must fall."

"By spring?" Nollin murmured. "Summer is already spent."

"Rachel, Io, Ferrin, Nedwin, Nollin, and Tark must join Galloran."

"Attack Felrook," Ferrin chuckled darkly, shaking his head.

"Jason Walker must find the abode of Darian the Pyromancer. My sight cannot find his dwelling. I do not know what will be learned. The last abode of Darian the Seer can be learned at the Celestine Library within the Inland Sea. This greatest of seers has vital knowledge. Make sure the secret can be shared."

"The Celestine Library is guarded," Ferrin said. "Inaccessible."

"Darian should have perished ages ago," Farfalee added softly.

The oracle blinked, her cheeks twitching. "Jasher, Farfalee, Drake, Aram, Corinne, and Nia must join Jason. The parallel quests must succeed. Many present will perish. You must stand united. Otherwise the children of Eldrin will be vanquished, as will the children of Certius, and an age of immeasurable darkness will choke the world. Spend the fall and winter here. Depart as winter wanes. Send a few ahead to prepare the way. The timing is crucial. I have seen and I have spoken."

"Felrook cannot be taken," Nollin scoffed mildly. "Not by ten times the number we could muster."

"I'm not leaving Jason," Tark griped. "Look again."

The oracle gasped, cheeks quivering. For a moment, her eyes were not hazy, and she peered desperately at Galloran. "I searched, but could not view the end. Nothing seen, everything glimpsed. You need one with a truer eye and a farther gaze." Her eyes rolled back, her face slackening. "A secret from the past can ransom the future. The servant will betray the master. The pleasant paths have crumbled. Lyrian must be purchased with sacrifice. Our hope is red, like the blood of heroes; black as the bowels of the earth; and white, like a flash of orantium."

Her eyelids fluttered rapidly. Drool leaked from the corners of her mouth. Hooded acolytes stormed into the room, armed with tools to cut the oracle from the clay. She died long before they succeeded.

ACKNOWLEDGMENTS

Two down, one to go. Many people have helped the Beyonders series to continue. My editor, Liesa Abrams, did much to improve the story. My agent, Simon Lipskar, arranged the practical side and offered editorial guidance.

The entire team at Simon & Schuster did a great job spreading the word about A World Without Heroes so that the series could find readers. I feel proud to be associated with them. Thanks go to Mara Anastas, Carolyn Swerdloff, Anna McKean, Paul Crichton, Bethany Buck, Matt Pantoliano, Fiona Simpson, and the rest of the team. These are not just people who do their jobs well—they are people I enjoy spending time with! The folks at Shadow Mountain have also been very supportive of this new series.

Early readers for this volume included some friends and family, namely Mary Mull, Cherie and Bryson Mull, Tiffany Mull, Pam Mull, Chris Schoebinger, Liz Saban, Jason and Natalie Conforto, and the ever vigilant eye of J. Tucker Davis Esq., M.D., J.D. Their tips, catches, and feedback were very beneficial. My talented cousin Mike Walton drew the map and some cool pictures for the website. Once again the design team produced a terrific cover—special thanks to Lisa Vega.

And thanks to Jeannie Ng for lending her close eye for consistency to the manuscript.

My family and friends are my secret weapon. My wife, Mary, is my first editor, and her insight and support have been a key ingredient to my success on every book, this one included. My kids bring a highly motivating joy into my life. And my siblings, parents, and friends help me put on my Salt Lake City launch parties and contribute in numerous other ways. My dad, Gary, has helped sell T-shirts; my mom, Pam, dresses up as Muriel the witch; my aunt Kim and sister Tiffany pose as fairies or Ephira; and my brother Ty drags his friends out to help with the event. My comedy friends from years past help make my launch parties cool and funny, including Summer Mull, Bryson Mull, Robert Marsh, Chad and Shelly Morris, Gavin and Maren McCaleb, and Joel Hilton, who does a killer Jack Sparrow impersonation.

Some people from the early days must also be shown gratitude. The Allen family, including Aaron, Robert, and Daryl, were very supportive of this concept back before I had ever published anything. Kjirstin Youngberg and Dean Hale also offered some advice in the past. And my brother-in-law Sean Fleming helped me overcome some doubts I had regarding the ending of book one. His support helped me resist taking the story in a safer, more predictable direction. With the benefit of hindsight, I feel that choice made the series cooler.

Among the others I thank, I must never forget you, the reader. Without you my books would serve no purpose. The story does not happen on the page. It happens in your mind. Thanks for bringing Beyonders to life by participating in the story with me. Thanks for telling others about the story. Most people find books through word of mouth. If you're enjoying Beyonders so far, I expect that you'll love the last volume, *Chasing the Prophecy*. I sure hope I'm right!

WHAT DOES THE FUTURE HOLD?

After *Seeds of Rebellion*, only one book remains to complete the Beyonders trilogy. The final volume, *Chasing the Prophecy*, will release in Spring 2013. I have been working on this series for more than ten years, and I'm passionate about ending it well. I'm unspeakably excited to share the conclusion.

In the meanwhile, I have some other books out there, and one other new story coming. My Fablehaven series is complete, and follows the adventures of Kendra and her brother, Seth, as they explore secret wildlife parks for magical creatures hidden around our world. All of the books are now in paperback, and I am pleased with how they turned out.

Between Fablehaven 2 and 3 I wrote a novel called *The Candy Shop War*. It is my only other novel besides the Beyonders and Fablehaven books. The story follows four young friends: Nate, Trevor, Summer, and Pigeon. When magicians come to their town and start sharing magical candy with certain kids, a lot of trouble follows. Between Beyonders 2 and 3 I will be releasing a sequel to *The Candy Shop War* called *The Arcade Catastrophe*.

I also have a lone picture book called *Pingo*. I had the pleasure of working with #1 *New York Times* bestselling illustrator Brandon Dorman on the project. The story follows a boy, Chad, whose imaginary friend becomes his imaginary enemy when he tries to stop believing in him. The story can be tricky to find in bookstores these days, but is usually available at the standard online outlets. I have a prequel to *Pingo* in development, where Chad and Pingo have a contest with other kids at school to see who has the best imaginary friend.

I will also start a brand-new series after Beyonders. The details are still a secret, but I'll try to sneak some info into the Author's Note of *Chasing the Prophecy*.

For updates or further details on my books and other projects, swing by my website, brandonmull.com. You can also find me on Twitter as brandonmull, or join one of my Facebook fan pages.

Dear Readers,

   As I thought about bonus content to include in the first-edition hardcover of *Seeds of Rebellion*, my mind turned immediately to the interviews with the oracle. The most important characters in this series had a chance to converse with her in private, and I thought it might be interesting to witness more of those exchanges. I selected three characters to follow.

ORACULAR INTERVIEWS

L ooking back, Tark received a reassuring nod from Galloran before opening the door and stepping into the room with the oracle. He reached to take off his hat before realizing he was not wearing one. Withered and small, the oracle reclined in a strange chair, gazing at him kindly.

"Should I close the door, Your Grace?" Tark asked.

"Please," she replied gently.

Tark complied and then went to stand awkwardly before her. Unsure of the etiquette involved, he fell to his knees.

"No," she scolded, extending a fragile, spotted hand. "Take a seat."

He rose and sat on the low, cushioned stool. "I'm not sure I belong here," Tark apologized.

"Nonsense," the oracle responded. "Give me your hand."

Tark held out his hand, palm upward. She took it in both of hers and squeezed, her head bowed. Then she traced a fingertip over some of the calluses and lines on his palm. She turned his hand over and inspected the back. He was aware that his fingernails were dirty. She released his hand and stared at him silently.

"I'm no hero," Tark confessed. "I'm sure you know that by now. But I mean well. Hopefully, you saw that too. I fell in with this company by accident. I'm no lord, not by any stretch of the imagination. I'm out of my element." She kept staring at him. "I also talk too much. At the wrong times, I mean. Should I go?"

"You are wrong," the oracle chided.

"No surprise there," Tark replied.

She stared.

"Wrong for this mission?"

"Wrong about your worth. Wrong about your role in the coming conflict."

Tark avoided her eyes. "Begging your pardon, I don't expect to have much of a role to play at all."

Her smile crinkled her wrinkles. "And you're wrong."

Tark cleared his throat uncomfortably. Unsure what to do with his hands, he gripped the sides of the plush stool. "What should I do?"

"The details evade me," the oracle explained. "I've glimpsed a few things. I feel that victory remains possible. Elusive and unlikely, but still available. Intuition can mislead, Tark, but there are certain instincts I have learned to trust, and those instincts insist you will have a key role to play. I doubt there can be victory without you."

Tark chuckled with embarrassment. "I'll serve Lord Jason as best I can, Your Grace."

"You're a better man than you are ready to believe. You did not kill your friends."

Tark shifted on the stool. "I suppose not. Still, Your Grace, a man doesn't get many chances to learn what he's made of.

I told my friends I would go off the falls with them. Then I escaped the raft when the opportunity came. I know now that Lord Jason was trying to save us. But I didn't know that at the time. All I knew was that I didn't want to head over those falls."

The oracle nodded.

"I tried to make up for it by fighting Maldor. Lord Jason helped me recognize that alternative. Then an invitation came. A summons to the Eternal Feast. I quit. Turned my back on my ideals. And again Lord Jason came for me."

The oracle motioned for him to continue.

"When we broke out of Harthenham, Lord Jason got left behind. Not by design. Everything happened so quickly. I knew I should go back for him. But I had the seed. Jasher's amar. And it was an excuse. I was secretly glad for that seed, Your Grace, because it let me run away. Take my meaning?"

"I do."

"I've shown courage a time or two," Tark said, eyes distant. "I'm not a complete craven. But I'm afraid that when it matters most, I don't quite measure up."

"I sent your friends off that waterfall," the oracle said.

"I know," Tark muttered. "You were right. We needed Jason. Our world, I mean. We need him."

"And we need you, Tark," the oracle said. "I'm not trying to console you. I'm not that nurturing. We all wrestle with doubts. Show me a man ready to walk glibly to his death and I will show you a fool who undervalues his life. You are no longer the same man who jumped off the raft. You cannot afford to be that man. Your comrades need you. Lyrian needs you."

"What must I do?"

"I expect you will know when the time comes."

"I'll try to do my part, Your Grace."

"I'm afraid you must, or the cause will be lost."

*　*　*　*　*

Nedwin entered the oracle's chamber and closed the door. The old woman stared at him expectantly. He heard her breath rattling faintly in her lungs. The room was small, with soft furnishings. It felt intimate. The smell bothered him.

"What am I to do?" Nedwin asked.

"You don't want to be here."

"I want to fulfill my duty."

"Let me see your hand."

"Is it necessary?"

The oracle nodded. "I must get a clear sense of you."

"You won't like it."

"Why not?"

"I'm not entirely . . . well."

"I can tell that from here. Let me have a closer look. I've lived a long time. I do not shock easily."

Nedwin crossed to her and sat on a low, cushioned cylinder. He held out his hand. She took it. Her mouth bent into a frown. Wrinkles bunched around her wispy eyebrows as they lowered into a scowl. She rocked gently from side to side, then dropped his hand as if it were hot. She gazed at him in dismay.

"Warned you," he said.

"In my long years, I've never sensed such suffering."

"I try not to dwell on it."

She took deep, cleansing breaths. Each inhalation rattled slightly, like the early onset of lungrot. Her calm returned. "The void left by the eye healed well."

Nedwin glanced at the puckered scar on his freckled hand. "I have experience with salves."

"Galloran will need you."

"It's why I'm alive."

She nodded. "You wish to die."

"Wouldn't you? Be honest."

There was pain in her eyes. "You refused to give up until you learned what had become of him."

"Galloran is my lifeline. I worshipped him as a child. I still do. He deserves it. The thought of him kept me going—keeps me going. I'm . . . better when he's near."

"I wish I could help," the oracle said earnestly. "What would you like to know?"

"Will I . . . can I hold myself together? Sometimes I worry."

"Give me your hand again."

"Are you sure?"

She nodded. She gripped his fingers with one hand, his wrist with the other. Sweat beaded on her crinkled brow. Again she released him as if he had burned her. "I don't know how you're standing here. Yet you haven't broken. Notwhere it matters. Having come this far, I'm not sure you can be broken."

"True, I think. What about the dreams? Anything to be done?"

"I'm sorry."

He shrugged for her benefit. "Are we finished?"

"I think so. I admire you, Nedwin."

"Find what needs to be done, and I'll do it."

Are you all right?" Ulani asked, her small hand still on his elbow.

"I have some experience moving about without my sight," Galloran replied.

"Leave us," the oracle said.

The delicate fingers slid away from his arm. He heard the door close. "Here we are," he said.

"Here we are," she answered. "Follow my voice. No obstacles stand between us except for your seat."

Galloran closed the distance with swift strides, then slowed until his shins felt the cushioned stool. Using a hand to confirm the position, he sat. "A husband without a wife, a father without a son, a hero without a quest, and a king without a country. Here we sit on the other side of it all. That boy you met years ago had no appreciation for how literal it would be."

"I speak what I see," the oracle said. "Not more, not less."

"Do we still have a chance?"

"I believe so."

"Are we wishing? Dreaming?"

"I believe enough to trade my remaining years to look deeper."

Galloran frowned. "This will kill you?"

"If I wish to see enough to be of service, yes. Even so, it might not suffice. Too many variables. I catch confusing glimpses. The least likely outcomes are the hardest to identify."

"Is success the least likely result?"

"I'm afraid so. I shall know more tomorrow. May I borrow your hand?"

He held his arm out. Her hands found his, her fingers feather soft. "Those eyes!" she exclaimed.

"Necessary evil," Galloran apologized.

"Interesting. I can feel the owners. They wonder what you're doing. Their attention is bent on you. They know you're here in the jungle. They pay close heed to every clue. They are very loyal to Maldor. Extremely committed."

"Any spark of me in here?"

She released his hand. "You have held up well, in spite of it all. As expected. Nonetheless remarkable."

"Don't flatter me, Esmira."

"Never."

"Plenty have suffered more."

"I feel for Nedwin, too."

Galloran leaned forward. "What about my companions? How can I help them? Where should I center my attention? Who is most important?"

"Which link of a chain is most vital?"

"All of them? Even the displacer?"

"Especially the displacer."

Galloran sighed. "If we have passed beyond hope, you will tell me."

"If we have passed beyond hope, I will seek to abort my vision before the toxins consume me. But I do not expect to survive."

Galloran stood. "You represent our final opportunity, Esmira. Without this vision, we'll have no allies, no compass."

"I am aware."

"I appreciate it. We all appreciate it."

"While you languished in dungeons, I dined in a tropical paradise. I know my duty. My sight has been the last hope of Lyrian for many years. My fate would be crueler if I could not be of service. Now go. Leave me to my preparations."

Galloran heard her mentally summon Ulani. He adjusted his blindfold, then smoothed his hands down his robe. "Blind before I could see. You do have a way with words."

BRANDON MULL

is the author of the Beyonders series, as well as the *New York Times*, *USA Today*, and *Wall Street Journal* bestselling Fablehaven series. He resides in Utah, in a happy little valley near the mouth of a canyon, with his wife and four children. Brandon's greatest regret is that he has but one life to give for Gondor.